Riverside Edition

THE WRITINGS OF

HARRIET BEECHER STOWE

*WITH BIOGRAPHICAL INTRODUCTIONS
PORTRAITS, AND OTHER
ILLUSTRATIONS*

IN SIXTEEN VOLUMES
VOLUME VII

The Writings of Harriet Beecher Stowe

Riverside Edition

HOUGHTON, MIFFLIN & CO.

AGNES OF SORRENTO

BY

HARRIET BEECHER STOWE

AMS Press, Inc.

New York

1967

AMS Press, Inc.
New York, N.Y. 10003
1967

Manufactured in the United States of America

CONTENTS

The frontispiece ("The Cavalier stood in the moonlight before Agnes," page 92) and the vignette were drawn by Malcolm Fraser.

INTRODUCTORY NOTE

In the summer of 1859, Mrs. Stowe made her third and last journey to Europe. During the summer, the whole family was abroad, save the youngest; but in the autumn Mr. Stowe and one of the daughters returned to America, leaving Mrs. Stowe with two daughters and a son to spend the winter in Italy. The residence there was mainly to establish the health of the family; but Mrs. Stowe had entered into engagements with the New York *Ledger* and the New York *Independent* to furnish contributions, with a design ultimately of collecting the papers and recasting them for a volume to be published in the spring of 1860 in America and England, under the title of *Leaves from Foreign Books for Home Reading.* She had indeed entered into an agreement with Sampson Low & Co., the London publishers of *Uncle Tom's Cabin* and *Dred,* for the publication of the volume, but a sudden change of plans brought her home before she had perfected her book, and it was never published.

Meanwhile her dramatic instinct had begun to work upon the material thus gathered. It was impossible for her, with her strong religious nature and her active interest in structural Christianity to avoid subjecting the great church so constantly in evidence to those tests of personal religion which had been familiar to her from childhood. Her stay in Florence brought vividly before her the figure of Savonarola, and her imagination, in seeking to recover the life of his day, instinctively invested it with the spiritual struggles so well known to her and her circle. There was no conscious protestantizing of the life, as one may say, but the story which she told naturally reflected the color of her own religious training. *Agnes of Sorrento* was begun in this Italian winter, and had its immediate origin, as she herself explains in the following note, in a friendly contest of story telling. It was not completed until some time after the return to America, finding its first publication in *The Atlantic Monthly* in America and *The Cornhill Magazine* in England. In *The Atlantic* it was begun in May, 1861, and finished in April, 1862.

In the party with Mrs. Stowe were Mr. and Mrs. Howard of Brooklyn, and their children. When the tale made its final appearance in book form, it was accompanied by the following passages from a letter to the publishers by Mrs. Stowe. The "Annie" referred to was Miss Annie Howard.

"The author was spending some weeks with a party of choice and very dear friends, on an excursion to southern Italy. Nothing could have been more fabulously and dreamily bright and beautiful than the whole time thus employed. Naples, Sorrento, Salerno, Pæstum, Pompeii, are names of enchantment which will never fade from the remembrance of any of that party. At Salerno, within a day's ride of Pæstum, the whole company were detained by a storm for a day and a night. The talents of the whole company were called in requisition to make the gloomy evening pass pleasantly with song and jest and story. The first chapters of this story were there written and read, to the accompanying dash of the Mediterranean. The plan of the whole future history was then sketched out. Whether it ever find much favor in the eyes of the world or not, sure it is, the story was a child of love in its infancy, and its flowery Italian cradle rocked it with an indulgent welcome.

"The writer and the party were, fresh from strolls and

rambles about charming Sorrento; they had explored the
gloomy gorge, and carried away golden boughs of fruits and
blossoms from her orange orchards. Under the shadow of
the old arched gateway they had seen, sitting at her orange
stand, a beautiful young girl, whose name became Agnes in
the story ; and in the shadows of the gorge they met that
woman straight and tall, with silver hair, Roman nose, and
dark eyes, whose name became Elsie. The whole golden
scene receded centuries back, and they saw them in a vision
as they might and must have been in other days.

"The author begs to say that this story is a mere dreamland, that it neither assumes nor will have responsibility
for historical accuracy. It merely reproduces to the reader
the visionary region that appeared to the writer ; and if
some critic says this date be wrong, or that incident out of
place, let us answer, ' Who criticises perspective and distances, that looks down into a purple lake at eventide ? All
dates shall give way to the fortunes of our story, and our
lovers shall have the benefit of fairyland ; and whoso wants
history will not find it here, except to our making, and as
it suits our purpose.'

"The story is dedicated to the dear friends, wherever
scattered, who first listened to it at Salerno.   Alas ! in
writing this, a sorrow falls upon us, — the brightest, in
youth and beauty, and in promise of happy life, who listened to that beginning, has passed to the land of silence.

"When our merry company left Sorrento, all the younger
members adorned themselves with profuse knots of roses,
which grew there so abundantly that it would seem no
plucking could exhaust them. A beautiful girl sat opposite the writer in the carriage and said, 'Now I will count
my roses; I have just seven knots, and in each seven roses.'
And in reply, another remarked, 'Seven is the perfect
number, and seven times seven is perfection.' 'It is no
emblem,' she said gayly, 'of what a perfect time of enjoy-

ment we have had.'   One month later, and this rose had
faded and passed away.

   " There be many who will understand and tenderly feel
the meaning, when we say that this little history is dedicated to the memory of ANNIE."

AGNES OF SORRENTO

CHAPTER I

THE OLD TOWN

THE setting sunbeams slant over the antique gateway of
Sorrento, fusing into a golden bronze the brown freestone
vestments of old Saint Antonio, who with his heavy stone
mitre and upraised hands has for centuries kept watch
thereupon.

A quiet time he has of it up there in the golden Italian
air, in petrified act of blessing, while orange lichens and
green mosses from year to year embroider quaint patterns
on the seams of his sacerdotal vestments, and small tassels
of grass volunteer to ornament the folds of his priestly
drapery, and golden showers of blossoms from some more
hardy plant fall from his ample sleeve-cuffs.   Little birds
perch and chitter and wipe their beaks unconcernedly, now
on the tip of his nose and now on the point of his mitre,
while the world below goes on its way pretty much as it
did when the good saint was alive, and, in despair of the
human brotherhood, took to preaching to the birds and
the fishes.

Whoever passed beneath this old arched gateway, thus
saint-guarded, in the year of our Lord's grace ——, might
have seen under its shadow, sitting opposite to a stand of
golden oranges, the little Agnes.

A very pretty picture was she, reader, — with such a

face as you sometimes see painted in those wayside shrines
of sunny Italy, where the lamp burns pale at evening, and
gillyflower and cyclamen are renewed with every morning.

She might have been fifteen or thereabouts, but was so
small of stature that she seemed yet a child. Her black
hair was parted in a white unbroken seam down to the high
forehead, whose serious arch, like that of a cathedral door,
spoke of thought and prayer. Beneath the shadows of this
brow lay brown, translucent eyes, into whose thoughtful
depths one might look as pilgrims gaze into the waters of
some saintly well, cool and pure down to the unblemished
sand at the bottom. The small lips had a gentle compres-
sion, which indicated a repressed strength of feeling; while
the straight line of the nose, and the flexible, delicate nos-
tril, were perfect as in those sculptured fragments of the
antique which the soil of Italy so often gives forth to the
day from the sepulchres of the past. The habitual pose of
the head and face had the shy uplooking grace of a violet;
and yet there was a grave tranquillity of expression, which
gave a peculiar degree of character to the whole figure.

At the moment at which we have called your attention,
the fair head is bent, the long eyelashes lie softly down on
the pale, smooth cheek; for the Ave Maria bell is sounding
from the Cathedral of Sorrento, and the child is busy with
her beads.

By her side sits a woman of some threescore years, tall,
stately, and squarely formed, with ample breadth of back
and size of chest, like the robust dames of Sorrento. Her
strong Roman nose, the firm, determined outline of her
mouth, and a certain energy in every motion, speak the
woman of will and purpose. There is a degree of vigor in
the decision with which she lays down her spindle and
bows her head, as a good Christian of those days would,
at the swinging of the evening bell.

But while the soul of the child in its morning freshness,

free from pressure or conscience of earthly care, rose like an illuminated mist to heaven, the words the white-haired woman repeated were twined with threads of worldly prudence, — thoughts of how many oranges she had sold, with a rough guess at the probable amount for the day, — and her fingers wandered from her beads a moment to see if the last coin had been swept from the stand into her capacious pocket, and her eyes wandering after them suddenly made her aware of the fact that a handsome cavalier was standing in the gate, regarding her pretty grandchild with looks of undisguised admiration.

"Let him look!" she said to herself, with a grim clasp on her rosary; "a fair face draws buyers, and our oranges must be turned into money; but he who does more than look has an affair with me; so gaze away, my master, and take it out in buying oranges! — *Ave Maria! ora pro nobis, nunc et,*" etc., etc.

A few moments, and the wave of prayer which had flowed down the quaint old shadowy street, bowing all heads as the wind bowed the scarlet tassels of neighboring clover-fields, was passed, and all the world resumed the work of earth just where they left off when the bell began.

"Good even to you, pretty maiden!" said the cavalier, approaching the stall of the orange-woman with the easy, confident air of one secure of a ready welcome, and bending down on the yet prayerful maiden the glances of a pair of piercing hazel eyes that looked out on each side of his aquiline nose with the keenness of a falcon's.

"Good even to you, pretty one! We shall take you for a saint, and worship you in right earnest, if you raise not those eyelashes soon."

"Sir! my lord!" said the girl, — a bright color flushing into her smooth brown cheeks, and her large dreamy eyes suddenly upraised with a flutter, as of a bird about to take flight.

"Agnes, bethink yourself!" said the white-haired dame; "the gentleman asks the price of your oranges; be alive, child!"

"Ah, my lord," said the young girl, "here are a dozen fine ones."

"Well, you shall give them me, pretty one," said the young man, throwing a gold piece down on the stand with a careless ring.

"Here, Agnes, run to the stall of Raphael the poulterer for change," said the adroit dame, picking up the gold.

"Nay, good mother, by your leave," said the unabashed cavalier; "I make my change with youth and beauty thus!" And with the word he stooped down and kissed the fair forehead between the eyes.

"For shame, sir!" said the elderly woman, raising her distaff, — her great glittering eyes flashing beneath her silver hair like tongues of lightning from a white cloud. "Have a care! — this child is named for blessed Saint Agnes, and is under her protection."

"The saints must pray for us, when their beauty makes us forget ourselves," said the young cavalier, with a smile. "Look me in the face, little one," he added; "say, wilt thou pray for me?"

The maiden raised her large serious eyes, and surveyed the haughty, handsome face with that look of sober inquiry which one sometimes sees in young children, and the blush slowly faded from her cheek, as a cloud fades after sunset.

"Yes, my lord," she answered, with a grave simplicity, "I will pray for you."

"And hang this upon the shrine of Saint Agnes for my sake," he added, drawing from his finger a diamond ring, which he dropped into her hand; and before mother or daughter could add another word or recover from their surprise, he had thrown the corner of his mantle over his shoulder and was off down the narrow street, humming the refrain of a gay song.

"You have struck a pretty dove with that bolt," said another cavalier, who appeared to have been observing the proceeding, and now, stepping forward, joined him.

"Like enough," said the first, carelessly.

"The old woman keeps her mewed up like a singing-bird," said the second; "and if a fellow wants speech of her, it's as much as his crown is worth; for Dame Elsie has a strong arm, and her distaff is known to be heavy."

"Upon my word," said the first cavalier, stopping and throwing a glance backward, "where do they keep her?"

"Oh, in a sort of pigeon's nest up above the Gorge; but one never sees her, except under the fire of her grandmother's eyes. The little one is brought up for a saint, they say, and goes nowhere but to mass, confession, and the sacrament."

"Humph!" said the other, "she looks like some choice old picture of Our Lady, — not a drop of human blood in her. When I kissed her forehead, she looked into my face as grave and innocent as a babe. One is tempted to try what one can do in such a case."

"Beware the grandmother's distaff!" said the other, laughing.

"I've seen old women before," said the cavalier, as they turned down the street and were lost to view.

Meanwhile the grandmother and grand-daughter were roused from the mute astonishment in which they were gazing after the young cavalier by a tittering behind them; and a pair of bright eyes looked out upon them from beneath a bundle of long, crimson-headed clover, whose rich carmine tints were touched to brighter life by setting sunbeams.

There stood Giulietta, the head coquette of the Sorrento girls, with her broad shoulders, full chest, and great black

eyes, rich and heavy as those of the silver-haired ox for
whose benefit she had been cutting clover. Her bronzed
cheek was smooth as that of any statue, and showed a color
like that of an open pomegranate; and the opulent, lazy
abundance of her ample form, with her leisurely movements,
spoke an easy and comfortable nature, — that is to say,
when Giulietta was pleased; for it is to be remarked that
there lurked certain sparkles deep down in her great eyes,
which might, on occasion, blaze out into sheet-lightning,
like her own beautiful skies, which, lovely as they are, can
thunder and sulk with terrible earnestness when the fit
takes them. At present, however, her face was running
over with mischievous merriment, as she slyly pinched little Agnes by the ear.

"So you know not yon gay cavalier, little sister?" she
said, looking askance at her from under her long lashes.

"No, indeed! What has an honest girl to do with
knowing gay cavaliers?" said Dame Elsie, bestirring herself with packing the remaining oranges into a basket,
which she covered trimly with a heavy linen towel of her
own weaving. "Girls never come to good who let their
eyes go walking through the earth, and have the names of
all the wild gallants on their tongues. Agnes knows no
such nonsense, — blessed be her gracious patroness, with
Our Lady and Saint Michael!"

"I hope there is no harm in knowing what is right before one's eyes," said Giulietta. "Anybody must be blind
and deaf not to know the Lord Adrian. All the girls in
Sorrento know him. They say he is even greater than he
appears, — that he is brother to the King himself; at any
rate, a handsomer and more gallant gentleman never wore
spurs."

"Let him keep to his own kind," said Elsie. "Eagles
make bad work in dove-cots. No good comes of such gallants for us."

"Nor any harm, that I ever heard of," said Giulietta. "But let me see, pretty one, — what did he give you? Holy Mother! what a handsome ring!"

"It is to hang on the shrine of Saint Agnes," said the younger girl, looking up with simplicity.

A loud laugh was the first answer to this communication. The scarlet clover-tops shook and quivered with the merriment.

"To hang on the shrine of Saint Agnes!" Giulietta repeated. "That is a little too good!"

"Go, go, you baggage!" said Elsie, wrathfully brandishing her spindle. "If ever you get a husband, I hope he'll give you a good beating! You need it, I warrant! Always stopping on the bridge there, to have cracks with the young men! Little enough you know of saints, I dare say! So keep away from *my* child! Come, Agnes," she said, as she lifted the orange-basket on to her head; and, straightening her tall form, she seized the girl by the hand to lead her away.

CHAPTER II

THE DOVE-COT

THE old town of Sorrento is situated on an elevated plateau, which stretches into the sunny waters of the Mediterranean, guarded on all sides by a barrier of mountains which defend it from bleak winds and serve to it the purpose of walls to a garden. Here, groves of oranges and lemons, with their almost fabulous coincidence of fruitage with flowers, fill the air with perfume, which blends with that of roses and jessamines; and the fields are so starred and enameled with flowers that they might have served as the type for those Elysian realms sung by ancient poets. The fervid air is fanned by continual sea-breezes, which give a delightful elasticity to the otherwise languid climate. Under all these cherishing influences, the human being develops a wealth and luxuriance of physical beauty unknown in less favored regions. In the region about Sorrento one may be said to have found the land where beauty is the rule and not the exception. The singularity there is not to see handsome points of physical proportion, but rather to see those who are without them. Scarce a man, woman, or child you meet who has not some personal advantage to be commended, while even striking beauty is common. Also, under these kindly skies, a native courtesy and gentleness of manner make themselves felt. It would seem as if humanity, rocked in this flowery cradle, and soothed by so many daily caresses and appliances of nursing Nature, grew up with all that is kindliest on the outward, — not repressed and beat in, as under the inclement atmosphere and stormy skies of the North.

The town of Sorrento itself overhangs the sea, skirting along rocky shores, which, hollowed here and there into picturesque grottoes, and fledged with a wild plumage of brilliant flowers and trailing vines, descend in steep precipices to the water. Along the shelly beach, at the bottom, one can wander to look out on the loveliest prospect in the world. Vesuvius rises with its two peaks softly clouded in blue and purple mists, which blend with its ascending vapors, — Naples and the adjoining villages at its base gleaming in the distance like a fringe of pearls on a regal mantle. Nearer by, the picturesque rocky shores of the island of Capri seem to pulsate through the dreamy, shifting mists that veil its sides; and the sea shimmers and glitters like the neck of a peacock with an iridescent mingling of colors: the whole air is a glorifying medium, rich in prismatic hues of enchantment.

The town on three sides is severed from the main land by a gorge two hundred feet in depth and forty or fifty in breadth, crossed by a bridge resting on double arches, the construction of which dates back to the time of the ancient Romans. This bridge affords a favorite lounging-place for the inhabitants, and at evening a motley assemblage may be seen lolling over its moss-grown sides, — men with their picturesque knit caps of scarlet or brown falling gracefully on one shoulder, and women with their shining black hair and the enormous pearl ear-rings which are the pride and heirlooms of every family. The present traveler at Sorrento may remember standing on this bridge and looking down the gloomy depths of the gorge, to where a fair villa, with its groves of orange-trees and gardens, overhangs the tremendous depths below.

Hundreds of years since, where this villa now stands was the simple dwelling of the two women whose history we have begun to tell you. There you might have seen a small stone cottage with a two-arched arcade in front,

gleaming brilliantly white out of the dusky foliage of an
orange-orchard.   The dwelling was wedged like a bird-box
between two fragments of rock, and behind it the land
rose rocky, high, and steep, so as to form a natural wall.
A small ledge or terrace of cultivated land here hung in
air, — below it, a precipice of two hundred feet down into
the Gorge of Sorrento.   A couple of dozen orange-trees,
straight and tall, with healthy, shining bark, here shot up
from the fine black volcanic soil, and made with their foliage a twilight shadow on the ground, so deep that no vege-
tation, save a fine velvet moss, could dispute their claim to
its entire nutritious offices.   These trees were the sole
wealth of the women and the sole ornament of the garden;
but, as they stood there, not only laden with golden fruit,
but fragrant with pearly blossoms, they made the little
rocky platform seem a perfect Garden of the Hesperides.
The stone cottage, as we have said, had an open, white-
washed arcade in front, from which one could look down
into the gloomy depths of the gorge, as into some mysterious underworld.   Strange and weird it seemed, with its
fathomless shadows and its wild grottoes, over which hung,
silently waving, long pendants of ivy, while dusky gray
aloes uplifted their horned heads from great rock-rifts, like
elfin spirits struggling upward out of the shade.   Nor was
wanting the usual gentle poetry of flowers; for white iris
leaned its fairy pavilion over the black void like a pale-
cheeked princess from the window of some dark enchanted
castle, and scarlet geranium and golden broom and crimson
gladiolus waved and glowed in the shifting beams of the
sunlight.   Also there was in this little spot what forms the
charm of Italian gardens always, — the sweet song and
prattle of waters.   A clear mountain-spring burst through
the rock on one side of the little cottage, and fell with a
lulling noise into a quaint moss-grown water-trough, which
had been in former times the sarcophagus of some old

Roman sepulchre. Its sides were richly sculptured with figures and leafy scrolls and arabesques, into which the sly-footed lichens with quiet growth had so insinuated themselves as in some places almost to obliterate the original design; while, round the place where the water fell, a veil of ferns and maiden's-hair, studded with tremulous silver drops, vibrated to its soothing murmur. The superfluous waters, drained off by a little channel on one side, were conducted through the rocky parapet of the garden, whence they trickled and tinkled from rock to rock, falling with a continual drip among the swaying ferns and pendent ivy wreaths, till they reached the little stream at the bottom of the gorge. This parapet or garden-wall was formed of blocks or fragments of what had once been white marble, the probable remains of the ancient tomb from which the sarcophagus was taken. Here and there a marble acanthus-leaf, or the capital of an old column, or a fragment of sculpture jutted from under the mosses, ferns, and grasses with which prodigal Nature had filled every interstice and carpeted the whole. These sculptured fragments everywhere in Italy seem to whisper, from the dust, of past life and death, of a cycle of human existence forever gone, over whose tomb the life of to-day is built.

"Sit down and rest, my dove," said Dame Elsie to her little charge, as they entered their little enclosure.

Here she saw for the first time, what she had not noticed in the heat and hurry of her ascent, that the girl was panting and her gentle bosom rising and falling in thick heartbeats, occasioned by the haste with which she had drawn her onward.

"Sit down, dearie, and I will get you a bit of supper."

"Yes, grandmother, I will. I must tell my beads once for the soul of the handsome gentleman that kissed my forehead to-night."

"How did you know that he was handsome, child?"
said the old dame, with some sharpness in her voice.

"He bade me look on him, grandmother, and I saw it."

"You must put such thoughts away, child," said the old
dame.

"Why must I?" said the girl, looking up with an eye
as clear and unconscious as that of a three-year-old child.

"If she does not think, why should I tell her?" said
Dame Elsie, as she turned to go into the house, and left
the child sitting on the mossy parapet that overlooked the
gorge. Thence she could see far off, not only down the
dim, sombre abyss, but out to the blue Mediterranean beyond, now calmly lying in swathing-bands of purple, gold,
and orange, while the smoky cloud that overhung Vesuvius
became silver and rose in the evening light.

There is always something of elevation and purity that
seems to come over one from being in an elevated region.
One feels morally as well as physically above the world,
and from that clearer air able to look down on it calmly
with disengaged freedom. Our little maiden sat for a few
moments gazing, her large brown eyes dilating with a
tremulous lustre, as if tears were half of a mind to start in
them, and her lips apart with a delicate earnestness, like
one who is pursuing some pleasing inner thought. Suddenly rousing herself, she began by breaking the freshest
orange-blossoms from the golden-fruited trees, and, kissing
and pressing them to her bosom, she proceeded to remove
the faded flowers of the morning from before a little rude
shrine in the rock, where, in a sculptured niche, was a
picture of the Madonna and Child, with a locked glass door
in front of it. The picture was a happy transcript of one
of the fairest creations of the religious school of Florence,
done by one of those rustic copyists of whom Italy is full,
who appear to possess the instinct of painting, and to
whom we owe many of those sweet faces which sometimes

look down on us by the wayside from rudest and home-
liest shrines.

The poor fellow by whom it had been painted was one
to whom years before Dame Elsie had given food and shelter for many months during a lingering illness; and he had
painted so much of his dying heart and hopes into it that
it had a peculiar and vital vividness in its power of affect-
ing the feelings. Agnes had been familiar with this picture from early infancy. No day of her life had the flowers
failed to be freshly placed before it. It had seemed to
smile down sympathy on her childish joys, and to cloud
over with her childish sorrows. It was less a picture to
her than a presence; and the whole air of the little orange-
garden seemed to be made sacred by it. When she had
arranged her flowers, she kneeled down and began to say
prayers for the soul of the young gallant.

"Holy Jesus," she said, "he is young, rich, handsome,
and a king's brother; and for all these things the Fiend
may tempt him to forget his God and throw away his soul.
Holy Mother, give him good counsel! "

"Come, child, to your supper," said Dame Elsie. "I
have milked the goats, and everything is ready."

CHAPTER III

THE GORGE

After her light supper was over, Agnes took her dis.
taff, wound with shining white flax, and went and seated
herself in her favorite place, on the low parapet that overlooked the gorge.

This ravine, with its dizzy depths, its waving foliage,
its dripping springs and the low murmur of the little
stream that pursued its way far down at the bottom, was
one of those things which stimulated her impressible imagination, and filled her with a solemn and vague delight.
The ancient Italian tradition made it the home of fauns and
dryads, wild woodland creatures, intermediate links between
vegetable life and that of sentiment and reasoning humanity. The more earnest faith that came in with Christianity, if it had its brighter lights in an immortality of blessedness, had also its deeper shadows in the intenser perceptions
it awakened of sin and evil, and of the mortal struggle by
which the human spirit must avoid endless woe and rise to
endless felicity. The myths with which the colored Italian
air was filled in mediæval ages no longer resembled those
graceful, floating, cloud-like figures one sees in the ancient
chambers of Pompeii, — the bubbles and rainbows of human
fancy, rising aimless and buoyant, with a mere freshness
of animal life, against a black background of ·utter and
hopeless ignorance as to man's past or future. They were
rather expressed by solemn images of mournful, majestic
angels and of triumphant saints, or fearful, warning presen-
tations of loathsome fiends. Each lonesome gorge and

sombre dell had tales no more of tricky fauns and dryads, but of those restless, wandering demons who, having lost their own immortality of blessedness, constantly lie in wait to betray frail humanity, and cheat it of that glorious inheritance bought by the Great Redemption.

The education of Agnes had been one which rendered her whole system peculiarly sensitive and impressible to all influences from the invisible and unseen. Of this education we shall speak more particularly hereafter. At present we see her sitting in the twilight on the moss-grown marble parapet, her distaff, with its silvery flax, lying idly in her hands, and her widening dark eyes gazing intently into the gloomy gorge below, from which arose the far-off complaining babble of the brook at the bottom and the shiver and sigh of evening winds through the trailing ivy. The white mist was slowly rising, wavering, undulating, and creeping its slow way up the sides of the gorge. Now it hid a tuft of foliage, and now it wreathed itself around a horned clump of aloes, and, streaming far down below it in the dimness, made it seem like the goblin robe of some strange, supernatural being.

The evening light had almost burned out in the sky; only a band of vivid red lay low in the horizon out to sea, and the round full moon was just rising like a great silver lamp, while Vesuvius with its smoky top began in the obscurity to show its faintly flickering fires. A vague agitation seemed to oppress the child; for she sighed deeply, and often repeated with fervor the Ave Maria.

At this moment there began to rise from the very depths of the gorge below her the sound of a rich tenor voice, with a slow, sad modulation, and seeming to pulsate upward through the filmy, shifting mists. It was one of those voices which seem fit to be the outpouring of some spirit denied all other gifts of expression, and rushing with passionate fervor through this one gate of utterance. So

distinctly were the words spoken, that they seemed each
one to rise as with a separate intelligence out of the mist,
and to knock at the door of the heart.

> Sad is my life, and lonely!
> No hope for me,
> Save thou, my love, my only,
> I see!
>
> Where art thou, O my fairest?
> Where art thou gone?
> Dove of the rock, I languish
> Alone!
>
> They say thou art so saintly,
> Who dare love thee?
> Yet bend thine eyelids holy
> On me!
>
> Though heaven alone possess thee,
> Thou dwell'st above,
> Yet heaven, didst thou but know it,
> Is love.

There was such an intense earnestness in these sounds,
that large tears gathered in the wide dark eyes, and fell
one after another upon the sweet alyssum and maiden's-hair
that grew in the crevices of the marble wall. She shivered
and drew away from the parapet, and thought of stories
she had heard the nuns tell of wandering spirits who sometimes in lonesome places pour forth such entrancing music
as bewilders the brain of the unwary listener, and leads
him to some fearful destruction.

"Agnes!" said the sharp voice of old Elsie, appearing
at the door, "here! where are you?"

"Here, grandmamma."

"Who's that singing this time o' night?"

"I don't know, grandmamma."

Somehow the child felt as if that singing were strangely
sacred to her, — a *rapport* between her and something
vague and invisible which might yet become dear.

"Is 't down in the gorge?" said the old woman, coming

with her heavy, decided step to the parapet, and looking over, her keen black eyes gleaming like dagger-blades into the mist. "If there's anybody there," she said, "let them go away, and not be troubling honest women with any of their caterwauling. Come, Agnes," she said, pulling the girl by the sleeve, "you must be tired, my lamb! and your evening prayers are always so long, best be about them, girl, so that old grandmamma may put you to bed. What ails the girl? Been crying! Your hand is cold as a stone."

"Grandmamma, what if that might be a spirit?" she said. "Sister Rosa told me stories of singing spirits that have been in this very gorge."

"Likely enough," said Dame Elsie; "but what's that to us? Let 'em sing! — so long as we don't listen, where's the harm done? We will sprinkle holy water all round the parapet, and say the office of Saint Agnes, and let them sing till they are hoarse."

Such was the triumphant view which this energetic good woman took of the power of the means of grace which her church placed at her disposal.

Nevertheless, while Agnes was kneeling at her evening prayers, the old dame consoled herself with a soliloquy, as with a brush she vigorously besprinkled the premises with holy water.

"Now, here's the plague of a girl! If she's handsome, — and nobody wants one that isn't, — why, then, it's a purgatory to look after her. This one is good enough, — none of your hussies, like Giulietta: but the better they are, the more sure to have fellows after them. A murrain on that cavalier, — king's brother, or what not! — it was he serenading, I'll be bound. I must tell Antonio, and have the girl married, for aught I see: and I don't want to give her to him either; he didn't bring her up. There's no peace for us mothers. Maybe I'll tell Father

Francesco about it. That's the way poor little Isella was carried away. Singing is of the Devil, I believe; it always bewitches girls. I'd like to have poured some hot oil down the rocks: I'd have made him squeak in another tone, I reckon. Well, well! I hope I shall come in for a good seat in paradise for all the trouble I've had with her mother, and am like to have with her, — that's all!"

In an hour more, the large, round, sober moon was shining fixedly on the little mansion in the rocks, silvering the glossy darkness of the orange-leaves, while the scent of the blossoms arose like clouds about the cottage. The moonlight streamed through the unglazed casement, and made a square of light on the little bed where Agnes was sleeping, in which square her delicate face was framed, with its tremulous and spiritual expression most resembling in its sweet plaintive purity some of the Madonna faces of Fra Angelico, — those tender wild flowers of Italian religion and poetry.

By her side lay her grandmother, with those sharp, hard, clearly cut features, so worn and bronzed by time, so lined with labor and care, as to resemble one of the Fates in the picture of Michel Angelo; and even in her sleep she held the delicate lily hand of the child in her own hard, brown one, with a strong and determined clasp.

While they sleep, we must tell something more of the story of the little Agnes, — of what she is, and what are the causes which have made her such.

CHAPTER IV

WHO AND WHAT

OLD Elsie was not born a peasant. Originally she was the wife of a steward in one of those great families of Rome whose estate and traditions were princely. Elsie, as her figure and profile and all her words and movements indicated, was of a strong, shrewd, ambitious, and courageous character, and well disposed to turn to advantage every gift with which Nature had endowed her.

Providence made her a present of a daughter whose beauty was wonderful, even in a country where beauty is no uncommon accident. In addition to her beauty, the little Isella had quick intelligence, wit, grace, and spirit. As a child she became the pet and plaything of the Princess whom Elsie served. This noble lady, pressed by the *ennui* which is always the moth and rust on the purple and gold of rank and wealth, had, as other noble ladies had in those days, and have now, sundry pets: greyhounds, white and delicate, that looked as if they were made of Sèvres china; spaniels with long silky ears and fringy paws; apes and monkeys, that made at times sad devastations in her wardrobe; and a most charming little dwarf, that was ugly enough to frighten the very owls, and spiteful as he was ugly. She had, moreover, peacocks, and macaws, and parrots, and all sorts of singing-birds, and falcons of every breed, and horses, and hounds, — in short, there is no saying what she did *not* have. One day she took it into her head to add the little Isella to the number of her acquisitions. With the easy grace of aristocracy, she reached out her jeweled hand and took Elsie's one flower to add to her conservatory, — and Elsie was only too proud to have it so.

Her daughter was kept constantly about the person of the Princess, and instructed in all the wisdom which would have been allowed her, had she been the Princess's own daughter, which, to speak the truth, was in those days nothing very profound, — consisting of a little singing and instrumentation, a little embroidery and dancing, with the power of writing her own name and of reading a love letter.

All the world knows that the very idea of a pet is something to be spoiled for the amusement of the pet-owner; and Isella was spoiled in the most particular and circumstantial manner. She had suits of apparel for every day in the year, and jewels without end, — for the Princess was never weary of trying the effect of her beauty in this and that costume; so that she sported through the great grand halls and down the long aisles of the garden much like a bright-winged humming-bird, or a damsel-fly all green and gold. She was a genuine child of Italy, — full of feeling, spirit, and genius, — alive in every nerve to the finger-tips; and under the tropical sunshine of her mistress's favor she grew as an Italian rosebush does, throwing its branches freakishly over everything in a wild labyrinth of perfume, brightness, and thorns.

For a while her life was a triumph, and her mother triumphed with her at an humble distance. The Princess was devoted to her with the blind fatuity with which ladies of rank at times will invest themselves in a caprice. She arrogated to herself all the praises of her beauty and wit, allowed her to flirt and make conquests to her heart's content, and engaged to marry her to some handsome young officer of her train, when she had done being amused with her.

Now we must not wonder that a young head of fifteen should have been turned by this giddy elevation, nor that an old head of fifty should have thought all things were possible in the fortune of such a favorite. Nor must we wonder that the young coquette, rich in the laurels of a hundred conquests, should have turned her bright eyes on the son and heir, when he came home from the University of Bologna. Nor is it to be wondered at, that this same son and heir, being a man as well as a Prince, should have done as other men did, — fallen desperately in love with this dazzling, sparkling, piquant mixture of matter and spirit, which no university can prepare a young man to comprehend, — which always seemed to run from him, and yet always threw a Parthian shot behind her as she fled. Nor is it to be wondered at, if this same Prince, after a week or two, did not know whether he was on his head or his heels, or whether the sun rose in the east or the south, or where he stood, or whither he was going.

In fact, the youthful pair very soon came into that dreamland where are no more any points of the compass, no more division of time, no more latitude and longitude, no more up and down, but only a general wandering among enchanted groves and singing nightingales.

It was entirely owing to old Elsie's watchful shrewdness and address that the lovers came into this paradise by the gate of marriage; for the young man was ready to offer anything at the feet of his divinity, as the old mother was not slow to perceive.

So they stood at the altar for the time being a pair of as true lovers as Romeo and Juliet: but then, what has true love to do with the son of a hundred generations and heir to a Roman principality?

Of course, the rose of love, having gone through all its stages of bud and blossom into full flower, must next begin to drop its leaves. Of course. Who ever heard of an immortal rose?

The time of discovery came. Isella was found to be a mother; and then the storm burst upon her and drabbled her in the dust as fearlessly as the summer wind sweeps down and besmirches the lily it has all summer been wooing and flattering.

The Princess was a very pious and moral lady, and of course threw her favorite out into the street as a vile weed, and virtuously ground her down under her jeweled highheeled shoes.

She could have forgiven her any common frailty; of course it was natural that the girl should have been seduced by the all-conquering charms of her son, — but aspire to marriage with their house! — pretend to be her son's wife! Since the time of Judas had such treachery ever been heard of?

Something was said of the propriety of walling up the culprit alive, — a mode of disposing of small family matters somewhat à la mode in those times. But the Princess acknowledged herself foolishly tender, and unable quite to allow this very obvious propriety in the case.

She contented herself with turning mother and daughter into the streets with every mark of ignominy, which was reduplicated by every one of her servants, lackeys, and court-companions, who, of course, had always known just how the thing must end.

As to the young Prince, he acted as a well-instructed young nobleman should, who understands the great difference there is between the tears of a duchess and those of low-born women. No sooner did he behold his conduct in the light of his mother's countenance than he turned his back on his low marriage with edifying penitence. He did not think it necessary to convince his mother of the real existence of a union whose very supposition made her so unhappy, and occasioned such an uncommonly disagreeable and tempestuous state of things in the well-bred circle where his birth called him to move. Being, however, a religious youth, he opened his mind to his family-confessor, by whose advice he sent a messenger with a large sum of money to Elsie, piously commending her and her daughter to the Divine protection. He also gave orders for an entire new suit of raiment for the Virgin Mary in the family chapel, including a splendid set of diamonds, and promised unlimited candles to the altar of a neighboring convent. If all this could not atone for a youthful error, it was a pity. So he thought, as he drew on his riding gloves and went off on a hunting party, like a gallant and religious young nobleman.

Elsie, meanwhile, with her forlorn and disgraced daughter, found a temporary asylum in a neighboring mountain village, where the poor, bedrabbled, broken-winged songbird soon panted and fluttered her little life away.

When the once beautiful and gay Isella had been hidden in the grave, cold and lonely, there remained a little wailing infant, which Elsie gathered to her bosom.

Grim, dauntless, and resolute, she resolved, for the sake of this hapless one, to look life in the face once more, and try the battle under other skies.

Taking the infant in her arms, she traveled with her far from the scene of her birth, and set all her energies at work to make for her a better destiny than that which had fallen to the lot of her unfortunate mother.

She set about to create her nature and order her fortunes with that sort of downright energy with which resolute people always attack the problem of a new human existence. This child should be happy: the rocks on which her mother was wrecked she should never strike upon, — they were all marked on Elsie's chart. Love had been the root of all poor Isella's troubles, — and Agnes never should know love, till taught it safely by a husband of Elsie's own choosing.

The first step of security was in naming her for the chaste Saint Agnes, and placing her girlhood under her special protection. Secondly, which was quite as much to the point, she brought her up laboriously in habits of incessant industry, — never suffering her to be out of her sight, or to have any connection or friendship, except such as could be carried on under the immediate supervision of her piercing black eyes. Every night she put her to bed as if she had been an infant, and, wakening her again in the morning, took her with her in all her daily toils, — of which, to do her justice, she performed all the hardest portion, leaving to the girl just enough to keep her hands employed and her head steady.

The peculiar circumstance which had led her to choose the old town of Sorrento for her residence, in preference to any of the beautiful villages which impearl that fertile plain, was the existence there of a flourishing convent dedicated to Saint Agnes, under whose protecting shadow her young charge might more securely spend the earlier years of her life.

With this view, having hired the domicile we have already described, she lost no time in making the favorable acquaintance of the sisterhood, — never coming to them empty-handed. The finest oranges of her garden, the whitest flax of her spinning, were always reserved as offerings at the shrine of the patroness whom she sought to propitiate for her grandchild.

In her earliest childhood the little Agnes was led toddling to the shrine by her zealous relative, and at the sight of her fair, sweet, awestruck face, with its viny mantle of encircling curls, the torpid bosoms of the sisterhood throbbed with a strange, new pleasure, which they humbly hoped was not sinful, — as agreeable things, they found, generally were. They loved the echoes of her little feet down the damp, silent aisles of their chapel, and her small, sweet, slender voice, as she asked strange baby-questions, which, as usual with baby-questions, hit all the insoluble points of philosophy and theology exactly on the head.

The child became a special favorite with the Abbess, Sister Theresa, a tall, thin, bloodless, sad-eyed woman, who looked as if she might have been cut out of one of the glaciers of Monte Rosa, but in whose heart the little fair one had made herself a niche, pushing her way up through, as you may have seen a lovely blue-fringed gentian standing in a snowdrift of the Alps with its little ring of melted snow around it.

Sister Theresa offered to take care of the child at any time when the grandmother wished to be about her labors; and so, during her early years, the little one was often domesticated for days together at the Convent. A perfect mythology of wonderful stories encircled her, which the good sisters were never tired of repeating to each other. They were the simplest sayings and doings of childhood, — handfuls of such wild flowers as bespread the green turf of nursery-life everywhere, but miraculous blossoms in the eyes of these good women, whom Saint Agnes had unwittingly deprived of any power of making comparisons or ever having Christ's sweetest parable of the heavenly kingdom enacted in homes of their own.

Old Jocunda, the portress, never failed to make a sensation with her one stock-story of how she found the child standing on her head and crying, — having been put into this reversed position in consequence of climbing up on a high stool to get her little fat hand into the vase of holy water, failing in which Christian attempt, her heels went up and her head down, greatly to her dismay.

"Nevertheless," said old Jocunda, gravely, "it showed an edifying turn in the child; and when I lifted the little thing up, it stopped crying the minute its little fingers touched the water, and it made a cross on its forehead as sensible as the oldest among us. Ah, sisters, there's grace there, or I'm mistaken."

All the signs of an incipient saint were, indeed, manifested in the little one. She never played the wild and noisy plays of common children, but busied herself in making altars and shrines, which she adorned with the prettiest flowers of the gardens, and at which she worked hour after hour in the quietest and happiest earnestness. Her dreams were a constant source of wonder and edification in the Convent, for they were all of angels and saints; and many a time, after hearing one, the sisterhood crossed themselves, and the Abbess said, "*Ex oribus parvulorum.*" Always sweet, dutiful, submissive, cradling herself every night with a lulling of sweet hymns and infant murmur of prayers, and found sleeping in her little white bed with her crucifix clasped to her bosom, it was no wonder that the Abbess thought her the special favorite of her divine patroness, and like her the subject of an early vocation to be the celestial bride of One fairer than the children of men, who should snatch her away from all earthly things, to be united to Him in a celestial paradise.

As the child grew older, she often sat at evening with wide, wondering eyes, listening over and over again to the story of the fair Saint Agnes, — how she was a princess, living in her father's palace, of such exceeding beauty and grace that none saw her but to love her, yet of such sweetness and humility as passed all comparison; and how, when a heathen prince would have espoused her to his son, she said, "Away from me, tempter! for I am betrothed to a lover who is greater and fairer than any earthly suitor, — he is so fair that the sun and moon are ravished by his beauty, so mighty that the angels of heaven are his servants;" how she bore meekly with persecutions and threatenings and death for the sake of this unearthly love; and when she had poured out her blood, how she came to her mourning friends in ecstatic vision, all white and glistening, with a fair lamb by her side, and bade them weep not for her, because she was reigning with Him whom on earth she had preferred to all other lovers. There was also the legend of the fair Cecilia, the lovely musician whom angels had rapt away to their choirs; the story of that queenly saint, Catharine, who passed through the courts of heaven, and saw the angels crowned with roses and lilies, and the Virgin on her throne, who gave her the wedding ring that espoused her to be the bride of the King Eternal.

Fed with such legends, it could not be but that a child with a sensitive, nervous organization and vivid imagination, should have grown up with an unworldly and spiritual character, and that a poetic mist should have enveloped all her outward perceptions similar to that palpitating veil of blue and lilac vapor that enshrouds the Italian landscape.

Nor is it to be marveled at, if the results of this system of education went far beyond what the good old grandmother intended. For, though a stanch good Christian, after the manner of those times, yet she had not the slightest mind to see her grand-daughter a nun; on the contrary, she was working day and night to add to her dowry, and had in her eye a reputable middle-aged blacksmith, who was a man of substance and prudence, to be the husband and keeper of her precious treasure. In a home thus established she hoped to enthrone herself, and provide for the rearing of a generation of stout-limbed girls and boys who should grow up to make a flourishing household in the land. This subject she had not yet broached to her grand-daughter, though daily preparing to do so, — deferring it, it must be told, from a sort of jealous, yearning craving to have wholly to herself the child for whom she had lived so many years.

Antonio, the blacksmith to whom this honor was destined, was one of those broad backed, full-chested, long-limbed fellows one shall often see around Sorrento, with great, kind, black eyes like those of an ox, and all the attributes of a healthy, kindly, animal nature. Contentedly he hammered away at his business; and certainly, had not Dame Elsie of her own providence elected him to be the husband of her fair grand-daughter, he would never have thought of the matter himself; but, opening the black eyes aforenamed upon the girl, he perceived that she was fair, and also received an inner light through Dame Elsie as to the amount of her dowry; and, putting these matters together, conceived a kindness for the maiden, and awaited with tranquillity the time when he should be allowed to commence his wooing.

CHAPTER V

THE next morning Elsie awoke, as was her custom, when the very faintest hue of dawn streaked the horizon. A hen who has seen a hawk balancing his wings and cawing in mid-air over her downy family could not have awakened with her feathers, metaphorically speaking, in a more bristling state of caution.

"Spirits in the gorge, quotha?" said she to herself, as she vigorously adjusted her dress. "I believe so, — spirits in good sound bodies, I believe; and next we shall hear, there will be rope-ladders, and climbings, and the Lord knows what. I shall go to confession this very morning, and tell Father Francesco the danger; and instead of taking her down to sell oranges, suppose I send her to the sisters to carry the ring and a basket of oranges?"

"Ah, ah!" she said, pausing, after she was dressed, and addressing a coarse print of Saint Agnes pasted against the wall, — "you look very meek there, and it was a great thing, no doubt, to die as you did; but if you'd lived to be married and bring up a family of girls, you'd have known something greater. Please, don't take offense with a poor old woman who has got into the way of speaking her mind freely! I'm foolish, and don't know much, — so, dear lady, pray for me!" And old Elsie bent her knee and crossed herself reverently, and then went out, leaving her young charge still sleeping.

It was yet dusky dawn when she might have been seen kneeling, with her sharp, clear-cut profile, at the grate of a confession-box in a church in Sorrento. Within was seated a personage who will have some influence on our story, and who must therefore be somewhat minutely introduced to the reader.

Il Padre Francesco had only within the last year arrived in the neighborhood, having been sent as superior of a brotherhood of Capuchins, whose convent was perched on a crag in the vicinity. With this situation came a pastoral care of the district; and Elsie and her grand-daughter found in him a spiritual pastor very different from the fat, jolly, easy Brother Girolamo, to whose place he had been appointed. The latter had been one of those numerous priests taken from the peasantry, who never rise above the average level of thought of the body from which they are drawn. Easy, gossipy, fond of good living and good stories, sympathetic in troubles and in joys, he had been a general favorite in the neighborhood, without exerting any particularly spiritualizing influence.

It required but a glance at Father Francesco to see that he was in all respects the opposite of this. It was evident that he came from one of the higher classes, by that indefinable air of birth and breeding which makes itself felt under every change of costume. Who he might be, what might have been his past history, what rank he might have borne, what part played in the great warfare of life, was all of course sunk in the oblivion of his religious profession, where, as at the grave, a man laid down name and fame and past history and worldly goods, and took up a coarse garb and a name chosen from the roll of the saints, in sign that the world that had known him should know him no more.

Imagine a man between thirty and forty, with that round, full, evenly developed head, and those chiseled features, which one sees on ancient busts and coins no less than in the streets of modern Rome. The cheeks were sunken and sallow; the large, black, melancholy eyes had a wistful, anxious, penetrative expression, that spoke a stringent, earnest spirit, which, however deep might be the grave in which it lay buried, had not yet found repose. The long, thin, delicately formed hands were emaciated and bloodless; they clasped with a nervous eagerness a rosary and crucifix of ebony and silver, — the only mark of luxury that could be discerned in a costume unusually threadbare and squalid. The whole picture of the man, as he sat there, had it been painted and hung in a gallery, was such as must have stopped every person of a certain amount of sensibility before it with the conviction that behind that strong, melancholy, earnest figure and face lay one of those hidden histories of human passion in which the vivid life of mediæval Italy was so fertile.

He was listening to Elsie, as she knelt, with that easy air of superiority which marks a practiced man of the world, yet with a grave attention which showed that her communication had awakened the deepest interest in his mind. Every few moments he moved slightly in his seat, and interrupted the flow of the narrative by an inquiry concisely put, in tones which, clear and low, had a solemn and severe distinctness, producing, in the still, dusky twilight of the church, an almost ghostly effect.

When the communication was over, he stepped out of the confessional and said to Elsie in parting, "My daughter, you have done well to take this in time. The devices of Satan in our corrupt times are numerous and artful, and they who keep the Lord's sheep must not sleep. Before many days I will call and examine the child; meanwhile I approve your course."

It was curious to see the awestruck, trembling manner in which old Elsie, generally so intrepid and commanding, stood before this man in his brown rough woolen gown with his corded waist; but she had an instinctive percep-

tion of the presence of the man of superior birth no less
than a reverence for the man of religion.

After she had departed from the church, the Capuchin
stood lost in thought; and to explain his revery, we must
throw some further light on his history.

Il Padre Francesco, as his appearance and manner inti-
mated, was in truth from one of the most distinguished
families of Florence.   He was one of those whom an
ancient writer characterizes as "men of longing desire."
Born with a nature of restless stringency that seemed to
doom him never to know repose, excessive in all things,
he had made early trial of ambition, of war, and of what
the gallants of his time called love, — plunging into all the
dissipated excesses of a most dissolute age, and outdoing in
luxury and extravagance the foremost of his companions.

The wave of a great religious impulse — which in our
times would have been called a revival — swept over the
city of Florence, and bore him, with multitudes of others,
to listen to the fervid preaching of the Dominican monk,
Jerome Savonarola; and amid the crowd that trembled,
wept, and beat their breasts under his awful denunciations,
he, too, felt within himself a heavenly call, — the death of
an old life, and the uprising of a new purpose.

The colder manners and more repressed habits of modern
times can give no idea of the wild fervor of a religious
revival among a people so passionate and susceptible to
impressions as the Italians.   It swept society like a spring
torrent from the sides of the Apennines, bearing all before
it.   Houses were sacked with religious fervor by penitent
owners, and licentious pictures and statuary and books, and
all the thousand temptations and appliances of a luxurious
age, were burned in the great public square.   Artists con-
victed of impure and licentious designs threw their palettes
and brushes into the expiatory flames, and retired to convents, till called forth by the voice of the preacher, and bid

to turn their art into higher channels. Since the days of
Saint Francis no such profound religious impulse had agitated the Italian community.

In our times a conversion is signalized by few outward
changes, however deep the inner life; but the life of the
Middle Ages was profoundly symbolical, and always required
the help of material images in its expression.

The gay and dissolute young Lorenzo Sforza took leave
of the world with rites of awful solemnity. He made his
will and disposed of all his worldly property, and assem-
bling his friends, bade them the farewell of a dying man.
Arrayed as for the grave, he was laid in his coffin, and
thus carried from his stately dwelling by the brethren of
the Misericordia, who, in their ghostly costume, with
mournful chants and lighted candles, bore him to the tomb
of his ancestors, where the coffin was deposited in the
vault, and its occupant passed the awful hours of the night
in darkness and solitude. Thence he was carried, the next
day, almost in a state of insensibility, to a neighboring
convent of the severest order, where, for some weeks, he
observed a penitential retreat of silence and prayer, neither
seeing nor hearing any living being but his spiritual director.

The effect of all this on an ardent and sensitive temperament can scarcely be conceived; and it is not to be wondered at that the once gay and luxurious Lorenzo Sforza,
when emerging from this tremendous discipline, was so
wholly lost in the worn and weary Padre Francesco that it
seemed as if in fact he had died and another had stepped
into his place. The face was ploughed deep with haggard
furrows, and the eyes were as those of a man who has seen
the fearful secrets of another life. He voluntarily sought
a post as far removed as possible from the scenes of his
early days, so as more completely to destroy his identity
with the past; and he devoted himself with enthusiasm to

the task of awakening to a higher spiritual life the indolent, self-indulgent monks of his order, and the ignorant peasantry of the vicinity.

But he soon discovered, what every earnest soul learns who has been baptized into a sense of things invisible, how utterly powerless and inert any mortal man is to inspire others with his own insights and convictions. With bitter discouragement and chagrin, he saw that the spiritual man must forever lift the dead weight of all the indolence and indifference and animal sensuality that surround him, — that the curse of Cassandra is upon him, forever to burn and writhe under awful visions of truths which no one around him will regard. In early life the associate only of the cultivated and the refined, Father Francesco could not but experience at times an insupportable *ennui* in listening to the confessions of people who had never learned either to think or to feel with any degree of distinctness, and whom his most fervent exhortations could not lift above the most trivial interests of a mere animal life. He was weary of the childish quarrels and bickerings of the monks, of their puerility, of their selfishness and self-indulgence, of their hopeless vulgarity of mind, and utterly discouraged with their inextricable labyrinths of deception. A melancholy deep as the grave seized on him, and he redoubled his austerities, in the hope that by making life painful he might make it also short.

But the first time that the clear, sweet tones of Agnes rang in his ears at the confessional, and her words, so full of unconscious poetry and repressed genius, came like a strain of sweet music through the grate, he felt at his heart a thrill to which it had long been a stranger, and which seemed to lift the weary, aching load from off his soul, as if some invisible angel had borne it up on his wings.

In his worldly days he had known women as the gallants in Boccaccio's romances knew them, and among them

one enchantress whose sorceries had kindled in his heart
one of those fatal passions which burn out the whole of a
man's nature, and leave it, like a sacked city, only a smoul-
dering heap of ashes. Deepest, therefore, among his vows
of renunciation had been those which divided him from all
womankind. The gulf that parted him and them was in
his mind deep as hell, and he thought of the sex only in
the light of temptation and danger. For the first time in
his life, an influence serene, natural, healthy, and sweet
breathed over him from the mind of a woman, — an influence so heavenly and peaceful that he did not challenge or
suspect it, but rather opened his worn heart insensibly to
it, as one in a fetid chamber naturally breathes freer when
the fresh air is admitted.

How charming it was to find his most spiritual exhortations seized upon with the eager comprehension of a nature
innately poetic and ideal! Nay, it sometimes seemed to
him as if the suggestions which he gave her dry and leaf-
less she brought again to him in miraculous clusters of
flowers, like the barren rod of Joseph, which broke into
blossoms when he was betrothed to the spotless Mary; and
yet, withal, she was so humbly unconscious, so absolutely
ignorant of the beauty of all she said and thought, that she
impressed him less as a mortal woman than as one of those
divine miracles in feminine form of which he had heard in
the legends of the saints.

Thenceforward his barren, discouraged life began to
blossom with wayside flowers, — and he mistrusted not the
miracle, because the flowers were all heavenly. The pious
thought or holy admonition that he saw trodden under the
swinish feet of the monks he gathered up again in hope, —
she would understand it; and gradually all his thoughts
became like carrier-doves, which, having once learned the
way to a favorite haunt, are ever fluttering to return
thither.

Such is the wonderful power of human sympathy, that the discovery even of the existence of a soul capable of understanding our inner life often operates as a perfect charm; every thought, and feeling, and aspiration carries with it a new value, from the interwoven consciousness that attends it of the worth it would bear to that other mind; so that, while that person lives, our existence is doubled in value, even though oceans divide us.

The cloud of hopeless melancholy which had brooded over the mind of Father Francesco lifted and sailed away, he knew not why, he knew not when. A secret joyfulness and alacrity possessed his spirits; his prayers became more fervent and his praises more frequent. Until now, his meditations had been most frequently those of fear and wrath, — the awful majesty of God, the terrible punishment of sinners, which he conceived with all that haggard, dreadful sincerity of vigor which characterized the modern Etruscan phase of religion of which the "Inferno" of Dante was the exponent and the outcome. His preachings and his exhortations had dwelt on that lurid world seen by the severe Florentine, at whose threshold hope forever departs, and around whose eternal circles of living torture the shivering spirit wanders dismayed and blasted by terror.

He had been shocked and discouraged to find how utterly vain had been his most intense efforts to stem the course of sin by presenting these images of terror: how hard natures had listened to them with only a coarse and cruel appetite, which seemed to increase their hardness and brutality; and how timid ones had been withered by them, like flowers scorched by the blast of a furnace; how, in fact, as in the case of those cruel executions and bloody tortures then universal in the jurisprudence of Europe, these pictures of eternal torture seemed to exert a morbid demoralizing influence which hurried on the growth of iniquity.

But since his acquaintance with Agnes, without his knowing exactly why, thoughts of the Divine Love had floated into his soul, filling it with a golden cloud like that which of old rested over the mercy-seat in that sacred inner temple where the priest was admitted alone. He became more affable and tender, more tolerant to the erring, more fond of little children; would stop sometimes to lay his hand on the head of a child, or to raise up one who lay overthrown in the street. The song of little birds and the voices of animal life became to him full of tenderness; and his prayers by the sick and dying seemed to have a melting power, such as he had never known before. It was spring in his soul, — soft, Italian spring, — such as brings out the musky breath of the cyclamen, and the faint, tender perfume of the primrose, in every moist dell of the Apennines.

A year passed in this way, perhaps the best and happiest of his troubled life, — a year in which, insensibly to himself, the weekly interviews with Agnes at the confessional became the rallying points around which the whole of his life was formed, and she the unsuspected spring of his inner being.

It was his duty, he said to himself, to give more than usual time and thought to the working and polishing of this wondrous jewel which had so unexpectedly been intrusted to him for the adorning of his Master's crown; and so long as he conducted with the strictest circumspection of his office, what had he to fear in the way of so delightful a duty? He had never touched her hand; never had even the folds of her passing drapery brushed against his garments of mortification and renunciation; never, even in pastoral benediction, had he dared lay his hand on that beautiful head. It is true, he had not forbidden himself to raise his glance sometimes when he saw her coming in at the church door and gliding up the aisle with downcast eyes, and thoughts evidently so far above earth that she seemed, like one of Fra Angelico's angels, to be moving on a cloud, so encompassed with stillness and sanctity that he held his breath as she passed.

But in the confession of Dame Elsie that morning he had received a shock which threw his whole interior being into a passionate agitation which dismayed and astonished him.

The thought of Agnes, his spotless lamb, exposed to lawless and licentious pursuit, of whose nature and probabilities his past life gave him only too clear an idea, was of itself a very natural source of anxiety. But Elsie had unveiled to him her plans for her marriage, and consulted him on the propriety of placing Agnes immediately under the protection of the husband she had chosen for her; and it was this part of her communication which had awakened the severest internal recoil, and raised a tumult of passions which the priest vainly sought either to assuage or understand.

As soon as his morning duties were over, he repaired to his convent, sought his cell, and, prostrate on his face before the crucifix, began his internal reckoning with himself. The day passed in fasting and solitude.

It is now golden evening, and on the square, flat roof of the convent, which, high-perched on a crag, overlooks the bay, one might observe a dark figure slowly pacing backward and forward. It is Father Francesco; and as he walks up and down, one could see by his large, bright, dilated eye, by the vivid red spot on either sunken cheek, and by the nervous energy of his movements, that he is in the very height of some mental crisis, — in that state of placid *extase* in which the subject supposes himself perfectly calm, because every nerve is screwed to the highest point of tension and can vibrate no more.

What oceans had that day rolled over him and swept

him, as one may see a little boat rocked on the capricious
surges of the Mediterranean! Were, then, all his strivings
and agonies in vain? Did he love this woman with any
earthly love? Was he jealous of the thought of a future
husband? Was it a tempting demon that said to him,
"Lorenzo Sforza might have shielded this treasure from
the profanation of lawless violence, from the brute grasp
of an inappreciative peasant, but Father Francesco cannot"?
There was a moment when his whole being vibrated with
a perception of what a marriage bond might have been that
was indeed a sacrament, and that bound together two pure
and loyal souls who gave life and courage to each other in
all holy purposes and heroic deeds; and he almost feared
that he had cursed his vows, — those awful vows, at whose
remembrance his inmost soul shivered through every nerve.

But after hours of prayer and struggle, and wave after
wave of agonizing convulsion, he gained one of those high
points in human possibility where souls can stand a little
while at a time, and where all things seem so transfigured
and pure that they fancy themselves thenceforward forever
victorious over evil.

As he walks up and down in the gold-and-purple evening twilight, his mind seems to him calm as that glowing
sea that reflects the purple shores of Ischia, and the quaint,
fantastic grottoes and cliffs of Capri. All is golden and
glowing; he sees all clear; he is delivered from his spiritual enemies; he treads them under his feet.

Yes, he says to himself, he loves Agnes, — loves her all-
sacredly as her guardian angel does, who ever beholdeth
the face of her Father in Heaven. Why, then, does he
shrink from her marriage? Is it not evident? Has that
tender soul, that poetic nature, that aspiring genius, anything in common with the vulgar coarse details of a peasant's life? Will not her beauty always draw the eye of
the licentious, expose her artless innocence to solicitation

which will annoy her and bring upon her head the incon-
siderate jealousy of her husband? Think of Agnes made
subject to the rude authority, to the stripes and correction,
which men of the lower class, under the promptings of
jealousy, do not scruple to inflict on their wives! What
career did society, as then organized, present to such a
nature, so perilously gifted in body and mind? He has
the answer. The Church has opened a career to woman
which all the world denies her.

He remembers the story of the dyer's daughter of Siena,
the fair Saint Catharine. In his youth he had often visited
the convent where one of the first artists of Italy has im-
mortalized her conflicts and her victories, and knelt with
his mother at the altar where she now communes with the
faithful. He remembered how, by her sanctity, her humility, and her holy inspirations of soul, she had risen to
the courts of princes, whither she had been sent as ambas-
sadress to arrange for the interests of the Church; and then
rose before his mind's eye the gorgeous picture of Pinturic-
chio, where, borne in celestial repose and purity amid all
the powers and dignitaries of the Church, she is canonized
as one of those that shall reign and intercede with Christ
in heaven.

Was it wrong, therefore, in him, though severed from
all womankind by a gulf of irrevocable vows, that he should
feel a kind of jealous property in this gifted and beautiful
creature? and though he might not, even in thought,
dream of possessing her himself, was there sin in the vehement energy with which his whole nature rose up in him
to say that no other man should, — that she should be the
bride of Heaven alone?

Certainly, if there were, it lurked far out of sight, and
the priest had a case that might have satisfied a conscience
even more fastidious; and he felt a sort of triumph in
the results of his mental scrutiny.

Yes, she should ascend from glory to glory, — but his should be the hand that should lead her upward. He would lead her within the consecrated grate, — he would pronounce the awful words that should make it sacrilege for all other men to approach her; and yet through life he should be the guardian and director of her soul, the one being to whom she should render an obedience as unlimited as that which belongs to Christ alone.

Such were the thoughts of this victorious hour, which, alas! were destined to fade as those purple skies and golden fires gradually went out, leaving, in place of their light and glory, only the lurid glow of Vesuvius.

CHAPTER VI

THE WALK TO THE CONVENT

ELSIE returned from the confessional a little after sunrise, much relieved and satisfied. Padre Francesco had shown such a deep interest in her narrative that she was highly gratified. Then he had given her advice which exactly accorded with her own views; and such advice is always regarded as an eminent proof of sagacity in the giver.

On the point of the marriage he had recommended delay, — a course quite in accordance with Elsie's desire, who, curiously enough, ever since her treaty of marriage with Antonio had been commenced, had cherished the most whimsical, jealous dislike of him, as if he were about to get away her grandchild from her; and this rose at times so high that she could scarcely speak peaceably to him, — a course of things which caused Antonio to open wide his great soft ox-eyes, and wonder at the ways of woman-kind; but he waited the event in philosophic tranquillity.

The morning sunbeams were shooting many a golden shaft among the orange-trees when Elsie returned and found Agnes yet kneeling at her prayers.

"Now, my little heart," said the old woman, when their morning meal was done, "I am going to give you a holiday to-day. I will go with you to the Convent, and you shall spend the day with the sisters, and so carry Saint Agnes her ring."

"Oh, thank you, grandmamma! how good you are!

May I stop a little on the way, and pick some cyclamen and myrtles and daisies for her shrine ? "

"Just as you like, child; but if you are going to do that, we must be off soon, for I must be at my stand betimes to sell oranges: I had them all picked this morning while my little darling was asleep."

"You always do everything, grandmamma, and leave me nothing to do: it is not fair. But, grandmamma, if we are going to get flowers by the way, let us follow down the stream, through the gorge, out upon the sea-beach, and so walk along the sands, and go by the back path up the rocks to the Convent: that walk is so shady and lovely at this time in the morning, and it is so fresh along by the seaside ! "

"As you please, dearie; but first fill a little basket with our best oranges for the sisters."

"Trust me for that ! " And the girl ran eagerly to the house, and drew from her treasures a little white wicker basket, which she proceeded to line curiously with orange-leaves, sticking sprays of blossoms in a wreath round the border.

"Now for some of our best blood-oranges ! " she said; "old Jocunda says they put her in mind of pomegranates. And here are some of these little ones, — see here, grandmamma ! " she exclaimed as she turned and held up a branch just broken, where five small golden balls grew together with a pearly spray of white buds just beyond them.

The exercise of springing up for the branch had sent a vivid glow into her clear brown cheek, and her eyes were dilated with excitement and pleasure; and as she stood joyously holding the branch, while the flickering shadows fell on her beautiful face, she seemed more like a painter's dream than a reality.

Her grandmother stood a moment admiring her.

"She's too good and too pretty for Antonio or any other

man: she ought to be kept to look at," she said to herself. "If I could keep her always, no man should have her; but death will come, and youth and beauty go, and so somebody must care for her."

When the basket was filled and trimmed, Agnes took it on her arm. Elsie raised and poised on her head the great square basket that contained her merchandise, and began walking erect and straight down the narrow rocky stairs that led into the gorge, holding her distaff with its white flax in her hands, and stepping as easily as if she bore no burden.

Agnes followed her with light, irregular movements, glancing aside from time to time, as a tuft of flowers or a feathery spray of leaves attracted her fancy. In a few moments her hands were too full, and her woolen apron of many-colored stripes was raised over one arm to hold her treasures, while a hymn to Saint Agnes, which she constantly murmured to herself, came in little ripples of sound, now from behind a rock, and now out of a tuft of bushes, to show where the wanderer was hid. The song, like many Italian ones, would be nothing in English, — only a musical repetition of sweet words to a very simple and childlike idea, the *bella, bella, bella* ringing out in every verse with a tender joyousness that seemed in harmony with the waving ferns and pendent flowers and long ivy-wreaths from among which its notes issued. "Beautiful and sweet Agnes," it said, in a thousand tender repetitions, "make me like thy little white lamb! Beautiful Agnes, take me to the green fields where Christ's lambs are feeding! Sweeter than the rose, fairer than the lily, take me where thou art!"

At the bottom of the ravine a little stream tinkles its way among stones so mossy in their deep, cool shadow as to appear all verdure; for seldom the light of the sun can reach the darkness where they lie. A little bridge, hewn from solid rock, throws across the shrunken stream an arch much wider than its waters seem to demand; for in spring and autumn, when the torrents wash down from the mountains, its volume is often suddenly increased.

This bridge was so entirely and evenly grown over with short thick moss that it might seem cut of some strange kind of living green velvet, and here and there it was quaintly embroidered with small blossoming tufts of white alyssum, or feathers of ferns and maiden's-hair which shook and trembled to every breeze. Nothing could be lovelier than this mossy bridge, when some stray sunbeam, slanting up the gorge, took a fancy to light it up with golden hues, and give transparent greenness to the tremulous thin leaves that waved upon it.

On this spot Elsie paused a moment, and called back after Agnes, who had disappeared into one of those deep grottoes with which the sides of the gorge are perforated, and which are almost entirely veiled by the pendent ivy-wreaths.

"Agnes! Agnes! wild girl! come quick!"

Only the sound of "*Bella, bella Agnella*" came out of the ivy-leaves to answer her; but it sounded so happy and innocent that Elsie could not forbear a smile, and in a moment Agnes came springing down with a quantity of the feathery lycopodium in her hands, which grows nowhere so well as in moist and dripping places.

Out of her apron were hanging festoons of golden broom, crimson gladiolus, and long, trailing sprays of ivy; while she held aloft in triumph a handful of the most superb cyclamen, whose rosy crowns rise so beautifully above their dark quaint leaves in moist and shady places.

"See, see, grandmother, what an offering I have! Saint Agnes will be pleased with me to-day; for I believe in her heart she loves flowers better than gems."

"Well, well, wild one, — time flies, we must hurry."

And crossing the bridge quickly, the grandmother struck into a mossy footpath that led them, after some walking, under the old Roman bridge at the gateway of Sorrento. Two hundred feet above their heads rose the mighty arches, enameled with moss and feathered with ferns all the way; and below this bridge the gorge grew somewhat wider, its sides gradually receding and leaving a beautiful flat tract of land, which was laid out as an orange-orchard. The golden fruit was shut in by rocky walls on either side which here formed a perfect hotbed, and no oranges were earlier or finer.

Through this beautiful orchard the two at length emerged from the gorge upon the sea-sands, where lay the blue Mediterranean swathed in bands of morning mist, its many-colored waters shimmering with a thousand reflected lights, and old Capri panting through sultry blue mists, and Vesuvius with his cloud-spotted sides and smoke-wreathed top burst into view. At a little distance a boat-load of bronzed fishermen had just drawn in a net, from which they were throwing out a quantity of sardines, which flapped and fluttered in the sunshine like scales of silver. The wind blowing freshly bore thousands of little purple waves to break one after another at the foamy line which lay on the sand.

Agnes ran gayly along the beach with her flowers and vines fluttering from her gay striped apron, and her cheeks flushed with exercise and pleasure, — sometimes stopping and turning with animation to her grandmother to point out the various floral treasures that enameled every crevice and rift of the steep wall of rock which rose perpendicularly above their heads in that whole line of the shore which is crowned with the old city of Sorrento: and surely never did rocky wall show to the open sea a face more picturesque and flowery. The deep red cliff was hollowed here and there into fanciful grottoes, draped with every varied hue and form of vegetable beauty. Here a crevice high in air was all abloom with purple gillyflower, and depending in festoons above it the golden blossoms of the broom; here a cleft seemed to be a nestling-place for a colony of gladiolus, with its crimson flowers and blade-like leaves; here the silver-frosted foliage of the miller-geranium, or of the wormwood, toned down the extravagant brightness of other blooms by its cooler tints. In some places it seemed as if a sort of floral cascade were tumbling confusedly over the rocks, mingling all hues and all forms in a tangled mass of beauty.

"Well, well," said old Elsie, as Agnes pointed to some superb gillyflowers which grew nearly half-way up the precipice, "is the child possessed? You have all the gorge in your apron already. Stop looking, and let us hurry on."

After a half-hour's walk, they came to a winding staircase cut in the rock, which led them a zigzag course up through galleries and grottoes looking out through curious windows and loop-holes upon the sea, till finally they emerged at the old sculptured portal of a shady garden which was surrounded by the cloistered arcades of the Convent of Saint Agnes.

The Convent of Saint Agnes was one of those monuments in which the piety of the Middle Ages delighted to commemorate the triumphs of the new Christianity over the old Heathenism.

The balmy climate and paradisiacal charms of Sorrento and the adjacent shores of Naples had made them favorite resorts during the latter period of the Roman Empire, — a period when the whole civilized world seemed to human view about to be dissolved in the corruption of universal sensuality. The shores of Baiæ were witnesses of the orgies and cruelties of Nero and a court made in his likeness, and the palpitating loveliness of Capri became the hotbed of the unnatural vices of Tiberius. The whole of Southern

Italy was sunk in a debasement of animalism and ferocity which seemed irrecoverable, and would have been so, had it not been for the handful of salt which a Galilean peasant had about that time cast into the putrid, fermenting mass of human society.

We must not wonder at the zeal which caused the artistic Italian nature to love to celebrate the passing away of an era of unnatural vice and demoniac cruelty by visible images of the purity, the tenderness, the universal benevolence which Jesus had brought into the world.

Sometime about the middle of the thirteenth century, it had been a favorite enterprise of a princess of a royal family in Naples to erect a convent to Saint Agnes, the guardian of female purity, out of the wrecks and remains of an ancient temple of Venus, whose white pillars and graceful acanthus-leaves once crowned a portion of the precipice on which the town was built, and were reflected from the glassy blue of the sea at its feet. It was said that this princess was the first lady abbess. Be that as it may, it proved to be a favorite retreat for many ladies of rank and religious aspiration, whom ill-fortune in some of its varying forms led to seek its quiet shades, and it was well and richly endowed by its royal patrons.

It was built after the manner of conventual buildings generally, — in a hollow square, with a cloistered walk around the inside looking upon a garden.

The portal at which Agnes and her grandmother knocked, after ascending the winding staircase cut in the precipice, opened through an arched passage into this garden.

As the ponderous door swung open, it was pleasant to hear the lulling sound of a fountain, which came forth with a gentle patter, like that of soft summer rain, and to see the waving of rose-bushes and golden jessamines, and smell the perfumes of orange-blossoms mingling with those of a thousand other flowers.

The door was opened by an odd-looking portress. She might be seventy-five or eighty; her cheeks were of the color of very yellow parchment drawn in dry wrinkles; her eyes were those large, dark, lustrous ones so common in her country, but seemed, in the general decay and shrinking of every other part of her face, to have acquired a wild, unnatural appearance; while the falling away of her teeth left nothing to impede the meeting of her hooked nose with her chin. Add to this, she was humpbacked, and twisted in her figure; and one needs all the force of her very good-natured, kindly smile to redeem the image of poor old Jocunda from association with that of some Thracian witch, and cause one to see in her the appropriate portress of a Christian institution.

Nevertheless, Agnes fell upon her neck and imprinted a very fervent kiss upon what was left of her withered cheek, and was repaid by a shower of those epithets of endearment which in the language of Italy fly thick and fast as the petals of the orange blossom from her groves.

"Well, well," said old Elsie, "I 'm going to leave her here to-day. You 've no objections, I suppose?"

"Bless the sweet lamb, no! She belongs here of good right. I believe blessed Saint Agnes has adopted her; for I 've seen her smile, plain as could be, when the little one brought her flowers."

"Well, Agnes," said the old woman, "I shall come for you after the Ave Maria." Saying which, she lifted her basket and departed.

The garden where the two were left was one of the most peaceful retreats that the imagination of a poet could create.

Around it ran on all sides the Byzantine arches of a cloistered walk, which, according to the quaint, rich fashion of that style, had been painted with vermilion, blue, and gold. The vaulted roof was spangled with gold stars on a blue ground, and along the sides was a series of fresco

pictures representing the various scenes in the life of Saint
Agnes; and as the foundress of the Convent was royal in
her means, there was no lack either of gold or gems or of
gorgeous painting.

Full justice was done in the first picture to the princely
wealth and estate of the fair Agnes, who was represented
as a pure-looking, pensive child, standing in a thoughtful
attitude, with long ripples of golden hair flowing down
over a simple white tunic, and her small hands clasping a
cross on her bosom, while, kneeling at her feet, obsequious
slaves and tire-women were offering the richest gems and
the most gorgeous robes to her serious and abstracted gaze.

In another, she was represented as walking modestly to
school, and winning the admiration of the son of the Roman Prætor, who fell sick — so says the legend — for the
love of her.

Then there was the demand of her hand in marriage by
the princely father of the young man, and her calm rejec-
tion of the gorgeous gifts and splendid gems which he had
brought to purchase her consent.

Then followed in order her accusation before the tribu-
nals as a Christian, her trial, and the various scenes of her
martyrdom.

Although the drawing of the figures and the treatment
of the subjects had the quaint stiffness of the thirteenth
century, their general effect, as seen from the shady bowers
of the garden, was of a solemn brightness, a strange and
fanciful richness, which was poetical and impressive.

In the centre of the garden was a fountain of white
marble, which evidently was the wreck of something that
had belonged to the old Greek temple. The statue of a
nymph sat on a green mossy pedestal in the midst of a
sculptured basin, and from a partially reversed urn on
which she was leaning, a clear stream of water dashed down
from one mossy fragment to another, till it lost itself in
the placid pool.

The figure and face of this nymph, in their classic finish of outline, formed a striking contrast to the drawing of the Byzantine paintings within the cloisters, and their juxtaposition in the same enclosure seemed a presentation of the spirit of a past and present era: the past so graceful in line, so perfect and airy in conception, so utterly without spiritual aspiration or life; the present limited in artistic power, but so earnest, so intense, seeming to struggle and burn, amid its stiff and restricted boundaries, for the expression of some diviner phase of humanity.

Nevertheless, the nymph of the fountain, different in style and execution as it was, was so fair a creature, that it was thought best, after the spirit of those days, to purge her from all heathen and improper histories by baptizing her in the waters of her own fountain, and bestowing on her the name of the saint to whose convent she was devoted. The simple sisterhood, little conversant in nice points of antiquity, regarded her as Saint Agnes dispensing the waters of purity to her convent; and marvelous and sacred properties were ascribed to the water, when taken fasting with a sufficient number of prayers and other religious exercises. All around the neighborhood of this fountain the ground was one bed of blue and white violets, whose fragrance filled the air, and which were deemed by the nuns to have come up there in especial token of the favor with which Saint Agnes regarded the conversion of this heathen relic to pious and Christian uses.

This nymph had been an especial favorite of the childhood of Agnes, and she had always had a pleasure which she could not exactly account for in gazing upon it. It is seldom that one sees in the antique conception of the immortals any trace of human feeling. Passionless perfection and repose seem to be their uniform character. But now and then from the ruins of Southern Italy fragments have been dug, not only pure in outline, but invested with a

strange pathetic charm, as if the calm, inviolable circle of
divinity had been touched by some sorrowing sense of that
unexplained anguish with which the whole lower creation
groans. One sees this mystery of expression in the face
of that strange and beautiful Psyche which still enchants
the Museum of Naples. Something of this charm of mournful pathos lingered on the beautiful features of this nymph,
— an expression so delicate and shadowy that it seemed to
address itself only to finer natures. It was as if all the
silent, patient woe and discouragement of a dumb antiquity
had been congealed into this memorial. Agnes was often
conscious, when a child, of being saddened by it, and yet
drawn towards it with a mysterious attraction.

About this fountain, under the shadow of bending rose
trees and yellow jessamines, was a circle of garden seats,
adopted also from the ruins of the past. Here a graceful
Corinthian capital, with every white acanthus-leaf perfect,
stood in a mat of acanthus-leaves of Nature's own making,
glossy green and sharply cut; and there was a long portion
of a frieze sculptured with graceful dancing figures; and in
another place a fragment of a fluted column, with lycopodium and colosseum vine hanging from its fissures in graceful draping. On these seats Agnes had dreamed away
many a tranquil hour, making garlands of violets, and listening to the marvelous legends of old Jocunda.

In order to understand anything of the true idea of conventual life in those days, we must consider that books
were as yet unknown, except as literary rarities, and reading and writing were among the rare accomplishments of
the higher classes; and that Italy, from the time that the
great Roman Empire fell and broke into a thousand shivers,
had been subject to a continual series of conflicts and struggles, which took from life all security. Norman, Dane,
Sicilian, Spaniard, Frenchman, and German mingled and
struggled, now up and now down; and every struggle was

attended by the little ceremonies of sacking towns, burning villages, and routing out entire populations to utter misery and wretchedness. During these tumultuous ages, those buildings consecrated by a religion recognized alike by all parties afforded to misfortune the only inviolable asylum, and to feeble and discouraged spirits the only home safe from the prospect of reverses.

If the destiny of woman is a problem that calls for grave attention even in our enlightened times, and if she is too often a sufferer from the inevitable movements of society, what must have been her position and needs in those ruder ages, unless the genius of Christianity had opened refuges for her weakness, made inviolable by the awful sanctions of religion?

What could they do, all these girls and women together, with the twenty-four long hours of every day, without reading or writing, and without the care of children? Enough; with their multiplied diurnal prayer periods, with each its chants and ritual of observances, — with the preparation for meals, and the clearing away thereafter, — with the care of the chapel, shrine, sacred gifts, drapery, and ornaments, — with embroidering altar-cloths and making sacred tapers, — with preparing conserves of rose leaves and curious spiceries, — with mixing drugs for the sick, — with all those mutual offices and services to each other which their relations in one family gave rise to, — and with divers feminine gossipries and harmless chatterings and cooings, one can conceive that these dove-cots of the Church presented often some of the most tranquil scenes of those convulsive and disturbed periods.

Human nature probably had its varieties there as otherwhere. There were there the domineering and the weak, the ignorant and the vulgar, and the patrician and the princess, and though professedly all brought on the footing of sisterly equality, we are not to suppose any Utopian

degree of perfection among them. The way of pure spirituality was probably, in the convent as well as out, that
strait and narrow one which there be few to find. There,
as elsewhere, the devotee who sought to progress faster
toward heaven than suited the paces of her fellow-travelers
was reckoned a troublesome enthusiast, till she got far
enough in advance to be worshiped as a saint.

Sister Theresa, the abbess of this convent, was the
youngest daughter in a princely Neapolitan family, who
from her cradle had been destined to the cloister, in order
that her brother and sister might inherit more splendid
fortunes and form more splendid connections. She had
been sent to this place too early to have much recollection
of any other mode of life; and when the time came to take
the irrevocable step, she renounced with composure a world
she had never known.

Her brother had endowed her with a *livre des heures*,
illuminated with all the wealth of blue and gold and divers
colors which the art of those times afforded, — a work ex-
ecuted by a pupil of the celebrated Fra Angelico; and the
possession of this treasure was regarded by her as a far
richer inheritance than that princely state of which she
knew nothing. Her neat little cell had a window that
looked down on the sea, — on Capri, with its fantastic
grottoes, — on Vesuvius, with its weird daily and nightly
changes. The light that came in from the joint reflection
of sea and sky gave a golden and picturesque coloring to
the simple and bare furniture, and in sunny weather she
often sat there, just as a lizard lies upon a wall, with the
simple, warm, delightful sense of living and being amid
scenes of so much beauty. Of the life that people lived in
the outer world, the struggle, the hope, the fear, the vivid
joy, the bitter sorrow, Sister Theresa knew nothing. She
could form no judgment and give no advice founded on
any such experience.

The only life she knew was a certain ideal one, drawn from the legends of the saints; and her piety was a calm, pure enthusiasm which had never been disturbed by a temptation or a struggle. Her rule in the Convent was even and serene; but those who came to her flock from the real world, from the trials and temptations of a real experience, were always enigmas to her, and she could scarcely comprehend or aid them.

In fact, since in the cloister, as everywhere else, character will find its level, it was old Jocunda who was the real governess of the Convent. Jocunda was originally a peasant woman, whose husband had been drafted to some of the wars of his betters, and she had followed his fortunes in the camp. In the sack of a fortress, she lost her husband and four sons, all the children she had, and herself received an injury which distorted her form, and so she took refuge in the Convent. Here her energy and *savoir-faire* rendered her indispensable in every department. She made the bargains, bought the provisions (being allowed to sally forth for these purposes), and formed the medium by which the timid, abstract, defenseless nuns accomplished those material relations with the world with which the utmost saintliness cannot afford to dispense. Besides and above all this, Jocunda's wide experience and endless capabilities of narrative made her an invaluable resource for enlivening any dull hours that might be upon the hands of the sisterhood; and all these recommendations, together with a strong mother-wit and native sense, soon made her so much the leading spirit in the Convent that Mother Theresa herself might be said to be under her dominion.

"So, so," she said to Agnes, when she had closed the gate after Elsie, — "you never come empty-handed. What lovely oranges! — worth double any that one can buy of anybody else but your grandmother."

"Yes, and these flowers I brought to dress the altar."

"Ah, yes! Saint Agnes has given you a particular grace for that," said Jocunda.

"And I have brought a ring for her treasury," said Agnes, taking out the gift of the Cavalier.

"Holy Mother! here is something, to be sure!" said Jocunda, catching it eagerly. "Why, Agnes, this is a diamond, — and as pretty a one as ever I saw. How it shines!" she added, holding it up. "That's a prince's present. How did you get it?"

"I want to tell our mother about it," said Agnes.

"You do?" said Jocunda. "You'd better tell me. I know fifty times as much about such things as she."

"Dear Jocunda, I will tell you, too; but I love Mother Theresa, and I ought to give it to her first."

"As you please, then," said Jocunda. "Well, put your flowers here by the fountain, where the spray will keep them cool, and we will go to her."

CHAPTER VII

THE Mother Theresa sat in a sort of withdrawing-room,
the roof of which rose in arches, starred with blue and
gold like that of the cloister, and the sides were frescoed
with scenes from the life of the Virgin. Over every door,
and in convenient places between the paintings, texts of
Holy Writ were illuminated in blue and scarlet and gold,
with a richness and fancifulness of outline, as if every
sacred letter had blossomed into a mystical flower. The
Abbess herself, with two of her nuns, was busily embroidering a new altar-cloth, with a lavish profusion of adornment; and, from time to time, their voices rose in the
musical tones of an ancient Latin hymn. The words were
full of that quaint and mystical pietism with which the
fashion of the times clothed the expression of devotional
feeling: —

> " Jesu, corona virginum,
> Quem mater illa concepit,
> Quæ sola virgo parturit,
> Hæc vota clemens accipe.
>
> " Qui pascis inter lilia
> Septus choreis virginum,
> Sponsus decoris gloria
> Sponsisque reddens præmia.
>
> " Quocunque pergis, virgines
> Sequuntur atque laudibus
> Post te canentes cursitant
> Hymnosque dulces personant." [1]

[1] " Jesus, crown of virgin spirits,
Whom a virgin mother bore,

This little canticle was, in truth, very different from the
hymns to Venus which used to resound in the temple which
the convent had displaced.   The voices which sung were
of a deep, plaintive contralto, much resembling the richness
of a tenor, and as they moved in modulated waves of chanting sound, the effect was soothing and dreamy.   Agnes
stopped at the door to listen.

"Stop, dear Jocunda," she said to the old woman, who
was about to push her way abruptly into the room, "wait
till it is over."

Jocunda, who was quite matter-of-fact in her ideas of
religion, made a little movement of impatience, but was
recalled to herself by observing the devout absorption with
which Agnes, with clasped hands and downcast head, was
mentally joining in the hymn with a solemn brightness in
her young face.

"If she has n't got a vocation, nobody ever had one,"
said Jocunda, mentally.   "Deary me, I wish I had more
of one myself!"

When the strain died away, and was succeeded by a
conversation on the respective merits of two kinds of gold
embroidering thread, Agnes and Jocunda entered the apartment.   Agnes went forward and kissed the hand of the
Mother reverentially.

Sister Theresa we have before described as tall, pale,
and sad-eyed, — a moonlight style of person, wanting in

> Graciously accept our praises
> While thy footsteps we adore.
>
> "Thee among the lilies feeding
> Choirs of virgins walk beside,
> Bridegroom crowned with glorious beauty
> Giving beauty to thy bride.
>
> "Where thou goest still they follow
> Singing, singing as they move,
> All those souls forever virgin
> Wedded only to thy love."

all those elements of warm color and physical solidity
which give the impression of a real vital human existence.
The strongest affection she had ever known had been that
which had been excited by the childish beauty and graces
of Agnes, and she folded her in her arms and kissed her
forehead with a warmth that had in it the semblance of
maternity.

"Grandmamma has given me a day to spend with you,
dear mother," said Agnes.

"Welcome, dear little child!" said Mother Theresa.
"Your spiritual home always stands open to you."

"I have something to speak to you of in particular, my
mother," said Agnes, blushing deeply.

"Indeed!" said the Mother Theresa, a slight movement
of curiosity arising in her mind as she signed to the two
nuns to leave the apartment.

"My mother," said Agnes, "yesterday evening, as grandmamma and I were sitting at the gate, selling oranges, a
young cavalier came up and bought oranges of me, and he
kissed my forehead and asked me to pray for him, and gave
me this ring for the shrine of Saint Agnes."

"Kissed your forehead!" said Jocunda, "here's a
pretty go! it isn't like you, Agnes, to let him."

"He did it before I knew," said Agnes. "Grandmamma reproved him, and then he seemed to repent, and
gave this ring for the shrine of Saint Agnes."

"And a pretty one it is, too," said Jocunda. "We
haven't a prettier in all our treasury. Not even the great
emerald the Queen gave is better in its way than this."

"And he asked you to pray for him?" said Mother
Theresa.

"Yes, mother dear; he looked right into my eyes and
made me look into his, and made me promise; and I knew
that holy virgins never refused their prayers to any one
that asked, and so I followed their example."

"I'll warrant me he was only mocking at you for a poor little fool," said Jocunda; "the gallants of our day don't believe much in prayers."

"Perhaps so, Jocunda," said Agnes, gravely; "but if that be the case, he needs prayers all the more."

"Yes," said Mother Theresa. "Remember the story of the blessed Saint Dorothea, — how a wicked young nobleman mocked at her, when she was going to execution, and said, 'Dorothea, Dorothea, I will believe, when you shall send me down some of the fruits and flowers of Paradise;' and she, full of faith, said, 'To-day I will send them;' and, wonderful to tell, that very day, at evening, an angel came to the young man with a basket of citrons and roses, and said, 'Dorothea sends thee these, wherefore believe.' See what grace a pure maiden can bring to a thoughtless young man, — for this young man was converted and became a champion of the faith."

"That was in the old times," said Jocunda, skeptically. "I don't believe setting the lamb to pray for the wolf will do much in our day. Prithee, child, what manner of man was this gallant?"

"He was beautiful as an angel," said Agnes, "only it was not a good beauty. He looked proud and sad, both, — like one who is not at ease in his heart. Indeed, I feel very sorry for him; his eyes made a kind of trouble in my mind that reminds me to pray for him often."

"And I will join my prayers to yours, dear daughter," said the Mother Theresa; "I long to have you with us, that we may pray together every day; say, do you think your grandmamma will spare you to us wholly before long?"

"Grandmamma will not hear of it yet," said Agnes; "and she loves me so, it would break her heart, if I should leave her, and she could not be happy here; but, mother, you have told me we could carry an altar always in our hearts, and adore in secret. When it is God's will I should come to you, He will incline her heart."

"Between you and me, little one," said Jocunda, "I think there will soon be a third person who will have something to say in the case."

"Whom do you mean?" said Agnes.

"A husband," said Jocunda; "I suppose your grandmother has one picked out for you. You are neither humpbacked nor cross-eyed, that you should n't have one as well as other girls."

"I don't want one, Jocunda; and I have promised to Saint Agnes to come here, if she will only get grandmother to consent."

"Bless you, my daughter!" said Mother Theresa; "only persevere and the way will be opened."

"Well, well," said Jocunda, "we 'll see. Come, little one, if you would n't have your flowers wilt, we must go back and look after them."

Reverently kissing the hand of the Abbess, Agnes withdrew with her old friend, and crossed again to the garden to attend to her flowers.

"Well now, childie," said Jocunda, "you can sit here and weave your garlands, while I go and look after the conserves of raisins and citrons that Sister Cattarina is making. She is stupid at anything but her prayers, is Cattarina. Our Lady be gracious to me! I think I got my vocation from Saint Martha, and if it was n't for me, I don't know what would become of things in the Convent. Why, since I came here, our conserves, done up in fig-leaf packages, have had quite a run at Court, and our gracious Queen herself was good enough to send an order for a hundred of them last week. I could have laughed to see how puzzled the Mother Theresa looked; much she knows about conserves! I suppose she thinks Gabriel brings them straight down from Paradise, done up in leaves of the tree of life. Old Jocunda knows what goes to their making up; she 's good for something, if she is old and twisted; many a scrubby old olive bears fat berries," said the old portress, chuckling.

"Oh, dear Jocunda," said Agnes, "why must you go this minute? I want to talk with you about so many things!"

"Bless the sweet child! it does want its old Jocunda, does it?" said the old woman, in the tone with which one caresses a baby. "Well, well, it should then! Just wait a minute, till I go and see that our holy Saint Cattarina has n't fallen a-praying over the conserving-pan. I 'll be back in a moment."

So saying, she hobbled off briskly, and Agnes, sitting down on the fragment sculptured with dancing nymphs, began abstractedly pulling her flowers towards her, shaking from them the dew of the fountain.

Unconsciously to herself, as she sat there, her head drooped into the attitude of the marble nymph, and her sweet features assumed the same expression of plaintive and dreamy thoughtfulness; her heavy dark lashes lay on her pure waxen cheeks like the dark fringe of some tropical flower. Her form, in its drooping outlines, scarcely yet showed the full development of womanhood, which after-years might unfold into the ripe fullness of her country-women. Her whole attitude and manner were those of an exquisitely sensitive and highly organized being, just struggling into the life of some mysterious new inner birth, — into the sense of powers of feeling and being hitherto unknown even to herself.

"Ah," she softly sighed to herself, "how little I am! how little I can do! Could I convert one soul! Ah, holy Dorothea, send down the roses of heaven into his soul, that he also may believe!"

"Well, my little beauty, you have not finished even one garland," said the voice of old Jocunda, bustling up behind her. "Praise to Saint Martha, the conserves are doing well, and so I catch a minute for my little heart."

So saying, she sat down with her spindle and flax by Agnes, for an afternoon gossip.

"Dear Jocunda, I have heard you tell stories about spirits that haunt lonesome places. Did you ever hear about any in the gorge?"

"Why, bless the child, yes, — spirits are always pacing up and down in lonely places. Father Anselmo told me that; and he had seen a priest once that had seen that in the Holy Scriptures themselves, — so it must be true."

"Well, did you ever hear of their making the most beautiful music?"

"Have n't I?" said Jocunda, — "to be sure I have, — singing enough to draw the very heart out of your body, — it 's an old trick they have. Why, I want to know if you never heard about the King of Amalfi's son coming home from fighting for the Holy Sepulchre? Why, there 's rocks not far out from this very town where the Sirens live; and if the King's son had n't had a holy bishop on board, who slept every night with a piece of the true cross under his pillow, the green ladies would have sung him straight into perdition. They are very fair-spoken at first, and sing so that a man gets perfectly drunk with their music, and longs to fly to them; but they suck him down at last under water, and strangle him, and that 's the end of him."

"You never told me about this before, Jocunda."

"Have n't I, child? Well, I will now. You see, this good bishop, he dreamed three times that they would sail past these rocks, and he was told to give all the sailors holy wax from an altar-candle to stop their ears, so that they should n't hear the music. Well, the King's son said he wanted to hear the music, so he would n't have his ears stopped; but he told 'em to tie him to the mast, so that he could hear it, but not to mind a word he said, if he begged 'em ever so hard to untie him.

"Well, you see they did it; and the old bishop, he had his ears sealed up tight, and so did all the men; but the young man stood tied to the mast, and when they sailed past he was like a demented creature. He called out that it was his lady who was singing, and he wanted to go to her, — and his mother, who they all knew was a blessed saint in paradise years before; and he commanded them to untie him, and pulled and strained on his cords to get free; but they only tied him the tighter, and so they got him past, — for, thanks to the holy wax, the sailors never heard a word, and so they kept their senses. So they all got safe home; but the young prince was so sick and pining that he had to be exorcised and prayed for seven times seven days before they could get the music out of his head."

"Why," said Agnes, "do those Sirens sing there yet?"

"Well, that was a hundred years ago. They say the old bishop, he prayed 'em down; for he went out a little after on purpose, and gave 'em a precious lot of holy water; most likely he got 'em pretty well under, though my husband's brother says he 's heard 'em singing in a small way, like frogs in springtime; but he gave 'em a pretty wide berth. You see, these spirits are what 's left of old heathen times, when, Lord bless us! the earth was just as full of 'em as a bit of old cheese is of mites. Now a Christian body, if they take reasonable care, can walk quit of 'em; and if they have any haunts in lonesome and doleful places, if one puts up a cross or a shrine, they know they have to go."

"I am thinking," said Agnes, "it would be a blessed work to put up some shrines to Saint Agnes and our good Lord in the gorge, and I 'll promise to keep the lamps burning and the flowers in order."

"Bless the child!" said Jocunda, "that is a pious and Christian thought."

"I have an uncle in Florence who is a father in the holy convent of San Marco, who paints and works in stone, — not for money, but for the glory of God; and when he comes this way I will speak to him about it," said Agnes. "About this time in the spring he always visits us."

"That's mighty well thought of," said Jocunda. "And now, tell me, little lamb, have you any idea who this grand cavalier may be that gave you the ring?"

"No," said Agnes, pausing a moment over the garland of flowers she was weaving, — "only Giulietta told me that he was brother to the King. Giulietta said everybody knew him."

"I'm not so sure of that," said Jocunda. "Giulietta always thinks she knows more than she does."

"Whatever he may be, his worldly state is nothing to me," said Agnes. "I know him only in my prayers."

"Ay, ay," muttered the old woman to herself, looking obliquely out of the corner of her eye at the girl, who was busily sorting her flowers; "perhaps he will be seeking some other acquaintance."

"You have n't seen him since?" said Jocunda.

"Seen him? Why, dear Jocunda, it was only last evening" —

"True enough. Well, child, don't think too much of him. Men are dreadful creatures, — in these times especially; they snap up a pretty girl as a fox does a chicken, and no questions asked."

"I don't think he looked wicked, Jocunda; he had a proud, sorrowful look. I don't know what could make a rich, handsome young man sorrowful; but I feel in my heart that he is not happy. Mother Theresa says that those who can do nothing but pray may convert princes without knowing it."

"Maybe it is so," said Jocunda, in the same tone in which thrifty professors of religion often assent to the same sort of truths in our days. "I 've seen a good deal of that sort of cattle in my day; and one would think, by their actions, that praying souls must be scarce where they came from."

Agnes abstractedly stooped and began plucking handfuls of lycopodium, which was growing green and feathery on one side of the marble frieze on which she was sitting; in so doing, a fragment of white marble, which had been over-grown in the luxuriant green, appeared to view. It was that frequent object in the Italian soil, — a portion of an old Roman tombstone. Agnes bent over, intent on the mystic "*Dis Manibus*," in old Roman letters.

"Lord bless the child! I 've seen thousands of them," said Jocunda; "it 's some old heathen's grave, that 's been in hell these hundred years."

"In hell?" said Agnes, with a distressful accent.

"Of course," said Jocunda. "Where should they be? Serves 'em right, too; they were a vile old set."

"Oh, Jocunda, it 's dreadful to think of, that they should have been in hell all this time."

"And no nearer the end than when they began," said Jocunda.

Agnes gave a shivering sigh, and, looking up into the golden sky that was pouring such floods of splendor through the orange trees and jasmines, thought, How could it be that the world could possibly be going on so sweet and fair over such an abyss?

"Oh, Jocunda!" she said, "it does seem too dreadful to believe! How could they help being heathen, — being born so, — and never hearing of the true Church?"

"Sure enough," said Jocunda, spinning away energeti-cally, "but that 's no business of mine; my business is to save *my* soul, and that 's what I came here for. The dear saints know I found it dull enough at first, for I'd been used to jaunting round with my old man and the boy; but what with marketing and preserving, and one thing and another, I get on better now, praise to Saint Agnes!"

The large, dark eyes of Agnes were fixed abstractedly on the old woman as she spoke, slowly dilating, with a sad, mysterious expression, which sometimes came over them.

"Ah! how can the saints themselves be happy?" she said. "One might be willing to wear sackcloth and sleep on the ground, one might suffer ever so many years and years, if only one might save some of them."

"Well, it does seem hard," said Jocunda; "but what's the use of thinking of it? Old Father Anselmo told us in one of his sermons that the Lord wills that his saints should come to rejoice in the punishment of all heathens and heretics; and he told us about a great saint once, who took it into his head to be distressed because one of the old heathen whose books he was fond of reading had gone to hell, — and he fasted and prayed, and wouldn't take no for an answer, till he got him out."

"He did, then?" said Agnes, clasping her hands in an ecstasy.

"Yes; but the good Lord told him never to try it again, — and He struck him dumb, as a kind of hint, you know. Why, Father Anselmo said that even getting souls out of purgatory was no easy matter. He told us of one holy nun who spent nine years fasting and praying for the soul of her prince, who was killed in a duel, and then she saw in a vision that he was only raised the least little bit out of the fire, — and she offered up her life as a sacrifice to the Lord to deliver him, but, after all, when she died he wasn't quite delivered. Such things made me think that a poor old sinner like me would never get out at all, if I didn't set about it in earnest, — though it ain't all nuns that save their souls either. I remember in Pisa I saw a great picture of the Judgment Day in the Campo Santo, and there were lots of abbesses, and nuns, and monks, and bishops, too, that the devils were clearing off into the fire."

"Oh, Jocunda, how dreadful that fire must be!"

"Yes," said Jocunda. "Father Anselmo said hell-fire was n't like any kind of fire we have here, — made to warm us and cook our food, — but a kind made especially to torment body and soul, and not made for anything else. I remember a story he told us about that. You see, there was an old duchess that lived in a grand old castle, — and a proud, wicked old thing enough; and her son brought home a handsome young bride to the castle, and the old duchess was jealous of her, — 'cause, you see, she hated to give up her place in the house, and the old family jewels, and all the splendid things, — and so one time, when the poor young thing was all dressed up in a set of the old family lace, what does the old hag do but set fire to it!"

"How horrible!" said Agnes.

"Yes; and when the young thing ran screaming in her agony, the old hag stopped her and tore off a pearl rosary that she was wearing, for fear it should be spoiled by the fire."

"Holy Mother! can such things be possible?" said Agnes.

"Well, you see, she got her pay for it. That rosary was of famous old pearls that had been in the family a hundred years; but from that moment the good Lord struck it with a curse, and filled it white-hot with hell-fire, so that if anybody held it a few minutes in their hand, it would burn to the bone. The old sinner made believe that she was in great affliction for the death of her daughter-in-law, and that it was all an accident, and the poor young man went raving mad, — but that awful rosary the old hag could n't get rid of. She could n't give it away, — she could n't sell it, — but back it would come every night, and lie right over her heart, all white-hot with the fire that burned in it. She gave it to a convent, and she sold it to a merchant, but back it came; and she locked it up in the heaviest chests, and she buried it down in the lowest vaults, but it always came back in the night, till she was worn to a skeleton; and at last the old thing died without confession or sacrament, and went where she belonged. She was found lying dead in her bed one morning, and the rosary was gone; but when they came to lay her out, they found the marks of it burned to the bone into her breast. Father Anselmo used to tell us this, to show us a little what hell-fire was like."

"Oh, please, Jocunda, don't let us talk about it any more," said Agnes.

Old Jocunda, with her tough, vigorous organization and unceremonious habits of expression, could not conceive the exquisite pain with which this whole conversation had vibrated on the sensitive being at her right hand, — that what merely awoke her hard-corded nerves to a dull vibration of not unpleasant excitement was shivering and tearing the tenderer chords of poor little Psyche beside her.

Ages before, beneath those very skies that smiled so sweetly over her, — amid the bloom of lemon and citron, and the perfume of jasmine and rose, the gentlest of old Italian souls had dreamed and wondered what might be the unknown future of the dead, and, learning his lesson from the glorious skies and gorgeous shores which witnessed how magnificent a Being had given existence to man, had recorded his hopes of man's future in the words — *Aut beatus, aut nihil;* but, singular to tell, the religion which brought with it all human tenderness and pities, — the hospital for the sick, the refuge for the orphan, the enfranchisement of the slave, — this religion brought also the news of the eternal, hopeless, living torture of the great majority of mankind, past and present. Tender spirits, like those of Dante, carried this awful mystery as a secret and unexplained anguish, saints wrestled with God and wept over it; but still the awful fact remained, spite of Church and sacrament, that the gospel was in effect, to the majority of the human race, not the glad tidings of salvation, but the sentence of unmitigable doom.

The present traveler in Italy sees with disgust the dim and faded frescoes in which this doom is portrayed in all its varied refinements of torture; and the vivid Italian mind ran riot in these lurid fields, and every monk who wanted to move his audience was in his small way a Dante. The poet and the artist give only the highest form of the ideas of their day, and he who cannot read the "Inferno" with firm nerves may ask what the same representations were likely to have been in the grasp of coarse and common minds.

The first teachers of Christianity in Italy read the Gospels by the light of those fiendish fires which consumed their fellows. Daily made familiar with the scorching, the searing, the racking, the devilish ingenuities of torture, they transferred them to the future hell of the torturers. The sentiment within us which asserts eternal justice and retribution was stimulated to a kind of madness by that first baptism of fire and blood, and expanded the simple and grave warnings of the gospel into a lurid poetry of physical torture. Hence, while Christianity brought multiplied forms of mercy into the world, it failed for many centuries to humanize the savage forms of justice; and rack and wheel, fire and fagot were the modes by which human justice aspired to a faint imitation of what divine justice was supposed to extend through eternity.

But it is remarkable always to observe the power of individual minds to draw out of the popular religious ideas of their country only those elements which suit themselves, and to drop others from their thought. As a bee can extract pure honey from the blossoms of some plants whose leaves are poisonous, so some souls can nourish themselves only with the holier and more ethereal parts of popular belief.

Agnes had hitherto dwelt only on the cheering and the joyous features of her faith; her mind loved to muse on the legends of saints and angels and the glories of paradise, which, with a secret buoyancy, she hoped to be the lot of every one she saw. The mind of the Mother Theresa was of the same elevated cast, and the terrors on which Jocunda dwelt with such homely force of language seldom made a part of her instructions.

Agnes tried to dismiss these gloomy images from her mind, and, after arranging her garlands, went to decorate the shrine and altar, — a cheerful labor of love, in which she delighted.

To the mind of the really spiritual Christian of those ages the air of this lower world was not as it is to us, in spite of our nominal faith in the Bible, a blank, empty space from which all spiritual sympathy and life have fled, but, like the atmosphere with which Raphael has surrounded the Sistine Madonna, it was full of sympathizing faces, a great "cloud of witnesses." The holy dead were not gone from earth; the Church visible and invisible were in close, loving, and constant sympathy, — still loving, praying, and watching together, though with a veil between.

It was at first with no idolatrous intention that the prayers of the holy dead were invoked in acts of worship. Their prayers were asked simply because they were felt to be as really present with their former friends and as truly sympathetic as if no veil of silence had fallen between. In time this simple belief had its intemperate and idolatrous exaggerations, — the Italian soil always seeming to have a

fiery and volcanic forcing power, by which religious ideas
overblossomed themselves, and grew wild and ragged with
too much enthusiasm; and, as so often happens with
friends on earth, these too much loved and revered invisible friends became eclipsing screens instead of transmitting
mediums of God's light to the soul.

Yet we can see in the hymns of Savonarola, who perfectly represented the attitude of the highest Christian of
those times, how perfect might be the love and veneration
for departed saints without lapsing into idolatry, and with
what an atmosphere of warmth and glory the true belief of
the unity of the Church, visible and invisible, could inspire
an elevated soul amid the discouragements of an unbelieving and gainsaying world.

Our little Agnes, therefore, when she had spread all her
garlands out, seemed really to feel as if the girlish figure
that smiled in sacred white from the altar-piece was a dear
friend who smiled upon her, and was watching to lead her
up the path to heaven.

Pleasantly passed the hours of that day to the girl, and
when at evening old Elsie called for her, she wondered that
the day had gone so fast.

Old Elsie returned with no inconsiderable triumph from
her stand.   The cavalier had been several times during the
day past her stall, and once, stopping in a careless way
to buy fruit, commented on the absence of her young
charge.   This gave Elsie the highest possible idea of her
own sagacity and shrewdness, and of the promptitude with
which she had taken her measures, so that she was in as
good spirits as people commonly are who think they have
performed some stroke of generalship.

As the old woman and young girl emerged from the
dark-vaulted passage that led them down through the rocks
on which the convent stood to the sea at its base, the light
of a most glorious sunset burst upon them, in all those

strange and magical mysteries of light which any one who has walked that beach of Sorrento at evening will never forget.

Agnes ran along the shore, and amused herself with picking up little morsels of red and black coral, and those fragments of mosaic pavements, blue, red, and green, which the sea is never tired of casting up from the thousands of ancient temples and palaces which have gone to wreck all around these shores.

As she was busy doing this, she suddenly heard the voice of Giulietta behind her.

"So ho, Agnes! where have you been all day?"

"At the Convent," said Agnes, raising herself from her work, and smiling at Giulietta, in her frank, open way.

"Oh, then you really did take the ring to Saint Agnes?"

"To be sure I did," said Agnes.

"Simple child!" said Giulietta, laughing; "that was n't what he meant you to do with it. He meant it for you, — only your grandmother was by. You never will have any lovers, if she keeps you so tight."

"I can do without," said Agnes.

"I could tell you something about this one," said Giulietta.

"You did tell me something yesterday," said Agnes.

"But I could tell you some more. I know he wants to see you again."

"What for?" said Agnes.

"Simpleton, he 's in love with you. You never had a lover; it 's time you had."

"I don't want one, Giulietta. I hope I never shall see him again."

"Oh, nonsense, Agnes! Why, what a girl you are! Why, before I was as old as you, I had half-a-dozen lovers."

"Agnes," said the sharp voice of Elsie, coming up from

behind, "don't run on ahead of me again; and you, Mistress Baggage, let my child alone."

"Who's touching your child?" said Giulietta, scornfully. "Can't a body say a civil word to her?"

"I know what you would be after," said Elsie, "filling her head with talk of all the wild, loose gallants; but she is for no such market, I promise you! Come, Agnes."

So saying, old Elsie drew Agnes rapidly along with her, leaving Giulietta rolling her great black eyes after them with an air of infinite contempt.

"The old kite!" she said; "I declare he shall get speech of the little dove, if only to spite her. Let her try her best, and see if we don't get round her before she knows it. Pietro says his master is certainly wild after her, and I have promised to help him."

Meanwhile, just as old Elsie and Agnes were turning into the orange orchard which led into the Gorge of Sorrento, they met the cavalier of the evening before.

He stopped, and, removing his cap, saluted them with as much deference as if they had been princesses. Old Elsie frowned, and Agnes blushed deeply; both hurried forward. Looking back, the old woman saw that he was walking slowly behind them, evidently watching them closely, yet not in a way sufficiently obtrusive to warrant an open rebuff.

CHAPTER VIII

THE CAVALIER

NOTHING can be more striking, in common Italian life, than the contrast between out-doors and in-doors. Without, all is fragrant and radiant; within, mouldy, dark, and damp. Except in the well-kept palaces of the great, houses in Italy are more like dens than habitations, and a sight of them is a sufficient reason to the mind of any inquirer, why their vivacious and handsome inhabitants spend their life principally in the open air. Nothing could be more perfectly paradisiacal than this evening at Sorrento. The sun had sunk, but left the air full of diffused radiance, which trembled and vibrated over the thousand many-colored waves of the sea. The moon was riding in a broad zone of purple, low in the horizon, her silver forehead somewhat flushed in the general rosiness that seemed to penetrate and suffuse every object. The fishermen, who were drawing in their nets, gayly singing, seemed to be floating on a violet-and-gold-colored flooring that broke into a thousand gems at every dash of the oar or motion of the boat. The old stone statue of Saint Antonio looked down in the rosy air, itself tinged and brightened by the magical colors which floated round it. And the girls and men of Sorrento gathered in gossiping knots on the old Roman bridge that spanned the gorge, looked idly down into its dusky shadows, talking the while, and playing the time - honored game of flirtation which has gone on in all climes and languages since man and woman began.

Conspicuous among them all was Giulietta, her blue-black hair recently braided and polished to a glossy radiance, and all her costume arranged to show her comely proportions to the best advantage, — her great pearl ear-rings shaking as she tossed her head, and showing the flash of the emerald in the middle of them. An Italian peasant-woman may trust Providence for her gown, but ear-rings she attends to herself, — for what is life without them? The great pearl ear-rings of the Sorrento women are accumulated, pearl by pearl, as the price of years of labor. Giulietta, however, had come into the world, so to speak, with a gold spoon in her mouth, — since her grandmother, a thriving, stirring, energetic body, had got together a pair of ear-rings of unmatched size, which had descended as heirlooms to her, leaving her nothing to do but display them, which she did with the freest good-will. At present she was busily occupied in coquetting with a tall and jauntily-dressed fellow, wearing a plumed hat and a red sash, who seemed to be mesmerized by the power of her charms, his large dark eyes following every movement, as she now talked with him gayly and freely, and now pretended errands to this and that and the other person on the bridge, stationing herself here and there, that she might have the pleasure of seeing herself followed.

"Giulietta," at last said the young man, earnestly, when he found her accidentally standing alone by the parapet, "I must be going to-morrow."

"Well, what is that to me?" said Giulietta, looking wickedly from under her eyelashes.

"Cruel girl! you know " —

"Nonsense, Pietro! I don't know anything about you;" but as Giulietta said this, her great, soft, dark eyes looked out furtively, and said just the contrary.

"You will go with me?"

"Did I ever hear anything like it? One can't be civil

to a fellow but he asks her to go to the world's end. Pray, how far is it to your dreadful old den?"

"Only two days' journey, Giulietta."

"Two days!"

"Yes, my life; and you shall ride."

"Thank you, sir, — I was n't thinking of walking. But seriously, Pietro, I am afraid it's no place for an honest girl to be in."

"There are lots of honest women there, — all our men have wives; and our captain has put his eye on one, too, or I'm mistaken."

"What! little Agnes?" said Giulietta. "He will be bright that gets her. That old dragon of a grandmother is as tight to her as her skin."

"Our captain is used to helping himself," said Pietro. "We might carry them both off some night, and no one the wiser; but he seems to want to win the girl to come to him of her own accord. At any rate, we are to be sent back to the mountains while he lingers a day or two more round here."

"I declare, Pietro, I think you all little better than Turks or heathens, to talk in that way about carrying off women; and what if one should be sick and die among you? What is to become of one's soul, I wonder?"

"Pshaw! don't we have priests? Why, Giulietta, we are all very pious, and never think of going out without saying our prayers. The Madonna is a kind Mother, and will wink very hard on the sins of such good sons as we are. There is n't a place in all Italy where she is kept better in candles, and in rings and bracelets, and everything a woman could want. We never come home without bringing her something; and then we have lots left to dress all our women like princesses; and they have nothing to do from morning till night but play the lady. Come now?"

At the moment this conversation was going on in the balmy, seductive evening air at the bridge, another was transpiring in the Albergo della Torre, one of those dark, musty dens of which we have been speaking. In a damp, dirty chamber, whose brick floor seemed to have been unsuspicious of even the existence of brooms for centuries, was sitting the cavalier whom we have so often named in connection with Agnes. His easy, high-bred air, his graceful, flexible form and handsome face formed a singular contrast to the dark and mouldy apartment, at whose single unglazed window he was sitting. The sight of this splendid man gave an impression of strangeness, in the general bareness, much as if some marvelous jewel had been unaccountably found lying on that dusty brick floor.

He sat deep in thought, with his elbow resting on a rickety table, his large, piercing dark eyes seeming intently to study the pavement.

The door opened, and a gray-headed old man entered, who approached him respectfully.

"Well, Paolo?" said the cavalier, suddenly starting.

"My Lord, the men are all going back to-night."

"Let them go, then," said the cavalier, with an impatient movement. "I can follow in a day or two."

"Ah, my Lord, if I might make so bold, why should you expose your person by staying longer? You may be recognized and" —

"No danger," said the other, hastily.

"My Lord, you must forgive me, but I promised my dear lady, your mother, on her death-bed" —

"To be a constant plague to me," said the cavalier, with a vexed smile and an impatient movement; "but speak on, Paolo, — for when you once get anything on your mind, one may as well hear it first as last."

"Well, then, my Lord, this girl, — I have made inquiries, and every one reports her most modest and pious,

— the only grandchild of a poor old woman. Is it worthy of a great lord of an ancient house to bring her to shame ? "

"Who thinks of bringing her to shame ? 'Lord of an ancient house!' " added the cavalier, laughing bitterly, — "a landless beggar, cast out of everything, — titles, estates, all! Am I, then, fallen so low that my wooing would disgrace a peasant-girl ? "

"My Lord, you cannot mean to woo a peasant-girl in any other way than one that would disgrace her, — one of the House of Sarelli, that goes back to the days of the old Roman Empire! "

"And what of the 'House of Sarelli that goes back to the days of the old Roman Empire' ? It is lying like weeds' roots uppermost in the burning sun. What is left to me but the mountains and my sword ? No, I tell you, Paolo, Agostino Sarelli, cavalier of fortune, is not thinking of bringing disgrace on a pious and modest maiden, unless it would disgrace her to be his wife."

"Now may the saints above help us! Why, my Lord, our house in days past has been allied to royal blood. I could tell you how Joachim VI." —

"Come, come, my good Paolo, spare me one of your chapters of genealogy. The fact is, my old boy, the world is all topsy-turvy, and the bottom is the top, and it is n't much matter what comes next. Here are shoals of noble families uprooted and lying round like those aloes that the gardener used to throw over the wall in springtime; and there is that great boar of a Cæsar Borgia turned in to batten and riot over our pleasant places."

"Oh, my Lord," said the old serving-man, with a distressful movement, "we have fallen on evil times, to be sure, and they say his Holiness has excommunicated us. Anselmo heard that in Naples yesterday."

"Excommunicated!" said the young man, — every fea-

ture of his fine face, and every nerve of his graceful form
seeming to quiver with the effort to express supreme contempt. "Excommunicated! I should hope so! One
would hope through Our Lady's grace to act so that Alexander, and his adulterous, incestuous, filthy, false-swearing,
perjured, murderous crew, would excommunicate us! In
these times, one's only hope of paradise lies in being excommunicated."

"Oh, my dear master," said the old man, falling on his
knees, "what is to become of us? That I should live to
hear you talk like an infidel and unbeliever!"

"Why, hear you, poor old fool! Did you never hear in
Dante of the Popes that are burning in hell? Wasn't
Dante a Christian, I beg to know?"

"Oh, my Lord, my Lord! a religion got out of poetry,
books, and romances won't do to die by. We have no
business with the affairs of the Head of the Church, — it's
the Lord's appointment. We have only to shut our eyes
and obey. It may all do well enough to talk so when you
are young and fresh; but when sickness and death come,
then we *must* have religion, — and if we have gone out of
the only true Roman Catholic Apostolic Church, what becomes of our souls? Ah, I misdoubted about your taking
so much to poetry, though my poor mistress was so proud
of it; but these poets are all heretics, my Lord, — that's
my firm belief. But, my Lord, if you do go to hell, I'm
going there with you; I'm sure I never could show my
face among the saints, and you not there."

"Well, come, then, my poor Paolo," said the cavalier,
stretching out his hand to his serving-man, "don't take it
to heart so. Many a better man than I has been excommunicated and cursed from toe to crown, and been never
a whit the worse for it. There's Jerome Savonarola there
in Florence — a most holy man, they say, who has had
revelations straight from heaven — has been excommuni-

cated; but he preaches and gives the sacraments all the same, and nobody minds it."

"Well, it's all a maze to me," said the old serving-man, shaking his white head. "I can't see into it. I don't dare to open my eyes for fear I should get to be a heretic; it seems to me that everything is getting mixed up together. But one must hold on to one's religion; because, after we have lost everything in this world, it would be too bad to burn in hell forever at the end of that."

"Why, Paolo, I am a good Christian. I believe, with all my heart, in the Christian religion, like the fellow in Boccaccio, — because I think it must be from God, or else the Popes and Cardinals would have had it out of the world long ago. Nothing but the Lord Himself could have kept it against them."

"There you are, my dear master, with your romances. Well, well, well! I don't know how it'll end. I say my prayers, and try not to inquire into what's too high for me. But now, dear master, will you stay lingering after this girl till some of our enemies hear where you are and pounce down upon us? Besides, the troop are never so well affected when you are away; there are quarrels and divisions."

"Well, well," said the cavalier, with an impatient movement, — "one day longer. I must get a chance to speak with her once more. I must see her."

CHAPTER IX

THE ARTIST MONK

ON the evening when Agnes and her grandmother returned from the Convent, as they were standing after supper looking over the garden parapet into the gorge, their attention was caught by a man in an ecclesiastical habit, slowly climbing the rocky pathway towards them.

"Isn't that Brother Antonio?" said Dame Elsie, leaning forward to observe more narrowly. "Yes, to be sure it is!"

"Oh, how glad I am!" exclaimed Agnes, springing up with vivacity, and looking eagerly down the path by which the stranger was approaching.

A few moments more of clambering, and the stranger met the two women at the gate with a gesture of benediction.

He was apparently a little past the middle point of life, and entering on its shady afternoon. He was tall and well proportioned, and his features had the spare delicacy of the Italian outline. The round brow, fully developed in all the perceptive and æsthetic regions, — the keen eye, shadowed by long, dark lashes, — the thin, flexible lips, — the sunken cheek, where, on the slightest emotion, there fluttered a brilliant flush of color, — all were signs telling of the enthusiast in whom the nervous and spiritual predominated over the animal.

At times, his eye had a dilating brightness, as if from the flickering of some inward fire which was slowly consuming the mortal part, and its expression was brilliant even to the verge of insanity.

His dress was the simple, coarse, white stuff-gown of the Dominican friars, over which he wore a darker traveling-garment of coarse cloth, with a hood, from whose deep shadows his bright mysterious eyes looked like jewels from a cavern. At his side dangled a great rosary and cross of black wood, and under his arm he carried a portfolio secured with a leathern strap, which seemed stuffed to bursting with papers.

Father Antonio, whom we have thus introduced to the reader, was an itinerant preaching monk from the Convent of San Marco in Florence, on a pastoral and artistic tour through Italy.

Convents in the Middle Ages were the retreats of multitudes of natures who did not wish to live in a state of perpetual warfare and offense, and all the elegant arts flourished under their protecting shadows. Ornamental gardening, pharmacy, drawing, painting, carving in wood, illumination, and calligraphy were not unfrequent occupations of the holy fathers, and the convent has given to the illustrious roll of Italian Art some of its most brilliant names. No institution in modern Europe had a more established reputation in all these respects than the Convent of San Marco in Florence. In its best days, it was as near an approach to an ideal community, associated to unite religion, beauty, and utility, as ever has existed on earth. It was a retreat from the commonplace prose of life into an atmosphere at once devotional and poetic; and prayers and sacred hymns consecrated the elegant labors of the chisel and the pencil, no less than the more homely ones of the still and the crucible. San Marco, far from being that kind of sluggish lagoon often imagined in conventual life, was rather a sheltered hotbed of ideas, fervid with intellectual and moral energy, and before the age in every radical movement. At this period, Savonarola, the poet and prophet of the Italian religious world of his day, was

superior of this convent, pouring through all the members
of the order the fire of his own impassioned nature, and
seeking to lead them back to the fervors of more primitive
and evangelical ages, and in the reaction of a worldly and
corrupt Church was beginning to feel the power of that
current which at last drowned his eloquent voice in the
cold waters of martyrdom. Savonarola was an Italian
Luther, — differing from the great Northern Reformer as
the more ethereally strung and nervous Italian differs from
the bluff and burly German; and like Luther, he became
in his time the centre of every living thing in society about
him. He inspired the pencils of artists, guided the counsels of statesmen, and, a poet himself, was an inspiration
to poets. Everywhere in Italy the monks of his order
were traveling, restoring the shrines, preaching against the
voluptuous and unworthy pictures with which sensual artists had desecrated the churches, and calling the people
back by their exhortations to the purity of primitive Christianity.

Father Antonio was a younger brother of Elsie, and had
early become a member of the San Marco, enthusiastic not
less in religion than in Art. His intercourse with his sister had few points of sympathy, Elsie being as decided a
utilitarian as any old Yankee female born in the granite
hills of New Hampshire, and pursuing with a hard and
sharp energy her narrow plan of life for Agnes. She
regarded her brother as a very properly religious person,
considering his calling, but was a little bored with his ex-
uberant devotion, and absolutely indifferent to his artistic
enthusiasm. Agnes, on the contrary, had from a child
attached herself to her uncle with all the energy of a sympathetic nature, and his yearly visits had been looked forward to on her part with intense expectation. To him
she could say a thousand things which she instinctively concealed from her grandmother; and Elsie was well pleased

with the confidence, because it relieved her a little from the vigilant guardianship that she otherwise held over the girl. When Father Antonio was near, she had leisure now and then for a little private gossip of her own, without the constant care of supervising Agnes.

"Dear uncle, how glad I am to see you once more!" was the eager salutation with which the young girl received the monk, as he gained the little garden. "And you have brought your pictures; oh, I know you have so many pretty things to show me!"

"Well, well, child," said Elsie, "don't begin upon that now. A little talk of bread and cheese will be more in point. Come in, brother, and wash your feet, and let me beat the dust out of your cloak, and give you something to stay Nature; for you must be fasting."

"Thank you, sister," said the monk; "and as for you, pretty one, never mind what she says. Uncle Antonio will show his little Agnes everything by-and-by. A good little thing it is, sister."

"Yes, yes, — good enough, — and too good," said Elsie, bustling about; "roses can't help having thorns, I suppose."

"Only our ever-blessed Rose of Sharon, the dear mystical Rose of Paradise, can boast of having no thorns," said the monk, bowing and crossing himself devoutly.

Agnes clasped her hands on her bosom and bowed also, while Elsie stopped with her knife in the middle of a loaf of black bread, and crossed herself with somewhat of impatience, — like a worldly-minded person of our day, who is interrupted in the midst of an observation by a grace.

After the rites of hospitality had been duly observed, the old dame seated herself contentedly in her door with her distaff, resigned Agnes to the safe guardianship of her uncle, and had a feeling of security in seeing them sitting together on the parapet of the garden, with the portfolio spread out between them, — the warm twilight glow of the evening sky lighting up their figures as they bent in ardent interest over its contents. The portfolio showed a fluttering collection of sketches, — fruits, flowers, animals, insects, faces, figures, shrines, buildings, trees, — all, in short, that might strike the mind of a man to whose eye nothing on the face of the earth is without beauty and significance.

"Oh, how beautiful!" said the girl, taking up one sketch, in which a bunch of rosy cyclamen was painted rising out of a bed of moss.

"Ah, that indeed, my dear!" said the artist. "Would you had seen the place where I painted it! I stopped there to recite my prayers one morning; 't was by the side of a beautiful cascade, and all the ground was covered with these lovely cyclamens, and the air was musky with their fragrance. Ah, the bright rose-colored leaves! I can get no color like them, unless some angel would bring me some from those sunset clouds yonder."

"And oh, dear uncle, what lovely primroses!" pursued Agnes, taking up another paper.

"Yes, child; but you should have seen them when I was coming down the south side of the Apennines; these were everywhere so pale and sweet, they seemed like the humility of our Most Blessed Mother in her lowly mortal state. I am minded to make a border of primroses to the leaf in the Breviary where is the 'Hail, Mary!' — for it seems as if that flower doth ever say, 'Behold the handmaid of the Lord!'"

"And what will you do with the cyclamen, uncle? does not that mean something?"

"Yes, daughter," replied the monk, readily entering into that symbolical strain which permeated all the heart and mind of the religious of his day, "I can see a meaning in it. For you see that the cyclamen puts forth its leaves in early spring deeply engraven with mystical characters, and loves cool shadows, and moist, dark places, but comes at length to wear a royal crown of crimson; and it seems to me like the saints who dwell in convents and other prayerful places, and have the word of God graven in their hearts in youth, till these blossom into fervent love, and they are crowned with royal graces."

"Ah!" sighed Agnes, "how beautiful and how blessed to be among such!"

"Thou sayest well, dear child. Blessed are the flowers of God that grow in cool solitudes, and have never been profaned by the hot sun and dust of this world!"

"I should like to be such a one," said Agnes. "I often think, when I visit the sisters at the Convent, that I long to be one of them."

"A pretty story!" said Dame Elsie, who had heard the last words, "go into a convent and leave your poor grandmother all alone, when she has toiled night and day for so many years to get a dowry for you and find you a worthy husband!"

"I don't want any husband in this world, grandmamma," said Agnes.

"What talk is this? Not want a good husband to take care of you when your poor old grandmother is gone? Who will provide for you?"

"He who took care of the blessed Saint Agnes, grandmamma."

"Saint Agnes, to be sure! That was a great many years ago, and times have altered since then; in these days girls must have husbands. Is n't it so, Brother Antonio?"

"But if the darling hath a vocation?" said the artist, mildly.

"Vocation! I 'll see to that! She sha'n't have a vocation! Suppose I 'm going to delve, and toil, and spin, and wear myself to the bone, and have her slip through my fingers at last with a vocation? No, indeed!"

"Indeed, dear grandmother, don't be angry!" said
Agnes. "I will do just as you say, — only I don't want
a husband."

"Well, well, my little heart, — one thing at a time;
you shan't have him till you say yes willingly," said
Elsie, in a mollified tone.

Agnes turned again to the portfolio and busied herself
with it, her eyes dilating as she ran over the sketches.

"Ah! what pretty, pretty bird is this?" she asked.

"Knowest thou not that bird, with his little red beak?"
said the artist. "When our dear Lord hung bleeding, and
no man pitied him, this bird, filled with tender love, tried
to draw out the nails with his poor little beak, — so much
better were the birds than we hard-hearted sinners! —
hence he hath honor in many pictures. See here, — I
shall put him into the office of the Sacred Heart, in a little
nest curiously built in a running vine of passion-flower.
See here, daughter, — I have a great commission to execute a Breviary for our house, and our holy Father was
pleased to say that the spirit of the blessed Angelico had
in some little humble measure descended on me, and now
I am busy day and night; for not a twig rustles, not a
bird flies, nor a flower blossoms, but I begin to see therein
some hint of holy adornment to my blessed work."

"Oh, Uncle Antonio, how happy you must be!" said
Agnes, her large eyes filling with tears.

"Happy! — child, am I not?" said the monk, looking
up and crossing himself. "Holy Mother, am I not? Do
I not walk the earth in a dream of bliss, and see the footsteps of my Most Blessed Lord and his dear Mother on
every rock and hill? I see the flowers rise up in clouds
to adore them. What am I, unworthy sinner, that such
grace is granted me? Often I fall on my face before the
humblest flower where my dear Lord hath written his
name, and confess I am unworthy the honor of copying his
sweet handiwork."

The artist spoke these words with his hands clasped and his fervid eyes upraised, like a man in an ecstasy; nor can our more prosaic English give an idea of the fluent naturalness and grace with which such images melt into that lovely tongue which seems made to be the natural language of poetry and enthusiasm.

Agnes looked up to him with humble awe, as to some celestial being; but there was a sympathetic glow in her face, and she put her hands on her bosom, as her manner often was when much moved, and, drawing a deep sigh, said, —

"Would that such gifts were mine!"

"They are thine, sweet one," said the monk. "In Christ's dear kingdom is no mine or thine, but all that each hath is the property of others. I never rejoice so much in my art as when I think of the communion of saints, and that all that our Blessed Lord will work through me is the property of the humblest soul in his kingdom. When I see one flower rarer than another, or a bird singing on a twig, I take note of the same, and say, ' This lovely work of God shall be for some shrine, or the border of a missal, or the foreground of an altar-piece, and thus shall his saints be comforted.' "

"But," said Agnes, fervently, "how little can a poor young maiden do! Ah, I do so long to offer myself up in some way to the dear Lord, who gave himself for us, and for his Most Blessed Church!"

As Agnes spoke these words, her cheek, usually so clear and pale, became suffused with a tremulous color, and her dark eyes had a deep, divine expression; a moment after, the color slowly faded, her head drooped, and her long, dark lashes fell on her cheek, while her hands were folded on her bosom. The eye of the monk was watching her with an enkindled glance.

"Is she not the very presentment of our Blessed Lady

in the Annunciation?" said he to himself. "Surely, this grace is upon her for this special purpose. My prayers are answered."

"Daughter," he began, in a gentle tone, "a glorious work has been done of late in Florence under the preaching of our blessed Superior. Could you believe it, daughter, in these times of backsliding and rebuke there have been found painters base enough to paint the pictures of vile, abandoned women in the character of our Blessed Lady; yea, and princes have been found wicked enough to buy them and put them up in churches, so that the people have had the Mother of all Purity presented to them in the guise of a vile harlot. Is it not dreadful?"

"How horrible!" said Agnes.

"Ah, but you should have seen the great procession through Florence, when all the little children were inspired by the heavenly preaching of our dear Master. These dear little ones, carrying the blessed cross and singing the hymns our Master had written for them, went from house to house and church to church, demanding that everything that was vile and base should be delivered up to the flames, — and the people, beholding, thought that the angels had indeed come down, and brought forth all their loose pictures and vile books, such as Boccaccio's romances and other defilements, and the children made a splendid bonfire of them in the Grand Piazza, and so thousands of vile things were consumed and scattered. And then our blessed Master exhorted the artists to give their pencils to Christ and his Mother, and to seek for her image among pious and holy women living a veiled and secluded life, like that our Lady lived before the blessed Annunciation. ' Think you,' he said, ' that the blessed Angelico obtained the grace to set forth our Lady in such heavenly wise by gazing about the streets on mincing women tricked out in all the world's bravery? — or did he not find her image in holy solitudes, among modest and prayerful saints?' "

"Ah," said Agnes, drawing in her breath with an expression of awe, "what mortal would dare to sit for the image of our Lady!"

"Dear child, there be women whom the Lord crowns with beauty when they know it not, and our dear Mother sheds so much of her spirit into their hearts that it shines out in their faces; and among such must the painter look. Dear little child, be not ignorant that our Lord hath shed this great grace on thee. I have received a light that thou art to be the model for the 'Hail Mary!' in my Breviary."

"Oh, no, no, no! it cannot be!" said Agnes, covering her face with her hands.

"My daughter, thou art very beautiful, and this beauty was given thee not for thyself, but to be laid like a sweet flower on the altar of thy Lord. Think how blessed, if, through thee, the faithful be reminded of the modesty and humility of Mary, so that their prayers become more fervent, — would it not be a great grace?"

"Dear uncle," said Agnes, "I am Christ's child. If it be as you say, — which I did not know, — give me some days to pray and prepare my soul, that I may offer myself in all humility."

During this conversation Elsie had left the garden and gone a little way down the gorge, to have a few moments of gossip with an old crony. The light of the evening sky had gradually faded away, and the full moon was pouring a shower of silver upon the orange-trees. As Agnes sat on the parapet, with the moonlight streaming down on her young, spiritual face, now tremulous with deep suppressed emotion, the painter thought he had never seen any human creature that looked nearer to his conception of a celestial being.

They both sat awhile in that kind of quietude which often falls between two who have stirred some deep fountain of emotion. All was so still around them, that the

drip and trickle of the little stream which fell from the
garden wall into the dark abyss of the gorge could well be
heard as it pattered from one rocky point to another, with
a slender, lulling sound.

Suddenly the reveries of the two were disturbed by the
shadow of a figure which passed into the moonlight and
seemed to rise from the side of the gorge. A man enveloped in a dark cloak with a peaked hood stepped across
the moss-grown garden parapet, stood a moment irresolute,
then the cloak dropped suddenly from him, and the cavalier stood in the moonlight before Agnes. He bore in his
hand a tall stalk of white lily, with open blossoms and
buds and tender fluted green leaves, such as one sees in a
thousand pictures of the Annunciation. The moonlight
fell full upon his face, revealing his haughty yet beautiful
features, agitated by some profound emotion. The monk
and the girl were both too much surprised for a moment to
utter a sound; and when, after an instant, the monk made
a half-movement as if to address him, the cavalier raised
his right hand with a sudden authoritative gesture which
silenced him. Then turning toward Agnes, he kneeled,
and kissing the hem of her robe, and laying the lily in her
lap, "Holiest and dearest," he said, "oh, forget not to pray
for me!" He rose again in a moment, and, throwing his
cloak around him, sprang over the garden wall, and was
heard rapidly descending into the shadows of the gorge.

All this passed so quickly that it seemed to both the
spectators like a dream. The splendid man, with his jeweled weapons, his haughty bearing, and air of easy command, bowing with such solemn humility before the peasant-girl, reminded the monk of the barbaric princes in the
wonderful legends he had read, who had been drawn by
some heavenly inspiration to come and render themselves
up to the teachings of holy virgins, chosen of the Lord, in
divine solitudes. In the poetical world in which he lived

all such marvels were possible. There were a thousand precedents for them in that devout dreamland, "The Lives of the Saints."

"My daughter," he said, after looking vainly down the dark shadows upon the path of the stranger, "have you ever seen this man before ? "

"Yes, uncle; yesterday evening I saw him for the first time, when sitting at my stand at the gate of the city. It was at the Ave Maria; he came up there and asked my prayers, and gave me a diamond ring for the shrine of Saint Agnes, which I carried to the convent to-day."

"Behold, my dear daughter, the confirmation of what I have just said to thee! It is evident that our Lady hath endowed thee with the great grace of a beauty which draws the soul upward towards the angels, instead of downward to sensual things, like the beauty of worldly women. What saith the blessed poet Dante of the beauty of the holy Beatrice ? — that it said to every man who looked on her, '*Aspire!*' [1] Great is the grace, and thou must give special praise therefor."

"I would," said Agnes, thoughtfully, "that I knew who this stranger is, and what is his great trouble and need, — his eyes are so full of sorrow. Giulietta said he was the King's brother, and was called the Lord Adrian. What

[1] I cannot forbear quoting Mr. Norton's beautiful translation of this sonnet in the *Atlantic Monthly* for February, 1859: —

> " So gentle and so modest doth appear
> My lady when she giveth her salute,
> That every tongue becometh trembling mute,
> Nor do the eyes to look upon her dare.
> And though she hears her praises, she doth go
> Benignly clothèd with humility,
> And like a thing come down she seems to be
> From heaven to earth, a miracle to show.
> So pleaseth she whoever cometh nigh her,
> She gives the heart a sweetness through the eyes
> Which none can understand who doth not prove.
> And from her lip there seems indeed to move
> A spirit sweet and in Love's very guise,
> Which goeth saying to the soul, ' Aspire ! ' "

sorrow can he have, or what need for the prayers of a poor
maid like me ? ''

"Perhaps the Lord hath pierced him with a longing
after the celestial beauty and heavenly purity of paradise,
and wounded him with a divine sorrow, as happened to
Saint Francis and to the blessed Saint Dominic," said the
monk. "Beauty is the Lord's arrow, wherewith he pierceth
to the inmost soul, with a divine longing and languishment
which find rest only in him. Hence thou seest the wounds
of love in saints are always painted by us with holy flames
ascending from them. Have good courage, sweet child,
and pray with fervor for this youth; for there be no prayers
sweeter before the throne of God than those of spotless
maidens. The Scripture saith, ' My beloved feedeth among
the lilies.' ''

At this moment the sharp, decided tramp of Elsie was
heard reëntering the garden.

"Come, Agnes," she said, "it is time for you to begin
your prayers, or, the saints know, I shall not get you to
bed till midnight. I suppose prayers are a good thing,"
she added, seating herself wearily; "but if one must have
so many of them, one must get about them early. There's
reason in all things."

Agnes, who had been sitting abstractedly on the parapet,
with her head drooped over the lily-spray, now seemed to
collect herself. She rose up in a grave and thoughtful
manner, and, going forward to the shrine of the Madonna,
removed the flowers of the morning, and holding the vase
under the spout of the fountain, all feathered with waving
maiden-hair, filled it with fresh water, the drops falling
from it in a thousand little silver rings in the moonlight.

"I have a thought," said the monk to himself, drawing
from his girdle a pencil and hastily sketching by the moonlight. What he drew was a fragile maiden form, sitting
with clasped hands on a mossy ruin, gazing on a spray of

white lilies which lay before her. He called it, The Blessed Virgin pondering the Lily of the Annunciation.

"Hast thou ever reflected," he said to Agnes, "what that lily might be like which the angel Gabriel brought to our Lady ? — for, trust me, it was no mortal flower, but grew by the river of life. I have often meditated thereon, that it was like unto living silver with a light in itself, like the moon, — even as our Lord's garments in the Transfiguration, which glistened like the snow. I have cast about in myself by what device a painter might represent so marvelous a flower."

"Now, brother Antonio," said Elsie, "if you begin to talk to the child about such matters, our Lady alone knows when we shall get to bed. I am sure I 'm as good a Christian as anybody; but, as I said, there 's reason in all things, and one cannot always be wondering and inquiring into heavenly matters, — as to every feather in Saint Michael's wings, and as to our Lady's girdle and shoestrings and thimble and work-basket; and when one gets through with our Lady, then one has it all to go over about her mother, the blessed Saint Anne (may her name be ever praised!). I mean no disrespect, but I am certain the saints are reasonable folk and must see that poor folk must live, and, in order to live, must think of something else now and then besides *them*. That 's my mind, brother."

"Well, well, sister," said the monk, placidly, "no doubt you are right. There shall be no quarreling in the Lord's vineyard; every one hath his manner and place, and you follow the lead of the blessed Saint Martha, which is holy and honorable."

"Honorable! I should think it might be!" said Elsie. "I warrant me, if everything had been left to Saint Mary's doings, our Blessed Lord and the Twelve Apostles might have gone supperless. But it 's Martha gets all the work, and Mary all the praise."

"Quite right, quite right," said the monk, abstractedly, while he stood out in the moonlight busily sketching the fountain. By just such a fountain, he thought, our Lady might have washed the clothes of the Blessed Babe. Doubtless there was some such in the court of her dwelling, all mossy, and with sweet waters forever singing a song of praise therein.

Elsie was heard within the house meanwhile making energetic commotion, rattling pots and pans, and producing decided movements among the simple furniture of the dwelling, probably with a view to preparing for the night's repose of the guest.

Meanwhile Agnes, kneeling before the shrine, was going through with great feeling and tenderness the various manuals and movements of nightly devotion which her own religious fervor and the zeal of her spiritual advisers had enjoined upon her. Christianity, when it entered Italy, came among a people every act of whose life was colored and consecrated by symbolic and ritual acts of heathenism. The only possible way to uproot this was in supplanting it by Christian ritual and symbolism equally minute and pervading. Besides, in those ages when the Christian preacher was utterly destitute of all the help which the press now gives in keeping under the eye of converts the great inspiring truths of religion, it was one of the first offices of every saint whose preaching stirred the heart of the people, to devise symbolic forms, signs, and observances, by which the mobile and fluid heart of the multitude might crystalize into habits of devout remembrance. The rosary, the crucifix, the shrine, the banner, the procession, were catechisms and tracts invented for those who could not read, wherein the substance of pages was condensed and gave itself to the eye and the touch. Let us not, from the height of our day, with the better appliances which a universal press gives us, sneer at the homely rounds of the ladder by which the first multitudes of the Lord's followers climbed heavenward.

If there seemed somewhat mechanical in the number of times which Agnes repeated the "Hail, Mary!" — in the prescribed number of times she rose or bowed or crossed herself or laid her forehead in low humility on the flags of the pavement, it was redeemed by the earnest fervor which inspired each action. However foreign to the habits of a Northern mind or education such a mode of prayer may be, these forms to her were all helpful and significant, her soul was borne by them Godward, — and often, as she prayed, it seemed to her that she could feel the dissolving of all earthly things, and the pressing nearer and nearer of the great cloud of witnesses who ever surround the humblest member of Christ's mystical body.

> " Sweet loving hearts around her beat,
>   Sweet helping hands are stirred,
>   And palpitates the veil between
>   With breathings almost heard."

Certain English writers, looking entirely from a worldly and philosophical standpoint, are utterly at a loss to account for the power which certain Italian women of obscure birth came to exercise in the councils of nations merely by the force of a mystical piety; but the Northern mind of Europe is entirely unfitted to read and appreciate the psychological religious phenomena of Southern races. The temperament which in our modern days has been called the mediïstic, and which with us is only exceptional, is more or less a race-peculiarity of Southern climates, and gives that objectiveness to the conception of spiritual things from which grew up a whole ritual and a whole world of religious Art. The Southern saints and religious artists were seers, — men and women of that peculiar fineness and delicacy of temperament which made them especially apt to receive and project outward the truths of the spiritual life; they

were in that state of "divine madness" which is favorable
to the most intense conception of the poet and artist, and
something of this influence descended through all the channels of the people.

When Agnes rose from prayer, she had a serene, exalted
expression, like one who walks with some unseen excellence
and meditates on some untold joy.   As she was crossing
the court to come towards her uncle, her eye was attracted
by the sparkle of something on the ground, and, stooping,
she picked up a heart-shaped locket, curiously made of a
large amethyst, and fastened with a golden arrow.   As she
pressed upon this, the locket opened and disclosed to her
view a folded paper.   Her mood at this moment was so
calm and elevated that she received the incident with no
start or shiver of the nerves.   To her it seemed a provi-
dential token, which would probably bring to her some
further knowledge of this mysterious being who had been
so especially confided to her intercessions.

Agnes had learned of the Superior of the Convent the
art of reading writing, which would never have been the
birthright of the peasant-girl in her times, and the moon
had that dazzling clearness which revealed every letter.
She stood by the parapet, one hand lying in the white
blossoming alyssum which filled its marble crevices, while
she read and seriously pondered the contents of the paper.

TO AGNES

Sweet saint, sweet lady, may a sinful soul
Approach thee with an offering of love,
And lay at thy dear feet a weary heart
That loves thee, as it loveth God above ?
If blessed Mary may without a stain
Receive the love of sinners most defiled,
If the fair saints that walk with her in white
Refuse not love from earth's most guilty child,
Shouldst thou, sweet lady, then that love deny
Which all-unworthy at thy feet is laid ?
Ah, gentlest angel, be not more severe
Than the dear heavens unto a loving prayer !

Howe'er unworthily that prayer be said,
Let thine acceptance be like that on high !

There might have been times in Agnes's life when the
reception of this note would have astonished and perplexed
her; but the whole strain of thought and conversation this
evening had been in exalted and poetical regions, and the
soft stillness of the hour, the wonderful calmness and clearness of the moonlight, all seemed in unison with the strange
incident that had occurred, and with the still stranger tenor
of the paper.   The soft melancholy, half-religious tone of
it was in accordance with the whole undercurrent of her
life, and prevented that start of alarm which any homage
of a more worldly form might have excited.   It is not to
be wondered at, therefore, that she read it many times with
pauses and intervals of deep thought, and then with a
movement of natural and girlish curiosity examined the rich
jewel which had enclosed it.   At last, seeming to collect
her thoughts, she folded the paper and replaced it in its
sparkling casket, and, unlocking the door of the shrine,
laid the gem with its enclosure beneath the lily-spray, as
another offering to the Madonna.   "Dear Mother," she
said, "if indeed it be so, may he rise from loving me to
loving thee and thy dear Son, who is Lord of all! Amen!"
Thus praying, she locked the door and turned thoughtfully
to her repose, leaving the monk pacing up and down in the
moonlit garden.

Meanwhile the cavalier was standing on the velvet mossy
bridge which spanned the stream at the bottom of the
gorge, watching the play of moonbeams on layer after layer
of tremulous silver foliage in the clefts of the black, rocky
walls on either side.   The moon rode so high in the deep
violet-colored sky, that her beams came down almost verti-
cally, making green and translucent the leaves through
which they passed, and throwing strongly marked shadows
here and there on the flower-embroidered moss of the old

bridge.   There was that solemn, plaintive stillness in the
air which makes the least sound — the hum of an insect's
wing, the cracking of a twig, the patter of falling water —
so distinct and impressive.

It needs not to be explained how the cavalier, following
the steps of Agnes and her grandmother at a distance, had
threaded the path by which they ascended to their little
sheltered nook, — how he had lingered within hearing of
Agnes's voice, and, moving among the surrounding rocks
and trees, and drawing nearer and nearer as evening shadows drew on, had listened to the conversation, hoping that
some unexpected chance might gain him a moment's speech
with his enchantress.

The reader will have gathered from the preceding chap-
ter that the conception which Agnes had formed as to the
real position of her admirer from the reports of Giulietta
was false, and that in reality he was not Lord Adrian, the
brother of the King, but an outcast and landless representative of one branch of an ancient and noble Roman family,
whose estates had been confiscated and whose relations had
been murdered, to satisfy the boundless rapacity of Cæsar
Borgia, the infamous favorite of the notorious Alexander
VI.

The natural temperament of Agostino Sarelli had been
rather that of the poet and artist than of the warrior.   In
the beautiful gardens of his ancestral home it had been his
delight to muse over the pages of Dante; to sing to the
lute, and to write, in the facile flowing rhyme of his native
Italian, the fancies of the dreamland of his youth.

He was the younger brother of the family, — the favorite son and companion of his mother, who, being of a tender and religious nature, had brought him up in habits of
the most implicit reverence and devotion for the institutions of his fathers.

The storm which swept over his house, and blasted all

his worldly prospects, blasted, too, and withered all those
religious hopes and beliefs by which alone sensitive and
affectionate natures can be healed of the wounds of adver-
sity without leaving distortion or scar.   For his house had
been overthrown, his elder brother cruelly and treacher-
ously murdered, himself and his retainers robbed and cast
out, by a man who had the entire sanction and support of
the Head of the Christian Church, the Vicar of Christ on
Earth.   So said the current belief of his times, — the faith
in which his sainted mother died; and the difficulty with
which a man breaks away from such ties is in exact proportion to the refinement and elevation of his nature.

In the mind of our young nobleman there was a double
current.   He was a Roman, and the traditions of his house
went back to the time of Mutius Scævola; and his old
nurse had often told him that grand story of how the
young hero stood with his right hand in the fire rather
than betray his honor.   If the legends of Rome's ancient
heroes cause the pulses of colder climes and alien races to
throb with sympathetic heroism, what must their power be
to one who says, "These were my fathers"?   Agostino
read Plutarch, and thought, "I, too, am a Roman!" and
then he looked on the power that held sway over the
Tarpeian Rock and the halls of the old "Sanctus Senatus,"
and asked himself, "By what right does it hold these?"
He knew full well that in the popular belief all those
hardy and virtuous old Romans whose deeds of heroism so
transported him were burning in hell for the crime of having been born before Christ; and he asked himself, as he
looked on the horrible and unnatural luxury and vice which
defiled the Papal chair and ran riot through every ecclesiastical order, whether such men, without faith, without conscience, and without even decency, were indeed the only
authorized successors of Christ and his Apostles?

To us, of course, from our modern standpoint, the ques-

tion has an easy solution, — but not so in those days, when
the Christianity of the known world was in the Romish
church, and when the choice seemed to be between that
and infidelity. Not yet had Luther flared aloft the bold,
cheery torch which showed the faithful how to disentangle
Christianity from Ecclesiasticism. Luther in those days
was a star lying low in the gray horizon of a yet unawak-
ened dawn.

All through Italy at this time there was the restless
throbbing and pulsating, the aimless outreach of the popular heart, which marks the decline of one cycle of religious
faith and calls for some great awakening and renewal.
Savonarola, the priest and prophet of this dumb desire, was
beginning to heave a great heart of conflict towards that
mighty struggle with the vices and immoralities of his time
in which he was yet to sink a martyr; and even now his
course was beginning to be obstructed by the full energy
of the whole aroused serpent brood which hissed and
knotted in the holy places of Rome.

Here, then, was our Agostino, with a nature intensely
fervent and poetic, every fibre of whose soul and nervous
system had been from childhood skillfully woven and inter-
twined with the ritual and faith of his fathers, yearning
towards the grave of his mother, yearning towards the
legends of saints and angels with which she had lulled his
cradle slumbers and sanctified his childhood's pillow, and
yet burning with the indignation of a whole line of old
Roman ancestors against an injustice and oppression wrought
under the full approbation of the head of that religion.
Half his nature was all the while battling the other half.
Would he be Roman, or would he be Christian? All the
Roman in him said "No!" when he thought of submission to the patent and open injustice and fiendish tyranny
which had disinherited him, slain his kindred, and held
its impure reign by torture and by blood. He looked on

the splendid snow-crowned mountains whose old silver senate engirdles Rome with an eternal and silent majesty of presence, and he thought how often in ancient times they had been a shelter to free blood that would not endure oppression; and so gathering to his banner the crushed and scattered retainers of his father's house, and offering refuge and protection to multitudes of others whom the crimes and rapacities of the Borgias had stripped of possessions and means of support, he fled to a fastness in the mountains between Rome and Naples, and became an independent chieftain, living by his sword.

The rapacity, cruelty, and misgovernment of the various regular authorities of Italy at this time made brigandage a respectable and honored institution in the eyes of the people, though it was ostensibly banned both by Pope and Prince. Besides, in the multitude of contending factions which were every day wrangling for supremacy, it soon became apparent, even to the ruling authorities, that a band of fighting men under a gallant leader, advantageously posted in the mountains and understanding all their passes, was a power of no small importance to be employed on one side or the other; and therefore it happened, that, though nominally outlawed or excommunicated, they were secretly protected on both sides, with a view to securing their assistance in critical turns of affairs.

Among the common people of the towns and villages their relations were of the most comfortable kind, their depredations being chiefly confined to the rich and prosperous, who, as they wrung their wealth out of the people, were not considered particular objects of compassion when the same kind of high-handed treatment was extended toward themselves.

The most spirited and brave of the young peasantry, if they wished to secure the smiles of the girls of their neighborhood, and win hearts past redemption, found no surer

avenue to favor than in joining the brigands. The leaders
of these bands sometimes piqued themselves on elegant
tastes and accomplishments; and one of them is said to
have sent to the poet Tasso, in his misfortunes and exile,
an offer of honorable asylum and protection in his mountain fortress.

Agostino Sarelli saw himself, in fact, a powerful chief,
and there were times when the splendid scenery of his
mountain fastness, its inspiring air, its wild eagle-like grandeur, independence, and security, gave him a proud con-
tentment, and he looked at his sword and loved it as a
bride.   But then again there were moods in which he felt
all that yearning and disquiet of soul which the man of
wide and tender moral organization must feel who has had
his faith shaken in the religion of his fathers.   To such a
man the quarrel with his childhood's faith is a never-end-
ing anguish; especially is it so with a religion so objective,
so pictorial, and so interwoven with the whole physical and
nervous nature of man, as that which grew up and flowered in modern Italy.

Agostino was like a man who lives in an eternal struggle
of self-justification, — his reason forever going over and
over with its plea before his regretful and never-satisfied
heart, which was drawn every hour of the day by some
chain of memory towards the faith whose visible adminis-
trators he detested with the whole force of his moral being.
When the vesper-bell, with its plaintive call, rose amid
the purple shadows of the olive-silvered mountains, — when
the distant voices of chanting priest and choir reached him
solemnly from afar, — when he looked into a church with
its cloudy pictures of angels, and its window-panes flaming
with venerable forms of saints and martyrs, — it roused a
yearning anguish, a pain and conflict, which all the efforts
of his reason could not subdue.   How to be a Christian
and yet defy the authorized Head of the Christian Church,

or how to be a Christian and recognize foul men of obscene
and rapacious deeds as Christ's representatives, was the inextricable Gordian knot, which his sword could not divide.
He dared not approach the Sacrament, he dared not pray,
and sometimes he felt wild impulses to tread down in riot-
ous despair every fragment of a religious belief which
seemed to live in his heart only to torture him.   He had
heard priests scoff over the wafer they consecrated, — he
had known them to mingle poison for rivals in the sacramental wine, — and yet God had kept silence and not
struck them dead; and like the Psalmist of old he said,
"Verily, I have cleansed my heart in vain, and washed
my hands in innocency.   Is there a God that judgeth in
the earth?"

The first time he saw Agnes bending like a flower in the
slanting evening sunbeams by the old gate of Sorrento,
while he stood looking down the kneeling street and striving to hold his own soul in the sarcastic calm of utter
indifference, he felt himself struck to the heart by an influence he could not define.   The sight of that young face,
with its clear, beautiful lines, and its tender fervor, recalled
a thousand influences of the happiest and purest hours of
his life, and drew him with an attraction he vainly strove
to hide under an air of mocking gallantry.

When she looked him in the face with such grave, surprised eyes of innocent confidence, and promised to pray
for him, he felt a remorseful tenderness as if he had
profaned a shrine.   All that was passionate, poetic, and
romantic in his nature was awakened to blend itself in a
strange mingling of despairing sadness and of tender veneration about this sweet image of perfect purity and faith.
Never does love strike so deep and immediate a root as in
a sorrowful and desolated nature; there it has nothing to
dispute the soil, and soon fills it with its interlacing fibres.

In this case it was not merely Agnes that he sighed for,

but she stood to him as the fair symbol of that life-peace, that rest of soul which he had lost, it seemed to him, forever.

"Behold this pure, believing child," he said to himself, — "a true member of that blessed Church to which thou art a rebel! How peacefully this lamb walketh the old ways trodden by saints and martyrs, while thou art an infidel and unbeliever!" And then a stern voice within him answered, "What then? Is the Holy Ghost indeed alone dispensed through the medium of Alexander and his scarlet crew of cardinals? Hath the power to bind and loose in Christ's Church been indeed given to whoever can buy it with the wages of robbery and oppression? Why does every prayer and pious word of the faithful reproach me? Why is God silent? Or is there any God? Oh, Agnes, Agnes! dear lily! fair lamb! lead a sinner into the green pastures where thou restest!"

So wrestled the strong nature, tempest-tossed in its strength, — so slept the trustful, blessed in its trust, — then in Italy, as now in all lands.

CHAPTER X

THE dreams of Agnes, on the night after her conversation with the monk and her singular momentary interview with the cavalier, were a strange mixture of images, indicating the peculiarities of her education and habits of daily thought.

She dreamed that she was sitting alone in the moonlight, and heard some one rustling in the distant foliage of the orange groves, and from them came a young man dressed in white of a dazzling clearness like sunlight; large pearly wings fell from his shoulders and seemed to shimmer with a phosphoric radiance; his forehead was broad and grave, and above it floated a thin, tremulous tongue of flame; his eyes had that deep, mysterious gravity which is so well expressed in all the Florentine paintings of celestial beings; and yet, singularly enough, this white-robed, glorified form seemed to have the features and lineaments of the mysterious cavalier of the evening before, — the same deep, mournful dark eyes, only that in them the light of earthly pride had given place to the calm, strong gravity of an assured peace, — the same broad forehead, — the same delicately chiseled features, but elevated and etherealized, glowing with a kind of interior ecstasy. He seemed to move from the shadow of the orange trees with a backward floating of his lustrous garments, as if borne on a cloud just along the surface of the ground; and in his hand he held the lily spray, all radiant with a silvery, living light, just as the monk had suggested to her a divine flower might be.

Agnes seemed to herself to hold her breath and marvel with a secret awe, and as often happens in dreams, she wondered to herself, "Was this stranger, then, indeed, not even mortal, not even a king's brother, but an angel? How strange," she said to herself, "that I should never have seen it in his eyes!"   Nearer and nearer the vision drew, and touched her forehead with the lily, which seemed dewy and icy cool; and with the contact it seemed to her that a delicious tranquillity, a calm ecstasy, possessed her soul, and the words were impressed in her mind, as if spoken in her ear, "The Lord hath sealed thee for his own!" — and then, with the wild fantasy of dreams, she saw the cavalier in his wonted form and garments, just as he had kneeled to her the night before, and he said, "Oh, Agnes! Agnes! little lamb of Christ, love me and lead me!" — and in her sleep it seemed to her that her heart stirred and throbbed with a strange, new movement in answer to those sad, pleading eyes, and thereafter her dream became more troubled.

The sea was beginning now to brighten with the reflection of the coming dawn in the sky, and the flickering fire of Vesuvius was waxing sickly and pale; and while all the high points of rocks were turning of a rosy purple, in the weird depths of the gorge were yet the unbroken shadows and stillness of night.   But at the earliest peep of dawn the monk had risen, and now, as he paced up and down the little garden, his morning hymn mingled with Agnes's dreams, — words strong with all the nerve of the old Latin, which, when they were written, had scarcely ceased to be the spoken tongue of Italy.

> "Splendor paternæ gloriæ,
> De luce lucem proferens,
> Lux lucis et fons luminis,
> Dies diem illuminans !
>
> "Votis vocemus et Patrem,
> Patrem potentis gratiæ,

Patrem perennis gloriæ:
Culpam releget lubricam !

" Confirmet actus strenuos,
Dentes retundat invidi,
Casus secundet asperos,
Donet gerendi gratiam !

" Christus nobis sit cibus,
Potusque noster sit fides:
Læti bibamus sobriam
Ebrietatem spiritus !

" Lætus dies hic transeat,
Pudor sit ut diluculum,
Fides velut meridies.
Crepusculum mens nesciat ! " [1]

The hymn in every word well expressed the character
and habitual pose of mind of the singer, whose views of
earthly matters were as different from the views of ordi-
nary working mortals as those of a bird, as he flits and
perches and sings, must be from those of the four-footed

[1] Splendor of the Father's glory,
Bringing light with cheering ray,
Light of light and fount of brightness,
Day, illuminating day !

In our prayers we call thee Father,
Father of eternal glory,
Father of a mighty grace:
Heal our errors, we implore thee!

Form our struggling, vague desires;
Power of spiteful spirits break;
Help us in life's straits, and give us
Grace to suffer for thy sake!

Christ for us shall be our food;
Faith in him our drink shall be;
Hopeful, joyful, let us drink
Soberness of ecstasy!

Joyful shall our day go by,
Purity its dawning light,
Faith its fervid noontide glow,
And for us shall be no night!

ox who plods. The "*sobriam ebrietatem spiritus*" was with him first constitutional, as a child of sunny skies, and then cultivated by every employment and duty of the religious and artistic career to which from childhood he had devoted himself. If perfect, unalloyed happiness has ever existed in this weary, work-day world of ours, it has been in the bosoms of some of those old religious artists of the Middle Ages, whose thoughts grew and flowered in prayerful shadows, bursting into thousands of quaint and fanciful blossoms on the pages of missal and breviary. In them the fine life of color, form, and symmetry, which is the gift of the Italian, formed a rich stock on which to graft the true vine of religious faith, and rare and fervid were the blossoms.

For it must be remarked in justice of the Christian religion, that the Italian people never rose to the honors of originality in the beautiful arts till inspired by Christianity. The Art of ancient Rome was a second-hand copy of the original and airy Greek, — often clever, but never vivid and self-originating. It is to the religious Art of the Middle Ages, to the Umbrian and Florentine schools particularly, that we look for the peculiar and characteristic flowering of the Italian mind. When the old Greek Art revived again in modern Europe, though at first it seemed to add richness and grace to this peculiar development, it smothered and killed it at last, as some brilliant tropical parasite exhausts the life of the tree it seems at first to adorn. Raphael and Michel Angelo mark both the perfected splendor and the commenced decline of original Italian Art; and just in proportion as their ideas grew less Christian and more Greek did the peculiar vividness and intense flavor of Italian nationality pass away from them. They became again like the ancient Romans, gigantic imitators and clever copyists, instead of inspired kings and priests of a national development.

The tones of the monk's morning hymn awakened both Agnes and Elsie, and the latter was on the alert instantly.

"Bless my soul!" she said, "brother Antonio has a marvelous power of lungs; he is at it the first thing in the morning. It always used to be so; when he was a boy, he would wake me up before daylight singing."

"He is happy, like the birds," said Agnes, "because he flies near heaven."

"Like enough: he was always a pious boy; his prayers and his pencil were ever uppermost: but he was a poor hand at work: he could draw you an olive-tree on paper; but set him to dress it, and any fool would have done better."

The morning rites of devotion and the simple repast being over, Elsie prepared to go to her business. It had occurred to her that the visit of her brother was an admirable pretext for withdrawing Agnes from the scene of her daily traffic, and of course, as she fondly supposed, keeping her from the sight of the suspected admirer.

Neither Agnes nor the monk had disturbed her serenity by recounting the adventure of the evening before. Agnes had been silent from the habitual reserve which a difference of nature ever placed between her and her grandmother, — a difference which made confidence on her side an utter impossibility. There are natures which ever must be silent to other natures, because there is no common language between them. In the same house, at the same board, sharing the same pillow even, are those forever strangers and foreigners, whose whole stock of intercourse is limited to a few brief phrases on the commonest material wants of life, and who, as soon as they try to go farther, have no words that are mutually understood.

"Agnes," said her grandmother, "I shall not need you at the stand to-day. There is that new flax to be spun, and you may keep company with your uncle. I 'll warrant me, you 'll be glad enough of that!"

"Certainly I shall," said Agnes, cheerfully. "Uncle's comings are my holidays."

"I will show you somewhat further on my Breviary," said the monk. "Praised be God, many new ideas sprang up in my mind last night, and seemed to shoot forth in blossoms. Even my dreams have often been made fruitful in this divine work."

"Many a good thought comes in dreams," said Elsie; "but, for my part, I work too hard and sleep too sound to get much that way."

"Well, brother," said Elsie, after breakfast, "you must look well after Agnes to-day; for there be plenty of wolves go round, hunting these little lambs."

"Have no fear, sister," said the monk, tranquilly; "the angels have her in charge. If our eyes were only clear-sighted, we should see that Christ's little ones are never alone."

"All that is fine talk, brother; but I never found that the angels attended to any of my affairs, unless I looked after them pretty sharp myself; and as for girls, the dear Lord knows they need a legion apiece to look after them. What with roystering fellows and smooth-tongued gallants, and with silly, empty-headed hussies like that Giulietta, one has much ado to keep the best of them straight. Agnes is one of the best, too, — a well-brought up, pious, obedient girl, and industrious as a bee. Happy is the husband who gets her. I would I knew a man good enough for her."

This conversation took place while Agnes was in the garden picking oranges and lemons, and filling the basket which her grandmother was to take to the town. The silver ripple of a hymn that she was singing came through the open door; it was part of a sacred ballad in honor of Saint Agnes: —

"Bring me no pearls to bind my hair,
  No sparkling jewels bring to me!
Dearer by far the blood-red rose
  That speaks of Him who died for me.

"Ah! vanish every earthly love,
  All earthly dreams forgotten be!
My heart is gone beyond the stars,
  To live with Him who died for me."

"Hear you now, sister," said the monk, "how the Lord keeps the door of this maiden's heart? There is no fear of her; and I much doubt, sister, whether you would do well to interfere with the evident call this child hath to devote herself wholly to the Lord."

"Oh, you talk, brother Antonio, who never had a child in your life, and don't know how a mother's heart warms towards her children and her children's children! The saints, as I said, must be reasonable, and ought n't to be putting vocations into the head of an old woman's only staff and stay; and if they ought n't to, why, then, they won't. Agnes is a pious child, and loves her prayers and hymns; and so she will love her husband, one of these days, as an honest woman should."

"But you know, sister, that the highest seats in Paradise are reserved for the virgins who follow the Lamb."

"Maybe so," said Elsie, stiffly; "but the lower seats are good enough for Agnes and me. For my part, I would rather have a little comfort as I go along, and put up with less in Paradise (may our dear Lady bring us safely there!) say I."

So saying, Elsie raised the large, square basket of golden fruit to her head, and turned her stately figure towards the scene of her daily labors.

The monk seated himself on the garden wall, with his portfolio by his side, and seemed busily sketching and retouching some of his ideas. Agnes wound some silvery-white flax round her distaff, and seated herself near him under an orange tree; and while her small fingers were twisting the flax, her large, thoughtful eyes were wandering off on the deep blue sea, pondering over and over the strange events of the day before, and the dreams of the night.

"Dear child," said the monk, "have you thought more of what I said to you?"

A deep blush suffused her cheek as she answered, —

"Yes, uncle; and I had a strange dream last night."

"A dream, my little heart? Come, then, and tell it to its uncle. Dreams are the hushing of the bodily senses, that the eyes of the Spirit may open."

"Well, then," said Agnes, "I dreamed that I sat pondering as I did last evening in the moonlight, and that an angel came forth from the trees" —

"Indeed!" said the monk, looking up with interest; "what form had he?"

"He was a young man, in dazzling white raiment, and his eyes were deep as eternity; and over his forehead was a silver flame, and he bore a lily-stalk in his hand, which was like what you told of, with light in itself."

"That must have been the holy Gabriel," said the monk, "the angel that came to our blessed Mother. Did he say aught?"

"Yes, he touched my forehead with the lily, and a sort of cool rest and peace went all through me, and he said, ' The Lord hath sealed thee for his own!'"

"Even so," said the monk, looking up, and crossing himself devoutly, "by this token I know that my prayers are answered."

"But, dear uncle," said Agnes, hesitating and blushing painfully, "there was one singular thing about my dream, — this holy angel had yet a strange likeness to the young man that came here last night, so that I could not but marvel at it."

"It may be that the holy angel took on him in part this likeness to show how glorious a redeemed soul might become, that you might be encouraged to pray. The holy Saint Monica thus saw the blessed Augustine standing clothed in white among the angels while he was yet a worldling and unbeliever, and thereby received the grace to continue her prayers for thirty years, till she saw him a holy bishop. This is a sure sign that this young man, whoever he may be, shall attain Paradise through your prayers. Tell me, dear little heart, is this the first angel thou hast seen?"

"I never dreamed of them before. I have dreamed of our Lady, and Saint Agnes, and Saint Catharine of Siena, and sometimes it seemed that they sat a long time by my bed, and sometimes it seemed that they took me with them away to some beautiful place where the air was full of music, and sometimes they filled my hands with such lovely flowers that when I waked I was ready to weep that they could no more be found. Why, dear uncle, do *you* see angels often?"

"Not often, dear child, but sometimes a little glimpse. But you should see the pictures of our holy Father Angelico, to whom the angels appeared constantly; for so blessed was the life he lived, that it was more in heaven than on earth. He would never cumber his mind with the things of this world, and would not paint for money, nor for princes' favor; nor would he take places of power and trust in the Church, or else, so great was his piety, they had made a bishop of him; but he kept ever aloof and walked in the shade. He used to say, 'They that would do Christ's work must walk with Christ.' His pictures of angels are indeed wonderful, and their robes are of all dazzling colors, like the rainbow. It is most surely believed among us that he painted to show forth what he saw in heavenly visions."

"Ah!" said Agnes, "how I wish I could see some of these things!"

"You may well say so, dear child. There is one picture of Paradise painted on gold, and there you may see our Lord in the midst of the heavens crowning his blessed Mother, and all the saints and angels surrounding; and the colors are so bright that they seem like the sunset clouds, — golden, and rosy, and purple, and amethystine, and green like the new, tender leaves of spring: for, you see, the angels are the Lord's flowers and birds that shine and sing to gladden his Paradise, and there is nothing bright on earth that is comparable to them, — so said the blessed Angelico, who saw them. And what seems worthy of note about them is their marvelous lightness, that they seem to float as naturally as the clouds do, and their garments have a divine grace of motion like vapor that curls and wavers in the sun. Their faces, too, are most wonderful; for they seem so full of purity and majesty, and withal humble, with an inexpressible sweetness; for, beyond all others it was given to the holy Angelico to paint the immortal beauty of the soul."

"It must be a great blessing and favor for you, dear uncle, to see all these things," said Agnes; "I am never tired of hearing you tell of them."

"There is one little picture," said the monk, "wherein he hath painted the death of our dear Lady; and surely no mortal could ever conceive anything like her sweet dying face, so faint and weak and tender that each man sees his own mother dying there, yet so holy that one feels that it can be no other than the mother of our Lord; and around her stand the disciples mourning; but above is our blessed Lord himself, who receives the parting spirit, as a tender new-born babe, into his bosom: for so the holy painters represented the death of saints, as of a birth in which each soul became a little child of heaven."

"How great grace must come from such pictures!" said Agnes. "It seems to me that the making of such holy things is one of the most blessed of good works. Dear uncle," she said, after a pause, "they say that this deep gorge is haunted by evil spirits, who often waylay and bewilder the unwary, especially in the hours of darkness."

"I should not wonder in the least," said the monk; "for you must know, child, that our beautiful Italy was of old so completely given up and gone over to idolatry that even her very soil casts up fragments of temples and stones that have been polluted. Especially around these shores there is scarcely a spot that hath not been violated in all times by vilenesses and impurities such as the Apostle saith it is a shame even to speak of. These very waters cast up marbles and fragments of colored mosaics from the halls which were polluted with devil-worship and abominable revelings; so that, as the Gospel saith that the evil spirits cast out by Christ walk through waste places, so do they cling to these fragments of their old estate."

"Well, uncle, I have longed to consecrate the gorge to Christ by having a shrine there, where I might keep a lamp burning."

"It is a most pious thought, child."

"And so, dear uncle, I thought that you would undertake the work. There is one Pietro hereabout who is a skillful worker in stone, and was a playfellow of mine, — though of late grandmamma has forbidden me to talk with him, — and I think he would execute it under your direction."

"Indeed, my little heart, it shall be done," said the monk, cheerfully; "and I will engage to paint a fair picture of our Lady to be within; and I think it would be a good thought to have a pinnacle on the outside, where should stand a statue of Saint Michael with his sword. Saint Michael is a brave and wonderful angel, and all the devils and vile spirits are afraid of him. I will set about the devices to-day." And cheerily the good monk began to intone a verse of an old hymn, —

> "Sub tutela Michaelis,
> Pax in terra, pax in cœlis." [1]

In such talk and work the day passed to Agnes; but we will not say that she did not often fall into deep musings on the mysterious visitor of the night before. Often while the good monk was busy at his drawing, the distaff would droop over her knee and her large dark eyes become intently fixed on the ground, as if she were pondering some absorbing subject.

Little could her literal, hard-working grandmother, or her artistic, simple-minded uncle, or the dreamy Mother Theresa, or her austere confessor, know of the strange forcing process which they were all together uniting to carry on in the mind of this sensitive young girl. Absolutely secluded by her grandmother's watchful care from any actual knowledge and experience of real life, she had no practical tests by which to correct the dreams of that inner world in which she delighted to live and move, and which was peopled with martyrs, saints, and angels, whose deeds were possible or probable only in the most exalted regions of devout poetry.

So she gave her heart at once and without reserve to an enthusiastic desire for the salvation of the stranger, whom Heaven, she believed, had directed to seek her intercessions; and when the spindle drooped from her hand, and her eyes became fixed on vacancy, she found herself wondering who he might really be, and longing to know yet a little more of him.

Towards the latter part of the afternoon, a hasty messenger came to summon her uncle to administer the last

---

[1] "'Neath Saint Michael's watch is given
   Peace on earth and peace in heaven."

rites to a man who had just fallen from a building, and
who, it was feared, might breathe his last unshriven.

"Dear daughter, I must hasten and carry Christ to this
poor sinner," said the monk, hastily putting all his sketches
and pencils into her lap. "Have a care of these till I
return, — that is my good little one!"

Agnes carefully arranged the sketches and put them into
the book, and then, kneeling before the shrine, began
prayers for the soul of the dying man.

She prayed long and fervently, and so absorbed did she
become, that she neither saw nor heard anything that passed
around her.

It was therefore with a start of surprise, as she rose
from prayer, that she saw the cavalier sitting on one end
of the marble sarcophagus, with an air so composed and
melancholy that he might have been taken for one of the
marble knights that sometimes are found on tombs.

"You are surprised to see me, dear Agnes," he said,
with a calm, slow utterance, like a man who has assumed
a position he means fully to justify; "but I have watched
day and night, ever since I saw you, to find one moment
to speak with you alone."

"My Lord," said Agnes, "I humbly wait your pleasure.
Anything that a poor maiden may rightly do, I will en-
deavor, in all loving duty."

"Whom do you take me for, Agnes, that you speak
thus?" said the cavalier, smiling sadly.

"Are you not the brother of our gracious King?" said
Agnes.

"No, dear maiden; and if the kind promise you lately
made me is founded on this mistake, it may be retracted."

"No, my Lord," said Agnes, "though I now know not
who you are, yet if in any strait or need you seek such
poor prayers as mine, God forbid I should refuse them!"

"I am, indeed, in strait and need, Agnes; the sun does

not shine on a more desolate man than I am, — one more
utterly alone in the world; there is no one left to love me.
Agnes, can you not love me a little? — let it be ever so
little, it shall content me."

It was the first time that words of this purport had ever
been addressed to Agnes; but they were said so simply, so
sadly, so tenderly, that they somehow seemed to her the
most natural and proper things in the world to be said;
and this poor handsome knight, who looked so earnest and
sorrowful, — how could she help answering, "Yes"?
From her cradle she had always loved everybody and everything, and why should an exception be made in behalf of
a very handsome, very strong, yet very gentle and submissive human being, who came and knocked so humbly at
the door of her heart? Neither Mary nor the saints had
taught her to be hard-hearted.

"Yes, my Lord," she said, "you may believe that I will
love and pray for you; but now, you must leave me, and
not come here any more, because grandmamma would not
be willing that I should talk with you, and it would be
wrong to disobey her, she is so very good to me."

"But, dear Agnes," began the cavalier, approaching her,
"I have many things to say to you, — I have much to tell
you."

"But I know grandmamma would not be willing," said
Agnes; "indeed you must not come here any more."

"Well, then," said the stranger, "at least you will meet
me at some time, — tell me only where."

"I cannot, — indeed I cannot," said Agnes, distressed
and embarrassed. "Even now, if grandmamma knew you
were here, she would be so angry."

"But how can you pray for me, when you know nothing
of me?"

"The dear Lord knoweth you," said Agnes; "and when
I speak of you, He will know what you need."

"Ah, dear child, how fervent is your faith! Alas for me! I have lost the power of prayer! I have lost the believing heart my mother gave me, — my dear mother who is now in heaven."

"Ah, how can that be?" said Agnes. "Who could lose faith in so dear a Lord as ours, and so loving a mother?"

"Agnes, dear little lamb, you know nothing of the world; and I should be most wicked to disturb your lovely peace of soul with any sinful doubts. Oh, Agnes, Agnes, I am most miserable, most unworthy!"

"Dear sir, should you not cleanse your soul by the holy sacrament of confession, and receive the living Christ within you? For he says, ' Without me ye can do nothing.' "

"Oh, Agnes, sacrament and prayer are not for such as me! It is only through your pure prayers I can hope for grace."

"Dear sir, I have an uncle, a most holy man, and gentle as a lamb. He is of the convent San Marco in Florence, where there is a most holy prophet risen up."

"Savonarola?" said the cavalier, with flashing eyes.

"Yes, that is he. You should hear my uncle talk of him, and how blessed his preaching has been to many souls. Dear sir, come sometime to my uncle."

At this moment the sound of Elsie's voice was heard ascending the path to the gorge outside, talking with Father Antonio, who was returning.

Both started, and Agnes looked alarmed.

"Fear nothing, sweet lamb," said the cavalier; "I am gone."

He kneeled and kissed the hand of Agnes, and disappeared at one bound over the parapet on the side opposite that which they were approaching.

Agnes hastily composed herself, struggling with that half-guilty feeling which is apt to weigh on a conscientious

nature that has been unwittingly drawn to act a part which
would be disapproved by those whose good opinion it habit-
ually seeks.   The interview had but the more increased
her curiosity to know the history of this handsome stranger.
Who, then, could he be?   What were his troubles?   She
wished the interview could have been long enough to satisfy her mind on these points.   From the richness of his
dress, from his air and manner, from the poetry and the
jewel that accompanied it, she felt satisfied that, if not
what she supposed, he was at least nobly born, and had
shone in some splendid sphere whose habits and ways were
far beyond her simple experiences.   She felt towards him
somewhat of the awe which a person of her condition in
life naturally felt toward that brilliant aristocracy which in
those days assumed the state of princes, and the members
of which were supposed to look down on common mortals
from as great a height as the stars regard the humblest
flowers of the field.

"How strange," she thought, "that he should think so
much of me!   What can he see in me?   And how can it
be that a great lord, who speaks so gently and is so rever-
ential to a poor girl, and asks prayers so humbly, can be so
wicked and unbelieving as he says he is?   Dear God, it
cannot be that he is an unbeliever; the great Enemy has
been permitted to try him, to suggest doubts to him, as he
has to holy saints before now.   How beautifully he spoke
about his mother! — tears glittered in his eyes then, — ah,
there must be grace there after all!"

"Well, my little heart," said Elsie, interrupting her
reveries, "have you had a pleasant day?"

"Delightful, grandmamma," said Agnes, blushing deeply
with consciousness.

"Well," said Elsie, with satisfaction, "one thing I know,
— I 've frightened off that old hawk of a cavalier with his
hooked nose.   I have n't seen so much as the tip of his

shoe-tie to-day. Yesterday he made himself very busy around our stall; but I made him understand that you never would come there again till the coast was clear."

The monk was busily retouching the sketch of the Virgin of the Annunciation. He looked up, and saw Agnes standing gazing towards the setting sun, the pale olive of her cheek deepening into a crimson flush. His head was too full of his own work to give much heed to the conversation that had passed, but, looking at the glowing face, he said to himself, —

"Truly, sometimes she might pass for the rose of Sharon as well as the lily of the valley!"

The moon that evening rose an hour later than the night before, yet found Agnes still on her knees before the sacred shrine, while Elsie, tired, grumbled at the draft on her sleeping-time.

"Enough is as good as a feast," she remarked between her teeth; still she had, after all, too much secret reverence for her grandchild's piety openly to interrupt her. But in those days, as now, there were the material and the spiritual, the souls who looked only on things that could be seen, touched, and tasted, and souls who looked on the things that were invisible.

Agnes was pouring out her soul in that kind of yearning, passionate prayer possible to intensely sympathetic people, in which the interests and wants of another seem to annihilate for a time personal consciousness, and make the whole of one's being seem to dissolve in an intense solicitude for something beyond one's self. In such hours prayer ceases to be an act of the will, and resembles more some overpowering influence which floods the soul from without, bearing all its faculties away on its resistless tide.

Brought up from infancy to feel herself in a constant circle of invisible spiritual agencies, Agnes received this wave of intense feeling as an impulse inspired and breathed

into her by some celestial spirit, that thus she should be
made an interceding medium for a soul in some unknown
strait or peril. For her faith taught her to believe in an
infinite struggle of intercession in which all the Church
Visible and Invisible were together engaged, and which
bound them in living bonds of sympathy to an interceding
Redeemer, so that there was no want or woe of human life
that had not somewhere its sympathetic heart, and its
never-ceasing prayer before the throne of Eternal Love.
Whatever may be thought of the actual truth of this belief,
it certainly was far more consoling than that intense indi-
vidualism of modern philosophy, which places every soul
alone in its life-battle, scarce even giving it a God to lean
upon.

CHAPTER XI

THE reader, if a person of any common knowledge of human nature, will easily see the direction in which a young, inexperienced, and impressible girl would naturally be tending under all the influences which we perceive to have come upon her.

But in the religious faith which Agnes professed there was a modifying force, whose power both for good and evil can scarcely be estimated.

The simple Apostolic direction, "Confess your faults one to another," and the very natural need of personal pastoral guidance and assistance to a soul in its heavenward journey, had in common with many other religious ideas been forced by the volcanic fervor of the Italian nature into a certain exaggerated proposition. Instead of brotherly confession one to another, or the pastoral sympathy of a fatherly elder, the religious mind of the day was instructed in an awful mysterious sacrament of confession, which gave to some human being a divine right to unlock the most secret chambers of the soul, to scrutinize and direct its most veiled and intimate thoughts, and, standing in God's stead, to direct the current of its most sensitive and most mysterious emotions.

Every young aspirant for perfection in the religious life had to commence by an unreserved surrender of the whole being in blind faith at the feet of some such spiritual director, all whose questions must be answered, and all whose injunctions obeyed, as from God himself. Thenceforward

was to be no soul-privacy, no retirement, nothing too sacred
to be expressed, too delicate to be handled and analyzed.
In reading the lives of those ethereally made and moulded
women who have come down to our day canonized as saints
in the Roman Catholic communion, one too frequently gets
the impression of most regal natures, gifted with all the
most divine elements of humanity, but subjected to a constant unnatural pressure from the ceaseless scrutiny and
ungenial pertinacity of some inferior and uncomprehending
person invested with the authority of a Spiritual Director.

That there are advantages attending this species of intimate direction, when wisely and skillfully managed, cannot
be doubted.   Groveling and imperfect natures have often
thus been lifted up and carried in the arms of superior wisdom and purity.   The confession administered by a Fénelon
or a Francis de Sales was doubtless a beautiful and most
invigorating ordinance; but the difficulty in its actual working is the rarity of such superior natures, — the fact that
the most ignorant and most incapable may be invested with
precisely the same authority as the most intelligent and
skillful.

He to whom the faith of Agnes obliged her to lay open
her whole soul, who had a right with probing-knife and
lancet to dissect all the finest nerves and fibres of her
womanly nature, was a man who had been through all the
wild and desolating experiences incident to a dissipated and
irregular life in those turbulent days.

It is true that he was now with most stringent and earnest solemnity striving to bring every thought and passion
into captivity to the spirit of his sacred vows; but still,
when a man has once lost that unconscious soul-purity
which exists in a mind unscathed by the fires of passion,
no after-tears can weep it back again.   No penance, no
prayer, no anguish of remorse can give back the simplicity
of a soul that has never been stained.

Il Padre Francesco had not failed to make those inquiries into the character of Agnes's mysterious lover which he assumed to be necessary as a matter of pastoral faithfulness.

It was not difficult for one possessing the secrets of the confessional to learn the real character of any person in the neighborhood, and it was with a kind of bitter satisfaction which rather surprised himself that the father learned enough ill of the cavalier to justify his using every possible measure to prevent his forming any acquaintance with Agnes. He was captain of a band of brigands, and, of course, in array against the State; he was excommunicated, and, of course, an enemy of the Church. What but the vilest designs could be attributed to such a man? Was he not a wolf prowling round the green, secluded pastures where as yet the Lord's lamb had been folded in unconscious innocence?

Father Francesco, when he next met Agnes at the confessional, put such questions as drew from her the whole account of all that had passed between her and the stranger. The recital on Agnes's part was perfectly translucent and pure, for she had said no word and had had no thought that brought the slightest stain upon her soul. Love and prayer had been the prevailing habit of her life, and in promising to love and pray, she had had no worldly or earthly thought. The language of gallantry, or even of sincere passion, had never reached her ear; but it had always been as natural to her to love every human being as for a plant with tendrils to throw them round the next plant, and therefore she entertained the gentle guest who had lately found room in her heart without a question or a scruple.

As Agnes related her childlike story of unconscious faith and love, her listener felt himself strangely and bitterly agitated. It was a vision of ignorant purity and uncon-

sciousness rising before him, airy and glowing as a child's
soap-bubble, which one touch might annihilate; but he
felt a strange remorseful tenderness, a yearning admiration,
at its unsubstantial purity.   There is something pleading
and pitiful in the simplicity of perfect ignorance, — a rare
and delicate beauty in its freshness, like the morning-glory
cup, which, once withered by the heat, no second morning
can restore.   Agnes had imparted to her confessor, by a
mysterious sympathy, something like the morning freshness of her own soul; she had redeemed the idea of womanhood from gross associations, and set before him a fair ideal
of all that female tenderness and purity may teach to man.
Her prayers, — well he believed in them, — but he set his
teeth with a strange spasm of inward passion, when he
thought of her prayers and love being given to another.
He tried to persuade himself that this was only the fervor
of pastoral zeal against a vile robber who had seized the
fairest lamb of the sheepfold; but there was an intensely
bitter, miserable feeling connected with it, that scorched
and burned his higher aspirations like a stream of lava running among fresh leaves and flowers.

The conflict of his soul communicated a severity of earnestness to his voice and manner which made Agnes tremble, as he put one probing question after another, designed
to awaken some consciousness of sin in her soul.   Still,
though troubled and distressed by his apparent disapproba-
tion, her answers came always clear, honest, unfaltering,
like those of one who *could* not form an idea of evil.

When the confession was over, he came out of his recess
to speak with Agnes a few words face to face.   His eyes
had a wild and haggard earnestness, and a vivid hectic
flush on either cheek told how extreme was his emotion.
Agnes lifted her eyes to his with an innocent wondering
trouble and an appealing confidence that for a moment
wholly unnerved him.   He felt a wild impulse to clasp

her in his arms; and for a moment it seemed to him he would sacrifice heaven and brave hell, if he could for one moment hold her to his heart, and say that he loved her, — her, the purest, fairest, sweetest revelation of God's love that had ever shone on his soul, — her, the only star, the only flower, the only dewdrop of a burning, barren, weary life. It seemed to him that it was not the longing, gross passion, but the outcry of his whole nature for something noble, sweet, and divine.

But he turned suddenly away with a sort of groan, and, folding his robe over his face, seemed engaged in earnest prayer. Agnes looked at him awestruck and breathless.

"Oh, my father!" she faltered, "what have I done?"

"Nothing, my poor child," said the father, suddenly turning toward her with recovered calmness and dignity; "but I behold in thee a fair lamb whom the roaring lion is seeking to devour. Know, my daughter, that I have made inquiries concerning this man of whom you speak, and find that he is an outlaw and a robber and a heretic, — a vile wretch stained by crimes that have justly drawn down upon him the sentence of excommunication from our Holy Father, the Pope."

Agnes grew deadly pale at this announcement.

"Can it be possible?" she gasped. "Alas! what dreadful temptations have driven him to such sins?"

"Daughter, beware how you think too lightly of them, or suffer his good looks and flattering words to blind you to their horror. You must from your heart detest him as a vile enemy."

"Must I, my father?"

"Indeed you must."

"But if the dear Lord loved us and died for us when we were his enemies, may we not pity and pray for unbelievers? Oh, say, my dear father, is it not allowed to us to pray for all sinners, even the vilest?"

"I do not say that you may not, my daughter," said the monk, too conscientious to resist the force of this direct appeal; "but, daughter," he added, with an energy that alarmed Agnes, "you must watch your heart; you must not suffer your interest to become a worldly love: remember that you are chosen to be the espoused of Christ alone."

While the monk was speaking thus, Agnes fixed on him her eyes with an innocent mixture of surprise and perplexity, which gradually deepened into a strong gravity of gaze, as if she were looking through him, through all visible things, into some far-off depth of mysterious knowledge.

"My Lord will keep me," she said; "my soul is safe in His heart as a little bird in its nest; but while I love Him, I cannot help loving everybody whom He loves, even His enemies: and, father, my heart prays within me for this poor sinner, whether I will or no; something within me continually intercedes for him."

"Oh, Agnes! Agnes! blessed child, pray for me also," said the monk, with a sudden burst of emotion which perfectly confounded his disciple. He hid his face with his hands.

"My blessed father!" said Agnes, "how could I deem that holiness like yours had any need of my prayers?"

"Child! child! you know nothing of me. I am a miserable sinner, tempted of devils, in danger of damnation."

Agnes stood appalled at this sudden burst, so different from the rigid and restrained severity of tone in which the greater part of the conversation had been conducted. She stood silent and troubled; while he, whom she had always regarded with such awful veneration, seemed shaken by some internal whirlwind of emotion whose nature she could not comprehend.

At length Father Francesco raised his head, and recovered his wonted calm severity of expression.

"My daughter," he said, "little do the innocent lambs of the flock know of the dangers and conflicts through which the shepherds must pass who keep the Lord's fold. We have the labors of angels laid upon us, and we are but men. Often we stumble, often we faint, and Satan takes advantage of our weakness. I cannot confer with you now as I would; but, my child, listen to my directions. Shun this young man; let nothing ever lead you to listen to another word from him; you must not even look at him, should you meet, but turn away your head and repeat a prayer. I do not forbid you to practice the holy work of intercession for his soul, but it must be on these conditions."

"My father," said Agnes, "you may rely on my obedience;" and, kneeling, she kissed his hand.

He drew it suddenly away, with a gesture of pain and displeasure.

"Pardon a sinful child this liberty," said Agnes.

"You know not what you do," said the father, hastily. "Go, my daughter, — go at once; I will confer with you some other time;" and hastily raising his hand in an attitude of benediction, he turned and went into the confessional.

"Wretch! hypocrite! whited sepulchre!" he said to himself, — "to warn this innocent child against a sin that is all the while burning in my own bosom! Yes, I do love her, — I do! I, that warn her against earthly love, I would plunge into hell itself to win hers! And yet, when I know that the care of her soul is only a temptation and a snare to me, I cannot, will not give her up! No, I cannot! — no, I will not! Why should I not love her? Is she not pure as Mary herself? Ah, blessed is he whom such a woman leads! And I — I — have condemned myself to the society of swinish, ignorant, stupid monks, — I must know no such divine souls, no such sweet communion! Help me, blessed Mary! — help a miserable sinner!"

Agnes left the confessional perplexed and sorrowful. The pale, proud, serious face of the cavalier seemed to look at her imploringly, and she thought of him now with the pathetic interest we give to something noble and great exposed to some fatal danger. "Could the sacrifice of my whole life," she thought, "rescue this noble soul from perdition, then I shall not have lived in vain. I am a poor little girl; nobody knows whether I live or die. He is a strong and powerful man, and many must stand or fall with him. Blessed be the Lord that gives to his lowly ones a power to work in secret places! How blessed should I be to meet him in Paradise all splendid as I saw him in my dream! Oh, that would be worth living for, — worth dying for!"

CHAPTER XII

AGNES returned from the confessional with more sadness than her simple life had ever known before. The agitation of her confessor, the tremulous eagerness of his words, the alternations of severity and tenderness in his manner to her, all struck her only as indications of the very grave danger in which she was placed, and the awfulness of the sin and condemnation which oppressed the soul of one for whom she was conscious of a deep and strange interest.

She had the undoubting, uninquiring reverence which a Christianly educated child of those times might entertain for the visible head of the Christian Church, all whose doings were to be regarded with an awful veneration which never even raised a question.

That the Papal throne was now filled by a man who had bought his election with the wages of iniquity, and dispensed its powers and offices with sole reference to the aggrandizement of a family proverbial for brutality and obscenity, was a fact well known to the reasoning and enlightened orders of society at this time; but it did not penetrate into those lowly valleys where the sheep of the Lord humbly pastured, innocently unconscious of the frauds and violence by which their dearest interests were bought and sold.

The Christian faith we now hold, who boast our enlightened Protestantism, has been transmitted to us through the hearts and hands of such, — who, while princes wrangled with Pope, and Pope with princes, knew nothing of it all, but in lowly ways of prayer and patient labor were one with us of modern times in the great central belief of the Christian heart, "Worthy is the Lamb that was slain."

As Agnes came slowly up the path towards the little garden, she was conscious of a burden and weariness of spirit she had never known before. She passed the little moist grotto, which in former times she never failed to visit to see if there were any new-blown cyclamen, without giving it even a thought. A crimson spray of gladiolus leaned from the rock and seemed softly to kiss her cheek, yet she regarded it not; and once stopping and gazing abstractedly upward on the flower-tapestried walls of the gorge, as they rose in wreath and garland and festoon above her, she felt as if the brilliant yellow of the broom and the crimson of the gillyflowers, and all the fluttering, nodding armies of brightness that were dancing in the sunlight, were too gay for such a world as this, where mortal sins and sorrows made such havoc with all that seemed brightest and best, and she longed to fly away and be at rest.

Just then she heard the cheerful voice of her uncle in the little garden above, as he was singing at his painting. The words were those of that old Latin hymn of Saint Bernard, which, in its English dress, has thrilled many a Methodist class meeting and many a Puritan conference, telling, in the welcome they meet in each Christian soul, that there is a unity in Christ's Church which is not outward, — a secret, invisible bond, by which, under warring names and badges of opposition, His true followers have yet been one in Him, even though they discerned it not.

> "Jesu dulcis memoria,
> Dans vera cordi gaudia:
> Sed super mel et omnia
> Ejus dulcis præsentia.
>
> "Nil canitur suavius,
> Nil auditur jocundius,
> Nil cogitatur dulcius,
> Quam Jesus Dei Filius.

"Jesu, spes pœnitentibus,
Quam pius es petentibus,
Quam bonus te quærentibus,
Sed quis invenientibus !

"Nec lingua valet dicere,
Nec littera exprimere :
Expertus potest credere
Quid sit Jesum diligere." [1]

The old monk sang with all his heart; and his voice,
which had been a fine one in its day, had still that power
which comes from the expression of deep feeling. One
often hears this peculiarity in the voices of persons of genius and sensibility, even when destitute of any real critical
merit. They seem to be so interfused with the emotions
of the soul, that they strike upon the heart almost like the
living touch of a spirit.

Agnes was soothed in listening to him. The Latin
words, the sentiment of which had been traditional in the
Church from time immemorial, had to her a sacred fragrance and odor; they were words apart from all common
usage, a sacramental language, never heard but in moments
of devotion and aspiration, — and they stilled the child's

[1] "Jesus, the very thought of thee
With sweetness fills my breast;
But sweeter far thy face to see,
And in thy presence rest !

"Nor voice can sing, nor heart can **frame,**
Nor can the memory find
A sweeter sound than thy blest **name,**
O Saviour of mankind !

"O hope of every contrite **heart,**
O joy of all the meek,
To those who fall how kind thou **art,**
How good to those who seek!

"But what to those who find! Ah, **this**
Nor tongue nor pen can show!
The love of Jesus, what it is
None but his loved ones know."

heart in its tossings and tempest, as when of old the Jesus they spake of walked forth on the stormy sea.

"Yes, He gave his life for us!" she said; "He is ever reigning for us!

> "'Jesu dulcissime, e throno gloriæ
> Ovem deperditam venisti quærere!
> Jesu suavissime, pastor fidissime,
> Ad te O trahe me, ut semper sequar te!'"[1]

"What, my little one!" said the monk, looking over the wall; "I thought I heard angels singing. Is it not a beautiful morning?"

"Dear uncle, it is," said Agnes. "And I have been so glad to hear your beautiful hymn! — it comforted me."

"Comforted you, little heart? What a word is that! When you get as far along on your journey as your old uncle, then you may talk of comfort. But who thinks of comforting birds or butterflies or young lambs?"

"Ah, dear uncle, I am not so very happy," said Agnes, the tears starting into her eyes.

"Not happy?" said the monk, looking up from his drawing. "Pray, what's the matter now? Has a bee stung your finger? or have you lost your nosegay over a rock? or what dreadful affliction has come upon you? — hey, my little heart?"

Agnes sat down on the corner of the marble fountain, and, covering her face with her apron, sobbed as if her heart would break.

"What has that old priest been saying to her in the confession?" said Father Antonio to himself. "I dare say he cannot understand her. She is as pure as a dewdrop on a cobweb, and as delicate; and these priests, half of them, don't know how to handle the Lord's lambs. Come now,

---

[1] Jesus most beautiful, from thrones in glory,
  Seeking thy lost sheep, thou didst descend!
Jesus most tender, shepherd most faithful,
  To thee, oh, draw thou me, that I may follow thee,
  Follow thee faithfully world without end!

little Agnes," he said, with a coaxing tone, "what is its trouble? — tell its old uncle, — there's a dear!"

"Ah, uncle, I can't!" said Agnes, between her sobs.

"Can't tell its uncle! — there's a pretty go! Perhaps you will tell grandmamma?"

"Oh, no, no, no! not for the world!" said Agnes, sobbing still more bitterly.

"Why, really, little heart of mine, this is getting serious," said the monk; "let your old uncle try to help you."

"It isn't for myself," said Agnes, endeavoring to check her feelings, — "it is not for myself, — it is for another, — for a soul lost. Ah, my Jesus, have mercy!"

"A soul lost? Our Mother forbid!" said the monk, crossing himself. "Lost in this Christian land, so overflowing with the beauty of the Lord? — lost out of this fair sheepfold of Paradise?"

"Yes, lost," said Agnes, despairingly, "and if somebody do not save him, lost forever; and it is a brave and noble soul, too, — like one of the angels that fell."

"Who is it, dear? — tell me about it," said the monk. "I am one of the shepherds whose place it is to go after that which is lost, even till I find it."

"Dear uncle, you remember the youth who suddenly appeared to us in the moonlight here a few evenings ago?"

"Ah, indeed!" said the monk, "what of him?"

"Father Francesco has told me dreadful things of him this morning."

"What things?"

"Uncle, he is excommunicated by our Holy Father the Pope."

Father Antonio, as a member of one of the most enlightened and cultivated religious orders of the times, and as an intimate companion and disciple of Savonarola, had a full understanding of the character of the reigning Pope, and therefore had his own private opinion of how much his excommunication was likely to be worth in the invisible world.   He knew that the same doom had been threatened towards his saintly master, for opposing and exposing the scandalous vices which disgraced the high places of the Church; so that, on the whole, when he heard that this young man was excommunicated, so far from being impressed with horror towards him, he conceived the idea that he might be a particularly honest fellow and good Christian.   But then he did not hold it wise to disturb the faith of the simple-hearted by revealing to them the truth about the head of the Church on earth.

While the disorders in those elevated regions filled the minds of the intelligent classes with apprehension and alarm, they held it unwise to disturb the trustful simplicity of the lower orders, whose faith in Christianity itself they supposed might thus be shaken.   In fact, they were themselves somewhat puzzled how to reconcile the patent and manifest fact, that the actual incumbent of the Holy See was not under the guidance of any spirit, unless it were a diabolical one, with the theory which supposed an infallible guidance of the Holy Spirit to attend as a matter of course on that position.   Some of the boldest of them did not hesitate to declare that the Holy City had suffered a foul invasion, and that a false usurper reigned in her sacred palaces in place of the Father of Christendom.   The greater part did as people now do with the mysteries and discrepancies of a faith which on the whole they revere: they turned their attention from the vexed question, and sighed and longed for better days.

Father Antonio did not, therefore, tell Agnes that the announcement which had filled her with such distress was far less conclusive with himself of the ill desert of the individual to whom it related.

"My little heart," he answered, gravely, "did you learn the sin for which this young man was excommunicated?"

"Ah, me! my dear uncle, I fear he is an infidel, — an unbeliever. Indeed, now I remember it, he confessed as much to me the other day."

"Where did he tell you this?"

"You remember, my uncle, when you were sent for to the dying man? When you were gone, I kneeled down to pray for his soul; and when I rose from prayer, this young cavalier was sitting right here, on this end of the fountain. He was looking fixedly at me, with such sad eyes, so full of longing and pain, that it was quite piteous; and he spoke to me so sadly, I could not but pity him."

"What did he say to you, child?"

"Ah, father, he said that he was all alone in the world, without friends, and utterly desolate, with no one to love him; but worse than that, he said he had lost his faith, that he could not believe."

"What did you say to him?"

"Uncle, I tried, as a poor girl might, to do him some good. I prayed him to confess and take the sacrament; but he looked almost fierce when I said so. And yet I cannot but think, after all, that he has not lost all grace, because he begged me so earnestly to pray for him; he said his prayers could do no good, and wanted mine. And then I began to tell him about you, dear uncle, and how you came from that blessed convent in Florence, and about your master Savonarola; and that seemed to interest him, for he looked quite excited, and spoke the name over, as if it were one he had heard before. I wanted to urge him to come and open his case to you; and I think perhaps I might have succeeded, but that just then you and grandmamma came up the path; and when I heard you coming, I begged him to go, because you know grandmamma would be very angry, if she knew that I had given speech to a man, even for a few moments; she thinks men are so dreadful."

"I must seek this youth," said the monk, in a musing tone; "perhaps I may find out what inward temptation hath driven him away from the fold."

"Oh, do, dear uncle, do!" said Agnes, earnestly. "I am sure that he has been grievously tempted and misled, for he seems to have a noble and gentle nature; and he spoke so feelingly of his mother, who is a saint in heaven; and he seemed so earnestly to long to return to the bosom of the Church."

"The Church is a tender mother to all her erring children," said the monk.

"And don't you think that our dear Holy Father the Pope will forgive him?" said Agnes. "Surely, he will have all the meekness and gentleness of Christ, who would rejoice in one sheep found more than in all the ninety-and-nine who went not astray."

The monk could scarcely repress a smile at imagining Alexander the Sixth in this character of a good shepherd, as Agnes's enthusiastic imagination painted the head of the Church; and then he gave an inward sigh, and said, softly, "Lord, how long?"

"I think," said Agnes, "that this young man is of noble birth, for his words and his bearing and his tones of voice are not those of common men; even though he speaks so humbly and gently, there is yet something princely that looks out of his eyes, as if he were born to command; and he wears strange jewels, the like of which I never saw, on his hands and at the hilt of his dagger, — yet he seems to make nothing of them. But yet, I know not why, he spoke of himself as one utterly desolate and forlorn. Father Francesco told me that he was captain of a band of robbers who live in the mountains. One cannot think it is so."

"Little heart," said the monk tenderly, "you can scarcely know what things befall men in these distracted times, when faction wages war with faction, and men pillage and

burn and imprison, first on this side, then on that. Many
a son of a noble house may find himself homeless and landless, and, chased by the enemy, may have no refuge but
the fastnesses of the mountains. Thank God, our lovely
Italy hath a noble backbone of these same mountains, which
afford shelter to her children in their straits."

"Then you think it possible, dear uncle, that this may
not be a bad man, after all?"

"Let us hope so, child. I will myself seek him out;
and if his mind have been chafed by violence or injustice,
I will strive to bring him back into the good ways of the
Lord. Take heart, my little one, — all will yet be well.
Come now, little darling, wipe your bright eyes, and look
at these plans I have been making for the shrine we were
talking of, in the gorge. See here, I have drawn a goodly
arch with a pinnacle. Under the arch, you see, shall be
the picture of our Lady with the blessed Babe. The arch
shall be cunningly sculptured with vines of ivy and passion-flower; and on one side of it shall stand Saint Agnes
with her lamb, — and on the other, Saint Cecilia, crowned
with roses; and on this pinnacle, above all, Saint Michael,
all in armor, shall stand leaning, — one hand on his sword,
and holding a shield with the cross upon it."

"Ah, that will be beautiful!" said Agnes.

"You can scarcely tell," pursued the monk, "from this
faint drawing, what the picture of our Lady is to be; but
I shall paint her to the highest of my art, and with many
prayers that I may work worthily. You see, she shall be
standing on a cloud with a background all of burnished
gold, like the streets of the New Jerusalem; and she shall
be clothed in a mantle of purest blue from head to foot, to
represent the unclouded sky of summer; and on her forehead she shall wear the evening star, which ever shineth
when we say the Ave Maria; and all the borders of her
blue vesture shall be cunningly wrought with fringes of

stars; and the dear Babe shall lean his little cheek to hers
so peacefully, and there shall be a clear shining of love
through her face, and a heavenly restfulness, that it shall
do one's heart good to look at her.   Many a blessed hour
shall I have over this picture, — many a hymn shall I sing
as my work goes on.   I must go about to prepare the
panels forthwith; and it were well, if there be that young
man who works in stone, to have him summoned to our
conference."

"I think," said Agnes, "that you will find him in the
town; he dwells next to the cathedral."

"I trust he is a youth of pious life and conversation,"
said the monk.   "I must call on him this afternoon; for
he ought to be stirring himself up by hymns and prayers,
and by meditations on the beauty of saints and angels, for
so goodly a work.   What higher honor or grace can befall
a creature than to be called upon to make visible to men that
beauty of invisible things which is divine and eternal?
How many holy men have given themselves to this work
in Italy, till, from being overrun with heathen temples,
it is now full of most curious and wonderful churches,
shrines, and cathedrals, every stone of which is a miracle
of beauty!   I would, dear daughter, you could see our
great Duomo in Florence, which is a mountain of precious
marbles and many-colored mosaics; and the Campanile that
riseth thereby is like a lily of Paradise, — so tall, so stately,
with such an infinite grace, and adorned all the way up
with holy emblems and images of saints and angels; nor is
there any part of it, within or without, that is not finished
sacredly with care, as an offering to the most perfect God.
Truly, our fair Florence, though she be little, is worthy, by
her sacred adornments, to be worn as the lily of our Lady's
girdle, even as she hath been dedicated to her."

Agnes seemed pleased with the enthusiastic discourse of
her uncle.   The tears gradually dried from her eyes as she

listened to him, and the hope so natural to the young and untried heart began to reassert itself. God was merciful, the world beautiful; there was a tender Mother, a reigning Saviour, protecting angels and ˌguardian saints: surely, then, there was no need to despair of the recall of any wanderer; and the softest supplication of the most ignorant and unworthy would be taken up by so many sympathetic voices in the invisible world, and borne on in so many waves of brightness to the heavenly throne, that the most timid must have hope in prayer.

In the afternoon, the monk went to the town to seek the young artist, and also to inquire for the stranger for whom his pastoral offices were in requisition, and Agnes remained alone in the little solitary garden.

It was one of those rich slumberous afternoons of spring that seem to bathe earth and heaven with an Elysian softness; and from her little lonely nook shrouded in dusky shadows by its orange-trees, Agnes looked down the sombre gorge to where the open sea lay panting and palpitating in blue and violet waves, while the little white sails of fishing-boats drifted hither and thither, now silvered in the sunshine, now fading away like a dream into the violet vapor bands that mantled the horizon. The weather would have been oppressively sultry but for the gentle breeze which constantly drifted landward with coolness in its wings. The hum of the old town came to her ear softened by distance and mingled with the patter of the fountain and the music of birds singing in the trees overhead. Agnes tried to busy herself with her spinning; but her mind constantly wandered away, and stirred and undulated with a thousand dim and unshaped thoughts and emotions, of which she vaguely questioned in her own mind. Why did Father Francesco warn her so solemnly against an earthly love? Did he not know her vocation? But still he was wisest and must know best; there must be danger, if he said so. But then, this knight had spoken so modestly, so humbly, — so differently from Giulietta's lovers! — for Giulietta had sometimes found a chance to recount to Agnes some of her triumphs. How could it be that a knight so brave and gentle, and so piously brought up, should become an infidel? Ah, uncle Antonio was right, — he must have had some foul wrong, some dreadful injury! When Agnes was a child, in traveling with her grandmother through one of the highest passes of the Apennines, she had chanced to discover a wounded eagle, whom an arrow had pierced, sitting all alone by himself on a rock, with his feathers ruffled, and a film coming over his great, clear, bright eye, — and, ever full of compassion, she had taken him to nurse, and had traveled for a day with him in her arms; and the mournful look of his regal eyes now came into her memory. "Yes," she said to herself, "he is like my poor eagle! The archers have wounded him, so that he is glad to find shelter even with a poor maid like me; but it was easy to see my eagle had been king among birds, even as this knight is among men. Certainly, God must love him, — he is so beautiful and noble! I hope dear uncle will find him this afternoon; he knows how to teach him; as for me I can only pray."

Such were the thoughts that Agnes twisted into the shining white flax, while her eyes wandered dreamily over the soft hazy landscape. At last, lulled by the shivering sound of leaves, and the bird-songs, and wearied with the agitations of the morning, her head lay back against the end of the sculptured fountain, the spindle slowly dropped from her hand, and her eyes were closed in sleep, the murmur of the fountain still sounding in her dreams. In her dreams she seemed to be wandering far away among the purple passes of the Apennines, where she had come years ago when she was a little girl; with her grandmother she pushed through old olive-groves, weird and twisted with many a quaint gnarl, and rustling their pale silvery leaves in noonday twilight. Sometimes she seemed to carry in her bosom a wounded eagle, and often she sat down to stroke it and to try to give it food from her hand, and as often it looked upon her with a proud, patient eye, and then her grandmother seemed to shake her roughly by the arm and bid her throw the silly bird away; — but then again the dream changed, and she saw a knight lie bleeding and dying in a lonely hollow, — his garments torn, his sword broken, and his face pale and faintly streaked with blood; and she kneeled by him, trying in vain to stanch a deadly wound in his side, while he said reproachfully, "Agnes, dear Agnes, why would you not save me ?" and then she thought he kissed her hand with his cold dying lips; and she shivered and awoke, — to find that her hand was indeed held in that of the cavalier, whose eyes met her own when first she unclosed them, and the same voice that spoke in her dream said, "Agnes, dear Agnes!"

For a moment she seemed stupefied and confounded, and sat passively regarding the knight, who kneeled at her feet and repeatedly kissed her hand, calling her his saint, his star, his life, and whatever other fair name poetry lends to love. All at once, however, her face flushed crimson red, she drew her hand quickly away, and, rising up, made a motion to retreat, saying, in a voice of alarm, —

"Oh, my Lord, this must not be! I am committing deadly sin to hear you. Please, please go! please leave a poor girl!"

"Agnes, what does this mean ?" said the cavalier. "Only two days since, in this place, you promised to love me; and that promise has brought me from utter despair to love of life. Nay, since you told me that, I have been able to pray once more; the whole world seems changed for me: and now will you take it all away, — you, who are all I have on earth ?"

"My Lord, I did not know then that I was sinning. Our dear Mother knows I said only what I thought was true and right, but I find it was a sin."

"A sin to love, Agnes? Heaven must be full of sin, then; for there they do nothing else."

"Oh, my Lord, I must not argue with you; I am forbidden to listen even for a moment. Please go. I will never forget you, sir, — never forget to pray for you, and to love you as they love in heaven; but I am forbidden to speak with you. I fear I have sinned in hearing and saying even this much."

"Who forbids you, Agnes? Who has the right to forbid your good, kind heart to love, where love is so deeply needed and so gratefully received?"

"My holy father, whom I am bound to obey as my soul's director," said Agnes. "He has forbidden me so much as to listen to a word, and yet I have listened to many. How could I help it?"

"Ever these priests!" said the cavalier, his brow darkening with an impatient frown; "wolves in sheep's clothing!"

"Alas!" said Agnes, sorrowfully, "why will you" —

"Why will I what?" he said, facing suddenly toward her and looking down with a fierce, scornful determination.

"Why will you be at war with the Holy Church? Why will you peril your eternal salvation?"

"Is there a Holy Church? Where is it? Would there were one! I am blind and cannot see it. Little Agnes, you promised to lead me; but you drop my hand in the darkness. Who will guide me, if you will not?"

"My Lord, I am most unfit to be your guide. I am a poor girl, without any learning; but there is my uncle I spoke to you of. Oh, my Lord, if you only would go to him, he is wise and gentle both. I must go in now, my

Lord, — indeed, I must. I must not sin further. I must do a heavy penance for having listened and spoken to you, after the holy father had forbidden me."

"No, Agnes, you shall not go in," said the cavalier, suddenly stepping before her and placing himself across the doorway; "you shall see me, and hear me too. I take the sin on myself; you cannot help it. How will you avoid me? Will you fly now down the path of the gorge? I will follow you, — I am desperate. I had but one comfort on earth, but one hope of heaven, and that through you; and you, cruel, are so ready to give me up at the first word of your priest!"

"God knows if I do it willingly," said Agnes; "but I know it is best; for I feel I should love you too well, if I saw more of you. My Lord, you are strong and can compel me, but I beg you to leave me."

"Dear Agnes, could you really feel it possible that you might love me too well?" said the cavalier, his whole manner changing. "Ah! could I carry you far away to my home in the mountains, far up in the beautiful blue mountains, where the air is so clear, and the weary, wrangling world lies so far below that one forgets it entirely, you should be my wife, my queen, my empress. You should lead me where you would, your word should be my law. I will go with you wherever you will, — to confession, to sacrament, to prayers, never so often; never will I rebel against your word; if you decree, I will bend my neck to king or priest; I will reconcile me with anybody or anything only for your sweet sake; you shall lead me all my life; and when we die, I ask only that you may lead me to our Mother's throne in heaven, and pray her to tolerate me for your sake. Come, now, dear, is not even one unworthy soul worth saving?"

"My Lord, you have taught me how wise my holy father was in forbidding me to listen to you. He knew better

than I how weak was my heart, and how I might be drawn
on from step to step till — My Lord, I must be no man's
wife. I follow the blessed Saint Agnes! May God give
me grace to keep my vows without wavering! — for then I
shall gain power to intercede for you and bring down bless-
ings on your soul. Oh, never, never speak to me so again,
my Lord! — you will make me very, *very* unhappy. If
there is any truth in your words, my Lord, if you really
love me, you will go, and you will never try to speak to
me again."

"Never, Agnes? never? Think what you are saying!"

"Oh, I do think! I know it must be best," said Agnes,
much agitated; "for, if I should see you often and hear
your voice, I should lose all my strength. I could never
resist, and I should lose heaven for you and me too.
Leave me, and I will never, never forget to pray for you;
and go quickly too, for it is time for my grandmother to
come home, and she would be so angry, — she would never
believe I had not been doing wrong, and perhaps she would
make me marry somebody that I do not wish to. She has
threatened that many times; but I beg her to leave me free
to go to my sweet home in the convent and my dear Mother
Theresa."

"They shall never marry you against your will, little
Agnes, I pledge you my knightly word. I will protect
you from that. Promise me, dear, that, if ever you be
man's wife, you will be mine. Only promise me that, and
I will go."

"Will you?" said Agnes, in an ecstasy of fear and
apprehension, in which there mingled some strange troubled gleams of happiness. "Well, then, I will. Ah! I
hope it is no sin!"

"Believe me, dearest, it is not," said the knight. "Say
it again, — say, that I may hear it, — say, 'If ever I am
man's wife, I will be thine,' — say it, and I will go."

"Well, then, my Lord, if ever I am man's wife, I will be thine," said Agnes. "But I will be no man's wife. My heart and hand are promised elsewhere. Come, now, my Lord, your word must be kept."

"Let me put this ring on your finger, lest you forget," said the cavalier. "It was my mother's ring, and never during her lifetime heard anything but prayers and hymns. It is saintly, and worthy of thee."

"No, my Lord, I may not. Grandmother would inquire about it. I cannot keep it; but fear not my forgetting; I shall never forget you."

"Will you ever want to see me, Agnes?"

"I hope not, since it is not best. But you do not go."

"Well, then, farewell, my little wife! farewell, till I claim thee!" said the cavalier, as he kissed her hand, and vaulted over the wall.

"How strange that I cannot make him understand!" said Agnes, when he was gone. "I must have sinned, I must have done wrong; but I have been trying all the while to do right. Why would he stay so, and look at me so with those deep eyes? I was very hard with him, — very! I trembled for him, I was so severe; and yet it has not discouraged him enough. How strange that he would call me so, after all, when I explained to him I never could marry! Must I tell all this to Father Francesco? How dreadful! How he looked at me before! How he trembled and turned away from me! What will he think now? Ah, me! why must I tell *him?* If I could only confess to my mother Theresa, that would be easier. We have a mother in heaven to hear us; why should we not have a mother on earth? Father Francesco frightens me so! His eyes burn me! They seem to burn into my soul, and he seems angry with me sometimes, and sometimes looks at me so strangely! Dear, blessed Mother," she said, kneeing at the shrine, "help thy little child! I do not want to do wrong: I want to do right. Oh that I could come and live with thee!"

Poor Agnes! a new experience had opened in her heretofore tranquil life, and her day was one of conflict. Do what she would, the words that had been spoken to her in the morning would return to her mind, and sometimes she awoke with a shock of guilty surprise at finding she had been dreaming over what the cavalier said to her of living with him alone, in some clear, high, purple solitude of those beautiful mountains which she remembered as an enchanted dream of her childhood. Would he really always love her, then, always go with her to prayers and mass and sacrament, and be reconciled to the Church, and should she indeed have the joy of feeling that this noble soul was led back to heavenly peace through her? Was not this better than a barren life of hymns and prayers in a cold convent? Then the very voice that said these words, that voice of veiled strength and manly daring, that spoke with such a gentle pleading, and yet such an undertone of authority, as if he had a right to claim her for himself, — she seemed to feel the tones of that voice in every nerve; — and then the strange thrilling pleasure of thinking that he loved her so. Why should he, this strange, beautiful knight? Doubtless he had seen splendid high-born ladies, — he had seen even queens and princesses, — and what could he find to like in her, a poor little peasant? Nobody ever thought so much of her before, and he was so unhappy without her; — it was strange he should be; but he said so, and it must be true. After all, Father Francesco might be mistaken about his being wicked. On the whole, she felt sure he was mistaken, at least in part. Uncle Antonio did not seem to be so much shocked at what she told him; he knew the temptations of men better, perhaps, because he did not stay shut up in one convent, but traveled all about, preaching and teaching. If

only he could see him, and talk with him, and make him
a good Christian, — why, then, there would be no further
need of her; and Agnes was surprised to find what a dreadful, dreary blank appeared before her when she thought of
this.   Why should she wish him to remember her, since
she never could be his? — and yet nothing seemed so dreadful as that he should forget her.   So the poor little innocent fly beat and fluttered in the mazes of that enchanted
web, where thousands of her frail sex have beat and fluttered before.

CHAPTER XIII

THE MONK AND THE CAVALIER

FATHER ANTONIO had been down through the streets of the old town of Sorrento, searching for the young stone-cutter, and finding him had spent some time in enlightening him as to the details of the work he wished him to execute.

He found him not so easily kindled into devotional fervors as he had fondly imagined, nor could all his most devout exhortations produce one quarter of the effect upon him that resulted from the discovery that it was the fair Agnes who originated the design and was interested in its execution. Then did the large black eyes of the youth kindle into something of sympathetic fervor, and he willingly promised to do his very best at the carving.

"I used to know the fair Agnes well, years ago," he said, "but of late she will not even look at me; yet I worship her none the less. Who can help it that sees her? I don't think she is so hard-hearted as she seems; but her grandmother and the priests won't so much as allow her to lift up her eyes when one of us young fellows goes by. Twice these five years past have I seen her eyes, and then it was when I contrived to get near the holy water when there was a press round it of a saint's day, and I reached some to her on my finger, and then she smiled upon me and thanked me. Those two smiles are all I have had to live on for all this time. Perhaps, if I work very well, she will give me another, and perhaps she will say, ' Thank you, my good Pietro! ' as she used to, when I brought her birds' eggs or helped her across the ravine, years ago."

"Well, my brave boy, do your best," said the monk, "and let the shrine be of the fairest white marble. I will be answerable for the expense; I will beg it of those who have substance."

"So please you, holy father," said Pietro, "I know of a spot, a little below here on the coast, where was a heathen temple in the old days; and one can dig therefrom long pieces of fair white marble, all covered with heathen images. I know not whether your Reverence would think them fit for Christian purposes."

"So much the better, boy! so much the better!" said the monk, heartily. "Only let the marble be fine and white, and it is as good as converting a heathen any time to baptize it to Christian uses. A few strokes of the chisel will soon demolish their naked nymphs and other such rubbish, and we can carve holy virgins, robed from head to foot in all modesty, as becometh saints."

"I will get my boat and go down this very afternoon," said Pietro; "and, sir, I hope I am not making too bold in asking you, when you see the fair Agnes, to present unto her this lily, in memorial of her old playfellow."

"That I will, my boy! And now I think of it, she spoke kindly of you as one that had been a companion in her childhood, but said her grandmother would not allow her to speak to you now."

"Ah, that is it!" said Pietro. "Old Elsie is a fierce old kite, with strong beak and long claws, and will not let the poor girl have any good of her youth. Some say she means to marry her to some rich old man, and some say she will shut her up in a convent, which I should say was a sore hurt and loss to the world. There are a plenty of women, whom nobody wants to look at, for that sort of work; and a beautiful face is a kind of psalm which makes one want to be good."

"Well, well, my boy, work well and faithfully for the

saints on this shrine, and I dare promise you many a smile from this fair maiden; for her heart is set upon the glory of God and his saints, and she will smile on any one who helps on the good work. I shall look in on you daily for a time, till I see the work well started."

So saying, the old monk took his leave. Just as he was passing out of the house, some one brushed rapidly by him, going down the street. As he passed, the quick eye of the monk recognized the cavalier whom he had seen in the garden but a few evenings before. It was not a face and form easily forgotten, and the monk followed him at a little distance behind, resolving, if he saw him turn in anywhere, to follow and crave an audience of him.

Accordingly, as he saw the cavalier entering under the low arch that led to his hotel, he stepped up and addressed him with a gesture of benediction.

"God bless you, my son!"

"What would you with me, father?" said the cavalier, with a hasty and somewhat suspicious glance.

"I would that you would give me an audience of a few moments on some matters of importance," said the monk, mildly.

The tones of his voice seemed to have excited some vague remembrance in the mind of the cavalier; for he eyed him narrowly, and seemed trying to recollect where he had seen him before. Suddenly a light appeared to flash upon his mind; for his whole manner became at once more cordial.

"My good father," he said, "my poor lodging and leisure are at your service for any communication you may see fit to make."

So saying, he led the way up the damp, ill-smelling stone staircase, and opened the door of the deserted room where we have seen him once before. Closing the door, and seating himself at the one rickety table which the room afforded, he motioned to the monk to be seated also; then taking off his plumed hat, he threw it negligently on the table beside him, and passing his white, finely formed hand through the black curls of his hair, he tossed them carelessly from his forehead, and, leaning his chin in the hollow of his hand, fixed his glittering eyes on the monk in a manner that seemed to demand his errand.

"My Lord," said the monk, in those gentle, conciliating tones which were natural to him, "I would ask a little help of you in regard of a Christian undertaking which I have here in hand. The dear Lord hath put it into the heart of a pious young maid of this vicinity to erect a shrine to the honor of our Lady and her dear Son in this gorge of Sorrento, hard by. It is a gloomy place in the night, and hath been said to be haunted by evil spirits; and my fair niece, who is full of all holy thoughts, desired me to draw the plan for this shrine, and, so far as my poor skill may go, I have done so. See, here, my Lord, are the drawings."

The monk laid them down on the table, his pale cheek flushing with a faint glow of artistic enthusiasm and pride, as he explained to the young man the plan and drawings.

The cavalier listened courteously, but without much apparent interest, till the monk drew from his portfolio a paper and said, —

"This, my Lord, is my poor and feeble conception of the most sacred form of our Lady, which I am to paint for the centre of the shrine."

He laid down the paper, and the cavalier, with a sudden exclamation, snatched it up, looking at it eagerly.

"It is she!" he said; "it is her very self! — the divine Agnes, — the lily flower, — the sweet star, — the only one among women!"

"I see you have recognized the likeness," said the monk, blushing. "I know it hath been thought a practice of doubtful edification to represent holy things under the image of aught earthly; but when any mortal seems especially gifted with a heavenly spirit outshining in the face, it may be that our Lady chooses that person to reveal herself in."

The cavalier was gazing so intently on the picture that he scarcely heard the apology of the monk; he held it up, and seemed to study it with a long admiring gaze.

"You have great skill with your pencil, my father," he said; "one would not look for such things from under a monk's hood."

"I belong to the San Marco in Florence, of which you may have heard," said Father Antonio, "and am an unworthy disciple of the traditions of the blessed Angelico, whose visions of heavenly things are ever before us; and no less am I a disciple of the renowned Savonarola, of whose fame all Italy hath heard before now."

"Savonarola?" said the other, with eagerness, — "he that makes these vile miscreants that call themselves Pope and cardinals tremble? All Italy, all Christendom, is groaning and stretching out the hand to him to free them from these abominations. My father, tell me of Savonarola: how goes he, and what success hath he?"

"My son, it is now many months since I left Florence; since which time I have been sojourning in by-places, repairing shrines and teaching the poor of the Lord's flock, who are scattered and neglected by the idle shepherds, who think only to eat the flesh and warm themselves with the fleece of the sheep for whom the Good Shepherd gave his life. My duties have been humble and quiet; for it is not given to me to wield the sword of rebuke and controversy, like my great master."

"And you have not heard, then," said the cavalier, eagerly, "that they have excommunicated him?"

"I knew that was threatened," said the monk, "but I did not think it possible that it could befall a man of such shining holiness of life, so signally and openly owned of

God that the very gifts of the first Apostles seem revived in him."

"Does not Satan always hate the Lord?" said the cavalier. "Alexander and his councils are possessed of the Devil, if ever men were, — and are sealed as his children by every abominable wickedness. The Devil sits in Christ's seat, and hath stolen his signet-ring, to seal decrees against the Lord's own followers. What are Christian men to do in such case?"

The monk sighed and looked troubled.

"It is hard to say," he answered. "So much I know, — that before I left Florence our master wrote to the King of France touching the dreadful state of things at Rome, and tried to stir him up to call a general council of the Church. I much fear me this letter may have fallen into the hands of the Pope."

"I tell you, father," said the young man, starting up and laying his hand on his sword, "we must fight! It is the sword that must decide this matter! Was not the Holy Sepulchre saved from the Infidels by the sword? — and once more the sword must save the Holy City from worse infidels than the Turks. If such doings as these are allowed in the Holy City, another generation there will be no Christians left on earth. Alexander and Cæsar Borgia and the Lady Lucrezia are enough to drive religion from the world. They make us long to go back to the traditions of our Roman fathers, — who were men of cleanly and honorable lives and of heroic deeds, scorning bribery and deceit. They honored God by noble lives, little as they knew of Him. But these men are a shame to the mothers that bore them."

"You speak too truly, my son," said the monk. "Alas! the creation groaneth and travaileth in pain with these things. Many a time and oft have I seen our master groaning and wrestling with God on this account. For it is to

small purpose that we have gone through Italy preaching
and stirring up the people to more holy lives, when from
the very hill of Zion, the height of the sanctuary, come
down these streams of pollution. It seems as if the time
had come that the world could bear it no longer."

"Well, if it come to the trial of the sword, as come it
must," said the cavalier, "say to your master that Agostino
Sarelli has a band of one hundred tried men and an im-
pregnable fastness in the mountains, where he may take
refuge, and where they will gladly hear the Word of God
from pure lips. They call us robbers, — us who have gone
out from the assembly of robbers, that we might lead honest and cleanly lives. There is not one among us that hath
not lost houses, lands, brothers, parents, children, or
friends through their treacherous cruelty. There be those
whose wives and sisters have been forced into the Borgia
harem; there be those whose children have been tortured
before their eyes, — those who have seen the fairest and
dearest slaughtered by these hell-hounds, who yet sit in
the seat of the Lord and give decrees in the name of Christ.
Is there a God? If there be, why is He silent?"

"Yea, my son, there is a God," said the monk; "but
His ways are not as ours. A thousand years in His sight
are but as yesterday, as a watch in the night. He shall
come, and shall not keep silence."

"Perhaps you do not know, father," said the young
man, "that I, too, am excommunicated. I am excommunicated, because, Cæsar Borgia having killed my oldest
brother, and dishonored and slain my sister, and seized on
all our possessions, and the Pope having protected and con-
firmed him therein, I declare the Pope to be not of God,
but of the Devil. I will not submit to him, nor be ruled
by him; and I and my fellows will make good our mountains against him and his crew with such right arms as the
good Lord hath given us."

"The Lord be with you, my son!" said the monk; "and the Lord bring His Church out of these deep waters! Surely, it is a lovely and beautiful Church, made dear and precious by innumerable saints and martyrs who have given their sweet lives up willingly for it; and it is full of records of righteousness, of prayers and alms and works of mercy that have made even the very dust of our Italy precious and holy. Why hast Thou abandoned this vine of Thy planting, O Lord? The boar out of the wood doth waste it; the wild beast of the field doth devour it. Return, we beseech Thee, and visit this vine of Thy planting!"

The monk clasped his hands and looked upward pleadingly, the tears running down his wasted cheeks. Ah, many such strivings and prayers in those days went up from silent hearts in obscure solitudes, that wrestled and groaned under that mighty burden which Luther at last received strength to heave from the heart of the Church.

"Then, father, you do admit that one may be banned by the Pope, and may utterly refuse and disown him, and yet be a Christian?"

"How can I otherwise?" said the monk. "Do I not see the greatest saint this age or any age has ever seen under the excommunication of the greatest sinner? Only, my son, let me warn you. Become not irreverent to the true Church, because of a false usurper. Reverence the sacraments, the hymns, the prayers all the more for this sad condition in which you stand. What teacher is more faithful in these respects than my master? Who hath more zeal for our blessed Lord Jesus, and a more living faith in Him? Who hath a more filial love and tenderness towards our blessed Mother? Who hath more reverent communion with all the saints than he? Truly, he sometimes seems to me to walk encompassed by all the armies of heaven, — such a power goes forth in his words, and such a holiness in his life."

"Ah," said Agostino, "would I had such a confessor! The sacraments might once more have power for me, and I might cleanse my soul from unbelief."

"Dear son," said the monk, "accept a most unworthy, but sincere follower of this holy prophet, who yearns for thy salvation. Let me have the happiness of granting to thee the sacraments of the Church, which, doubtless, are thine by right as one of the flock of the Lord Jesus. Come to me some day this week in confession, and thereafter thou shalt receive the Lord within thee, and be once more united to Him."

"My good father," said the young man, grasping his hand, and much affected, "I will come. Your words have done me good; but I must think more of them. I will come soon; but these things cannot be done without pondering; it will take some time to bring my heart into charity with all men."

The monk rose up to depart, and began to gather up his drawings.

"For this matter, father," said the cavalier, throwing several gold pieces upon the table, "take these, and as many more as you need ask for your good work. I would willingly pay any sum," he added, while a faint blush rose to his cheek, "if you would give me a copy of this. Gold would be nothing in comparison with it."

"My son," said the monk, smiling, "would it be to thee an image of an earthly or a heavenly love?"

"Of both, father," said the young man. "For that dear face has been more to me than prayer or hymn; it has been even as a sacrament to me, and through it I know not what of holy and heavenly influences have come to me."

"Said I not well," said the monk, exulting, "that there were those on whom our Mother shed such grace that their very beauty led heavenward? Such are they whom the artist looks for, when he would adorn a shrine where the faithful shall worship. Well, my son, I must use my poor art for you; and as for gold, we of our convent take it not except for the adorning of holy things, such as this shrine."

"How soon shall it be done?" said the young man, eagerly.

"Patience, patience, my Lord! Rome was not built in a day, and our art must work by slow touches; but I will do my best. But wherefore, my Lord, cherish this image?"

"Father, are you of near kin to this maid?"

"I am her grandmother's only brother."

"Then I say to you, as the nearest of her male kin, that I seek this maid in pure and honorable marriage; and she hath given me her promise, that, if ever she be wife of mortal man, she will be mine."

"But she looks not to be wife of any man," said the monk; "so, at least, I have heard her say; though her grandmother would fain marry her to a husband of her choosing. 'T is a willful woman, is my sister Elsie, and a worldly, — not easy to persuade, and impossible to drive."

"And she hath chosen for this fair angel some base peasant churl who will have no sense of her exceeding loveliness? By the saints, if it come to this, I will carry her away with the strong arm!"

"That is not to be apprehended just at present. Sister Elsie is dotingly fond of the girl, which hath slept in her bosom since infancy."

"And why should I not demand her in marriage of your sister?" said the young man.

"My Lord, you are an excommunicated man, and she would have horror of you. It is impossible; it would not be to edification to make the common people judges in such

matters. It is safest to let their faith rest undisturbed,
and that they be not taught to despise ecclesiastical cen-
sures. This could not be explained to Elsie; she would
drive you from her doors with her distaff, and you would
scarce wish to put your sword against it. Besides, my
Lord, if you were not excommunicated, you are of noble
blood, and this alone would be a fatal objection with my
sister, who hath sworn on the holy cross that Agnes shall
never love one of your race."

"What is the cause of this hatred?"

"Some foul wrong which a noble did her mother," said
the monk; "for Agnes is of gentle blood on her father's
side."

"I might have known it," said the cavalier to himself;
"her words and ways are unlike anything in her class.
Father," he added, touching his sword, "we soldiers are
fond of cutting all Gordian knots, whether of love or religion, with this. The sword, father, is the best theologian,
the best casuist. The sword rights wrongs and punishes
evil doers, and some day the sword may cut the way out
of this embarrass also."

"Gently, my son! gently!" said the monk; "nothing is
lost by patience. See how long it takes the good Lord to
make a fair flower out of a little seed; and He does all
quietly, without bluster. Wait on Him a little in peacefulness and prayer, and see what He will do for thee."

"Perhaps you are right, my father," said the cavalier,
cordially. "Your counsels have done me good, and I shall
seek them further. But do not let them terrify my poor
Agnes with dreadful stories of the excommunication that
hath befallen me. The dear saint is breaking her good
little heart for my sins, and her confessor evidently hath
fobidden her to speak to me or look at me. If her heart
were left to itself, it would fly to me like a little tame
bird, and I would cherish it forever; but now she sees sin

in every innocent, womanly thought, — poor little dear child-angel that she is!"

"Her confessor is a Franciscan," said the monk, who, good as he was, could not escape entirely from the ruling prejudice of his order, "and from what I know of him, I should think might be unskillful in what pertaineth to the nursing of so delicate a lamb. It is not every one to whom is given the gift of rightly directing souls."

"I'd like to carry her off from him!" said the cavalier, between his teeth. "I will, too, if he is not careful!" Then he added aloud, "Father, Agnes is mine, — mine by the right of the truest worship and devotion that man could ever pay to woman, — mine because she loves me. For I know she loves me; I know it far better than she knows it herself, the dear, innocent child! and I will not have her torn from me to waste her life in a lonely, barren convent, or to be the wife of a stolid peasant. I am a man of my word, and I will vindicate my right to her in the face of God and man."

"Well, well, my son, as I said before, patience, — one thing at a time. Let us say our prayers and sleep to-night, to begin with, and to-morrow will bring us fresh counsel."

"Well, my father, you will be for me in this matter?" said the young man.

"My son, I wish you all happiness; and if this be for your best good and that of my dear niece, I wish it. But, as I said, there must be time and patience. The way must be made clear. I will see how the case stands; and you may be sure, when I can in good conscience, I will befriend you."

"Thank you, my father, thank you!" said the young man, bending his knee to receive the monk's parting benediction.

"It seems to me not best," said the monk, turning once

more, as he was leaving the threshold, "that you should come to me at present where I am, — it would only raise a storm that I could not allay; and so great would be the power of the forces they might bring to bear on the child, that her little heart might break and the saints claim her too soon."

"Well, then, father, come hither to me to-morrow at this same hour, if I be not too unworthy of your pastoral care."

"I shall be too happy, my son," said the monk.   "So be it."

And he turned from the door just as the bell of the cathedral struck the Ave Maria, and all in the street bowed in the evening act of worship.

CHAPTER XIV

THE golden sunshine of the spring morning was deadened to a sombre tone in the shadowy courts of the Capuchin convent. The reddish brown of the walls was flecked with gold and orange spots of lichen; and here and there, in crevices, tufts of grass, or even a little bunch of gold-blooming flowers, looked hardily forth into the shadowy air. A covered walk, with stone arches, inclosed a square filled with dusky shrubbery. There were tall, funereal cypresses, whose immense height and scraggy profusion of decaying branches showed their extreme old age. There were gaunt, gnarled olives, with trunks twisted in immense serpent folds, and boughs wreathed and knotted into wild, unnatural contractions, as if their growth had been a series of spasmodic convulsions, instead of a calm and gentle development of Nature. There were overgrown clumps of aloes, with the bare skeletons of former flower-stalks standing erect among their dusky horns or lying rotting on the ground beside them. The place had evidently been intended for the culture of shrubbery and flowers, but the growth of the trees had long since so intercepted the sunlight and fresh air that not even grass could find root beneath their branches. The ground was covered with a damp green mould, strewn here and there with dead boughs, or patched with tufts of fern and lycopodium, throwing out their green hairy roots into the moist soil. A few half-dead roses and jasmines, remnants of former days of flowers, still maintained a struggling existence, but

looked wan and discouraged in the effort, and seemed to
stretch and pine vaguely for a freer air. In fact, the whole
garden might be looked upon as a sort of symbol of the life
by which it was surrounded, — a life stagnant, unnatural,
and unhealthy, cut off from all those thousand stimulants
to wholesome development which are afforded by the open
plain of human existence, where strong natures grow distorted in unnatural efforts, though weaker ones find in its
lowly shadows a congenial refuge.

We have given the brighter side of conventual life in
the days we are describing: we have shown it as often a
needed shelter of woman's helplessness during ages of po-
litical uncertainty and revolution; we have shown it as the
congenial retreat where the artist, the poet, the student,
and the man devoted to ideas found leisure undisturbed
to develop themselves under the consecrating protection of
religion. The picture would be unjust to truth, did we
not recognize, what, from our knowledge of human nature,
we must expect, a conventual life of far less elevated and
refined order. We should expect that institutions which
guaranteed to each individual a livelihood, without the
necessity of physical labor or the responsibility of supporting a family, might in time come to be incumbered with
many votaries in whom indolence and improvidence were
the only impelling motives. In all ages of the world the
unspiritual are the majority, — the spiritual the exceptions.
It was to the multitude that Jesus said, "Ye seek me not
because ye saw the miracles, but because ye did eat and
were filled," — and the multitude has been much of the
same mind from that day to this.

The convent of which we speak had been for some years
under the lenient rule of the jolly Brother Girolamo, — an
easy, wide-spread, loosely organized body, whose views of
the purpose of human existence were decidedly Anacreontic.
Fasts he abominated, — night-prayers he found unfavorable

to his constitution; but he was a judge of olives and good wine, and often threw out valuable hints in his pastoral visits on the cooking of macaroni, for which he had himself elaborated a savory recipe; and the cellar and larder of the convent, during his pastorate, presented so many urgent solicitations to conventual repose, as to threaten an inconvenient increase in the number of others. The monks in his time lounged in all the sunny places of the convent like so many loose sacks of meal, enjoying to the full the *dolce far niente* which seems to be the universal rule of Southern climates. They ate and drank and slept and snored; they made pastoral visits through the surrounding community which were far from edifying; they gambled, and tippled, and sang most unspiritual songs; and keeping all the while their own private pass-key to Paradise tucked under their girdles, were about as jolly a set of sailors to Eternity as the world had to show. In fact, the climate of Southern Italy and its gorgeous scenery are more favorable to voluptuous ecstasy than to the severe and grave warfare of the true Christian soldier. The sunny plains of Capua demoralized the soldiers of Hannibal, and it was not without a reason that ancient poets made those lovely regions the abode of Sirens whose song maddened by its sweetness, and of a Circe who made men drunk with her sensual fascinations, till they became sunk to the form of brutes. Here, if anywhere, is the lotos-eater's paradise, — the purple skies, the enchanted shores, the soothing gales, the dreamy mists, which all conspire to melt the energy of the will, and to make existence either a half doze of dreamy apathy or an awaking of mad delirium.

It was not from dreamy, voluptuous Southern Italy that the religious progress of the Italian race received any vigorous impulses. These came from more northern and more mountainous regions, from the severe, clear heights of Florence, Perugia, and Assisi, where the intellectual and the moral both had somewhat of the old Etruscan earnestness and gloom.

One may easily imagine the stupid alarm and helpless confusion of these easy-going monks, when their new Superior came down among them hissing with a white heat from the very hottest furnace fires of a new religious experience, burning and quivering with the terrors of the world to come, — pale, thin, eager, tremulous, and yet with all the martial vigor of the former warrior, and all the habits of command of a former princely station. His reforms gave no quarter to right or left; sleepy monks were dragged out to midnight prayers, and their devotions enlivened with vivid pictures of hell-fire and ingenuities of eternal torment enough to stir the blood of the most torpid. There was to be no more gormandizing, no more wine-bibbing; the choice old wines were placed under lock and key for the use of the sick and poor in the vicinity; and every fast of the Church, and every obsolete rule of the order, were revived with unsparing rigor. It is true, they hated their new Superior with all the energy which laziness and good-living had left them, but they every soul of them shook in their sandals before him; for there is a true and established order of mastery among human beings, and when a man of enkindled energy and intense will comes among a flock of irresolute commonplace individuals, he subjects them to himself by a sort of moral paralysis similar to what a great, vigorous gymnotus distributes among a fry of inferior fishes. The bolder ones, who made motions of rebellion, were so energetically swooped upon, and consigned to the discipline of dungeon and bread-and-water, that less courageous natures made a merit of siding with the more powerful party, mentally resolving to carry by fraud the points which they despaired of accomplishing by force.

On the morning we speak of, two monks might have been seen lounging on a stone bench by one of the arches, looking listlessly into the sombre garden-path we have described. The first of these, Father Anselmo, was a corpulent fellow, with an easy swing of gait, heavy animal features, and an eye of shrewd and stealthy cunning: the whole air of the man expressed the cautious, careful voluptuary. The other, Father Johannes, was thin, wiry, and elastic, with hands like birds' claws, and an eye that reminded one of the crafty cunning of a serpent. His smile was a curious blending of shrewdness and malignity. He regarded his companion from time to time obliquely from the corners of his eyes, to see what impression his words were making, and had a habit of jerking himself up in the middle of a sentence and looking warily round to see if any one were listening, which indicated habitual distrust.

"Our holy Superior is out a good while this morning," he said, at length.

The observation was made in the smoothest and most silken tones, but they carried with them such a singular suggestion of doubt and inquiry that they seemed like an accusation.

"Ah?" replied the other, perceiving evidently some intended undertone of suspicion lurking in the woods, but apparently resolved not to commit himself to his companion.

"Yes," said the first; "the zeal of the house of the Lord consumes him, the blessed man!"

"Blessed man!" echoed the second, rolling up his eyes, and giving a deep sigh, which shook his portly proportions so that they quivered like jelly.

"If he goes on in this way much longer," continued Father Johannes, "there will soon be very little mortal left of him; the saints will claim him."

Father Anselmo gave something resembling a pious groan, but darted meanwhile a shrewd observant glance at the speaker.

"What would become of the convent, were he gone?"
said Father Johannes. "All these blessed reforms which
he has brought about would fall back; for our nature is
fearfully corrupt, and ever tends to wallow in the mire of
sin and pollution. What changes hath he wrought in us
all! To be sure, the means were sometimes severe. I
remember, brother, when he had you under ground for
more than ten days. My heart was pained for you; but I
suppose you know that it was necessary, in order to bring
you to that eminent state of sanctity where you now stand."

The heavy, sensual features of Father Anselmo flushed
up with some emotion, whether of anger or of fear it was
hard to tell; but he gave one hasty glance at his companion, which, if a glance could kill, would have struck him
dead, and then there fell over his countenance, like a veil,
an expression of sanctimonious humility as he replied, —

"Thank you for your sympathy, dearest brother. I remember, too, how I felt for you that week when you were
fed only on bread and water, and had to take it on your
knees off the floor, while the rest of us sat at table. How
blessed it must be to have one's pride brought down in
that way! When our dear, blessed Superior first came,
brother, you were as a bullock unaccustomed to the yoke,
but now what a blessed change! It must give you so much
peace! How you must love him!"

"I think we love him about equally," said Father Johannes, his dark, thin features expressing the concentration
of malignity. "His labors have been blessed among us.
Not often does a faithful shepherd meet so loving a flock.
I have been told that the great Peter Abelard found far
less gratitude. They tried to poison him in the most holy
wine."

"How absurd!" interrupted Father Anselmo, hastily;
"as if the blood of the Lord, as if our Lord himself could
be made poison!"

"Brother, it is a fact," insisted the former, in tones silvery with humility and sweetness.

"A fact that the most holy blood can be poisoned?" replied the other, with horror evidently genuine.

"I grieve to say, brother," said Father Johannes, "that in my profane and worldly days I tried that experiment on a dog, and the poor brute died in five minutes. Ah, brother," he added, observing that his obese companion was now thoroughly roused, "you see before you the chief of sinners. Judas was nothing to me; and yet, such are the triumphs of grace, I am an unworthy member of this most blessed and pious brotherhood; but I do penance daily in sackcloth and ashes for my offense."

"But, Brother Johannes, was it really so? did it really happen?" inquired Father Anselmo, looking puzzled. "Where, then, is our faith?"

"Doth our faith rest on human reason, or on the evidence of our senses, Brother Anselmo? I bless God that I have arrived at that state where I can adoringly say, ' I believe, because it is impossible.' Yea, brother, I know it to be a fact that the ungodly have sometimes destroyed holy men, like our Superior, who could not be induced to taste wine for any worldly purpose, by drugging the blessed cup; so dreadful are the ragings of Satan in our corrupt nature!"

"I can't see into that," said Father Anselmo, still looking confused.

"Brother," answered Father Johannes, "permit an unworthy sinner to remind you that you must not try to see into anything; all that is wanted of you in our most holy religion is to shut your eyes and believe; all things are possible to the eye of faith. Now, humanly speaking," he added, with a peculiarly meaning look, "who would believe that you kept all the fasts of our order, and all the extraordinary ones which it hath pleased our blessed Superior to lay upon us, as you surely do? A worldling might swear, to look at you, that such flesh and color must come in some way from good meat and good wine; but we remember how the three children throve on the pulse and rejected the meat from the king's table."

The countenance of Father Anselmo expressed both anger and alarm at this home-thrust, and the changes did not escape the keen eye of Father Johannes, who went on.

"I directed the eyes of our holy father upon you as a striking example of the benefits of abstemious living, showing that the days of miracles are not yet past in the Church, as some skeptics would have us believe. He seemed to study you attentively. I have no doubt he will honor you with some more particular inquiries, — the blessed saint!"

Father Anselmo turned uneasily on his seat and stealthily eyed his companion, to see, if possible, how much real knowledge was expressed by his words, and then answered on quite another topic.

"How this garden has fallen to decay! We miss old Father Angelo sorely, who was always trimming and cleaning it. Our Superior is too heavenly-minded to have much thought for earthly things, and so it goes."

Father Johannes watched this attempt at diversion with a glitter of stealthy malice, and, seeming to be absorbed in contemplation, broke out again exactly where he had left off on the unwelcome subject.

"I mind me now, Brother Anselmo, that, when you came out of your cell to prayers, the other night, your utterance was thick, and your eyes heavy and watery, and your gait uncertain. One would swear that you had been drunken with new wine; but we knew it was all the effect of fasting and devout contemplation, which inebriates the soul with holy raptures, as happened to the blessed Apostles on the day of Pentecost. I remarked the same to our holy father, and he seemed to give it earnest heed, for I saw him watching you through all the services. How blessed is such watchfulness!"

"The Devil take him!" said Father Anselmo, suddenly thrown off his guard; but checking himself, he added, confusedly, — "I mean" —

"I understand you, brother," said Father Johannes; "it is a motion of the old nature not yet entirely subdued. A little more of the discipline of the lower vaults, which you have found so precious, will set all that right."

"You would not inform against me?" said Father Anselmo, with an expression of alarm.

"It would be my duty, I suppose," said Father Johannes, with a sigh; "but, sinner that I am, I never could bring my mind to such proceedings with the vigor of our blessed father. Had I been Superior of the convent, as was talked of, how differently might things have proceeded! I should have erred by a sinful laxness. How fortunate that it was he, instead of such a miserable sinner as myself!"

"Well, tell me, then, Father Johannes, — for your eyes are shrewd as a lynx's, — *is* our good Superior so perfect as he seems? or does he have his little private comforts sometimes, like the rest of us? Nobody, you know, can stand it to be always on the top round of the ladder to Paradise. For my part, between you and me, I never believed all that story they read to us so often about Saint Simeon Stylites, who passed so many years on the top of a pillar and never came down. Trust me, the old boy found his way down sometimes, when all the world was asleep, and got somebody to do duty for him meantime, while he took a little something comfortable. Is it not so?"

"I am told to believe, and I do believe," said Father Johannes, casting down his eyes, piously; "and, dear brother, it ill befits a sinner like me to reprove; but it seemeth

to me as if you make too much use of the eyes of carnal
inquiry.   Touching the life of our holy father, I cannot
believe the most scrupulous watch can detect anything in
his walk or conversation other than appears in his profession.   His food is next to nothing, — a little chopped
spinach or some bitter herb cooked without salt for ordi-
nary days, and on fast days he mingles this with ashes,
according to a saintly rule.   As for sleep, I believe he
does without it; for at no time of the night, when I have
knocked at the door of his cell, have I found him sleeping.
He is always at his prayers or breviary.   His cell hath
only a rough, hard board for a bed, with a log of rough
wood for a pillow; yet he complains of that as tempting to
indolence."

Father Anselmo shrugged his fat shoulders, ruefully.

"It's all well enough," he said, "for those that want to
take this hard road to Paradise; but why need they drive
the flock up with them?"

"True enough, Brother Anselmo," said Father Johannes;
"but the flock will rejoice in it in the end, doubtless.   I
understand he is purposing to draw yet stricter the reins
of discipline.   We ought to be thankful."

"Thankful?   We can't wink but six times a week
now," said Father Anselmo; "and by and by he won't let
us wink at all."

"Hist! hush! here he comes," said Father Johannes.
"What ails him? he looks wild, like a man distraught."

In a moment more, in fact, Father Francesco strode hastily through the corridor, with his deep-set eyes dilated
and glittering, and a vivid hectic flush on his hollow
cheeks.   He paid no regard to the salutation of the obsequious monks; in fact, he seemed scarcely to see them,
but hurried in a disordered manner through the passages
and gained the room of his cell, which he shut and locked
with a violent clang.

"What has come over him now?" said Father Anselmo.

Father Johannes stealthily followed some distance, and then stood with his lean neck outstretched and his head turned in the direction where the Superior had disappeared. The whole attitude of the man, with his acute glittering eye, might remind one of a serpent making an observation before darting after his prey.

"Something is working him," he said to himself; "what may it be?"

Meanwhile that heavy oaken door had closed on a narrow cell, bare of everything which could be supposed to be a matter of convenience in the abode of a human being. A table of the rudest and most primitive construction was garnished with a skull, whose empty eye-holes and grinning teeth were the most conspicuous objects in the room. Behind this stood a large crucifix, manifestly the work of no common master, and bearing evident traces in its workmanship of Florentine art: it was, perhaps, one of the relics of the former wealth of the nobleman who had buried his name and worldly possessions in this living sepulchre. A splendid manuscript breviary, richly illuminated, lay open on the table; and the fair fancy of its flowery letters, the lustre of gold and silver on its pages, formed a singular contrast to the squalid nakedness of everything else in the room. This book, too, had been a family heirloom; some lingering shred of human and domestic affection sheltered itself under the protection of religion in making it the companion of his self-imposed life of penance and renunciation.

Father Francesco had just returned from the scene in the confessional we have already described. That day had brought to him one of those pungent and vivid inward revelations which sometimes overset in a moment some delusion that has been the cherished growth of years. Henceforth the reign of self-deception was past, — there

was no more self-concealment, no more evasion.   He loved
Agnes, — he knew it; he said it over and over again to himself with a stormy intensity of energy; and in this hour
the whole of his nature seemed to rise in rebellion against
the awful barriers which hemmed in and threatened this
passion.   He now saw clearly that all that he had been
calling fatherly tenderness, pastoral zeal, Christian unity,
and a thousand other evangelical names, was nothing more
nor less than a passion that had gone to the roots of existence and absorbed into itself all that there was of him.
Where was he to look for refuge?   What hymn, what
prayer, had he not blent with her image?   It was this that
he had given to her as a holy lesson, — it was that that
she had spoken of to him as the best expression of her
feelings.   This prayer he had explained to her; he remembered just the beautiful light in her eyes, which were
fixed on his so trustingly.   How dear to him had been
that unquestioning devotion, that tender, innocent humility! — how dear, and how dangerous!

We have read of flowing rivulets, wandering peacefully
without ripple or commotion, so long as no barrier stayed
their course, suddenly chafing in angry fury when an impassable dam was thrown across their waters.   So any
affection, however genial and gentle in its own nature, may
become an ungovernable, ferocious passion, by the interven-
tion of fatal obstacles in its course.   In the case of Father
Francesco, the sense of guilt and degradation fell like a
blight over all the past that had been so ignorantly happy.
He thought he had been living on manna, but found it
poison.   Satan had been fooling him, leading him on blind-
fold, and laughing at his simplicity, and now mocked at
his captivity.   And how nearly had he been hurried by a
sudden and overwhelming influence to the very brink of
disgrace!   He felt himself shiver and grow cold to think
of it.   A moment more, and he had blasted that pure ear

with forbidden words of passion; and even now he remembered, with horror, the look of grave and troubled surprise in those confiding eyes, that had always looked up to him trustingly, as to God. A moment more, and he had betrayed the faith he taught her, shattered her trust in the holy ministry, and perhaps imperiled her salvation. He breathed a sigh of relief when he thought of it, — he had not betrayed himself, he had not fallen in her esteem, he still stood on that sacred vantage-ground where his power over her was so great, and where at least he possessed her confidence and veneration. There was still time for recollection, for self-control, for a vehement struggle which should set all right again: but, alas! how shall a man struggle who finds his whole inner nature boiling in furious rebellion against the dictates of his conscience, — self against self?

It is true, also, that no passions are deeper in their hold, more pervading and more vital to the whole human being, than those that make their first entrance through the higher nature, and, beginning with a religious and poetic ideality, gradually work their way through the whole fabric of the human existence. From grosser passions, whose roots lie in the senses, there is always a refuge in man's loftier nature. He can cast them aside with contempt, and leave them as one whose lower story is flooded can remove to a higher loft, and live serenely with a purer air and wider prospect. But to love that is born of ideality, of intellectual sympathy, of harmonies of the spiritual and immortal natures, of the very poetry and purity of the soul, if it be placed where reason and religion forbid its exercise and expression, what refuge but the grave, — what hope but that wide eternity where all human barriers fall, all human relations end, and love ceases to be a crime? A man of the world may struggle by change of scene, place, and employment. He may put oceans between himself and the things that speak of what he desires to forget. He may fill the void in his life with the stirring excitement of the battle-field, or the whirl of travel from city to city, or the press of business and care. But what help is there for him whose life is tied down to the narrow sphere of the convent, — to the monotony of a bare cell, to the endless repetition of the same prayers, the same chants, the same prostrations, especially when all that ever redeemed it from monotony has been that image and that sympathy which conscience now bids him forget?

When Father Francesco precipitated himself into his cell and locked the door, it was with the desperation of a man who flies from a mortal enemy. It seemed to him that all eyes saw just what was boiling within him, — that the wild thoughts that seemed to scream their turbulent importunities in his ears were speaking so loud that all the world would hear. He should disgrace himself before the brethren whom he had so long been striving to bring to order and to teach the lessons of holy self-control. He saw himself pointed at, hissed at, degraded, by the very men who had quailed before his own reproofs; and scarcely, when he had bolted the door behind him, did he feel himself safe. Panting and breathless, he fell on his knees before the crucifix, and, bowing his head in his hands, fell forward upon the floor. As a spent wave melts at the foot of a rock, so all his strength passed away, and he lay awhile in a kind of insensibility, — a state in which, though consciously existing, he had no further control over his thoughts and feelings. In that state of dreamy exhaustion his mind seemed like a mirror, which, without vitality or will of its own, simply lies still and reflects the objects that may pass over it. As clouds sailing in the heavens cast their images, one after another, on the glassy floor of a waveless sea, so the scenes of his former life drifted in vivid pictures athwart his memory. He saw his father's palace, — the wide, cool, marble halls, — the gardens resounding with the voices of falling waters. He saw the fair face of his mother, and played with the jewels upon her hands. He saw again the picture of himself, in all the flush of youth and health, clattering on horseback through the streets of Florence with troops of gay young friends, now dead to him as he to them. He saw himself in the bowers of gay ladies, whose golden hair, lustrous eyes, and siren wiles came back shivering and trembling in the waters of memory in a thousand undulating reflections. There were wild revels, — orgies such as Florence remembers with shame to this day. There was intermingled the turbulent din of arms, — the haughty passion, the sudden provocation, the swift revenge. And then came the awful hour of conviction, the face of that wonderful man whose preaching had stirred all souls; and then those fearful days of penance, — that darkness of the tomb, — that dying to the world, — those solemn vows, and the fearful struggles by which they had been followed.

"Oh, my God!" he cried, "is it all in vain? — so many prayers? so many struggles? — and shall I fail of salvation at last?"

He seemed to himself as a swimmer, who, having exhausted his last gasp of strength in reaching the shore, is suddenly lifted up on a cruel wave and drawn back into the deep. There seemed nothing for him but to fold his arms and sink.

For he felt no strength now to resist, he felt no wish to conquer; he only prayed that he might lie there and die. It seemed to him that the love which possessed him and tyrannized over his very being was a doom, — a curse sent upon him by some malignant fate with whose power it was vain to struggle. He detested his work, — he detested his duties, — he loathed his vows; and there was not a thing in his whole future to which he looked forward

otherwise than with the extreme of aversion, except one,
to which he clung with a bitter and defiant tenacity, —
the spiritual guidance of Agnes.   Guidance! — he laughed
aloud, in the bitterness of his soul, as he thought of this.
He was her guide, her confessor; to him she was bound
to reveal every change of feeling; and this love that he too
well perceived rising in her heart for another, — he would
wring from her own confessions the means to repress and
circumvent it.   If she could not be his, he might at least
prevent her from belonging to any other, — he might at
least keep her always within the sphere of his spiritual
authority.   Had he not a right to do this? had he not a
right to cherish an evident vocation, — a right to reclaim
her from the embrace of an excommunicated infidel, and
present her as a chaste bride at the altar of the Lord?
Perhaps, when that was done, when an irrevocable barrier
should separate her from all possibility of earthly love,
when the awful marriage-vow should have been spoken
which should seal her heart for heaven alone, he might
recover some of the blessed calm which her influence once
brought over him, and these wild desires might cease, and
these feverish pulses be still.

Such were the vague images and dreams of the past and
future that floated over his mind, as he lay in a heavy sort
of lethargy on the floor of his cell, and hour after hour
passed away.   It grew afternoon, and the radiance of
evening came on.   The window of the cell overlooked the
broad Mediterranean, all one blue glitter of smiles and
sparkles.   The white-winged boats were flitting lightly
to and fro, like gauzy-winged insects in the summer air;
the song of the fishermen drawing their nets on the beach
floated cheerily upward.   Capri lay like a half-dissolved
opal in shimmering clouds of mist, and Naples gleamed out
pearly clear in the purple distance.   Vesuvius, with its
cloud-spotted sides, its garlanded villas and villages, its

silvery crown of vapor, seemed a warm-hearted and genial old giant lying down in his gorgeous repose, and holding all things on his heaving bosom in a kindly embrace.

So was the earth flooded with light and glory, that the tide poured into the cell, giving the richness of an old Venetian painting to its bare and squalid furniture. The crucifix glowed along all its sculptured lines with rich golden hues. The breviary, whose many-colored leaves fluttered as the wind from the sea drew inward, was yet brighter in its gorgeous tints. It seemed a sort of devotional butterfly perched before the grinning skull, which was bronzed by the enchanted light into warmer tones of color, as if some remembrance of what once it saw and felt came back upon it. So, also, the bare, miserable board which served for the bed, and its rude pillow, were glorified. A stray sunbeam, too, fluttered down on the floor like a pitying spirit, to light up that pale, thin face, whose classic outlines had now a sharp, yellow setness, like that of swooning or death; it seemed to linger compassionately on the sunken, wasted cheeks, on the long black lashes that fell over the deep hollows beneath the eyes like a funereal veil. Poor man! lying crushed and torn, like a piece of rockweed wrenched from its rock by a storm, and thrown up withered upon the beach!

From the leaves of the breviary there depends, by a fragment of gold braid, a sparkling something that wavers and glitters in the evening light. It is a cross of the cheapest and simplest material, that once belonged to Agnes. She lost it from her rosary at the confessional, and Father Francesco saw it fall, yet would not warn her of the loss, for he longed to possess something that had belonged to her. He made it a mark to one of her favorite hymns; but she never knew where it had gone. Little could she dream, in her simplicity, what a power she held over the man who seemed to her an object of such awful

veneration. Little did she dream that the poor little tinsel
cross had such a mighty charm with it, and that she herself, in her childlike simplicity, her ignorant innocence,
her peaceful tenderness and trust, was raising such a turbulent storm of passion in the heart which she supposed to
be above the reach of all human changes.

And now, through the golden air, the Ave Maria is
sounding from the convent-bells, and answered by a thousand tones and echoes from the churches of the old town,
and all Christendom gives a moment's adoring pause to
celebrate the moment when an angel addressed to a mortal
maiden words that had been wept and prayed for during
thousands of years. Dimly they sounded through his ear,
in that half-deadly trance, — not with plaintive sweetness
and motherly tenderness, but like notes of doom and vengeance. He felt rebellious impulses within, which rose up
in hatred against them, and all that recalled to his mind
the faith which seemed a tyranny, and the vows which
appeared to him such a hopeless and miserable failure.

But now there came other sounds nearer and more
earthly. His quickened senses perceive a busy patter of
sandaled feet outside his cell, and a whispering of consul-
tation, — and then the silvery, snaky tones of Father Johannes, which had that oily, penetrative quality which
passes through all substances with such distinctness.

"Brethren," he said, "I feel bound in conscience to
knock. Our blessed Superior carries his mortifications altogether too far. His faithful sons must beset him with
filial inquiries."

The condition in which Father Francesco was lying, like
many abnormal states of extreme exhaustion, seemed to be
attended with a mysterious quickening of the magnetic
forces and intuitive perceptions. He felt the hypocrisy of
those tones, and they sounded in his ear like the suppressed
hiss of a deadly serpent. He had always suspected that

this man hated him to the death; and he felt now that he was come with his stealthy tread and his almost supernatural power of prying observation, to read the very inmost secrets of his heart. He knew that he longed for nothing so much as the power to hurl him from his place and to reign in his stead; and the instinct of self-defense roused him. He started up as one starts from a dream, waked by a whisper in the ear, and, raising himself on his elbow, looked towards the door.

A cautious rap was heard, and then a pause. Father Francesco smiled with a peculiar and bitter expression. The rap became louder, more energetic, stormy at last, intermingled with vehement calls on his name.

Father Francesco rose at length, settled his garments, passed his hands over his brow, and then, composing himself to an expression of deliberate gravity, opened the door and stood before them. .

"Holy father," said Father Johannes, "the hearts of your sons have been saddened. A whole day have you withdrawn your presence from our devotions. We feared you might have fainted, your pious austerities so often transcend the powers of Nature."

"I grieve to have saddened the hearts of such affectionate sons," said the Superior, fixing his eye keenly on Father Johannes; "but I have been performing a peculiar office of prayer to-day for a soul in deadly peril, and have been so absorbed therein that I have known nothing that passed. There is a soul among us, brethren," he added, "that stands at this moment so near to damnation that even the most blessed Mother of God is in doubt for its salvation, and whether it can be saved at all, God only knows."

These words, rising up from a tremendous groundswell of repressed feeling, had a fearful, almost supernatural earnestness that made the body of the monks tremble. Most of them were conscious of living but a shabby, shambling, dissembling life, evading in every possible way the efforts of their Superior to bring them up to the requirements of their profession; and therefore, when these words were bolted out among them with such a glowing intensity, every one of them began mentally feeling for the key of his own private and interior skeleton-closet, and wondering which of their ghastly occupants was coming to light now.

Father Johannes alone was unmoved, because he had long since ceased to have a conscience. A throb of moral pulsation had for years been an impossibility to the dried and hardened fibre of his inner nature. He was one of those real, genuine, thorough unbelievers in all religion and all faith and all spirituality, whose unbelief grows only more callous by the constant handling of sacred things. Ambition was the ruling motive of his life, and every faculty was sharpened into such acuteness under its action that his penetration seemed at times almost preternatural.

While he stood with downcast eyes and hands crossed upon his breast, listening to the burning words which remorse and despair wrung from his Superior, he was calmly and warily studying to see what could be made of the evident interior conflict that convulsed him. Was there some secret sin? Had that sanctity at last found the temptation that was more than a match for it? And what could it be?

To a nature with any strong combative force there is no tonic like the presence of a secret and powerful enemy, and the stealthy glances of Father Johannes's serpent eye did more towards restoring Father Francesco to self-mastery than the most conscientious struggles could have done. He grew calm, resolved, determined. Self-respect was dear to him, — and dear to him no less that reflection of self-respect which a man reads in other eyes. He would not forfeit his conventual honor, or bring a stain on his order, or, least of all, expose himself to the scoffing eye of a triumphant enemy. Such were the motives that now came to his aid, while as yet the whole of his inner nature rebelled at the thought that he must tear up by the roots and wholly extirpate this love that seemed to have sent its fine fibres through every nerve of his being. "No!" he said to himself, with a fierce interior rebellion, "*that* I will not do! Right or wrong, come heaven, come hell, I *will* love her: and if lost I must be, lost I will be!" And while this determination lasted, prayer seemed to him a mockery. He dared not pray alone now, when most he needed prayer; but he moved forward with dignity towards the convent chapel to lead the vesper devotions of his brethren. Outwardly he was calm and rigid as a statue; but as he commenced the service, his utterance had a terrible meaning and earnestness that were felt even by the most drowsy and leaden of his flock. It is singular how the dumb, imprisoned soul, locked within the walls of the body, sometimes gives such a piercing power to the tones of the voice during the access of a great agony. The effect is entirely involuntary and often against the most strenuous opposition of the will, but one sometimes hears another reading or repeating words with an intense vitality, a living force, which tells of some inward anguish or conflict of which the language itself gives no expression.

Never were the long-drawn intonations of the chants and prayers of the Church pervaded by a more terrible, wild fervor than the Superior that night breathed into them. They seemed to wail, to supplicate, to combat, to menace, to sink in despairing pauses of helpless anguish, and anon to rise in stormy agonies of passionate importunity; and the monks quailed and trembled, they scarce knew why, with forebodings of coming wrath and judgment.

In the evening exhortation, which it had been the

Superior's custom to add to the prayers of the vesper-hour, he dwelt with a terrible and ghastly eloquence on the loss of the soul.

"Brethren," he said, "believe me, the very first hour of a damned.spirit in hell will outweigh all the prosperities of the most prosperous life. If you could gain the whole world, that one hour of hell would outweigh it all; how much more such miserable, pitiful scraps and fragments of the world as they gain who for the sake of a little fleshly ease neglect the duties of a holy profession! There is a broad way to hell through a convent, my brothers, where miserable wretches go who have neither the spirit to serve the Devil wholly, nor the patience to serve God; there be many shaven crowns that gnash their teeth in hell to-night, — many a monk's robe is burning on its owner in living fire, and the devils call him a fool for choosing to be damned in so hard a way. 'Could you not come here by some easier road than a cloister?' they ask. 'If you must sell your soul, why did you not get something for it?' Brethren, there be devils waiting for some of us; they are laughing at your paltry shifts and evasions, at your efforts to make things easy, — for they know how it will all end at last. Rouse yourselves! Awake! Salvation is no easy matter, — nothing to be got between sleeping and waking. Watch, pray, scourge the flesh, fast, weep, bow down in sackcloth, mingle your bread with ashes, if by any means ye may escape the everlasting fire!"

"Bless me!" said Father Anselmo, when the services were over, casting a half-scared glance after the retreating figure of the Superior as he left the chapel, and drawing a long breath; "it's enough to make one sweat to hear him go on. What has come over him? Anyhow, I'll give myself a hundred lashes this very night: something must be done."

"Well," said another, "I confess I did hide a cold wing

of fowl in the sleeve of my gown last fast-day. My old aunt gave it to me, and I was forced to take it for relation's sake; but I 'll do so no more, as I 'm a living sinner I 'll do a penance this very night."

Father Johannes stood under one of the arches that looked into the gloomy garden, and, with his hands crossed upon his breast, and his cold, glittering eye fixed stealthily now on one and now on another, listened with an ill-disguised sneer to these hasty evidences of fear and remorse in the monks, as they thronged the corridor on the way to their cells. Suddenly turning to a young brother who had lately joined the convent, he said to him, —

"And what of the pretty Clarice, my brother?"

The blood flushed deep into the pale cheek of the young monk, and his frame shook with some interior emotion as he answered, —

"She is recovering."

"And she sent for thee to shrive her?"

"My God!" said the young man, with an imploring, wild expression in his dark eyes, "she did; but I would not go."

"Then Nature is still strong," said Father Johannes, pitilessly eyeing the young man.

"When will it ever die?" said the stripling, with a despairing gesture; "it heeds neither heaven nor hell."

"Well, patience, boy! if you have lost an earthly bride, you have gained a heavenly one. The Church is our espoused in white linen. Bless the Lord, without ceasing, for the exchange."

There was an inexpressible mocking irony in the tones in which this was said, that made itself felt to the finely vitalized spirit of the youth, though to all the rest it sounded like the accredited average pious talk which is more or less the current coin of religious organizations.

Now no one knows through what wanton deviltry Father

Johannes broached this painful topic with the poor youth;
but he had a peculiar faculty, with his smooth tones and
his sanctimonious smiles, of thrusting red-hot needles into
any wounds which he either knew or suspected under the
coarse woolen robes of his brethren. He appeared to do
it in all coolness, in a way of psychological investigation.

He smiled, as the youth turned away, and a moment
after, started as if a thought had suddenly struck him.

"I have it!" he said to himself. "There may be a
woman at the bottom of this discomposure of our holy father; for he is wrought upon by something to the very
bottom of his soul. I have not studied human nature so
many years for nothing. Father Francesco hath been
much in the guidance of women. His preaching hath
wrought upon them, and perchance among them. Aha!"
he said to himself, as he paced up and down. "I have it!
I'll try an experiment upon him!"

CHAPTER XV

THE SERPENT'S EXPERIMENT

FATHER FRANCESCO sat leaning his head on his hand by the window of his cell, looking out upon the sea as it rose and fell, with the reflections of the fast coming stars glittering like so many jewels on its breast. The glow of evening had almost faded, but there was a wan, tremulous light from the moon, and a clearness produced by the reflection of such an expanse of water, which still rendered objects in his cell quite discernible.

In the terrible denunciations and warnings just uttered, he had been preaching to himself, striving to bring a force on his own soul by which he might reduce its interior rebellion to submission; but, alas! when was ever love cast out by fear? He knew not as yet the only remedy for such sorrow, — that there is a love celestial and divine, of which earthly love in its purest form is only the sacramental symbol and emblem, and that this divine love can by God's power so outflood human affections as to bear the soul above all earthly idols to its only immortal rest. This great truth rises like a rock amid stormy seas, and many is the sailor struggling in salt and bitter waters who cannot yet believe it is to be found. A few saints like Saint Augustine had reached it, — but through what buffetings, what anguish!

At this moment, however, there was in the heart of the father one of those collapses which follow the crisis of some mortal struggle. He leaned on the window-sill, exhausted and helpless.

Suddenly, a kind of illusion of the senses came over him, such as is not infrequent to sensitive natures in severe crises of mental anguish. He thought he heard Agnes singing, as he had sometimes heard her when he had called in his pastoral ministrations at the little garden and paused awhile outside that he might hear her finish a favorite hymn, which, like a shy bird, she sung all the more sweetly for thinking herself alone.

Quite as if they were sung in his ear, and in her very tones, he heard the words of Saint Bernard, which we have already introduced to our reader: —

> " Jesu dulcis memoria,
> Dans vera cordi gaudia :
> Sed super mel et omnia
> Ejus dulcis præsentia.
>
> " Jesu, spes pœnitentibus,
> Quam pius es petentibus,
> Quam bonus te quærentibus,
> Sed quis invenientibus ! "

Soft and sweet and solemn was the illusion, as if some spirit breathed them with a breath of tenderness over his soul; and he threw himself with a burst of tears before the crucifix.

"O Jesus, where, then, art Thou? Why must I thus suffer? She is not the one altogether lovely; it is Thou, — Thou, her Creator and mine. Why, why cannot I find Thee? Oh, take from my heart all other love but Thine alone ! "

Yet even this very prayer, this very hymn, were blent with the remembrance of Agnes; for was it not she who first had taught him the lesson of heavenly love? Was not she the first one who had taught him to look upward to Jesus other than as an avenging judge? Michel Angelo has embodied in a fearful painting, which now deforms the Sistine Chapel, that image of stormy vengeance which a religion debased by force and fear had substituted for the tender, good shepherd of earlier Christianity. It was only in the heart of a lowly maiden that Christ had been made manifest to the eye of the monk, as of old he was revealed to the world through a virgin. And how could he, then, forget her, or cease to love her, when every prayer and hymn, every sacred round of the ladder by which he must climb, was so full of memorials of her? While crying and panting for the supreme, the divine, the invisible love, he found his heart still craving the visible one, — the one so well known, revealing itself to the senses, and bringing with it the certainty of visible companionship.

As he was thus kneeling and wrestling with himself, a sudden knock at his door startled him. He had made it a point, never, at any hour of the day or night, to deny himself to a brother who sought him for counsel, however disagreeable the person and however unreasonable the visit. He therefore rose and unbolted the door, and saw Father Johannes standing with folded arms and downcast head, in an attitude of composed humility.

"What would you with me, brother?" he asked, calmly.

"My father, I have a wrestling of mind for one of our brethren whose case I would present to you."

"Come in, my brother," said the Superior. At the same time he lighted a little iron lamp, of antique form, such as are still in common use in that region, and seating himself on the board which served for his couch, made a motion to Father Johannes to be seated also.

The latter sat down, eyeing, as he did so, the whole interior of the apartment, so far as it was revealed by the glimmer of the taper.

"Well, my son," said Father Francesco, "what is it?"

"I have my doubts of the spiritual safety of Brother Bernard," said Father Johannes.

"Wherefore?" asked the Superior, briefly.

"Holy father, you are aware of the history of the brother, and of the worldly affliction that drove him to this blessed profession ? "

"I am," replied the Superior, with the same brevity.

"He narrated it to me fully," said Father Johannes. "The maiden he was betrothed to was married to another in his absence on a long journey, being craftily made to suppose him dead."

"I tell you I know the circumstances," said the Superior.

"I merely recalled them, because, moved doubtless by your sermon, he dropped words to me to-night which led me to suppose that this sinful, earthly love was not yet extirpated from his soul. Of late the woman was sick and nigh unto death, and sent for him."

"But he did not go ? " interposed Father Francesco.

"No, he did not, — grace was given him thus far; but he dropped words to me to the effect, that in secret he still cherished the love of this woman; and the awful words your Reverence has been speaking to us to-night have moved me with fear for the youth's soul, of the which I, as an elder brother, have had some charge, and I came to consult with you as to what help there might be for him."

Father Francesco turned away his head a moment and there was a pause; at last he said, in a tone that seemed like the throb of some deep, interior anguish, —

"The Lord help him!"

"Amen!" said Father Johannes, taking keen note of the apparent emotion.

"You must have experience in these matters, my father," he added, after a pause, — "so many hearts have been laid open to you. I would crave to know of you what you think is the safest and most certain cure for this love of woman, if once it hath got possession of the heart."

"*Death !* " said Father Francesco, after a solemn pause.

"I do not understand you," said Father Johannes.

"My son," said Father Francesco, rising up with an air

of authority, "you do *not* understand, — there is nothing in you by which you should understand. This unhappy brother hath opened his case to me, and I have counseled him all I know of prayer and fastings and watchings and mortifications. Let him persevere in the same; and if all these fail, the good Lord will send the other in His own time. There is an end to all things in this life, and that end shall certainly come at last. Bid him persevere and hope in this. And now, brother," added the Superior, with dignity, "if you have no other query, time flies and eternity comes on, — go, watch and pray, and leave me to my prayers, also."

He raised his hand with a gesture of benediction, and Father Johannes, awed in spite of himself, felt impelled to leave the apartment.

"Is it so, or is it not?" he said. "I cannot tell. He did seem to wince and turn away his head when I proposed the case; but then he made fight at last. I cannot tell whether I have got any advantage or not; but patience! we shall see!"

CHAPTER XVI

ELSIE PUSHES HER SCHEME

THE good Father Antonio returned from his conference with the cavalier with many subjects for grave pondering. This man, as he conjectured, so far from being an enemy either of Church or State, was in fact in many respects in the same position with his revered master, — as nearly so as the position of a layman was likely to resemble that of an ecclesiastic. His denial of the Visible Church, as represented by the Pope and cardinals, sprang not from an irreverent, but from a reverent spirit. To accept *them* as exponents of Christ and Christianity was to blaspheme and traduce both, and therefore he only could be counted in the highest degree Christian who stood most completely opposed to them in spirit and practice.

His kind and fatherly heart was interested in the brave young nobleman. He sympathized fully with the situation in which he stood, and he even wished success to his love; but then how was he to help him with Agnes, and above all with her old grandmother, without entering on the awful task of condemning and exposing that sacred authority which all the Church had so many years been taught to regard as infallibly inspired? Long had all the truly spiritual members of the Church who gave ear to the teachings of Savonarola felt that the nearer they followed Christ the more open was their growing antagonism to the Pope and the Cardinals; but still they hung back from the responsibility of inviting the people to an open revolt.

Father Antonio felt his soul deeply stirred with the

news of the excommunication of his saintly master; and
he marveled, as he tossed on his restless bed through the
night, how he was to meet the storm.   He might have
known, had he been able to look into a crowded assembly
in Florence about this time, when the unterrified monk
thus met the news of his excommunication: —

"There have come decrees from Rome, have there?
They call me a son of perdition.   Well, thus may you
answer: He to whom you give this name hath neither
favorites nor concubines, but gives himself solely to preaching Christ.   His spiritual sons and daughters, those who
listen to his doctrine, do not pass their time in infamous
practices.   They confess, they receive the communion,
they live honestly.   This man gives himself up to exalt
the Church of Christ: you to destroy it.   The time approaches for opening the secret chamber: we will give but
one turn of the key, and there will come out thence such
an infection, such a stench of this city of Rome, that the
odor shall spread through all Christendom, and all the
world shall be sickened."

But Father Antonio was of himself wholly unable to
come to such a courageous result, though capable of following to the death the master who should do it for him.
His was the true artist nature, as unfit to deal with rough
human forces as a bird that flies through the air is unfitted
to a hand-to-hand grapple with the armed forces of the
lower world.   There is strength in these artist natures.
Curious computations have been made of the immense mus-
cular power that is brought into exercise when a swallow
skims so smoothly through the blue sky; but the strength
is of a kind unadapted to mundane uses, and needs the
ether for its display.   Father Antonio could create the
beautiful; he could warm, could elevate, could comfort;
and when a stronger nature went before him, he could follow with an unquestioning tenderness of devotion: but he

wanted the sharp, downright power of mind that could cut and cleave its way through the rubbish of the past, when its institutions, instead of a commodious dwelling, had come to be a loathsome prison. Besides, the true artist has ever an enchanted island of his own; and when this world perplexes and wearies him, he can sail far away and lay his soul down to rest, as Cytherea bore the sleeping Ascanius far from the din of battle, to sleep on flowers and breathe the odor of a hundred undying altars to Beauty.

Therefore, after a restless night, the good monk arose in the first purple of the dawn, and instinctively betook him to a review of his drawings for the shrine, as a refuge from troubled thought. He took his sketch of the Madonna and Child into the morning twilight and began meditating thereon, while the clouds that lined the horizon were glowing rosy purple and violet with the approaching day.

"See there!" he said to himself, "yonder clouds have exactly the rosy purple of the cyclamen which my little Agnes loves so much; — yes, I am resolved that this cloud on which our Mother standeth shall be of a cyclamen color. And there is that star, like as it looked yesterday evening, when I mused upon it. Methought I could see our Lady's clear brow, and the radiance of her face, and I prayed that some little power might be given to show forth that which transports me."

And as the monk plied his pencil, touching here and there, and elaborating the outlines of his drawing, he sung, —

> "Ave, Maris Stella,
> Dei mater alma,
> Atque semper virgo,
> Felix cœli porta !
>
> "Virgo singularis,
> Inter omnes mitis,
> Nos culpis solutos
> Mites fac et castos!

"Vitam præsta puram,
Iter para tutum,
Ut videntes Jesum
Semper collætemur!"[1]

As the monk sung, Agnes soon appeared at the door.

"Ah, my little bird, you are there!" he said looking up.

"Yes," said Agnes, coming forward, and looking over his shoulder at his work.

"Did you find that young sculptor?" she asked.

"That I did, — a brave boy, too, who will row down the coast and dig us marble from an old heathen temple, which we will baptize into the name of Christ and his Mother."

"Pietro was always a good boy," said Agnes.

"Stay," said the monk, stepping into his little sleeping room; "he sent you this lily; see, I have kept it in water all night."

"Poor Pietro, that was good of him!" said Agnes. "I would thank him, if I could. But, uncle," she added, in a hesitating voice, "did you see anything of that — other one?"

"That I did, child, — and talked long with him."

"Ah, uncle, is there any hope for him?"

[1] Hail, thou Star of Ocean,
Thou forever virgin,
Mother of the Lord!
Blessed gate of Heaven,
Take our heart's devotion!

Virgin one and only,
Meekest 'mid them all,
From our sins set free,
Make us pure like thee,
Freed from passion's thrall!

Grant that in pure living,
Through safe paths below,
Forever seeing Jesus,
Rejoicing we may go!

"Yes, there is hope, — great hope. In fact, he has promised to receive me again, and I have hopes of leading him to the sacrament of confession, and after that " —

"And then the Pope will forgive him!" said Agnes, joyfully.

The face of the monk suddenly fell; he was silent, and went on retouching his drawing.

"Do you not think he will?" said Agnes, earnestly. "You said the Church was ever ready to receive the repentant."

"The True Church will receive him," said the monk, evasively; "yes, my little one, there is no doubt of it."

"And it is not true that he is captain of a band of robbers in the mountains?" said Agnes. "May I tell Father Francesco that it is not so?"

"Child, this young man hath suffered a grievous wrong and injustice; for he is lord of an ancient and noble estate, out of which he hath been driven by the cruel injustice of a most wicked and abominable man, the Duke di Valentinos,[1] who hath caused the death of his brothers and sisters, and ravaged the country around with fire and sword, so that he hath been driven with his retainers to a fortress in the mountains."

"But," said Agnes, with flushed cheeks, "why does not our blessed Father excommunicate this wicked duke? Surely this knight hath erred; instead of taking refuge in the mountains, he ought to have fled with his followers to Rome, where the dear Father of the Church hath a house for all the oppressed. It must be so lovely to be the father of all men, and to take in and comfort all those who are distressed and sorrowful, and to right the wrongs of all that are oppressed, as our dear Father at Rome doth!"

The monk looked up at Agnes's clear glowing face with a sort of wondering pity.

---

[1] Cæsar Borgia was created Duc de Valentinois by Louis XII. of France.

"Dear little child," he said, "there is a Jerusalem above which is mother of us all, and these things are done there.

'Cœlestis urbs Jerusalem,
Beata pacis visio,
Quæ celsa de viventibus
Saxis ad astra tolleris
Sponsæque ritu cingeris
Mille angelorum millibus! ' "

The face of the monk glowed as he repeated this ancient hymn of the Church,[1] as if the remembrance of that general assembly and church of the first-born gave him comfort in his depression.

Agnes felt perplexed, and looked earnestly at her uncle as he stooped over his drawing, and saw that there were deep lines of anxiety on his usually clear, placid face, — a look as of one who struggles mentally with some untold trouble.

"Uncle," she said, hesitatingly, "may I tell Father Francesco what you have been telling me of this young man ? "

"No, my little one, — it were not best. In fact, dear child, there be many things in his case impossible to explain, even to you; — but he is not so altogether hopeless as you thought; in truth, I have great hopes of him. I have admonished him to come here no more, but I shall see him again this evening."

Agnes wondered at the heaviness of her own little heart, as her kind old uncle spoke of his coming there no more. Awhile ago she dreaded his visits as a most fearful temptation, and thought perhaps he might come at any hour; now she was sure he would not, and it was astonishing what a weight fell upon her.

[1] This very ancient hymn is the fountain-head from which through various languages have trickled the various hymns of the Celestial City such as —

"Jerusalem, my happy home !"

and Quarles's —

" O mother dear, Jerusalem !"

"Why am I not thankful?" she asked herself. "Why am I not joyful? Why should I wish to see him again, when I should only be tempted to sinful thoughts, and when my dear uncle, who can do so much for him, has his soul in charge? And what is this which is so strange in his case? There is some mystery, after all, — something, perhaps, which I ought not to wish to know. Ah, how little can we know of this great wicked world, and of the reasons which our superiors give for their conduct! It is ours humbly to obey, without a question or a doubt. Holy Mother, may I not sin through a vain curiosity or self-will! May I ever say, as thou didst, 'Behold the handmaid of the Lord! be it unto me according to His word!'"

And Agnes went about her morning devotions with fervent zeal, and did not see the monk as he dropped the pencil, and, covering his face with his robe, seemed to wrestle in some agony of prayer.

"Shepherd of Israel," he said, "why hast Thou forgotten this vine of Thy planting? The boar out of the wood doth waste it, the wild beast of the field doth devour it. Dogs have encompassed Thy beloved; the assembly of the violent have surrounded him. How long, O Lord, holy and true, dost Thou not judge and avenge?"

"Now, really, brother," said Elsie, coming towards him, and interrupting his meditations in her bustling, business way, yet speaking in a low tone that Agnes should not hear, "I want you to help me with this child in a good common-sense fashion: none of your high-flying notions about saints and angels, but a little good common talk for every-day people that have their bread and salt to look after. The fact is, brother, this girl must be married. I went last night to talk with Antonio's mother, and the way is all open as well as any living girl could desire. Antonio is a trifle slow, and the high-flying hussies call him stupid; but his mother says a better son never

breathed, and he is as obedient to all her orders now as
when he was three years old.   And she has laid up plenty
of household stuff for him, and good hard gold pieces to
boot: she let me count them myself, and I showed her that
which I had scraped together, and she counted it, and we
agreed that the children that come of such a marriage
would come into the world with something to stand on.
Now Agnes is fond of you, brother, and perhaps it would
be well for you to broach the subject.   The fact is, when
I begin to talk, she gets her arms round my old neck and
falls to weeping and kissing me at such a rate as makes a
fool of me.   If the child would only be rebellious, one
could do something; but this love takes all the stiffness
out of one's joints; and she tells me she never wants a
husband, and she will be content to live with me all her
life.   The saints know it is n't for my happiness to put her
out of my old arms; but I can't last forever, — my old
back grows weaker every year; and Antonio has strong
arms to defend her from all these roystering fellows who
fear neither God nor man, and swoop up young maids as
kites do chickens.   And then he is as gentle and manage-
able as a this-year ox; Agnes can lead him by the horn, —
she will be a perfect queen over him; for he has been
brought up to mind the women."

"Well, sister," said the monk, "hath our little maid
any acquaintance with this man?   Have they ever spoken
together?"

"Not much.   I have never brought them to a very close
acquaintance; and that is what is to be done.   Antonio is
not much of a talker; to tell the truth, he does not know
as much to say as our Agnes: but the man's place is not
to say fine things, but to do the hard work that shall support the household."

"Then Agnes hath not even seen him?"

"Yes, at different times I have bid her regard him, and

said to her, 'There goes a proper man and a good Christian, — a man who minds his work and is obedient to his old mother: such a man will make a right good husband for some girl some day.'"

"And did you ever see that her eye followed him with pleasure?"

"No, neither him nor any other man, for my little Agnes hath no thought of that kind; but, once married, she will like him fast enough. All I want is to have you begin the subject, and get it into her head a little."

Father Antonio was puzzled how to meet this direct urgency of his sister. He could not explain to her his own private reasons for believing that any such attempt would be utterly vain, and only bring needless distress on his little favorite. He therefore answered, —

"My good sister, all such thoughts lie so far out of the sphere of us monks, that you could not choose a worse person for such an errand. I have never had any other communings with the child than touching the beautiful things of my art, and concerning hymns and prayers and the lovely world of saints and angels, where they neither marry nor are given in marriage; and so I should only spoil your enterprise, if I should put my unskillful hand to it."

"At any rate," said Elsie, "don't you approve of my plan?"

"I should approve of anything that would make our dear little one safe and happy, but I would not force the matter against her inclinations. You will always regret it, if you make so good a child shed one needless tear. After all, sister, what need of haste? 'T is a young bird yet. Why push it out of the nest? When once it is gone, you will never get it back. Let the pretty one have her little day to play and sing and be happy. Does she not make this garden a sort of Paradise with her little ways and her sweet words? Now, my sister, these all belong to you;

but, once she is given to another, there is no saying what may come. One thing only may you count on with certainty: that these dear days, when she is all day by your side and sleeps in your bosom all night, are over, — she will belong to you no more, but to a strange man who hath neither toiled nor wrought for her, and all her pretty ways and dutiful thoughts must be for him."

"I know it — I know it," said Elsie, with a sudden wrench of that jealous love which is ever natural to strong, passionate natures. "I'm sure it isn't for my own sake I urge this. I grudge him the girl. After all, he is but a stupid head. What has he ever done, that such good fortune should befall him? He ought to fall down and kiss the dust of my shoes for such a gift, and I doubt me much if he will ever think to do it. These men think nothing too good for them. I believe, if one of the crowned saints in heaven were offered them to wife, they would think it all quite natural, and not a whit less than their requirings."

"Well, then, sister," said the monk, soothingly, "why press this matter? why hurry? The poor little child is young; let her frisk like a lamb, and dance like a butterfly, and sing her hymns every day like a bright bird. Surely the Apostle saith, 'He that giveth his maid in marriage doeth well, but he that giveth her not doeth better.'"

"But I have opened the subject already to old Meta," said Elsie; "and if I don't pursue it, she will take it into her head that her son is lightly regarded, and then her back will be up, and one may lose the chance; and on the whole, considering the money and the fellow, I don't know a safer way to settle the girl."

"Well, sister, as I have remarked," said the monk, "I could not order my speech to propose anything of this kind to a young maid; I should so bungle that I might spoil all. You must even propose it yourself."

"I would not have undertaken it," said Elsie, "had I

not been frightened by that hook-nosed old kite of a cavalier that has been sailing and perching round. We are
two lone women here, and the times are unsettled, and one
never knows, that hath so fair a prize, but she may be carried off, and then no redress from any quarter."

"You might lodge her in the convent," said the monk.

"Yes, and then, the first thing I should know, they
would have got her away from me entirely. I have been
well pleased to have her much with the sisters hitherto,
because it kept her from hearing the foolish talk of girls
and gallants, — and such a flower would have had every
wasp and bee buzzing round it. But now the time is
coming to marry her, I much doubt these nuns. There's
old Jocunda is a sensible woman, who knew something of
the world before she went there, — but the Mother Theresa
knows no more than a baby; and they would take her in,
and make her as white and as thin as that moon yonder
now the sun has risen; and little good should I have of
her, for I have no vocation for the convent, — it would
kill me in a week. No, — she has seen enough of the
convent for the present. I will even take the risk of
watching her myself. Little has this gallant seen of her,
though he has tried hard enough! But to-day I may venture to take her down with me."

Father Antonio felt a little conscience-smitten in listening to these triumphant assertions of old Elsie; for he
knew that she would pour all her vials of wrath on his
head, did she know, that, owing to his absence from his
little charge, the dreaded invader had managed to have two
interviews with her grandchild, on the very spot that Elsie
deemed the fortress of security; but he wisely kept his own
counsel, believing in the eternal value of silence. In
truth, the gentle monk lived so much in the unreal and
celestial world of Beauty, that he was by no means a skillful guide for the passes of common life. Love, other than

that ethereal kind which aspires towards Paradise, was a
stranger to his thoughts, and he constantly erred in attri-
buting to other people natures and purposes as unworldly
and spiritual as his own.   Thus had he fallen, in his utter
simplicity, into the attitude of a go-between protecting the
advances of a young lover with the shadow of his monk's
gown, and he became awkwardly conscious that, if Elsie
should find out the whole truth, there would be no possibility of convincing her that what had been done in such
sacred simplicity on all sides was not the basest manœu-
vring.

Elsie took Agnes down with her to the old stand in the
gateway of the town.   On their way, as had probably been
arranged, Antonio met them.   We may have introduced
him to the reader before, who likely enough has forgotten
by this time our portraiture; so we shall say again, that
the man was past thirty, tall, straight, well-made, even to
the tapering of his well-formed limbs, as are the generality
of the peasantry of that favored region.   His teeth were
white as sea-pearl; his cheek, though swarthy, had a deep,
healthy flush; and his great velvet black eyes looked
straight out from under their long silky lashes, just as do
the eyes of the beautiful oxen of his country, with a languid, changeless tranquillity, betokening a good digestion,
and a well-fed, kindly animal nature.   He was evidently
a creature that had been nourished on sweet juices and
developed in fair pastures, under genial influences of sun
and weather, — one that would draw patiently in harness,
if required, without troubling his handsome head how he
came there, and, his labor being done, would stretch his
healthy body to rumination, and rest with serene, even
unreflecting quietude.

He had been duly lectured by his mother, this morning,
on the propriety of commencing his wooing, and was coming towards them with a bouquet in his hand.

"See there," said Elsie, "there is our young neighbor
Antonio coming towards us. There is a youth whom I am
willing you should speak to; none of your ruffian gallants,
but steady as an ox at his work, and as kind at the crib.
Happy will the girl be that gets him for a husband!"

Agnes was somewhat troubled and saddened this morning, and absorbed in cares quite new to her life before;
but her nature was ever kindly and social, and it had been
laid under so many restrictions by her grandmother's close
method of bringing up, that it was always ready to rebound
in favor of anybody to whom she allowed her to show kindness. So, when the young man stopped and shyly reached
forth to her a knot of scarlet poppies intermingled with
bright vetches and wild blue larkspurs, she took it gra-
ciously, and, frankly beaming a smile into his face, said, —

"Thank you, my good Antonio!" Then fastening them
in the front of her bodice, "There, they are beautiful!"
she said, looking up with the simple satisfaction of a child.

"They are not half so beautiful as you are," said the
young peasant; "everybody likes you."

"You are very kind, I am sure," said Agnes. "I like
everybody, as far as grandmamma thinks it best."

"I am glad of that," said Antonio, "because then I
hope you will like me."

"Oh, yes, certainly, I do; grandmamma says you are
very good, and I like all good people."

"Well, then, pretty Agnes," said the young man, "let
me carry your basket."

"Oh, you don't need to; it does not tire me."

"But I should like to do something for you," insisted
the young man, blushing deeply.

"Well, you may, then," said Agnes, who began to wonder at the length of time her grandmother allowed this
conversation to go on without interrupting it, as she generally had done when a young man was in the case. Quite

to her astonishment, her venerable relative, instead of sticking as close to her as her shadow, was walking forward very fast without looking behind.

"Now, Holy Mother," said that excellent matron, "do help this young man to bring this affair out straight, and give an old woman, who has had a world of troubles, a little peace in her old age!"

Agnes found herself, therefore, quite unusually situated, alone in the company of a handsome young man, and apparently with the consent of her grandmother. Some girls might have felt emotions of embarrassment, or even alarm, at this new situation; but the sacred loneliness and seclusion in which Agnes had been educated had given her a confiding fearlessness, such as voyagers have found in the birds of bright foreign islands which have never been invaded by man. She looked up at Antonio with a pleased, admiring smile, — much such as she would have given, if a great handsome stag, or other sylvan companion, had stepped from the forest and looked a friendship at her through his large liquid eyes. She seemed, in an innocent, frank way, to like to have him walking by her, and thought him very good to carry her basket, — though, as she told him, he need not do it, it did not tire her in the least.

"Nor does it tire me, pretty Agnes," said he, with an embarrassed laugh. "See what a great fellow I am, — how strong! Look, — I can bend an iron bar in my hands! I am as strong as an ox, — and I should like always to use my strength for you."

"Should you? How very kind of you! It is very Christian to use one's strength for others, like the good Saint Christopher."

"But I would use my strength for you because — I love you, gentle Agnes!"

"That is right, too," replied Agnes. "We must all love one another, my good Antonio."

"You must know what I mean," said the young man. "I mean that I want to marry you."

"I am sorry for that, Antonio," replied Agnes, gravely; "because I do not want to marry you. I am never going to marry anybody."

"Ah, girls always talk so, my mother told me; but nobody ever heard of a girl that did not want a husband; that is impossible," said Antonio, with simplicity.

"I believe girls generally do, Antonio; but I do not: my desire is to go to the convent."

"To the convent, pretty Agnes? Of all things, what should you want to go to the convent for? You never had any trouble. You are young, and handsome, and healthy, and almost any of the fellows would think himself fortunate to get you."

"I would go there to live for God and pray for souls," said Agnes.

"But your grandmother will never let you; she means you shall marry me. I heard her and my mother talking about it last night; and my mother bade me come on, for she said it was all settled."

"I never heard anything of it," said Agnes, now for the first time feeling troubled. "But, my good Antonio, if you really do like me and wish me well, you will not want to distress me?"

"Certainly not."

"Well, it *will* distress me very, very much, if you persist in wanting to marry me, and if you say any more on the subject."

"Is that really so?" said Antonio, fixing his great velvet eyes with an honest stare on Agnes.

"Yes, it is so, Antonio; you may rely upon it."

"But look here, Agnes, are you quite sure? Mother says girls do not always know their mind."

"But I know mine, Antonio. Now you really will

distress and trouble me very much, if you say anything more of this sort."

"I declare, I am sorry for it," said the young man. "Look ye, Agnes, I did not care half as much about it this morning as I do now. Mother has been saying this great while that I must have a wife, that she was getting old; and this morning she told me to speak to you. I thought you would be all ready, — indeed I did."

"My good Antonio, there are a great many very handsome girls who would be glad, I suppose, to marry you. I believe other girls do not feel as I do. Giulietta used to laugh and tell me so."

"That Giulietta was a splendid girl," said Antonio. "She used to make great eyes at me, and try to make me play the fool; but my mother would not hear of her. Now she has gone off with a fellow to the mountains."

"Giulietta gone?"

"Yes, haven't you heard of it? She's gone with one of the fellows of that dashing young robber-captain that has been round our town so much lately. All the girls are wild after these mountain fellows. A good, honest boy like me, that hammers away at his trade, they think nothing of; whereas one of these fellows with a feather in his cap has only to twinkle his finger at them, and they are off like a bird."

The blood rose in Agnes's cheeks at this very unconscious remark; but she walked along for some time with a countenance of grave reflection.

They had now gained the street of the city, where old Elsie stood at a little distance waiting for them.

"Well, Agnes," said Antonio, "so you really are in earnest?"

"Certainly I am."

"Well, then, let us be good friends, at any rate," said the young man.

"Oh, to be sure, I will," said Agnes, smiling with all the brightness her lovely face was capable of. "You are a kind, good man, and I like you very much. I will always remember you kindly."

"Well, good-by, then," said Antonio, offering his hand.

"Good-by," said Agnes, cheerfully giving hers.

Elsie, beholding the cordiality of this parting, comforted herself that all was right, and ruffled all her feathers with the satisfied pride of a matron whose family plans are succeeding.

"After all," she said to herself, "brother was right, — best let young folks settle these matters themselves. Now see the advantage of such an education as I have given Agnes! Instead of being betrothed to a good, honest, forehanded fellow, she might have been losing her poor silly heart to some of these lords or gallants who throw away a girl as one does an orange when they have sucked it. Who knows what mischief this cavalier might have done, if I had not been so watchful? Now let him come prying and spying about, she will have a husband to defend her. A smith's hammer is better than an old woman's spindle, any day."

Agnes took her seat with her usual air of thoughtful gravity, her mind seeming to be intensely preoccupied, and her grandmother, though secretly exulting in the supposed cause, resolved not to open the subject with her till they were at home or alone at night.

"I have my defense to make to Father Francesco, too," she said to herself, "for hurrying on this betrothal against his advice; but one must manage a little with these priests, — the saints forgive me! I really think sometimes, because they can't marry themselves, they would rather see every pretty girl in a convent than with a husband. It's natural enough, too. Father Francesco will be like the rest of the world: when he can't help a thing, he will see the will of the Lord in it."

Thus prosperously the world seemed to go with old Elsie. Meantime, when her back was turned, as she was kneeling over her basket, sorting out lemons, Agnes happened to look up, and there, just under the arch of the gateway, where she had seen him the first time, sat the cavalier on a splendid horse, with a white feather streaming backward from his black riding-hat and dark curls.

He bowed low and kissed his hand to her, and before she knew it her eyes met his, which seemed to flash light and sunshine all through her; and then he turned his horse and was gone through the gate, while she, filled with self-reproach, was taking her little heart to task for the instantaneous throb of happiness which had passed through her whole being at that sight. She had not turned away her head nor said a prayer, as Father Francesco told her to do, because the whole thing had been sudden as a flash; but now it was gone, she prayed, "My God, help me not to love him! — let me love Thee alone!" But many times in the course of the day, as she twisted her flax, she found herself wondering whither he could be going. Had he really gone to that enchanted cloud-land, in the old purple Apennines, whither he wanted to carry her, — gone, perhaps, never to return? That was best. But was he reconciled with the Church? Was that great, splendid soul that looked out of those eyes to be forever lost, or would the pious exhortations of her uncle avail? And then she thought he had said to her, that, if she would go with him, he would confess and take the sacrament, and be reconciled with the Church, and so his soul be saved.

She resolved to tell this to Father Francesco. Perhaps he would — No, — she shivered as she remembered the severe, withering look with which the holy father had spoken of him, and the awfulness of his manner, — he would never consent.   And then her grandmother —   No, there was no possibility.

Meanwhile Agnes's good old uncle sat in the orange-shaded garden, busily perfecting his sketches; but his mind was distracted, and his thoughts wandered, — and often he rose, and, leaving his drawings, would pace up and down the little place, absorbed in earnest prayer.   The thought of his master's position was hourly growing upon him. The real world with its hungry and angry tide was each hour washing higher and higher up on the airy shore of the ideal, and bearing the pearls and enchanted shells of fancy out into its salt and muddy waters.

"Oh, my master! my father!" he said, "is the martyr's crown of fire indeed waiting thee?   Will God desert His own?   But was not Christ crucified? — and the disciple is not above his master, nor the servant above his lord.   But surely Florence will not consent.   The whole city will make a stand for him; — they are ready, if need be, to pluck out their eyes and give them to him.   Florence will certainly be a refuge for him.   But why do I put confidence in man?   In the Lord alone have I righteousness and strength."

And the old monk raised the psalm, "*Quare fremunt gentes*," and his voice rose and fell through the flowery recesses and dripping grottoes of the old gorge, sad and earnest like the protest of the few and feeble of Christ's own against the rushing legions of the world.   Yet, as he sang, courage and holy hope came into his soul from the sacred words, — just such courage as they brought to Luther and to the Puritans in later times.

CHAPTER XVII

THE MONK'S DEPARTURE

THE three inhabitants of the little dove-cot were sitting in their garden after supper, enjoying the cool freshness. The place was perfumed with the smell of orange-blossoms, brought out by gentle showers that had fallen during the latter part of the afternoon, and all three felt the tranquillizing effects of the sweet evening air. The monk sat bending over his drawings, resting the frame on which they lay on the mossy garden-wall, so as to get the latest advantage of the rich golden twilight which now twinkled through the sky. Agnes sat by him on the same wall, — now glancing over his shoulder at his work, and now leaning thoughtfully on her elbow, gazing pensively down into the deep shadows of the gorge, or out where the golden light of evening streamed under the arches of the old Roman bridge, to the wide, bright sea beyond.

Old Elsie bustled about with unusual content in the lines of her keen, wrinkled face. Already her thoughts were running on household furnishing and bridal finery. She unlocked an old chest, which from its heavy, quaint carvings of dark wood must have been some relic of the fortunes of her better days, and, taking out of a little till of the same a string of fine, silvery pearls, held them up admiringly to the evening light. A splendid pair of pearl ear-rings also was produced from the same receptacle.

She sighed at first, as she looked at these things, and then smiled with rather an air of triumph, and, coming to where Agnes reclined on the wall, held them up playfully before her.

"See here, little one!" she said.

"Oh, what pretty things! — where did they come from?" said Agnes, innocently.

"Where did they? Sure enough! Little did you or any one else know old Elsie had things like these! But she meant her little Agnes should hold up her head with the best. No girl in Sorrento will have such wedding finery as this!"

"Wedding finery, grandmamma," said Agnes, faintly, "what does that mean?"

"What does that mean, sly-boots? Ah, you know well enough! What were you and Antonio talking about all the time this morning? Did he not ask you to marry him?"

"Yes, grandmamma; but I told him I was not going to marry. You promised me, dear grandmother, right here, the other night, that I should not marry till I was willing; and I told Antonio I was not willing."

"The girl says but true, sister," said the monk; "you remember you gave her your word that she should not be married till she gave her consent willingly."

"But, Agnes, my pretty one, what can be the objection?" said old Elsie, coaxingly. "Where will you find a better-made man, or more honest, or more kind? — and he is handsome; — and you will have a home that all the girls will envy."

"Grandmamma, remember, you promised me, — you *promised* me," said Agnes, looking distressed, and speaking earnestly.

"Well, well, child! but can't I ask a civil question, if I did? What is your objection to Antonio?"

"Only that I don't want to be married."

"Now you know, child," said Elsie, "I never will consent to your going to a convent. You might as well put a knife through my old heart as talk to me of that. And if you don't go, you must marry somebody; and who could be better than Antonio?"

"Oh, grandmamma, am I not a good girl? What have I done, that you are so anxious to get me away from you?" said Agnes. "I like Antonio well enough, but I like you ten thousand times better. Why cannot we live together just as we do now? I am strong. I can work a great deal harder than I do. You ought to let me work more, so that you need not work so hard and tire yourself, — let me carry the heavy basket, and dig round the trees."

"Pooh! a pretty story!" said Elsie. "We are two lone women, and the times are unsettled; there are robbers and loose fellows about, and we want a protector."

"And is not the good Lord our protector? — has He not always kept us, grandmother?" said Agnes.

"Oh, that's well enough to say, but folks can't always get along so; it's far better trusting the Lord with a good strong man about, — like Antonio, for instance. I should like to see the man that would dare be uncivil to *his* wife. But go your ways; it's no use toiling away one's life for children, who, after all, won't turn their little finger for you."

"Now, dear grandmother," said Agnes, "have I not said I would do everything for you, and work hard for you? Ask me to do anything else in the world, grandmamma; I will do anything to make you happy, except marry this man, — that I cannot."

"And that is the only thing I want you to do. Well, I suppose I may as well lock up these things; I see my gifts are not cared for."

And the old soul turned and went in quite testily, leaving Agnes with a grieved heart, sitting still by her uncle.

"Never weep, little one," said the kind old monk, when he saw the silent tears falling one after another; "your grandmother loves you, after all, and will come out of this, if we are quiet."

"This is such a beautiful world," said Agnes, "who would think it would be such a hard one to live in?— such battles and conflicts as people have here!"

"You say well, little heart; but great is the glory to be revealed; so let us have courage."

"Dear uncle, have you heard any ill-tidings of late?" asked Agnes. "I noticed this morning you were cast down, and to-night you look so tired and sad."

"Yes, dear child,—heavy tidings have indeed come. My dear master at Florence is hard beset by wicked men, and in great danger,—in danger, perhaps, of falling a martyr to his holy zeal for the blessed Jesus and his Church."

"But cannot our holy father, the Pope, protect him? You should go to Rome directly and lay the case before him."

"It is not always possible to be protected by the Pope," said Father Antonio, evasively. "But I grieve much, dear child, that I can be with you no longer. I must gird up my loins and set out for Florence, to see with my own eyes how the battle is going for my holy master."

"Ah, must I lose you, too, my dear, best friend?" said Agnes. "What shall I do?"

"Thou hast the same Lord Jesus, and the same dear Mother, when I am gone. Have faith in God, and cease not to pray for His Church,—and for me, too."

"That I will, dear uncle! I will pray for you more than ever, for prayer now will be all my comfort. But," she added, with hesitation, "oh, uncle, you promised to visit *him!*"

"Never fear, little Agnes, I will do that. I go to him this very night,—now even,—for the daylight waxes too scant for me to work longer."

"But you will come back and stay with us to-night, uncle?"

"Yes, I will,—but to-morrow morning I must be up

and away with the birds; and I have labored hard all day to finish the drawings for the lad who shall carve the shrine, that he may busy himself thereon in my absence."

"Then you will come back?"

"Certainly, dear heart, I will come back; of that be assured. Pray God it be before long, too."

So saying, the good monk drew his cowl over his head, and, putting his portfolio of drawings under his arm, began to wend his way towards the old town.

Agnes watched him departing, her heart in a strange flutter of eagerness and solicitude. What were these dreadful troubles which were coming upon her good uncle? — who those enemies of the Church that beset that saintly teacher he so much looked up to? And why was lawless violence allowed to run such riot in Italy, as it had in the case of the unfortunate cavalier? As she thought things over, she was burning with a repressed desire to *do* something herself to abate these troubles.

"I am not a knight," she said to herself, "and I cannot fight for the good cause. I am not a priest, and I cannot argue for it. I cannot preach and convert sinners. What, then, can I do? I can pray. Suppose I should make a pilgrimage? Yes, — that would be a good work, and I will. I will walk to Rome, praying at every shrine and holy place; and then, when I come to the Holy City, whose very dust is made precious with the blood of the martyrs and saints, I will seek the house of our dear father, the Pope, and entreat his forgiveness for this poor soul. He will not scorn me, for he is in the place of the blessed Jesus, and the richest princess and the poorest maiden are equal in his sight. Ah, that will be beautiful! Holy Mother," she said, falling on her knees before the shrine, "here I vow and promise that I will go praying to the Holy City. Smile on me and help me!"

And by the twinkle of the flickering lamp which threw

its light upon the picture, Agnes thought surely the placid face brightened to a tender maternal smile, and her enthusiastic imagination saw in this an omen of success.

Old Elsie was moody and silent this evening, — vexed at the thwarting of her schemes. It was the first time that the idea had ever gained a foothold in her mind, that her docile and tractable grandchild could really have for any serious length of time a will opposed to her own, and she found it even now difficult to believe it. Hitherto she had shaped her life as easily as she could mould a biscuit, and it was all plain sailing before her. The force and decision of this young will rose as suddenly upon her as the one rock in the middle of the ocean which a voyager unexpectedly discovered by striking on it.

But Elsie by no means regarded the game as lost. She mentally went over the field, considering here and there what was yet to be done.

The subject had fairly been broached. Agnes had listened to it, and parted in friendship from Antonio. Now his old mother must be soothed and pacified; and Antonio must be made to persevere.

"What is a girl worth that can be won at the first asking?" quoth Elsie. "Depend upon it, she will fall to thinking of him, and the next time she sees him she will give him a good look. The girl never knew what it was to have a lover. No wonder she does n't take to it at first; there 's where her bringing up comes in, so different from other girls'. Courage, Elsie! Nature will speak in its own time."

Thus soliloquizing, she prepared to go a few steps from their dwelling, to the cottage of Meta and Antonio, which was situated at no great distance.

"Nobody will think of coming here this time o' night," she said, "and the girl is in for a good hour at least with her prayers, and so I think I may venture. I don't really like to leave her, but it's not a great way, and I shall be back in a few moments. I want just to put a word into old Meta's ear, that she may teach Antonio how to demean himself."

And so the old soul took her spinning and away she went, leaving Agnes absorbed in her devotions.

The solemn starry night looked down steadfastly on the little garden. The evening wind creeping with gentle stir among the orange-leaves, and the falling waters of the fountain dripping their distant, solitary way down from rock to rock through the lonely gorge, were the only sounds that broke the stillness.

The monk was the first of the two to return; for those accustomed to the habits of elderly cronies on a gossiping expedition of any domestic importance will not be surprised that Elsie's few moments of projected talk lengthened imperceptibly into hours.

Agnes came forward anxiously to meet her uncle. He seemed wan and haggard, and trembling with some recent emotion.

"What is the matter with you, dear uncle?" she asked. "Has anything happened?"

"Nothing, child, nothing. I have only been talking on painful subjects, deep perplexities, out of which I can scarcely see my way. Would to God this night of life were past, and I could see morning on the mountains!"

"My uncle, have you not, then, succeeded in bringing this young man to the bosom of the True Church?"

"Child, the way is hedged up, and made almost impassable by difficulties you little wot of. They cannot be told to you; they are enough to destroy the faith of the very elect."

Agnes's heart sank within her; and the monk, sitting down on the wall of the garden, clasped his hands over one knee and gazed fixedly before him.

The sight of her uncle, — generally so cheerful, so elastic, so full of bright thoughts and beautiful words, — so utterly cast down, was both a mystery and a terror to Agnes.

"Oh, my uncle," she said, "it is hard that I must not know, and that I can do nothing, when I feel ready to die for this cause! What is one little life? Ah, if I had a thousand to give, I could melt them all into it, like little drops of rain in the sea! Be not utterly cast down, good uncle! Does not our dear Lord and Saviour reign in the heavens yet?"

"Sweet little nightingale!" said the monk, stretching his hand towards her. "Well did my master say that he gained strength to his soul always by talking with Christ's little children!"

"And all the dear saints and angels, they are not dead or idle either," said Agnes, her face kindling: "they are busy all around us. I know not what this trouble is you speak of; but let us think what legions of bright angels and holy men and women are caring for us."

"Well said, well said, dear child! There is, thank God, a Church Triumphant, — a crowned queen, a glorious bride; and the poor, struggling Church Militant shall rise to join her! What matter, then, though our way lie through dungeon and chains, through fire and sword, if we may attain to that glory at last?"

"Uncle, are there such dreadful things really before you?"

"There may be, child. I say of my master, as did the holy Apostles: 'Let us also go, that we may die with him.' I feel a heavy presage. But I must not trouble you, child. Early in the morning I will be up and away. I go with this youth, whose pathway lies a certain distance along mine, and whose company I seek for his good as well as my pleasure."

"You go with *him?*" said Agnes, with a start of surprise.

"Yes; his refuge in the mountains lies between here and Rome, and he hath kindly offered to bring me on my way faster than I can go on foot; and I would fain see our beautiful Florence as soon as may be. O Florence, Florence, Lily of Italy! wilt thou let thy prophet perish?"

"But, uncle, if he die for the faith, he will be a blessed martyr. That crown is worth dying for," said Agnes.

"You say well, little one, — you say well! '*Ex oribus parvulorum.*' But one shrinks from that in the person of a friend which one could cheerfully welcome for one's self. Oh, the blessed cross! never is it welcome to the flesh, and yet how joyfully the spirit may walk under it!"

"Dear uncle, I have made a solemn vow before our Holy Mother this night," said Agnes, "to go on a pilgrimage to Rome, and at every shrine and holy place to pray that these great afflictions which beset all of you may have a happy issue."

"My sweet heart, what have you done? Have you considered the unsettled roads, the wild, unruly men that are abroad, the robbers with which the mountains are filled?"

"These are all Christ's children and my brothers," said Agnes; "for them was the most holy blood shed, as well as for me. They cannot harm one who prays for them."

"But, dear heart of mine, these ungodly brawlers think little of prayer; and this beautiful, innocent little face will but move the vilest and most brutal thoughts and deeds."

"Saint Agnes still lives, dear uncle, — and He who kept her in worse trial. I shall walk through them all pure as snow, — I am assured I shall. The star which led the wise men and stood over the young child and his mother will lead me, too."

"But your grandmother?"

"The Lord will incline her heart to go with me. Dear

uncle, it does not beseem a child to reflect on its elders, yet I cannot but see that grandmamma loves this world and me too well for her soul's good. This journey will be for her eternal repose."

"Well, well, dear one, I cannot now advise. Take advice of your confessor, and the blessed Lord and his holy Mother be with you! But come now, I would soothe myself to sleep; for I have need of good rest to-night. Let us sing together our dear master's hymn of the Cross."

And the monk and the maiden sung together: —

> "Iesù, sommo conforto,
> Tu sei tutto il mio amore
> E 'l mio beato porto,
> E santo Redentore.
>   O gran bontà,
>   Dolce pietà,
>   Felice quel che teco unito sta!
>
> "Deh, quante volte offeso
> T' ha l' alma e 'l cor meschino,
> E tu sei in croce steso
> Per salvar me, tapino!
>
> "Iesù, fuss' io confitto
> Sopra quel duro ligno,
> Dove ti vedo afflitto,
> Iesù, Signor benigno !
>
> "O croce, fammi loco,
> E le mie membra prendi,
> Che del tuo dolce foco
> Il cor e l' alma accendi!
>
> "Infiamma il mio cor tanto
> Dell' amor tuo divino,
> Ch' io arda tutto quanto,
> Che paia un serafino!
>
> "La croce e 'l Crocifisso
> Sia nel mio cor scolpito,
> Ed io sia sempre affisso
> In gloria ov' egli è ito!" [1]

[1] Jesus, best comfort of my soul,
    Be Thou my only love,

As the monk sung, his soul seemed to fuse itself into the sentiment with that natural grace peculiar to his nation. He walked up and down the little garden, apparently forgetful of Agnes or of any earthly presence, and in the last verses stretched his hands towards heaven with streaming tears and a fervor of utterance indescribable.

The soft and passionate tenderness of the Italian words must exhale in an English translation, but enough may remain to show that the hymns with which Savonarola at this time sowed the mind of Italy often mingled the Moravian quaintness and energy with the Wesleyan purity and tenderness. One of the great means of popular reform which he proposed was the supplanting of the obscene and licentious songs, which at that time so generally defiled the

> My sacred saviour from my sins,
>   My door to heaven above!
> O lofty goodness, love divine,
>   Blest is the soul made one with thine!
>
> Alas, how oft this sordid heart
>   Hath wounded thy pure eye!
> Yet for this heart upon the cross
>   Thou gav'st thyself to die!
>
> Ah, would I were extended there
>   Upon that cold, hard tree,
> Where I have seen Thee, gracious Lord,
>   Breathe out thy life for me!
>
> Cross of my Lord, give room! give room!
>   To Thee my flesh be given!
> Cleansed in thy fires of love and pain,
>   My soul rise pure to heaven!
>
> Burn in my heart, celestial flame,
>   With memories of Him,
> Till, from earth's dross refined, I rise
>   To join the seraphim!
>
> Ah, vanish each unworthy trace
>   Of earthly care or pride,
> Leave only, graven on my heart,
>   The Cross, the Crucified!

minds of the young, by religious words and melodies. The children and young people brought up under his influence were sedulously stored with treasures of sacred melody, as the safest companions of leisure hours, and the surest guard against temptation.

"Come now, my little one," said the monk, after they had ceased singing, as he laid his hand on Agnes's head. "I am strong now; I know where I stand. And you, my little one, you are one of my master's ' Children of the Cross.' You must sing the hymns of our dear master, that I taught you, when I am far away. A hymn is a singing angel, and goes walking through the earth, scattering the devils before it. Therefore he who creates hymns imitates the most excellent and lovely works of our Lord God, who made the angels. These hymns watch our chamber-door, they sit upon our pillow, they sing to us when we awake; and therefore our master was resolved to sow the minds of his young people with them, as our lovely Italy is sown with the seeds of all colored flowers. How lovely has it often been to me, as I sat at my work in Florence, to hear the little children go by, chanting of Jesus and Mary, — and young men singing to young maidens, not vain flatteries of their beauty, but the praises of the One only Beautiful, whose smile sows heaven with stars like flowers! Ah, in my day I have seen blessed times in Florence! Truly was she worthy to be called the Lily City! — for all her care seemed to be to make white her garments to receive her Lord and Bridegroom. Yes, though she had sinned like the Magdalen, yet she loved much, like her. She washed His feet with her tears, and wiped them with the hair of her head. Oh, my beautiful Florence, be true to thy vows, be true to thy Lord and Governor, Jesus Christ, and all shall be well!"

"Amen, dear uncle!" said Agnes. "I will not fail to pray day and night, that thus it may be. And now, if you must travel so far, you must go to rest. Grandmamma has gone long ago. I saw her steal by as we were singing."

"And is there any message from my little Agnes to this young man?" asked the monk.

"Yes. Say to him that Agnes prays daily that he may be a worthy son and soldier of the Lord Jesus."

"Amen, sweet heart! Jesus and His sweet Mother bless thee!"

CHAPTER XVIII

THE PENANCE

THE course of our story requires us to return to the Capuchin convent, and to the struggles and trials of its Superior; for in his hands is the irresistible authority which must direct the future life of Agnes.

From no guilty compliances, no heedless running into temptation, had he come to love her. The temptation had met him in the direct path of duty; the poison had been breathed in with the perfume of sweetest and most life-giving flowers: nor could he shun that temptation, nor cease to inhale that fatal sweetness, without confessing himself vanquished in a point where, in his view, to yield was to be lost. The subtle and deceitful visit of Father Johannes to his cell had the effect of thoroughly rousing him to a complete sense of his position, and making him feel the immediate, absolute necessity of bringing all the energy of his will, all the resources of his nature, to bear on its present difficulties. For he felt, by a fine intuition, that already he was watched and suspected; any faltering step now, any wavering, any change in his mode of treating his female penitents, would be maliciously noted. The military education of his early days had still left in his mind a strong residuum of personal courage and honor, which made him regard it as dastardly to flee when he ought to conquer, and therefore he set his face as a flint for victory.

But reviewing his interior world, and taking a survey of the work before him, he felt that sense of a divided personality which often becomes so vivid in the history of individuals of strong will and passion. It seemed to him that there were two men within him: the one turbulent, passionate, demented; the other vainly endeavoring by authority, reason, and conscience to bring the rebel to subjection. The discipline of conventual life, the extraordinary austerities to which he had condemned himself, the monotonous solitude of his existence, all tended to exalt the vivacity of the nervous system, which, in the Italian constitution, is at all times disproportionately developed; and when those weird harp-strings of the nerves are once thoroughly unstrung, the fury and tempest of the discord sometimes utterly bewilders the most practiced self-government.

But he felt that *something* must be done with himself, and done immediately; for in a few days he must again meet Agnes at the confessional. He must meet her, not with weak tremblings and passionate fears, but calm as Fate, inexorable as the Judgment-Day. He must hear her confession, not as man, but as God; he must pronounce his judgments with a divine dispassionateness. He must dive into the recesses of her secret heart, and, following with subtile analysis all the fine courses of those fibres which were feeling their blind way towards an earthly love, must tear them remorselessly away. Well could he warn her of the insidiousness of earthly affections; better than any one else he could show her how a name that was blended with her prayers and borne before the sacred shrine in her most retired and solemn hours might at last come to fill all her heart with a presence too dangerously dear. He must direct her gaze up those mystical heights where an unearthly marriage awaited her, its sealed and spiritual bride; he must hurry her footsteps onward to the irrevocable issue.

All this was before him. But ere it could be done, he must subdue himself, — he must become calm and pulseless, in deadly resolve; and what prayer, what penance,

might avail for this? If all that he had already tried had
so miserably failed, what hope? He resolved to quit for
a season all human society, and enter upon one of those
desolate periods of retreat from earthly converse well known
in the annals of saintship as most prolific in spiritual victories.

Accordingly, on the day after the conversation with
Father Johannes, he startled the monks by announcing to
them that he was going to leave them for several days.

"My brothers," he said, "the weight of a fearful penance is laid upon me, which I must work out alone. I
leave you to-day, and charge you not to seek to follow my
footsteps; but, as you hope to escape hell, watch and
wrestle for me and yourselves during the time I am gone.
Before many days I hope to return to you with renewed
spiritual strength."

That evening, while Agnes and her uncle were sitting
together in their orange-garden, mingling their parting
prayers and hymns, scenes of a very different description
surrounded the Father Francesco.

One who looks on the flowery fields and blue seas of this
enchanting region thinks that the Isles of the Blest could
scarcely find on earth a more fitting image; nor can he
realize, till experience proves it to him, that he is in the
immediate vicinity of a weird and dreary region which
might represent no less the goblin horrors of the damned.

Around the foot of Vesuvius lie fair villages and villas,
garlanded with roses and flushing with grapes, whose juice
gains warmth from the breathing of its subterraneous fires,
while just above them rises a region more awful than can
be created by the action of any common causes of sterility.
There, immense tracts sloping gradually upward show a
desolation so peculiar, so utterly unlike every common solitude of Nature, that one enters upon it with the shudder
we give at that which is wholly unnatural. On all sides

are gigantic serpent convolutions of black lava, their immense folds rolled into every conceivable contortion, as if, in their fiery agonies, they had struggled and wreathed and knotted together, and then grown cold and black with the imperishable signs of those terrific convulsions upon them. Not a blade of grass, not a flower, not even the hardiest lichen, springs up to relieve the utter deathliness of the scene. The eye wanders from one black, shapeless mass to another, and there is ever the same suggestion of hideous monster life, of goblin convulsions and strange fiend-like agonies in some age gone by. One's very footsteps have an unnatural, metallic clink, and one's garments brushing over the rough surface are torn and fretted by its sharp, remorseless touch, as if its very nature were so pitiless and acrid that the slightest contact revealed it.

The sun was just setting over the beautiful Bay of Naples, — with its enchanted islands, its jeweled city, its flowery villages, all bedecked and bedropped with strange shiftings and flushes of prismatic light and shade, as if they belonged to some fairy-land of perpetual festivity and singing, — when Father Francesco stopped in his toilsome ascent up the mountain, and seating himself on ropy ridges of black lava, looked down on the peaceful landscape.

Above his head, behind him, rose the black cone of the mountain, over whose top the lazy clouds of thin white smoke were floating, tinged with the evening light; around him, the desolate convulsed waste, so arid, so supernaturally dreary; and below, like a soft enchanted dream, the beautiful bay, the gleaming white villas and towers, the picturesque islands, the gliding sails, flecked and streaked and dyed with the violet and pink and purple of the evening sky. The thin new moon and one glittering star trembled through the rosy air.

The monk wiped from his brow the sweat that had been caused by the toil of his hurried journey, and listened

to the bells of the Ave Maria pealing from the different
churches of Naples, filling the atmosphere with a soft tremble of solemn dropping sound, as if spirits in the air took
up and repeated over and over the angelic salutation which
a thousand earthly lips were just then uttering.   Mechanically he joined in the invocation which at that moment
united the hearts of all Christians, and as the words passed
his lips, he thought, with a sad, desolate longing, of the
hour of death of which they spake.

"It must come at last," he said.   "Life is but a moment.   Why am I so cowardly? why so unwilling to suffer
and to struggle?   Am I a warrior of the Lord, and do I
shrink from the toils of the camp, and long for the ease of
the court before I have earned it?   Why do we clamor for
happiness?   Why should we sinners be happy?   And yet,
O God, why is the world made so lovely as it lies there,
why so rejoicing, and so girt with splendor and beauty, if
we are never to enjoy it?   If penance and toil were all
we were sent here for, why not make a world grim and
desolate as this around me? — then there would be nothing
to seduce us.   But our path is a constant fight; Nature is
made only to be resisted; we must walk the sharp blade of
the sword over the fiery chasm to Paradise.   Come, then!
— no shrinking! — let me turn my back on everything dear
and beautiful, as now on this landscape!"

He rose and commenced the perpendicular ascent of the
cone, stumbling and climbing over the huge sliding blocks
of broken lava, which grated and crunched beneath his feet
with a harsh metallic ring.   Sometimes a broken fragment
or two would go tinkling down the rough path behind him,
and sometimes it seemed as if the whole loose black mass
from above were about to slide, like an avalanche, down
upon his head; — he almost hoped it would.   Sometimes
he would stop, overcome by the toil of the ascent, and seat
himself for a moment on a black fragment, and then his

eye would wander over the wide and peaceful panorama below. He seemed to himself like a fly perched upon some little roughness of a perpendicular wall, and felt a strange airy sense of pleasure in being thus between earth and heaven. A sense of relief, of beauty, and peacefulness would steal over him, as if he were indeed something disfranchised and disembodied, a part of the harmonious and beautiful world that lay stretched out beneath him; in a moment more he would waken himself with a start, and resume his toilsome journey with a sullen and dogged perseverance.

At last he gained the top of the mountain, — that weird, strange region where the loose, hot soil, crumbling beneath his feet, was no honest foodful mother-earth, but an acrid mass of ashes and corrosive minerals. Arsenic, sulphur, and many a sharp and bitter salt were in all he touched, every rift in the ground hissed with stifling steam, while rolling clouds of dun sullen smoke, and a deep hollow booming, like the roar of an immense furnace, told his nearness to the great crater. He penetrated the sombre tabernacle, and stood on the very brink of a huge basin, formed by a wall of rocks around a sunken plain, in the midst of which rose the black cone of the subterraneous furnace, which crackled and roared, and from time to time spit up burning stones and cinders, or oozed out slow ropy streams of liquid fire.

The sulphurous cliffs were dyed in many a brilliant shade of brown and orange by the admixture of various ores, but their brightness seemed strange and unnatural, and the dizzying whirls of vapor, now enveloping the whole scene in gloom, now lifting in this spot and now in that, seemed to magnify the dismal pit to an indefinite size. Now and then there would come up from the very entrails of the mountain a sort of convulsed sob of hollow sound, and the earth would quiver beneath his feet, and fragments

from the surrounding rocks would scale off and fall with
crashing reverberations into the depth beneath; at such
moments it would seem as if the very mountain were about
to crush in and bear him down in its ruins.

Father Francesco, though blinded by the smoke and
choked by the vapor, could not be content without descending into the abyss and exploring the very *penetralia* of its
mysteries.   Steadying his way by means of a cord which
he fastened to a firm projecting rock, he began slowly and
painfully clambering downward.   The wind was sweeping
across the chasm from behind, bearing the noxious vapors
away from him, or he must inevitably have been stifled.
It took him some little time, however, to effect his descent;
but at length he found himself fairly landed on the dark
floor of the gloomy enclosure.

The ropy, pitch-black undulations of lava yawned here
and there in red-hot cracks and seams, making it appear to
be only a crust over some fathomless depth of molten fire,
whose moanings and boilings could be heard below.   These
dark congealed billows creaked and bent as the monk
stepped upon them, and burned his feet through his coarse
sandals; yet he stumbled on.   Now and then his foot
would crush in, where the lava had hardened in a thinner
crust, and he would draw it suddenly back from the lurid
red-hot metal beneath.   The staff on which he rested was
constantly kindling into a light blaze as it slipped into
some heated hollow, and he was fain to beat out the fire
upon the cooler surface.   Still he went on half-stifled by
the hot and pungent vapor, but drawn by that painful,
unnatural curiosity which possesses one in a nightmare
dream.   The great cone in the centre was the point to
which he wished to attain, — the nearest point which man
can gain to this eternal mystery of fire.   It was trembling
with a perpetual vibration, a hollow, pulsating undertone
of sound like the surging of the sea before a storm, and

the lava that boiled over its sides rolled slowly down with a strange creaking; it seemed the condensed, intensified essence and expression of eternal fire, rising and still rising from some inexhaustible fountain of burning.

Father Francesco drew as near as he could for the stifling heat and vapor, and, resting on his staff, stood gazing intently. The lurid light of the fire fell with an unearthly glare on his pale, sunken features, his wild, haggard eyes, and his torn and disarranged garments. In the awful solitude and silence of the night he felt his heart stand still, as if indeed he had touched with his very hand the gates of eternal woe, and felt its fiery breath upon his cheek. He half-imagined that the seams and clefts which glowed in lurid lines between the dark billows would gape yet wider and show the blasting secrets of some world of fiery despair below. He fancied that he heard behind and around the mocking laugh of fiends, and that confused clamor of mingled shrieks and lamentions which Dante describes as filling the dusky approaches to that forlorn realm where hope never enters.

"Ah, God," he exclaimed, "for this vain life of man! They eat, they drink, they dance, they sing, they marry and are given in marriage, they have castles and gardens and villas, and the very beauty of Paradise seems over it all, — and yet how close by burns and roars the eternal fire! Fools that we are, to clamor for indulgence and happiness in this life, when the question is, to escape everlasting burnings! If I tremble at this outer court of God's wrath and justice, what must be the fires of hell? These are but earthly fires; they can but burn the body: those are made to burn the soul; they are undying as the soul is. What would it be to be dragged down, down, down, into an abyss of soul-fire hotter than this for ages on ages? This might bring merciful death in time: that will have no end."

The monk fell on his knees and breathed out piercing supplications. Every nerve and fibre within him seemed tense with his agony of prayer. It was not the outcry for purity and peace, not a tender longing for forgiveness, not a filial remorse for sin, but the nervous anguish of him who shrieks in the immediate apprehension of an unendurable torture. It was the cry of a man upon the rack, the despairing scream of him who feels himself sinking in a burning dwelling. Such anguish has found an utterance in Stradella's celebrated "Pietà, Signore," which still tells to our ears, in its wild moans and piteous shrieks, the religious conceptions of his day; for there is no phase of the Italian mind that has not found expression in its music.

When the oppression of the heat and sulphurous vapor became too dreadful to be borne, the monk retraced his way and climbed with difficulty up the steep sides of the crater, till he gained the summit above, where a comparatively free air revived him. All night he wandered up and down in that dreary vicinity, now listening to the mournful roar and crackle of the fire, and now raising his voice in penitential psalms or the notes of that terrific "Dies Iræ" which sums up all the intense fear and horror with which the religion of the Middle Ages clothed the idea of the final catastrophe of humanity. Sometimes prostrating himself with his face towards the stifling soil, he prayed with agonized intensity till Nature would sink in a temporary collapse, and sleep, in spite of himself, would steal over him.

So waned the gloomy hours of the night away, till the morning broke in the east, turning all the blue wavering floor of the sea to crimson brightness, and bringing up, with the rising breeze, the barking of dogs, the lowing of kine, the songs of laborers and boatmen, all fresh and breezy from the repose of the past night.

Father Francesco heard the sound of approaching foot-steps climbing the lava path, and started with a nervous trepidation. Soon he recognized a poor peasant of the vicinity, whose child he had tended during a dangerous illness. He bore with him a little basket of eggs, with a melon and a fresh green salad.

"Good-morning, holy father," he said, bowing humbly. "I saw you coming this way last night, and I could hardly sleep for thinking of you; and my good woman, Teresina, would have it that I should come out to look after you. I have taken the liberty to bring a little offering; — it was the best we had."

"Thank you, my son," said the monk, looking wistfully at the fresh, honest face of the peasant. "You have taken too much trouble for such a sinner. I must not allow myself such indulgences."

"But your Reverence must live. Look you," said the peasant, "at least your Reverence will take an egg. See here, how handily I can cook one," he added, striking his stick into a little cavity of a rock, from which, as from an escape-valve, hissed a jet of hot steam, — "see here, I nestle the egg in this little cleft, and it will be done in a twinkling. Our good God gives us our fire for nothing here."

There was something wholesomely kindly and cheerful in the action and expression of the man, which broke upon the overstrained and disturbed musings of the monk like daylight on a ghastly dream. The honest, loving heart sees love in everything; even the fire is its fatherly helper, and not its avenging enemy.

Father Francesco took the egg, when it was done, with a silent gesture of thanks.

"If I might make bold to say," said the peasant, en-couraged, "your Reverence should have some care for your-self. If a man will not feed himself, the good God will not feed him; and we poor people have too few friends already to let such as you die. Your hands are trembling, and you look worn out. Surely you should take something more, for the very love of the poor."

"My son, I am bound to do a heavy penance, and to work out a great conflict. I thank you for your undeserved kindness. Leave me now to myself, and come no more to disturb my prayers. Go, and God bless you!"

"Well," said the peasant, putting down the basket and melon, "I shall leave these things here, any way, and I beg your Reverence to have a care of yourself. Teresina fretted all night for fear something might come to you. The *bambino* that you cured is grown a stout little fellow, and eats enough for two, — and it is all of you; so she cannot forget it. She is a busy little woman, is Teresina; and when she gets a thought in her head, it buzzes, buzzes, like a fly in a bottle, and she will have it your Reverence is killing yourself by inches, and says she, ' What will all the poor do when he is gone?' So your Reverence must pardon us. We mean it all for the best."

So saying, the man turned and began sliding and slipping down the steep ashy sides of the mountain cone with a dexterity which carried him to the bottom in a few moments; and on he went, sending back after him a cheerful little air, the refrain of which is still to be heard in our days in that neighborhood. A word or two of the gay song fluttered back on the ear of the monk, —

" Tutta gioja, tutta festa."

So gay and airy it was in its ringing cadence that it seemed a musical laugh springing from sunny skies, and came fluttering into the dismal smoke and gloom of the mountain-top like a very butterfly of sound. It struck on the sad, leaden ear of the monk much as we might fancy the carol of a robin over a grave might seem, could the cold sleeper

below wake one moment to its perception. If it woke one
regretful sigh and drew one wandering look downward to
the elysian paradise that lay smiling at the foot of the
mountain, he instantly suppressed the feeling and set his
face in its old deathly stillness.

CHAPTER XIX

CLOUDS DEEPENING

AFTER the departure of her uncle to Florence, the life of Agnes was troubled and harassed from a variety of causes.

First, her grandmother was sulky and moody, and though saying nothing directly on the topic nearest her heart, yet intimating by every look and action that she considered Agnes as a most ungrateful and contumacious child. Then there was a constant internal perplexity, — a constant wearying course of self-interrogation and self-distrust, the pain of a sensitive spirit which doubts at every moment whether it may not be falling into sin. The absence of her kind uncle at this time took from her the strongest support on which she had leaned in her perplexities. Cheerful, airy, and elastic in his temperament, always full of fresh-springing and beautiful thoughts, as an Italian dell is of flowers, the charming old man seemed, while he stayed with Agnes, to be the door of a new and fairer world, where she could walk in air and sunshine, and find utterance for a thousand thoughts and feelings which at all other times lay in cold repression in her heart. His counsels were always so wholesome, his sympathies so quick, his devotion so fervent and cheerful, that while with him Agnes felt the burden of her life insensibly lifted and carried for her as by some angel guide.

Now they had all come back upon her, heavier a thousand-fold than ever they had been before. Never did she so much need counsel and guidance, — never had she so much within herself to be solved and made plain to her

own comprehension; yet she thought with a strange shiver
of her next visit to her confessor. That austere man, so
chilling, so awful, so far above all conception of human
weaknesses, how should she dare to lay before him all the
secrets of her breast, especially when she must confess to
having disobeyed his most stringent commands? She had
had another interview with this forbidden son of perdition,
but how it was she knew not. How could such things
have happened? Instead of shutting her eyes and turning
her head and saying prayers, she had listened to a passionate declaration of love, and his last word had called her his
wife. Her heart thrilled every time she thought of it;
and somehow she could not feel sure that it was exactly
a thrill of penitence. It was all like a strange dream to
her; and sometimes she looked at her little brown hands
and wondered if he really had kissed them, — he, the splendid strange vision of a man, the prince from fairy-land!
Agnes had never read romances, it is true, but she had
been brought up on the legends of the saints, and there
never was a marvel possible to human conception that had
not been told there. Princes had come from China and
Barbary and Abyssinia and every other strange out-of-the-
way place, to kneel at the feet of fair, obdurate saints who
would not even turn the head to look at them; but she
had acted, she was conscious, after a much more mortal
fashion, and so made herself work for confession and penance. Yet certainly she had not meant to do so; the interview came on her so suddenly, so unexpectedly; and
somehow he *would* speak, and he would not go when she
asked him to; and she remembered how he looked when
he stood right before her in the door-way and told her she
should hear him, — how the color flushed up in his cheeks,
what a fire there was in his great dark eyes; he looked as
if he were going to do something desperate then; it made
her hold her breath even now to think of it.

"These princes and nobles," she thought, "are so used to command, it is no wonder they make us feel as if they must have their will. I have heard grandmother call them wolves and vultures, that are ready to tear us poor folk to pieces; but I am sure he seems gentle. I'm sure it isn't wicked or cruel for him to want to make me his wife; and he couldn't know, of course, why it wasn't right he should; and it really is beautiful of him to love me so. Oh, if I were only a princess, and he loved me that way, how glad I should be to give up everything and go to him alone! And then we would pray together; and I really think that would be much better than praying all alone. He said men had so much more to tempt them. Ah, that is true! How can little moles that grub in the ground know of the dangers of eagles that fly to the very sun? Holy Mother, look mercifully upon him and save his soul!"

Such were the thoughts of Agnes the day when she was preparing for her confession; and all the way to church she found them floating and dissolving and reappearing in new forms in her mind, like the silvery smoke-clouds which were constantly veering and sailing over Vesuvius.

Only one thing was firm and never changing, and that was the purpose to reveal everything to her spiritual director. When she kneeled at the confessional with closed eyes, and began her whispered acknowledgments, she tried to feel as if she were speaking in the ear of God alone, — that God whose spirit she was taught to believe, for the time being, was present in His minister before whom her inmost heart was to be unveiled.

He who sat within had just returned from his lonely retreat with his mind and nerves in a state of unnatural tension, — a sort of ecstatic clearness and calmness, which he mistook for victory and peace. During those lonely days when he had wandered afar from human converse, and was surrounded only by objects of desolation and gloom, he had passed through as many phases of strange, unnatural experience as there were flitting smoke-wreaths eddying about him.

There are depths in man's nature and his possibilities which no plummet has ever sounded, — the wild, lonely joys of fanatical excitement, the perfectly ravenous appetite for self-torture, which seems able, in time, to reverse the whole human system, and make a heaven of hell. How else can we understand the facts related both in Hindoo and in Christian story, of those men and women who have found such strange raptures in slow tortures, prolonged from year to year, till pain became a habit of body and mind? It is said that after the tortures of the rack, the reaction of the overstrained nerves produces a sense of the most exquisite relief and repose; and so when mind and body are harrowed, harassed to the very outer verge of endurance, come wild throbbings and transports, and strange celestial clairvoyance, which the mystic hails as the descent of the New Jerusalem into his soul.

It had seemed to Father Francesco, when he came down from the mountain, that he had left his body behind him, — that he had left earth and earthly things; his very feet touching the ground seemed to tread not on rough, resisting soil, but on an elastic cloud. He saw a strange excess of beauty in every flower, in every leaf, in the wavering blue of the sea, in the red grottoed rocks that overhung the shore, with their purple, green, orange, and yellow hangings of flower-and-leaf tapestry. The songs of the fishermen on the beach, the peasant-girls cutting flowery fodder for the cattle, all seemed to him to have an unnatural charm. As one looking through a prism sees a fine bordering of rainbow on every object, so he beheld a glorified world. His former self seemed to him something forever past and gone. He looked at himself as at another person,

who had sinned and suffered, and was now resting in beati-
fied repose; and he fondly thought all this was firm reality, and believed that he was now proof against all earthly
impressions, able to hear and to judge with the dispassion-
ate calmness of a disembodied spirit.   He did not know
that this high-strung calmness, this fine clearness, were
only the most intense forms of nervous sensibility, and as
vividly susceptible to every mortal impression as is the
vitalized chemical plate to the least action of the sun's
rays.

When Agnes began her confession, her voice seemed to
nim to pass through every nerve; it seemed as if he could
feel her presence thrilling through the very wood of the
confessional.   He was astonished and dismayed at his own
emotion.   But when she began to speak of the interview
with the cavalier, he trembled from head to foot with
uncontrollable passion.   Nature long repressed came back
in a tempestuous reaction.   He crossed himself again and
again, he tried to pray, and blessed those protecting shadows
which concealed his emotion from the unconscious one by
his side.   But he set his teeth in deadly resolve, and his
voice, as he questioned her, came forth cutting and cold as
ice crystals.

"Why did you listen to a word?"

"My father, it was so sudden.   He wakened me from
sleep.   I answered him before I thought."

"You should not have been sleeping.   It was a sinful
indolence."

"Yes, my father."

"See now to what it led.   The enemy of your soul, ever
watching, seized this moment to tempt you."

"Yes, my father."

"Examine your soul well," said Father Francesco, in a
tone of austere severity that made Agnes tremble.   "Did
you not find a secret pleasure in his words?"

"My father, I fear I did," said she, with a trembling voice.

"I knew it! I knew it!" the priest muttered to himself, while the great drops started on his forehead, in the intensity of the conflict he repressed. Agnes thought the solemn pause that followed was caused by the horror that had been inspired by her own sinfulness.

"You did not, then, heartily and truly wish him to go from you?" pursued the cold, severe voice.

"Yes, my father, I did. I wished him to go with all my soul."

"Yet you say you found pleasure in his being near you," said Father Francesco, conscious how every string of his own being, even in this awful hour, was vibrating with a sort of desperate, miserable joy in being once more near to her.

"Ah," sighed Agnes, "that is true, my father, — woe is me! Please tell me how I could have helped it. I was pleased before I knew it."

"And you have been thinking of what he said to you with pleasure since?" pursued the confessor, with an intense severity of manner, deepening as he spoke.

"I *have* thought of it," faltered Agnes.

"Beware how you trifle with the holy sacrament! Answer frankly. You have thought of it *with pleasure.* Confess it."

"I do not understand myself exactly," said Agnes. "I have thought of it partly with pleasure and partly with pain."

"Would you like to go with him and be his wife, as he said?"

"If it were right, father, — not otherwise."

"Oh, foolish child! oh, blinded soul! to think of right in connection with an infidel and heretic! Do you not see that all this is an artifice of Satan? He can transform

himself into an angel of light. Do you suppose this heretic would be brought back to the Church by a foolish girl?
Do you suppose it is your prayers he wants? Why does
he not seek the prayers of the Church, — of holy men who
have power with God? He would bait his hook with this
pretense that he may catch your soul. Do you believe
me?"

"I am bound to believe you, my father."

"But you do not. Your heart is going after this wicked
man."

"Oh, my father, I do not wish it should. I never wish
or expect to see him more. I only pray for him that his
soul may not be lost."

"He has gone, then?"

"Yes, my father. And he went with my uncle, a most
holy monk, who has undertaken the work of his salvation.
He listens to my uncle, who has hopes of restoring him to
the Church."

"That is well. And now, my daughter, listen to me.
You must root out of your thought every trace and remembrance of these words of sinful earthly love which he hath
spoken. Such love would burn your soul to all eternity
with fire that never could be quenched. If you can tear
away all roots and traces of this from your heart, if by
fasting and prayer and penance you can become worthy to
be a bride of your divine Lord, then your prayers will gain
power, and you may prevail to secure his eternal salvation.
But listen to me, daughter, — listen and tremble! If ever
you should yield to his love and turn back from this heavenly marriage to follow him, you will accomplish his damnation and your own; to all eternity he will curse you,
while the fire rages and consumes him, — he will curse the
hour that he first saw you."

These words were spoken with an intense vehemence
which seemed almost supernatural. Agnes shivered and

trembled; a vague feeling of guilt overwhelmed and dis-
heartened her; she seemed to herself the most lost and
abandoned of human beings.

"My father, I shall think no penance too severe that
may restore my soul from this sin. I have already made
a vow to the blessed Mother that I will walk on foot to
the Holy City, praying in every shrine and holy place;
and I humbly ask your approval."

This announcement brought to the mind of the monk a
sense of relief and deliverance. He felt already, in the
terrible storm of agitation which this confession had aroused
within him, that nature was not dead, and that he was in-
finitely farther from the victory of passionless calm than he
had supposed. He was still a man, — torn with human
passions, with a love which he must never express, and a
jealousy which burned and writhed at every word which
he had wrung from its unconscious object. Conscience
had begun to whisper in his ear that there would be no
safety to him in continuing this spiritual dictatorship to
one whose every word unmanned him, — that it was laying
himself open to a ceaseless temptation, which in some
blinded, dreary hour of evil might hurry him into acts of
horrible sacrilege; and he was once more feeling that wild,
stormy revolt of his inner nature that so distressed him
before he left the convent.

This proposition of Agnes's struck him as a compromise.
It would take her from him only for a season, she would
go under his care and direction, and he would gradually
recover his calmness and self-possession in her absence.
Her pilgrimage to the holy places would be a most proper
and fit preparation for the solemn marriage-rite which
should forever sunder her from all human ties, and make
her inaccessible to all solicitations of human love. Therefore, after an interval of silence, he answered, —

"Daughter, your plan is approved. Such pilgrimages

have ever been held meritorious works in the Church, and there is a special blessing upon them."

"My father," said Agnes, "it has always been in my heart from my childhood to be the bride of the Lord; but my grandmother, who brought me up, and to whom I owe the obedience of a daughter, utterly forbids me; she will not hear a word of it. No longer ago than last Monday she told me I might as well put a knife into her heart as speak of this."

"And you, daughter, do you put the feelings of any earthly friend before the love of your Lord and Creator who laid down His life for you? Hear what He saith: 'He that loveth father or mother more than me is not worthy of me.'"

"But my poor old grandmother has no one but me in the world, and she has never slept a night without me; she is getting old, and she has worked for me all her good days;—it would be very hard for her to lose me."

"Ah, false, deceitful heart! Has, then, thy Lord not labored for thee? Has He not borne thee through all the years of thy life? And wilt thou put the love of any mortal before His?"

"Yes," replied Agnes, with a sort of hardy sweetness, "but my Lord does not need me as grandmother does; He is in glory, and will never be old or feeble; I cannot work for Him and tend Him as I shall her. I cannot see my way clear at present; but when she is gone, or if the saints move her to consent, I shall then belong to God alone."

"Daughter, there is some truth in your words; and if your Lord accepts you, He will dispose her heart. Will she go with you on this pilgrimage?"

"I have prayed that she might, father, — that her soul may be quickened; for I fear me, dear old grandmamma has found her love for me a snare, — she has thought too much of my interests and too little of her own soul, poor grandmamma!"

"Well, child, I shall enjoin this pilgrimage on her as a penance."

"I have grievously offended her lately," said Agnes, "in rejecting an offer of marriage with a man on whom she had set her heart, and therefore she does not listen to me as she is wont to do."

"You have done right in refusing, my daughter. I will speak to her of this, and show her how great is the sin of opposing a holy vocation in a soul whom the Lord calls to Himself, and enjoin her to make reparation by uniting with you in this holy work."

Agnes departed from the confessional without even looking upon the face of her director, who sat within listening to the rustle of her dress as she rose, — listening to the soft fall of her departing footsteps, and praying that grace might be given him not to look after her: and he did not, though he felt as if his life were going with her.

Agnes tripped round the aisle to a little side-chapel where a light was always kept burning by her before a picture of Saint Agnes, and, kneeling there, waited till her grandmother should be through with her confession.

"Ah, sweet Saint Agnes," she said, "pity me! I am a poor ignorant young girl, and have been led into grievous sin; but I did not mean to do wrong, — I have been trying to do right; pray for me, that I may overcome as you did. Pray our dear Lord to send you with us on this pilgrimage, and save us from all wicked and brutal men who would do us harm. As the Lord delivered you in sorest straits, keeping soul and body pure as a lily, ah, pray Him to keep me! I love you dearly, — watch over me and guide me."

In those days of the Church, such addresses to the glorified saints had become common among all Christians. They

were not regarded as worship, any more than a similar outpouring of confidence to a beloved and revered friend yet
in the body.   Among the hymns of Savonarola is one addressed to Saint Mary Magdalen, whom he regarded with
an especial veneration.   The great truth, that God is not
the God of the dead, but of the living, that *all* live to
Him, was in those ages with the truly religious a part of
spiritual consciousness.   The saints of the Church Triumphant, having become one with Christ as He is one with the
Father, were regarded as invested with a portion of his
divinity, and as the ministering agency through which his
mediatorial government on earth was conducted; and it
was thought to be in the power of the sympathetic heart
to attract them by the outflow of its affections, so that
their presence often overshadowed the walks of daily life
with a cloud of healing and protecting sweetness.

If the enthusiasm of devotion in regard to these invisible friends became extravagant and took the language due
to God alone, it was no more than the fervid Italian nature
was always doing with regard to visible objects of affection.
Love with an Italian always tends to become worship, and
some of the language of the poets addressed to earthly loves
rises into intensities of expression due only to the One,
Sovereign, Eternal Beauty.   One sees even in the writings
of Cicero that this passionate adoring kind of love is not
confined to modern times.   When he loses the daughter in
whom his heart is garnered up, he finds no comfort except
in building a temple to her memory, — a blind outreaching
towards the saint-worship of modern times.

Agnes rose from her devotions, and went with downcast
eyes, her lips still repeating prayers, to the font of holy
water, which was in a dim shadowy corner, where a painted
window cast a gold and violet twilight.   Suddenly there
was a rustle of garments in the dimness, and a jeweled
hand essayed to pass holy water to her on the tip of its

finger. This mark of Christian fraternity, common in those times, Agnes almost mechanically accepted, touching her slender finger to the one extended, and making the sign of the cross, while she raised her eyes to see who stood there. Gradually the haze cleared from her mind, and she awoke to the consciousness that it was the cavalier! He moved to come towards her, with a bright smile on his face; but suddenly she became pale as one who has seen a spectre, and, pushing from her with both hands, she said faintly, "Go, go!" and turned and sped up the aisle silently as a sunbeam, joining her grandmother, who was coming from the confessional with a gloomy and sullen brow.

Old Elsie had been enjoined to unite with her grand-child in this scheme of a pilgrimage, and received the direc-tion with as much internal contumacy as would a thriving church-member of Wall Street a proposition to attend a protracted meeting in the height of the business season. Not but that pilgrimages were holy and gracious works, — she was too good a Christian not to admit that, — but why must holy and gracious works be thrust on her in particu-lar? There were saints enough who liked such things; and people *could* get to heaven without, — if not with a very abundant entrance, still in a modest way, — and Elsie's ambition for position and treasure in the spiritual world was of a very moderate cast.

"Well, now, I hope you are satisfied," she said to Ag-nes, as she pulled her along with no very gentle hand; "you 've got me sent off on a pilgrimage, — and my old bones must be rattling up and down all the hills between here and Rome, — and who 's to see to the oranges? — they 'll all be stolen, every one."

"Grandmother" — began Agnes in a pleading voice.

"Oh, you hush up! I know what you 're going to say. 'The good Lord will take care of them.' I wish He may. He has his hands full, with all the people that go cawing and psalm-singing like so many crows, and leave all their affairs to Him!'"

Agnes walked along disconsolate, with her eyes full of tears, which coursed one another down her pale cheeks.

"There's Antonio," pursued Elsie, "would perhaps look after things a little. He is a good fellow, and only yesterday was asking if he couldn't do something for us. It's you he does it for, — but little you care who loves you, or what they do for you!"

At this moment they met old Jocunda, whom we have before introduced to the reader as portress of the Convent. She had on her arm a large square basket, which she was storing for its practical uses.

"Well, well, Saint Agnes be praised, I have found you at last," she said. "I was wanting to speak about some of your blood-oranges for conserving. An order has come down from our dear gracious lady, the Queen, to prepare a lot for her own blessed eating, and you may be sure I would get none of anybody but you. But what's this, my little heart, my little lamb? — crying? — tears in those sweet eyes? What's the matter now?"

"Matter enough for me!" said Elsie. "It's a weary world we live in. A body can't turn any way and not meet with trouble. If a body brings up a girl one way, why, every fellow is after her, and one has no peace; and if a body brings her up another way, she gets her head in the clouds, and there's no good of her in this world. Now look at that girl, — doesn't everybody say it's time she were married? — but no marrying for her! Nothing will do but we must off to Rome on a pilgrimage, — and what's the good of that, I want to know? If it's praying that's to be done, the dear saints know she's at it from morning till night, — and lately she's up and down three or four times a night with some prayer or other."

"Well, well," said Jocunda, "who started this idea?"

"Oh, Father Francesco and she got it up between them, and nothing will do but I must go, too."

"Well, now, after all, my dear," said Jocunda, "do you know, I made a pilgrimage once, and it is n't so bad. One gets a good deal by it, first and last. Everybody drops something into your hand as you go, and one gets treated as if one were somebody a little above the common; and then in Rome one has a princess or a duchess or some noble lady who washes one's feet, and gives one a good supper, and perhaps a new suit of clothes, and all that, — and ten to one there comes a pretty little sum of money to boot, if one plays one's cards well. A pilgrimage is n't bad, after all; one sees a world of fine things, and something new every day."

"But who is to look after our garden and dress our trees ? "

"Ah, now, there 's Antonio, and old Meta his mother," said Jocunda, with a knowing wink at Agnes. "I fancy there are friends there that would lend a hand to keep things together against the little one comes home. If one is going to be married, a pilgrimage brings good luck in the family. All the saints take it kindly that one comes so far to see them, and are more ready to do a good turn for one when one needs it. The blessed saints are like other folks, they like to be treated with proper attention."

This view of pilgrimages from the material standpoint had more effect on the mind of Elsie than the most elaborate appeals of Father Francesco. She began to acquiesce, though with a reluctant air.

Jocunda, seeing her words had made some impression, pursued her advantage on the spiritual ground.

"To be sure," she added, "I don't know how it is with you; but I know that I have, one way and another, rolled up quite an account of sins in my life. When I was tramping up and down with my old man through the coun-

try, — now in this castle and then in that camp, and now
and then in at the sacking of a city or village, or something
of the kind, — the saints forgive us! — it does seem as if
one got into things that were not of the best sort, in such
times. It's true, it's been wiped out over and over by the
priest; but then a pilgrimage is a good thing to make all
sure, in case one's good works should fall short of one's sins
at last. I can tell you, a pilgrimage is a good round weight
to throw into the scale; and when it comes to heaven and
hell, you know, my dear, why, one cannot be too careful."

"Well, that may be true enough," said Elsie, "though
as to my sins, I have tried to keep them regularly squared
up and balanced as I went along. I have always been
regular at confession, and never failed a jot or tittle in
what the holy father told me. But there may be something in what you say; one can't be too sure; and so I'll
e'en school my old bones into taking this tramp."

That evening, as Agnes was sitting in the garden at
sunset, her grandmother bustling in and out, talking,
groaning, and hurrying in her preparations for the antici-
pated undertaking, suddenly there was a rustling in the
branches overhead, and a bouquet of rosebuds fell at her
feet. Agnes picked it up, and saw a scrip of paper coiled
among the flowers. In a moment, remembering the apparition of the cavalier in the church in the morning, she
doubted not from whom it came. So dreadful had been
the effect of the scene at the confessional, that the thought
of the near presence of her lover brought only terror. She
turned pale; her hands shook. She shut her eyes, and
prayed that she might not be left to read the paper; and
then, summoning all her resolution, she threw the bouquet
with force over the wall. It dropped down, down, down
the gloomy, shadowy abyss, and was lost in the damp caverns below.

The cavalier stood without the wall, waiting for some

responsive signal in reply to his missive. It had never occurred to him that Agnes would not even read it, and he stood confounded when he saw it thrown back with such apparent rudeness. He remembered her pale, terrified look on seeing him in the morning. It was not indifference or dislike, but mortal fear, that had been shown in that pale face.

"These wretches are practicing on her," he said, in wrath, "filling her head with frightful images, and torturing her sensitive conscience till she sees sin in the most natural and innocent feelings."

He had learned from Father Antonio the intention of Agnes to go on a pilgrimage, and he longed to see and talk with her, that he might offer her his protection against dangers which he understood far better than she. It had never even occurred to him that the door for all possible communication would be thus suddenly barred in his face.

"Very well," he said to himself, with a darkening brow, "let them have it their own way here. She must pass through my dominions before she can reach Rome, and I will find a place where I *can* be heard, without priest or grandmother to let or hinder. She is mine, and I will care for her."

But poor Agnes had the woman's share of the misery to bear, in the fear and self-reproach and distress which every movement of this kind cost her. The involuntary thrill at seeing her lover, at hearing from him, the conscious struggle which it cost her to throw back his gift, were all noted by her accusing conscience as so many sins. The next day she sought again her confessor, and began an entrance on those darker and more chilly paths of penance, by which, according to the opinion of her times, the peculiarly elect of the Lord were supposed to be best trained. Hitherto her religion had been the cheerful and natural expression of her tender and devout nature, according to the more beautiful and engaging devotional forms of her Church. During the year when her confessor had been, unconsciously to himself, led by her instead of leading, her spiritual food had been its beautiful old hymns and prayers, which she found no weariness in often repeating. But now an unnatural conflict was begun in her mind, directed by a spiritual guide in whom every natural and normal movement of the soul had given way before a succession of morbid and unhealthful experiences. From that day Agnes wore upon her heart one of those sharp instruments of torture which in those items were supposed to be a means of inward grace, — a cross with seven steel points for the seven sorrows of Mary. She fasted with a severity which alarmed her grandmother, who in her inmost heart cursed the day that ever she had placed her in the way of saintship.

"All this will just end in spoiling her beauty, — making her as thin as a shadow," said Elsie; "and she was good enough before."

But it did not spoil her beauty, it only changed its character. The roundness and bloom melted away, but there came in their stead that solemn, transparent clearness of countenance, that spiritual light and radiance, which the old Florentine painters gave to their Madonnas.

It is singular how all religious exercises and appliances take the character of the nature that uses them. The pain and penance, which so many in her day bore as a cowardly expedient for averting divine wrath, seemed, as she viewed them, a humble way of becoming associated in the sufferings of her Redeemer. "*Jesu dulcis memoria,*" was the thought that carried a redeeming sweetness with every pain. Could she thus, by suffering with her Lord, gain power like Him to save, — a power which should save that soul so dear and so endangered! "Ah," she thought, "I would give my life-blood, drop by drop, if only it might avail for his salvation!"

CHAPTER XX

It was drawing towards evening, as two travelers, approaching Florence from the south, checked their course on the summit of one of the circle of hills which command a view of the city, and seemed to look down upon it with admiration. One of these was our old friend Father Antonio, and the other the cavalier. The former was mounted on an ambling mule, whose easy pace suited well with his meditative habits; while the other reined in a high-mettled steed, who, though now somewhat jaded under the fatigue of a long journey, showed by a series of little lively motions of his ears and tail, and by pawing the ground impatiently, that he had the inexhaustible stock of spirits which goes with good blood.

"There she lies, my Florence," said the monk, stretching his hands out with enthusiasm. "Is she not indeed a sheltered lily growing fair among the hollows of the mountains? Little she may be, sir, compared to old Rome; but every inch of her is a gem, — every inch!"

And, in truth, the scene was worthy of the artist's enthusiasm. All the overhanging hills that encircle the city with their silvery olive-gardens and their pearl-white villas were now lighted up with evening glory. The old gray walls of the convents of San Miniato and the Monte Oliveto were touched with yellow; and even the black obelisks of the cypresses in their cemeteries had here and there streaks and dots of gold, fluttering like bright birds among their gloomy branches. The distant snow-peaks of the Apennines, which even in spring long wear their icy mantles, were shimmering and changing like an opal ring with tints of violet, green, blue, and rose, blended in inexpressible softness by that dreamy haze which forms the peculiar feature of Italian skies.

In this loving embrace of mountains lay the city, divided by the Arno as by a line of rosy crystal barred by the graceful arches of its bridges.   Amid the crowd of palaces and spires and towers rose central and conspicuous the great Duomo, just crowned with that magnificent dome which was then considered a novelty and a marvel in architecture, and which Michel Angelo looked longingly back upon when he was going to Rome to build that more wondrous orb of Saint Peter's.   White and stately by its side shot up the airy shaft of the Campanile; and the violet vapor swathing the whole city in a tender indistinctness, these two striking objects, rising by their magnitude far above it, seemed to stand alone in a sort of airy grandeur.

And now the bells of the churches were sounding the Ave Maria, filling the air with sweet and solemn vibrations, as if angels were passing to and fro overhead, harping as they went; and ever and anon the great bell of the Campanile came pulsing in with a throb of sound of a quality so different that one hushed one's breath to hear.   It might be fancied to be the voice of one of those kingly archangels that one sees drawn by the old Florentine religious artists, — a voice grave and unearthly, and with a plaintive undertone of divine mystery.

The monk and the cavalier bent low in their saddles, and seemed to join devoutly in the worship of the hour.

One need not wonder at the enthusiasm of the returning pilgrim of those days for the city of his love, who feels the charm that lingers around that beautiful place even in modern times.   Never was there a spot to which the heart could insensibly grow with a more home-like affection, —

never one more thoroughly consecrated in every stone by the sacred touch of genius.

A republic, in the midst of contending elements, the history of Florence, in the Middle Ages, was a history of what shoots and blossoms the Italian nature might send forth, when rooted in the rich soil of liberty. It was a city of poets and artists. Its statesmen, its merchants, its common artisans, and the very monks in its convents, were all pervaded by one spirit. The men of Florence in its best days were men of a large, grave, earnest mould. What the Puritans of New England wrought out with severest earnestness in their reasonings and their lives, these early Puritans of Italy embodied in poetry, sculpture, and painting. They built their Cathedral and their Campanile, as the Jews of old built their Temple, with awe and religious fear, that they might thus express by costly and imperishable monuments their sense of God's majesty and beauty. The modern traveler who visits the churches and convents of Florence, or the museums where are preserved the fading remains of its early religious Art, if he be a person of any sensibility, cannot fail to be affected with the intense gravity and earnestness which pervade them. They seem less to be paintings for the embellishment of life than eloquent picture-writing by which burning religious souls sought to preach the truths of the invisible world to the eye of the multitude. Through all the deficiencies of perspective, coloring, and outline incident to the childhood and early youth of Art, one feels the passionate purpose of some lofty soul to express ideas of patience, self-sacrifice, adoration, and aspiration far transcending the limits of mortal capability.

The angels and celestial beings of these grave old painters are as different from the fat little pink Cupids or lovely laughing children of Titian and Correggio as are the sermons of President Edwards from the love-songs of Tom

Moore.   These old seers of the pencil give you grave, radiant beings, strong as man, fine as woman, sweeping downward in lines of floating undulation, and seeming by the
ease with which they remain poised in the air to feel none
of that earthly attraction which draws material bodies earth-
ward.   Whether they wear the morning star on their forehead or bear the lily or the sword in their hand, there is
still that suggestion of mystery and power about them, that
air of dignity and repose, that speak the children of a nobler race than ours.   One could well believe such a being
might pass in his serene poised majesty of motion through
the walls of a gross material dwelling without deranging
one graceful fold of his swaying robe or unclasping the
hands folded quietly on his bosom.   Well has a modern
master of art and style said of these old artists, "Many
pictures are ostentatious exhibitions of the artist's power of
speech, the clear and vigorous elocution of useless and
senseless words; while the earlier efforts of Giotto and
Cimabue are the burning messages of prophecy delivered by
the stammering lips of infants."

But at the time of which we write, Florence had passed
through her ages of primitive religious and republican simplicity, and was fast hastening to her downfall.   The genius,
energy, and prophetic enthusiasm of Savonarola had made,
it is true, a desperate rally on the verge of the precipice;
but no one man has ever power to turn back the downward
slide of a whole generation.

When Father Antonio left Sorrento in company with
the cavalier, it was the intention of the latter to go with
him only so far as their respective routes should lie together.   The band under the command of Agostino was
posted in a ruined fortress in one of those airily perched
old mountain-towns which form so picturesque and characteristic a feature of the Italian landscape.   But before they
reached this spot, the simple, poetic, guileless monk, with

his fresh artistic nature, had so won upon his traveling companion that a most enthusiastic friendship had sprung up between them, and Agostino could not find it in his heart at once to separate from him. Tempest-tossed and homeless, burning with a sense of wrong, alienated from the faith of his fathers through his intellect and moral sense, yet clinging to it with his memory and imagination, he found in the tender devotional fervor of the artist monk a reconciling and healing power. He shared, too, in no small degree, the feelings which now possessed the breast of his companion for the great reformer whose purpose seemed to meditate nothing less than the restoration of the Church of Italy to the primitive apostolic simplicity. He longed to see him, — to listen to the eloquence of which he had heard so much. Then, too, he had thoughts that but vaguely shaped themselves in his mind. This noble man, so brave and courageous, menaced by the forces of a cruel tyranny, might he not need the protection of a good sword ? He recollected, too, that he had an uncle high in the favor of the King of France, to whom he had written a full account of his own situation. Might he not be of use in urging this uncle to induce the French King to throw before Savonarola the shield of his protection ? At all events, he entered Florence this evening with the burning zeal of a young neophyte who hopes to effect something himself for a glorious and sacred cause embodied in a leader who commands his deepest veneration.

"My son," said Father Antonio, as they raised their heads after the evening prayer, "I am at this time like a man who, having long been away from his home, fears, on returning, that he shall hear some evil tidings of those he hath left. I long, yet dread, to go to my dear Father Girolamo and the beloved brothers in our house. There is a presage that lies heavy on my heart, so that I cannot shake it off. Look at our glorious old Duomo; — doth she

not sit there among the houses and palaces as a queen-
mother among nations, — worthy, in her greatness and
beauty, to represent the Church of the New Jerusalem, the
Bride of the Lord? Ah, I have seen it thronged and
pressed with the multitude who came to crave the bread of
life from our master!"

"Courage, my friend!" said Agostino; "it cannot be
that Florence will suffer her pride and glory to be trodden
down. Let us hasten on, for the shades of evening are
coming fast, and there is a keen wind sweeping down from
your snowy mountains." And the two soon found themselves plunging into the shadows of the streets, threading
their devious way to the convent.

At length they drew up before a dark wall, where the
Father Antonio rung a bell.

A door was immediately opened, a cowled head appeared,
and a cautious voice asked, —

"Who is there?"

"Ah, is that you, good Brother Angelo?" said Father
Antonio, cheerily.

"And is it you, dear Brother Antonio? Come in! come
in!" was the cordial response, as the two passed into the
court; "truly, it will make all our hearts leap to see you."

"And, Brother Angelo, how is our dear father? I have
been so anxious about him!"

"Oh, fear not! — he sustains himself in God, and is full
of sweetness to us all."

"But do the people stand by him, Angelo, and the
Signoria?"

"He has strong friends as yet, but his enemies are like
ravening wolves. The Pope hath set on the Franciscans,
and they hunt him as dogs do a good stag. But whom
have you here with you?" added the monk, raising his
torch and regarding the knight.

"Fear him not; he is a brave knight and good Christian,

who comes to offer his sword to our father and seek his counsels."

"He shall be welcome," said the porter, cheerfully. "We will have you into the refectory forthwith, for you must be hungry."

The young cavalier, following the flickering torch of his conductor, had only a dim notion of long cloistered corridors, out of which now and then, as the light flared by, came a golden gleam from some quaint old painting, where the pure angel forms of Angelico stood in the gravity of an immortal youth, or the Madonna, like a bending lily, awaited the message of Heaven; but when they entered the refectory, a cheerful voice addressed them, and Father Antonio was clasped in the embrace of the father so much beloved.

"Welcome, welcome, my dear son!" said that rich voice which had thrilled so many thousand Italian hearts with its music. "So you are come back to the fold again. How goes the good work of the Lord?"

"Well, everywhere," said Father Antonio, and then, recollecting his young friend, he suddenly turned and said, —

"Let me present to you one son who comes to seek your instructions, — the young Signor Agostino, of the noble house of Sarelli."

The Superior turned to Agostino with a movement full of a generous frankness, and warmly extended his hand, at the same time fixing upon him the mesmeric glance of a pair of large, deep blue eyes, which might, on slight observation, have been mistaken for black, so great was their depth and brilliancy.

Agostino surveyed his new acquaintance with that mingling of ingenuous respect and curiosity with which an ardent young man would regard the most distinguished leader of his age, and felt drawn to him by a certain atmosphere of vital cordiality such as one can feel better than describe.

"You have ridden far to-day, my son, — you must be weary," said the Superior, affably; "but here you must feel yourself at home; command us in anything we can do for you. The brothers will attend to those refreshments which are needed after so long a journey; and when you have rested and supped, we shall hope to see you a little more quietly."

So saying, he signed to one or two brothers who stood by, and, commending the travelers to their care, left the apartment.

In a few moments a table was spread with a plain and wholesome repast, to which the two travelers sat down with appetites sharpened by their long journey.

During the supper, the brothers of the convent, among whom Father Antonio had always been a favorite, crowded around him in a state of eager excitement.

"You should have been here the last week," said one; "such a turmoil as we have been in!"

"Yes," said another, "the Pope hath set on the Franciscans, who, you know, are always ready enough to take up with anything against our order, and they have been pursuing our father like so many hounds."

"There hath been a whirlwind of preaching here and there," said a third, "in the Duomo, and Santa Croce, and San Lorenzo; and they have battled to and fro, and all the city is full of it."

"Tell him about yesterday, about the ordeal," shouted an eager voice.

Two or three voices took up the story at once, and began to tell it, all the others correcting, contradicting, or adding incidents. From the confused fragments here and there Agostino gathered that there had been on the day before a popular spectacle in the grand piazza, in which, according to an old superstition of the Middle Ages, Fra Girolamo Savonarola and his opponents were expected to prove the truth of their words by passing unhurt through the fire; that two immense piles of combustibles had been constructed with a narrow passage between, and the whole magistracy of the city convened, with a throng of the populace, eager for the excitement of the spectacle; that the day had been spent in discussions, and scruples, and preliminaries; and that, finally, in the afternoon, a violent storm of rain arising had dispersed the multitude and put a stop to the whole exhibition.

"But the people are not satisfied," said Father Angelo; "and there are enough mischief-makers among them to throw all the blame on our father."

"Yes," said one, "they say he wanted to burn the Holy Sacrament, because he was going to take it with him into the fire."

"As if it could burn!" said another voice.

"It would to all human appearance, I suppose," said a third.

"Any way," said a fourth, "there is some mischief brewing; for here is our friend Prospero Rondinelli just come in, who says, when he came past the Duomo, he saw people gathering, and heard them threatening us: there were as many as two hundred, he thought."

"We ought to tell Father Girolamo," exclaimed several voices.

"Oh, he will not be disturbed!" said Father Angelo. "Since these affairs, he hath been in prayer in the chapter-room before the blessed Angelico's picture of the Cross. When we would talk with him of these things, he waves us away, and says only, 'I am weary; go and tell Jesus.'"

"He bade me come to him after supper," said Father Antonio. "I will talk with him."

"Do so, — that is right," said two or three eager voices as the monk and Agostino, having finished their repast, arose to be conducted to the presence of the father.

CHAPTER XXI

THEY found him in a large and dimly lighted apartment, sitting absorbed in pensive contemplation before a picture of the Crucifixion by Fra Angelico, which, whatever might be its *naïve* faults of drawing and perspective, had an intense earnestness of feeling, and, though faded and dimmed by the lapse of centuries, still stirs in some faint wise even the practiced *dilettanti* of our day.

The face upon the cross, with its majestic patience, seemed to shed a blessing down on the company of saints of all ages who were grouped by their representative men at the foot. Saint Dominic, Saint Ambrose, Saint Augustin, Saint Jerome, Saint Francis, and Saint Benedict were depicted as standing before the Great Sacrifice in company with the Twelve Apostles, the two Maries, and the fainting mother of Jesus, — thus expressing the unity of the Church Universal in that great victory of sorrow and glory. The painting was enclosed above by a semicircular bordering composed of medallion heads of the Prophets, and below was a similar medallion border of the principal saints and worthies of the Dominican order. In our day such pictures are visited by tourists with red guide-books in their hands, who survey them in the intervals of careless conversation; but they were painted by the simple artist on his knees, weeping and praying as he worked, and the sight of them was accepted by like simple-hearted Christians as a perpetual sacrament of the eye, by which they received Christ into their souls.

So absorbed was the father in the contemplation of this picture, that he did not hear the approaching footsteps of the knight and monk. When at last they came so near as almost to touch him, he suddenly looked up, and it became apparent that his eyes were full of tears.

He rose, and, pointing with a mute gesture toward the painting, said, —

"There is more in that than in all Michel Angelo Buonarotti hath done yet, though he be a God-fearing youth, — more than in all the heathen marbles in Lorenzo's gardens. But sit down with me here. I have to come here often, where I can refresh my courage."

The monk and knight seated themselves, the latter with his attention riveted on the remarkable man before him. The head and face of Savonarola are familiar to us by many paintings and medallions, which, however, fail to impart what must have been that effect of his personal presence which so drew all hearts to him in his day. The knight saw a man of middle age, of elastic, well-knit figure, and a flexibility and grace of motion which seemed to make every nerve, even to his finger-ends, vital with the expression of his soul. The close-shaven crown and the plain white Dominican robe gave a severe and statuesque simplicity to the lines of his figure. His head and face, like those of most of the men of genius whom modern Italy has produced, were so strongly cast in the antique mould as to leave no doubt of the identity of modern Italian blood with that of the great men of ancient Italy. His low, broad forehead, prominent Roman nose, well-cut, yet fully outlined lips, and strong, finely moulded jaw and chin, all spoke the old Roman vigor and energy, while the flexible delicacy of all the muscles of his face and figure gave an inexpressible fascination to his appearance. Every emotion and changing thought seemed to flutter and tremble over his countenance as the shadow of leaves over sunny water.

His eye had a wonderful dilating power, and when he was excited seemed to shower sparks; and his voice possessed a surprising scale of delicate and melodious inflections, which could take him in a moment through the whole range of human feeling, whether playful and tender or denunciatory and terrible. Yet, when in repose among his friends, there was an almost childlike simplicity and artlessness of manner which drew the heart by an irresistible attraction. At this moment it was easy to see by his pale cheek and the furrowed lines of his face that he had been passing through severe struggles; but his mind seemed stayed on some invisible centre, in a solemn and mournful calm.

"Come, tell me something of the good works of the Lord in our Italy, brother," he said, with a smile which was almost playful in its brightness. "You have been through all the lowly places of the land, carrying our Lord's bread to the poor, and repairing and beautifying shrines and altars by the noble gift that is in you."

"Yes, father," said the monk; "and I have found that there are many sheep of the Lord that feed quietly among the mountains of Italy, and love nothing so much as to hear of the dear Shepherd who laid down His life for them."

"Even so, even so," said the Superior, with animation; "and it is the thought of these sweet hearts that comforts me when my soul is among lions. The foundation standeth sure, — the Lord knoweth them that are his."

"And it is good and encouraging," said Father Antonio, "to see the zeal of the poor, who will give their last penny for the altar of the Lord, and who flock so to hear the word and take the sacraments. I have had precious seasons of preaching and confessing, and have worked in blessedness many days restoring and beautifying the holy pictures and statues whereby these little ones have been comforted. What with the wranglings of princes and

the factions and disturbances in our poor Italy, there be
many who suffer in want and loss of all things, so that no
refuge remains to them but the altars of our Jesus, and
none cares for them but He."

"Brother," said the Superior, "there be thousands of
flowers fairer than man ever saw that grow up in waste
places and in deep dells and shades of mountains; but God
bears each one in his heart, and delighteth Himself in
silence with them: and so doth He with these poor, simple, unknown souls. The True Church is not a flaunting
queen who goes boldly forth among men displaying her
beauties, but a veiled bride, a dove that is in the cleft of
the rocks, whose voice is known only to the Beloved.
Ah! when shall the great marriage-feast come, when all
shall behold her glorified? I had hoped to see the day
here in Italy: but now " —

The father stopped, and seemed to lapse into unconscious
musing, — his large eye growing fixed and mysterious in
its expression.

"The brothers have been telling me somewhat of the
tribulations you have been through," said Father Antonio,
who thought he saw a good opening to introduce the subject nearest his heart.

"No more of that! — no more!" said the Superior,
turning away his head with an expression of pain and
weariness, "rather let us look up. What think you, brother, are all *these* doing now?" he said, pointing to the
saints in the picture. "They are all alive and well, and
see clearly through our darkness." Then, rising up, he
added, solemnly, "Whatever man may say or do, it is
enough for me to feel that my dearest Lord and his blessed
Mother and all the holy archangels, the martyrs and prophets and apostles, are with me. The end is coming."

"But, dearest father," said Antonio, "think you the
Lord will suffer the wicked to prevail?"

"It may be for a time," said Savonarola. "As for me,
I am in His hands only as an instrument. He is master
of the forge and handles the hammer, and when He has
done using it He casts it from Him. Thus He did with
Jeremiah, whom He permitted to be stoned to death when
his preaching mission was accomplished; and thus He may
do with *this* hammer when He has done using it."

At this moment a monk rushed into the room with a
face expressive of the utmost terror, and called out, —

"Father, what shall we do? The mob are surrounding
the convent! Hark! hear them at the doors!"

In truth, a wild, confused roar of mingled shrieks,
cries, and blows came in through the open door of the
apartment; and the pattering sound of approaching footsteps was heard like showering rain-drops along the cloisters.

"Here come Messer Nicolo de' Lapi, and Francesco
Valori!" called out a voice.

The room was soon filled with a confused crowd, consisting of distinguished Florentine citizens, who had gained
admittance through a secret passage, and the excited novices
and monks.

"The streets outside the convent are packed close with
men," cried one of the citizens; "they have stationed
guards everywhere to cut off our friends who might come
to help us."

"I saw them seize a young man who was quietly walking, singing psalms, and slay him on the steps of the
Church of the Innocents," said another; "they cried and
hooted, 'No more psalm-singing!'"

"And there 's Arnolfo Battista," said a third; — "he
went out to try to speak to them, and they have killed
him, — cut him down with their sabres."

"Hurry! hurry! barricade the door! arm yourselves!"
was the cry from other voices.

"Shall we fight, father?   Shall we defend ourselves?"
cried others, as the monks pressed around their Superior.

When the crowd first burst into the room, the face of
the Superior flushed, and there was a slight movement of
surprise; then he seemed to recollect himself, and murmur-
ing, "I expected this, but not so soon," appeared lost in
mental prayer.   To the agitated inquiries of his flock, he
answered, "No, brothers; the weapons of monks must be
spiritual, not carnal."   Then lifting on high a crucifix,
he said, "Come with me, and let us walk in solemn procession to the altar, singing the praises of our God."

The monks, with the instinctive habit of obedience, fell
into procession behind their leader, whose voice, clear and
strong, was heard raising the Psalm, "*Quare fremunt
gentes:*" —

"Why do the heathen rage, and the people imagine a
vain thing?

"The kings of the earth set themselves, and the rulers
take counsel together, against the Lord, and against his
Anointed, saying, —

"Let us break their bands asunder, and cast away their
cords from us.

"He that sitteth in the heavens shall laugh: the Lord
shall have them in derision."

As one voice after another took up the chant, the solemn
enthusiasm rose and deepened, and all present, whether
ecclesiastics or laymen, fell into the procession and joined
in the anthem.   Amid the wild uproar, the din and clatter
of axes, the thunders of heavy battering-implements on the
stone walls and portals, came this long-drawn solemn wave
of sound, rising and falling, — now drowned in the savage
clamors of the mob, and now bursting out clear and full
like the voices of God's chosen amid the confusion and
struggles of all the generations of this mortal life.

White-robed and grand the procession moved on, while

the pictured saints and angels on the walls seemed to smile calmly down upon them from a golden twilight. They passed thus into the sacristy, where with all solemnity and composure they arrayed their Father and Superior for the last time in his sacramental robes, and then, still chanting, followed him to the high altar, where all bowed in prayer. And still, whenever there was a pause in the stormy uproar and fiendish clamor, might be heard the clear, plaintive uprising of that strange singing, "O Lord, save thy people, and bless thine heritage!"

It needs not to tell in detail what history has told of that tragic night: how the doors at last were forced, and the mob rushed in; how citizens and friends, and many of the monks themselves, their instinct of combativeness overcoming their spiritual beliefs, fought valiantly, and used torches and crucifixes for purposes little contemplated when they were made.

Fiercest among the combatants was Agostino, who three times drove back the crowd as they were approaching the choir, where Savonarola and his immediate friends were still praying. Father Antonio, too, seized a sword from the hand of a fallen man and laid about him with an impetuosity which would be inexplicable to any who do not know what force there is in gentle natures when the objects of their affections are assailed. The artist monk fought for his master with the blind desperation with which a woman fights over the cradle of her child.

All in vain! Past midnight, and the news comes that artillery is planted to blow down the walls of the convent, and the magistracy, who up to this time have lifted not a finger to repress the tumult, send word to Savonarola to surrender himself to them, together with the two most active of his companions, Fra Domenico da Pescia and Fra Silvestro Maruffi, as the only means of averting the destruction of the whole order. They offer him assurances of protection and safe return, which he does not in the least believe: nevertheless, he feels that his hour is come, and gives himself up.

His preparations were all made with a solemn method which showed that he felt he was approaching the last act in the drama of life. He called together his flock, scattered and forlorn, and gave them his last words of fatherly advice, encouragement, and comfort, — ending with the remarkable declaration, "A Christian's life consists in doing good and suffering evil." "I go with joy to this marriage-supper," he said, as he left the church for the last sad preparations. He and his doomed friends then confessed and received the sacrament, and after that he surrendered himself into the hands of the men who he felt in his prophetic soul had come to take him to torture and to death.

As he gave himself into their hands, he said, "I commend to your care this flock of mine, and these good citizens of Florence who have been with us;" and then once more turning to his brethren, said, "Doubt not, my brethren. God will not fail to perfect His work. Whether I live or die, He will aid and console you."

At this moment there was a struggle with the attendants in the outer circle of the crowd, and the voice of Father Antonio was heard crying out earnestly, "Do not hold me! I will go with him! I must go with him!"

"Son," said Savonarola, "I charge you on your obedience not to come. It is I and Fra Domenico who are to die for the love of Christ." And thus, at the ninth hour of the night, he passed the threshold of San Marco.

As he was leaving, a plaintive voice of distress was heard from a young novice who had been peculiarly dear to him, who stretched his hands after him, crying, "Father! father! why do you leave us desolate?" Whereupon he turned back a moment, and said, "God will be your help.

If we do not see each other again in this world, we surely shall in heaven."

When the party had gone forth, the monks and citizens stood looking into each other's faces, listening with dismay to the howl of wild ferocity that was rising around the departing prisoner.

"What shall we do?" was the outcry from many voices.

"I know what I shall do," said Agostino. "If any man here will find me a fleet horse, I will start for Milan this very hour; for my uncle is now there on a visit, and he is a counselor of weight with the King of France: we must get the King to interfere."

"Good! good! good!" rose from a hundred voices.

"I will go with you," said Father Antonio. "I shall have no rest till I do something."

"And I," quoth Jacopo Niccolini, "will saddle for you, without delay, two horses of part Arabian blood, swift of foot, and easy, and which will travel day and night without sinking."

CHAPTER XXII

THE CATHEDRAL

THE rays of the setting sun were imparting even more than their wonted cheerfulness to the airy and bustling streets of Milan. There was the usual rush and roar of busy life which mark the great city, and the display of gay costumes and brilliant trappings proper to a ducal capital which at that time gave the law to Europe in all matters of taste and elegance, even as Paris does now. It was, in fact, from the reputation of this city in matters of external show that our English term Milliner was probably derived; and one might well have believed this, who saw the sweep of the ducal cortege at this moment returning in pomp from the afternoon airing. Such glittering of gold-embroidered mantles, such bewildering confusion of colors, such flashing of jewelry from cap and dagger-hilt and finger-ring, and even from bridle and stirrup, testified that the male sex at this period in Italy were no whit behind the daughters of Eve in that passion for personal adornment which our age is wont to consider exclusively feminine. Indeed, all that was visible to the vulgar eye of this pageant was wholly masculine; though no one doubted that behind the gold-embroidered curtains of the litters which contained the female notabilities of the court still more dazzling wonders might be concealed. Occasionally a white jeweled hand would draw aside one of these screens, and a pair of eyes brighter than any gems would peer forth; and then there would be tokens of a visible commotion among the plumed and gemmed cavaliers around, and one young head would

nod to another with jests and quips, and there would be
bowing and curveting and all the antics and caracolings
supposable among gay young people on whom the sun shone
brightly, and who felt the world going well around them,
and deemed themselves the observed of all observers.

Meanwhile, the mute, subservient common people looked
on all this as a part of their daily amusement. Meek
dwellers in those dank, noisome caverns, without any opening but a street-door, which are called dwelling-places in
Italy, they lived in uninquiring good-nature, contentedly
bringing up children on coarse bread, dirty cabbage-stumps,
and other garbage, while all that they could earn was sucked
upward by capillary attraction to nourish the extravagance
of those upper classes on which they stared with such blind
and ignorant admiration.

This was the lot they believed themselves born for, and
which every exhortation of their priests taught them to
regard as the appointed ordinance of God. The women, to
be sure, as women always will be, were true to the instinct
of their sex, and crawled out of the damp and vile-smelling
recesses of their homes with solid gold ear-rings shaking in
their ears, and their blue-black lustrous hair ornamented
with a glittering circle of steel pins or other quaint coiffure.
There was sense in all this: for had not even Dukes of
Milan been found so condescending and affable as to admire
the charms of the fair in the lower orders, whence had
come sons and daughters who took rank among princes and
princesses? What father, or what husband, would be in-
sensible to prospects of such honor? What priest would
not readily absolve such sin? Therefore one might have
observed more than one comely dark-eyed woman, brilliant
as some tropical bird in the colors of her peasant dress,
who cast coquettish glances toward high places, not un-
acknowledged by patronizing nods in return, while mothers
and fathers looked on in triumph. These were the days

for the upper classes; the Church bore them all in her
bosom as a tender nursing-mother, and provided for all
their little peccadilloes with even grandmotherly indulgence, and in return the world was immensely deferential
towards the Church; and it was only now and then some
rugged John Baptist, in raiment of camel's hair, like Savonarola, who dared to speak an indecorous word of God's
truth in the ear of power, and Herod and Herodias had
ever at hand the good old recipe for quieting such disturbances. John Baptist was beheaded in prison, and then
all the world and all the Scribes and Pharisees applauded;
and only a few poor disciples were found to take up the
body and go and tell Jesus.

The whole piazza around the great Cathedral is at this
moment full of the dashing cavalcade of the ducal court,
looking as brilliant in the evening light as a field of poppy,
corn-flower, and scarlet clover at Sorrento; and there, amid
the flutter and rush, the amours and intrigues, the court
scandal, the laughing, the gibing, the glitter, and dazzle,
stands that wonderful Cathedral, that silent witness, that
strange, pure, immaculate mountain of airy, unearthly loveliness, — the most striking emblem of God's mingled vast-
ness and sweetness that ever it was given to human heart
to devise or hands to execute. If there be among the
many mansions of our Father above, among the houses not
made with hands, aught purer and fairer, it must be the
work of those grand spirits who inspired and presided over
the erection of this celestial miracle of beauty. In the
great, vain, wicked city, all alive with the lust of the flesh,
the lust of the eye, and the pride of life, it seemed to stand
as much apart and alone as if it were in the solemn desolation of the Campagna, or in one of the wide deserts of
Africa, — so little part or lot did it appear to have in anything earthly, so little to belong to the struggling, bustling
crowd who beneath its white dazzling pinnacles seemed

dwarfed into crawling insects.   They who could look up
from the dizzy, frivolous life below saw far, far above
them, in the blue Italian air, thousands of glorified saints
standing on a thousand airy points of brilliant whiteness,
ever solemnly adoring.   The marble which below was
somewhat touched and soiled with the dust of the street
seemed gradually to refine and brighten as it rose into the
pure regions of the air, till at last in those thousand distant
pinnacles it had the ethereal translucence of wintry frost-
work, and now began to glow with the violet and rose
hues of evening, in solemn splendor.

The ducal cortege sweeps by; but we have mounted the
dizzy, dark staircase that leads to the roof, where, amid the
bustling life of the city there is a promenade of still and
wondrous solitude.   One seems to have ascended in those
few moments far beyond the tumult and dust of earthly
things, to the silence, the clearness, the tranquillity of
ethereal regions.   The noise of the rushing tides of life
below rises only in a soft and distant murmur; while
around, in the wide, clear distance, is spread a prospect
which has not on earth its like or its equal.   The beautiful
plains of Lombardy lie beneath like a map, and the northern horizon-line is glittering with the entire sweep of the
Alps, like a solemn senate of archangels with diamond mail
and glittering crowns.   Mont Blanc, Monte Rosa with its
countenance of light, the Jungfrau and all the weird brothers of the Oberland, rise one after another to the delighted gaze, and the range of the Tyrol melts far off into
the blue of the sky.   On another side, the Apennines,
with their picturesque outlines and cloud-spotted sides,
complete the enclosure.   All around, wherever the eye
turns, is the unbroken phalanx of mountains; and this
temple, with its thousand saintly statues standing in attitudes of ecstasy and prayer, seems like a worthy altar and
shrine for the beautiful plain which the mountains enclose:
it seems to give all Northern Italy to God.

The effect of the statues in this high, pure air, in this solemn, glorious scenery, is peculiar. They seem a meet companionship for these exalted regions. They seem to stand exultant on their spires, poised lightly as ethereal creatures, the fit inhabitants of the pure blue sky. One feels that they have done with earth; one can fancy them a band of white-robed kings and priests forever ministering in that great temple of which the Alps and the Apennines are the walls and the Cathedral the heart and centre. Never were Art and Nature so majestically married by Religion in so worthy a temple.

One form could be discerned standing in rapt attention, gazing from a platform on the roof upon the far-distant scene. He was enveloped in the white coarse woolen gown of the Dominican monks, and seemed wholly absorbed in meditating on the scene before him, which appeared to move him deeply; for, raising his hands, he repeated aloud from the Latin Vulgate the words of an Apostle : —

"Accessistis ad Sion montem et civitatem Dei viventis, Jerusalem cælestem, et multorum millium angelorum frequentiam, ecclesiam primitivorum, qui inscripti sunt in cælis."[1]

At this moment the evening worship commenced within the Cathedral, and the whole building seemed to vibrate with the rising swell of the great organ, while the grave, long-drawn tones of the Ambrosian Liturgy rose surging in waves and dying away in distant murmurs, like the rolling of the tide on some ocean-shore. The monk turned and drew near to the central part of the roof to listen, and as he turned he disclosed the well-known features of Father Antonio.

Haggard, weary, and travel-worn, his first impulse, on

[1] " Ye are come unto Mount Sion, and unto the city of the living God, the heavenly Jerusalem, and to an innumerable company of angels, to the general assembly and church of the first-born, which are written in heaven."

entering the city, was to fly to this holy solitude, as the
wandering sparrow of sacred song sought her nest amid the
altars of God's temple.   Artist no less than monk, he
found in this wondrous shrine of beauty a repose both for
his artistic and his religious nature; and while waiting for
Agostino Sarelli to find his uncle's residence, he had determined to pass the interval in this holy solitude.   Many
hours had he paced alone up and down the long prome-
nades of white marble which run everywhere between for-
ests of dazzling pinnacles and flying buttresses of airy lightness.   Now he rested in fixed attention against the wall
above the choir, which he could feel pulsating with throbs
of sacred sound, as if a great warm heart were beating
within the fair marble miracle, warming it into mysterious
life and sympathy.

"I would now that boy were here to worship with me,"
he said.   "No wonder the child's faith fainteth: it takes
such monuments as these of the Church's former days to
strengthen one's hopes.   Ah, woe unto those by whom such
offense cometh!"

At this moment the form of Agostino was seen ascending
the marble staircase.

The eye of the monk brightened as he came towards
him.   He put out one hand eagerly to take his, and raised
the other with a gesture of silence.

"Look," he said, "and listen!   Is it not the sound of
many waters and mighty thunderings?"

Agostino stood subdued for the moment by the magnificent sights and sounds; for, as the sun went down, the
distant mountains grew every moment more unearthly in
their brilliancy; and as they lay in a long line, jeweled
brightness mingling with the cloud-wreaths of the far horizon, one might have imagined that he in truth beheld the
foundations of that celestial city of jasper, pearl, and translucent gold which the Apostle saw, and that the risings

and fallings of choral sound which seemed to thrill and pulsate through the marble battlements were indeed that song like many waters sung by the Church Triumphant above.

For a few moments the monk and the young man stood in silence, till at length the monk spoke.

"You have told me, my son, that your heart often troubles you in being more Roman than Christian; that you sometimes doubt whether the Church on earth be other than a fiction or a fable. But look around us. Who are these, this great multitude who praise and pray continually in this temple of the upper air? These are they who have come out of great tribulation, having washed their robes and made them white in the blood of the Lamb. These are not the men that have sacked cities, and made deserts, and written their triumphs in blood and carnage. These be men that have sheltered the poor, and built houses for orphans, and sold themselves into slavery to redeem their brothers in Christ. These be pure women who have lodged saints, brought up children, lived holy and prayerful lives. These be martyrs who have laid down their lives for the testimony of Jesus. There were no such churches in old Rome, — no such saints."

"Well," said Agostino, "one thing is certain. If such be the True Church, the Pope and the Cardinals of our day have no part in it; for they are the men who sack cities and make desolations, who devour widows' houses and for a pretense make long prayers. Let us see one of *them* selling himself into slavery for the love of anybody, while they seek to keep all the world in slavery to themselves!"

"That is the grievous declension our master weeps over," said the monk. "Ah, if the Bishops of the Church now were like brave old Saint Ambrose, strong alone by faith and prayer, showing no more favor to an unrepentant Emperor than to the meanest slave, then would the Church be a reality and a glory! Such is my master. Never is he afraid of the face of king or lord, when he has God's truth to speak. You should have heard how plainly he dealt with our Lorenzo de' Medici on his death-bed, — how he refused him absolution, unless he would make restitution to the poor and restore the liberties of Florence."

"I should have thought," said the young man, sarcastically, "that Lorenzo the Magnificent might have got absolution cheaper than that. Where were all the bishops in his dominion, that he must needs send for Jerome Savonarola?"

"Son, it is ever so," replied the monk. "If there be a man that cares neither for Duke nor Emperor, but for God alone, then Dukes and Emperors would give more for his good word than for a whole dozen of common priests."

"I suppose it is something like a rare manuscript or a singular gem: these *virtuosi* have no rest till they have clutched it. The thing they cannot get is always the thing they want."

"Lorenzo was always seeking our master," said the monk. "Often would he come walking in our gardens, expecting surely he would hasten down to meet him; and the brothers would run all out of breath to his cell to say, 'Father, Lorenzo is in the garden.' 'He is welcome,' would he answer, with his pleasant smile. 'But, father, will you not descend to meet him?' 'Hath he asked for me?' 'No.' 'Well, then, let us not interrupt his meditations,' he would answer, and remain still at his reading, so jealous was he lest he should seek the favor of princes and forget God, as does all the world in our day."

"And because he does not seek the favor of the men of this world he will be trampled down and slain. Will the God in whom he trusts defend him?"

The monk pointed expressively upward to the statues that stood glorified above them, still wearing a rosy radiance, though the shadows of twilight had fallen on all the city below.

"My son," he said, "the victories of the True Church are not in time, but in eternity. How many around us were conquered on earth that they might triumph in heaven! What saith the Apostle? 'They were tortured, not accepting deliverance, that they might obtain a better resurrection.'"

"But, alas!" said Agostino, "are we never to see the right triumph here? I fear that this noble name is written in blood, like so many of whom the world is not worthy. Can one do nothing to help it?"

"How is that? What have you heard?" said the monk, eagerly. "Have you seen your uncle?"

"Not yet; he is gone into the country for a day, — so say his servants. I saw, when the Duke's court passed, my cousin, who is in his train, and got a moment's speech with him; and he promised, that, if I would wait for him here, he would come to me as soon as he could be let off from his attendance. When he comes, it were best that we confer alone."

"I will retire to the southern side," said the monk, "and await the end of your conference;" and with that he crossed the platform on which they were standing, and, going down a flight of white marble steps, was soon lost to view amid the wilderness of frost-like carved work.

He had scarcely vanished, before footsteps were heard ascending the marble staircase on the other side, and the sound of a voice humming a popular air of the court.

The stranger was a young man of about five-and-twenty, habited with all that richness and brilliancy of coloring which the fashion of the day permitted to a young exquisite. His mantle of purple velvet falling jauntily off from one shoulder disclosed a doublet of amber satin richly embroidered with gold and seed-pearl. The long white plume which drooped from his cap was held in its place by a large diamond which sparkled like a star in the evening twilight. His finely moulded hands were loaded with rings, and ruffles of the richest Venetian lace encircled his wrists. He had worn over all a dark cloak with a peaked hood, the usual evening disguise in Italy; but as he gained the top-stair of the platform, he threw it carelessly down and gayly offered his hand.

"Good even to you, cousin mine! So you see I am as true to my appointment as if your name were Leonora or Camilla instead of Agostino. How goes it with you? I wanted to talk with you below, but I saw we must have a place without listeners. Our friends the saints are too high in heavenly things to make mischief by eavesdropping."

"Thank you, Cousin Carlos, for your promptness. And now to the point. Did your father, my uncle, get the letter I wrote him about a month since?"

"He did; and he bade me treat with you about it. It 's an abominable snarl, this, they have got you into. My father says, your best way is to come straight to him in France, and abide till things take a better turn: he is high in favor with the King and can find you a very pretty place at court, and he takes it upon him in time to reconcile the Pope. Between you and me, the old Pope has no special spite in the world against *you :* he merely wants your lands for his son, and as long as you prowl round and lay claim to them, why, you must stay excommunicated; but just clear the coast and leave them peaceably and he will put you back into the True Church, and my father will charge himself with your success. Popes don't last forever, or there may come another falling out with the King of France, and either way there will be a chance of your being one day put back into your rights; meanwhile, a young fellow might do worse than have a good place in our court."

During this long monologue, which the young speaker uttered with all the flippant self-sufficiency of worldly people with whom the world is going well, the face of the young nobleman who listened presented a picture of many strong contending emotions.

"You speak," he said, "as if man had nothing to do in this world but seek his own ease and pleasure. What lies nearest my heart is not that I am plundered of my estates, and my house uprooted, but it is that my beautiful Rome, the city of my fathers, is a prisoner under the heel of the tyrant. It is that the glorious religion of Christ, the holy faith in which my mother died, the faith made venerable by all these saints around us, is made the tool and instrument of such vileness and cruelty that one is tempted to doubt whether it were not better to have been born of heathen in the good old times of the Roman Republic, — God forgive me for saying so! Does the most Christian King of France know that the man who pretends to rule in the name of Christ is not a believer in the Christian religion, — that he does not believe even in a God, — that he obtained the holy seat by simony, — that he uses all its power to enrich a brood of children whose lives are so indecent that it is a shame to modest lips even to *say* what they do ? "

"Why, of course," said the other, "the King of France is pretty well informed about all these things. You know old King Charles, when he marched through Italy, had more than half a mind, they say, to pull the old Pope out of his place; and he might have done it easily. My father was in his train at that time, and he says the Pope was frightened enough. Somehow they made it all up among them, and settled about their territories, which is the main thing, after all; and now our new King, I fancy, does not like to meddle with him: between you and me, he has his eye in another direction here. This gay city would suit

him admirably, and he fancies he can govern it as well as
it is governed now. My father does not visit here with
his eyes shut, I can tell you. But as to the Pope —
Well, you see such things are delicate to handle. After
all, my dear Agostino, we are not priests, — our business
is with this world; and, no matter how they came by them,
these fellows have the keys of the kingdom of heaven, and
one cannot afford to quarrel with them, — we must have
the ordinances, you know, or what becomes of our souls?
Do you suppose, now, that I should live as gay and easy
a life as I do, if I thought there were any doubt of my
salvation? It's a mercy to us sinners that the ordinances
are not vitiated by the sins of the priests; it would go hard
with us, if they were: as it is, if they will live scandalous
lives, it is their affair, not ours."

"And is it nothing," replied the other, "to a true man
who has taken the holy vows of knighthood on him,
whether his Lord's religion be defamed and dishonored
and made a scandal and a scoffing? Did not all Europe go
out to save Christ's holy sepulchre from being dishonored
by the feet of the Infidel? and shall we let infidels have
the very house of the Lord, and reign supreme in his holy
dwelling-place? There has risen a holy prophet in Italy,
the greatest since the time of Saint Francis, and his preaching hath stirred all hearts to live more conformably with
our holy faith; and now for his pure life and good works
he is under excommunication of the Pope, and they have
seized and imprisoned him, and threaten his life."

"Oh, you mean Savonarola," said the other. "Yes, we
have heard of him, — a most imprudent, impracticable fellow, who will not take advice nor be guided. My father,
I believe, thought well of him once, and deemed that in
the distracted state of Italy he might prove serviceable in
forwarding some of his plans: but he is wholly wrapt up
in his own notions; he heeds no will but his own."

"Have you heard anything," said Agostino, "of a letter which he wrote to the King of France lately, stirring him up to call a General Council of the Christian Church to consider what is to be done about the scandals at Rome?"

"Then he has written one, has he?" replied the young man; "then the story that I have heard whispered about here must be true. A man who certainly is in a condition to know told me day before yesterday that the Duke had arrested a courier with some such letter, and sent it on to the Pope: it is likely, for the Duke hates Savonarola. If that be true, it will go hard with him yet; for the Pope has a long arm for an enemy."

"And so," said Agostino, with an expression of deep concern, "that letter, from which the good man hoped so much, and which was so powerful, will only go to increase his danger!"

"The more fool he! — he might have known that it was of no use. Who was going to take his part against the Pope?"

"The city of Florence has stood by him until lately," said Agostino, "and would again, with a little help."

"Oh, no! never think it, my dear Agostino! Depend upon it, it will end as such things always do, and the man is only a madman that undertakes it. Hark ye, cousin, what have *you* to do with this man? Why do you attach yourself to the side that is *sure* to lose? I cannot conceive what you would be at. This is no way to mend your fortunes. Come to-night to my father's palace: the Duke has appointed us princely lodgings, and treats us with great hospitality, and my father has plans for your advantage. Between us, there is a fair young ward of his, of large estates and noble blood, whom he designs for you. So you see, if you turn your attention in this channel, there may come a reinforcement of the family property, which will enable you to hold out until the Pope dies, or

some prince or other gets into a quarrel with him, which is
always happening, and then a move may be made for you.
My father, I'll promise you, is shrewd enough, and always
keeps his eye open to see where there is a joint in the harness, and have a trusty dagger-blade all whetted to stick
under. Of course, he means to see you righted; he has
the family interest at heart, and feels as indignant as you
could at the rascality which has been perpetrated; but
I am quite sure he will tell you that the way is not to
come out openly against the Pope and join this fanatical
party."

Agostino stood silent, with the melancholy air of a man
who has much to say, and is deeply moved by considera-
tions which he perceives it would be utterly idle and useless to attempt to explain. If the easy theology of his
friend were indeed true, — if the treasures of the heavenly
kingdom, glory, honor, and immortality, could indeed be
placed in unholy hands, to be bought and sold and traded
in, — if holiness of heart and life, and all those nobler
modes of living and being which were witnessed in the
histories of the thousand saints around him, were indeed
but a secondary thing in the strife for worldly place and
territory, — what, then, remained for the man of ideas, of
aspirations? In such a state of society, his track must be
like that of the dove in sacred history, who found no rest
for the sole of her foot.

Agostino folded his arms and sighed deeply, and then
made answer mechanically, as one whose thoughts are afar
off.

"Present my duty," he said, "to my uncle, your father,
and say to him that I will wait on him to-night."

"Even so," said the young man, picking up his cloak
and folding it about him. "And now, you know, I must
go. Don't be discouraged; keep up a good heart; you
shall see what it is to have powerful friends to stand by

you; all will be right yet. Come, will you go with me now?"

"Thank you," said Agostino, "I think I would be alone a little while. My head is confused, and I would fain think over matters a little quietly."

"Well, *au revoir*, then. I must leave you to the company of the saints. But be sure and come early."

So saying, he threw his cloak over his shoulder and sauntered carelessly down the marble steps, humming again the gay air with which he had ascended.

Left alone, Agostino once more cast a glance on the strangely solemn and impressive scene around him. He was standing on a platform of the central tower which overlooked the whole building. The round, full moon had now risen in the horizon, displacing by her solemn brightness the glow of twilight; and her beams were reflected by the delicate frost-work of the myriad pinnacles which rose in a bewildering maze at his feet. It might seem to be some strange enchanted garden of fairy-land, where a luxuriant and freakish growth of Nature had been suddenly arrested and frozen into eternal stillness. Around in the shadows at the foot of the Cathedral, the lights of the great gay city twinkled and danced and veered and fluttered like fireflies in the damp, dewy shadows of some moist meadow in summer. The sound of clattering hoofs and rumbling wheels, of tinkling guitars and gay roundelays, rose out of that obscure distance, seeming far off and plaintive like the dream of a life that is past. The great church seemed a vast world; the long aisles of statued pinnacles with their pure floorings of white marble appeared as if they might be the corridors of heaven; and it seemed as if the crowned and sceptred saints in their white marriage-garments might come down and walk there, without ever a spot of earth on their unsullied whiteness.

In a few moments Father Antonio had glided back to

the side of the young man, whom he found so lost in reverie that not till he laid his hand upon his arm did he
awaken from his meditations.

"Ah!" he said, with a start, "my father, is it you?"

"Yes, my son.   What of your conference?   Have you
learned anything?"

"Father, I have learned far more than I wished to
know."

"What is it, my son?   Speak it at once."

"Well, then, I fear that the letter of our holy father to
the King of France has been intercepted here in Milan,
and sent to the Pope."

"What makes you think so?" said the monk, with an
eagerness that showed how much he felt the intelligence.

"My cousin tells me that a person of consideration in
the Duke's household, who is supposed to be in a position
to know, told him that it was so."

Agostino felt the light grasp which the monk had laid
upon his arm gradually closing with a convulsive pressure,
and that he was trembling with intense feeling.

"Even so, Father, for so it seemed good in thy sight!"
he said, after a few moments of silence.

"It is discouraging," said Agostino, "to see how little
these princes care for the true interests of religion and the
service of God, — how little real fealty there is to our Lord
Jesus."

"Yes," said the monk, "all seek their own, and not the
things that are Christ's.   It is well written, ' Put not your
trust in princes.' "

"And what prospect, what hope do you see for him?"
said Agostino.   "Will Florence stand firm?"

"I could have thought so once," said the monk, "in
those days when I have seen counselors and nobles and
women of the highest degree all humbly craving to hear
the word of God from his lips, and seeming to seek nothing

so much as to purify their houses, their hands, and their hearts, that they might be worthy citizens of that commonwealth which has chosen the Lord Jesus for its gonfalonier. I have seen the very children thronging to kiss the hem of his robe, as he walked through the streets; but, oh, my friend, did not Jerusalem bring palms and spread its garments in the way of Christ only four days before he was crucified?"

The monk's voice here faltered. He turned away, and seemed to wrestle with a tempest of suppressed sobbing. A moment more, he looked heavenward and pointed up with a smile.

"Son," he said, "you ask what hope there is. I answer, There is hope of such crowns as these wear who came out of great tribulation and now reign with Christ in glory."

CHAPTER XXIII

THE PILGRIMAGE

THE morning sun rose clear and lovely on the old red rocks of Sorrento, and danced in a thousand golden scales and ripples on the wide Mediterranean. The shadows of the gorge were pierced by long golden shafts of light, here falling on some moist bed of crimson cyclamen, there shining through a waving tuft of gladiolus, or making the abundant yellow fringes of the broom more vivid in their brightness. The velvet-mossy old bridge, in the far shadows at the bottom, was lit up by a chance beam, and seemed as if it might be something belonging to fairy-land.

There had been a bustle and stir betimes in the little dove-cot, for to-morrow the inmates were to leave it for a long, adventurous journey.

To old Elsie, the journey back to Rome, the city of her former days of prosperity, the place which had witnessed her ambitious hopes, her disgrace and downfall, was full of painful ideas. There arose to her memory, like a picture, those princely halls, with their slippery, cold mosaic floors, their long galleries of statues and paintings, their enchanting gardens, musical with the voice of mossy fountains, fragrant with the breath of roses and jasmines, where the mother of Agnes had spent the hours of her youth and beauty. She seemed to see her flitting hither and thither down the stately ilex-avenues, like some gay singing-bird, to whom were given gilded cages and a constant round of caresses and sweets, or like the flowers in the parterres, which lived and died only as the graceful accessories of the grandeur of an old princely family.

She compared, mentally, the shaded and secluded life which Agnes had led with the specious and fatal brilliancy which had been the lot of her mother, — her simple peasant garb with those remembered visions of jewelry and silk and embroideries with which the partial patronage of the Duchess or the ephemeral passion of her son had decked out the poor Isella; and then came swelling at her heart a tumultuous thought, one which she had repressed and kept down for years with all the force of pride and hatred. Agnes, peasant-girl though she seemed, had yet the blood of that proud old family in her veins; the marriage had been a true one; she herself had witnessed it.

"Yes, indeed," she said to herself, "were justice done, she would now be a princess, — a fit mate for the nobles of the land; and here I ask no more than to mate her to an honest smith, — I that have seen a prince kneel to kiss her mother's hand, — yes, he did, — entreat her on his knees to be his wife, — I saw 'it. But then, what came of it? Was there ever one of these nobles that kept oath or promise to us of the people, or that cared for us longer than the few moments we could serve his pleasure? Old Elsie, you have done wisely! keep your dove out of the eagle's nest: it is foul with the blood of poor innocents whom he has torn to pieces in his cruel pride!"

These thoughts swelled in silence in the mind of Elsie, while she was busy sorting and arranging her household stores, and making those thousand-and-one preparations known to every householder, whether of much or little, who meditates a long journey.

To Agnes she seemed more than ever severe and hard; yet probably there never was a time when every pulse of her heart was beating more warmly for the child, and every thought of the future was more entirely regulated with reference to her welfare. It is no sinecure to have the entire devotion of a strong, enterprising, self-willed friend, as Agnes had all her life found. One cannot gather grapes of thorns or figs of thistles, and the affection of thorny and thistly natures has often as sharp an acid and as long prickers as wild gooseberries; yet it is their best, and must be so accepted.

Agnes tried several times to offer her help to her grandmother, but was refused so roughly that she dared not offer again, and therefore went to her favorite station by the parapet in the garden, whence she could look up and down the gorge, and through the arches of the old mossy Roman bridge that spanned it far down by the city-wall. All these things had become dear to her by years of familiar silent converse. The little garden, with its old sculptured basin and the ever-lulling dash of falling water; the tremulous draperies of maiden's-hair, always beaded with shining drops; the old shrine, with its picture, its lamp, and flower-vase; the tall, dusky orange-trees, so full of blossoms and fruit, so smooth and shining in their healthy bark, — all seemed to her as so many dear old friends whom she was about to leave, perhaps forever.

What this pilgrimage would be like, she scarcely knew: days and weeks of wandering, — over mountain-passes; in deep, solitary valleys, — as years ago, when her grandmother brought her, a little child, from Rome.

In the last few weeks, Agnes seemed to herself to have become wholly another being. Silently, insensibly, her feet had crossed the enchanted river that divides childhood from womanhood, and all the sweet ignorant joys of that first early paradise lay behind her. Up to this time her life had seemed to her a charming dream, full of blessed visions and images: legends of saints, and hymns, and prayers had blended with flower-gatherings in the gorge, and light daily toils.

Now a new, strange life had been born within her, —
a life full of passions, contradictions, and conflicts. A
love had sprung up in her heart, strange and wonderful,
for one who till within these few weeks had been entirely
unknown to her, who had never toiled for, or housed, or
clothed, or cared for her as her grandmother had, and yet
whom a few short interviews, a few looks, a few words,
had made to seem nearer and dearer than the old, tried
friends of her childhood. In vain she confessed it as a
sin, in vain she strove against it; it came back to her in
every hymn, in every prayer. Then she would press the
sharp cross to her breast, till a thousand stings of pain
would send the blood in momentary rushes to her pale
cheek, and cause her delicate lips to contract with an expression of stern endurance, and pray that by any penance
and anguish she might secure his salvation.

To save one such glorious soul, she said to herself, was
work enough for one little life. She was willing to spend
it all in endurance, unseen by him, unknown to him, so
that at last he should be received into that Paradise which
her ardent imagination conceived so vividly. Surely, there
she should meet him, radiant as the angel of her dream;
and then she would tell him that it was all for his sake
that she had refused to listen to him here. And these
sinful longings to see him once more, these involuntary
reachings of her soul after an earthly companionship, she
should find strength to overcome in this pilgrimage. She
should go to Rome, — the very city where the blessed Paul
poured out his blood for the Lord Jesus, — where Peter
fed the flock, till his time, too, came to follow his Lord in
the way of the cross. She should even come near to her
blessed Redeemer; she should go up, on her knees, those
very steps to Pilate's hall where He stood bleeding, crowned
with thorns, — His blood, perhaps, dropping on the very
stones. Ah, could any mortal love distract her there?

Should she not there find her soul made free of every earthly thrall to love her Lord alone, — as she had loved Him in the artless and ignorant days of her childhood, — but better, a thousand times?

"Good-morning to you, pretty dove!" said a voice from without the garden-wall; and Agnes, roused from her reverie, saw old Jocunda.

"I came down to help you off," she said, as she came into the little garden. "Why, my dear little saint! you are looking white as a sheet, and with those tears! What's it all for, baby?"

"Ah, Jocunda! grandmamma is angry with me all the time now. I wish I could go once more to the convent and see my dear Mother Theresa. She is angry, if I but name it; and yet she will not let me do anything here to help her, and so I don't know *what* to do."

"Well, at any rate, don't cry, pretty one! Your grandmamma is worked with hard thoughts. We old folks are twisted and crabbed and full of knots with disappointment and trouble, like the mulberry-trees that they keep for vines to run on. But I'll speak to her; I know her ways; she shall let you go; I'll bring her round."

"So-ho, sister!" said the old soul, hobbling to the door and looking in at Elsie, who was sitting flat on the stone floor of her cottage, sorting a quantity of flax that lay around her. The severe Roman profile was thrown out by the deep shadows of the interior, — and the piercing black eyes, the silver-white hair, and the strong, compressed lines of the mouth, as she worked, and struggled with the ghosts of her former life, made her look like no unapt personification of one of the Fates reviewing her flax before she commenced the spinning of some new web of destiny.

"Good-morning to you, sister!" said Jocunda. "I heard you were off to-morrow, and I came to see what I could do to help you."

"There's nothing to be done for me, but to kill me," said Elsie. "I am weary of living."

"Oh, never say that! Shake the dice again, my old man used to say, — God rest his soul! Please Saint Agnes, you'll have a brave pilgrimage."

"Saint Agnes be hanged!" said Elsie, gruffly. "I'm out with her. It was she put all these notions into my girl's head. Because she didn't get married herself, she don't want any one else to. She has no consideration. I've done with her: I told her so this morning. The candles I've burned and the prayers I've gone through with, that she might prosper me in this one thing! and it's all gone against me. She's a baggage, and shall never see another penny of mine, — that's flat!"

Such vituperation of saints and sacred images may be heard to this day in Italy, and is a common feature of idol-worship in all lands; for, however the invocation of the saints could be vitalized in the hearts of the few spiritual, there is no doubt that in the mass of the common people it had all the well-defined symptoms of the grossest idolatry, among which fits of passionate irreverence are one. The feeling which tempts the enlightened Christian in sore disappointment and vexation to rise in rebellion against a wise Providence, in the childish twilight of uncultured natures finds its full expression unawed by reverence or fear.

"Oh, hush, now!" said Jocunda. "What is the use of making her angry just as you are going to Rome, where she has the most power? All sorts of ill-luck will befall you. Make up with her before you start, or you may get the fever in the marshes and die, and then who will take care of poor Agnes?"

"Let Saint Agnes look after her; the girl loves her better than she does me, or anybody else," said Elsie. "If she cared anything about me, she'd marry and settle down, as I want her to."

"Oh, there you are wrong," said Jocunda. "Marrying is like your dinner: one is not always in stomach for it, and one's meat is another's poison. Now who knows but this pilgrimage may be the very thing to bring the girl round? I've seen people cured of too much religion by going to Rome. You know things ain't there as our little saint fancies. Why, between you and me, the priests themselves have their jokes on those who come so far to so little purpose. More shame for 'em, say I, too; but we common people mustn't look into such things too closely. Now take it cheerfully, and you'll see the girl will come back tired of tramping and able to settle down in a good home with a likely husband. I have a brother in Naples who is turning a pretty penny in the fisheries; I will give you directions to find him; his wife is a wholesome Christian woman; and if the little one be tired by the time you get there, you might do worse than stop two or three days with them. It's a brave city; seems made to have a good time in. Come, you let her just run up to the convent to bid good-by to the Mother Theresa and the sisters."

"I don't care where she goes," said Elsie, ungraciously.

"There, now!" said Jocunda, coming out, "Agnes, your grandmother bids you go to the convent to say good-by to the sisters; so run along, there's a little dear. The Mother Theresa talks of nothing else but you since she heard that you meditated this; and she has broken in two her own piece of the True Cross which she's carried in the gold and pearl reliquary that the Queen sent her, and means to give it to you. One doesn't halve such gifts, without one's whole heart goes with them."

"Dear mother!" said Agnes, her eyes filling with tears, "I will take her some flowers and oranges for the last time. Do you know, Jocunda, I feel that I never shall come back here to this dear little home where I have been so happy,

— everything sounds so mournful and looks so mournful!
— I love everything here so much!"

"Oh, dear child, never give in to such fancies, but pluck
up heart. You will be sure to have luck, wherever you
go, — especially since the mother will give you that holy
relic. I myself had a piece of Saint John Baptist's thumb-
nail sewed up in a leather bag, which I wore day and night
all the years I was tramping up and down with my old
man; but when he died, I had it buried with him to ease
his soul. For you see, dear, he was a trooper, and led
such a rackety up-and-down life, that I doubt but his confessions were but slipshod, and he needed all the help he
could get, poor old soul! It's a comfort to think he has
it."

"Ah, Jocunda, seems to me it were better to trust to
the free love of our dear Lord who died for us, and pray
to Him, without ceasing, for his soul."

"Like enough, dearie; but then, one can't be too sure,
you know. And there isn't the least doubt in my mind
that that was a true relic, for I got it in the sack of the
city of Volterra, out of the private cabinet of a noble lady,
with a lot of jewels and other matters that made quite a
little purse for us. Ah, that was a time, when that city
was sacked! It was hell upon earth for three days, and
all our men acted like devils incarnate; but then they always will in such cases. But go your ways now, dearie,
and I'll stay with your grandmamma; for, please God, you
must be up and away with the sun to-morrow."

Agnes hastily arranged a little basket of fruit and flowers, and took her way down through the gorge, under the
Roman bridge, through an orange-orchard, and finally came
out upon the seashore, and so along the sands below the
cliffs on which the old town of Sorrento is situated.

So cheating and inconsistent is the human heart, especially in the feminine subject, that she had more than once

occasion to chide herself for the thrill with which she remembered passing the cavalier once in this orange-garden,
and the sort of vague hope which she detected that somewhere along this road he might appear again.

"How perfectly wicked and depraved I must be," she
said to herself, "to find any pleasure in such a thought of
one I should pray never to meet again!"

And so the little soul went on condemning herself in
those exaggerated terms which the religious vocabulary of
conventual life furnished ready-made for the use of penitents of every degree, till by the time she arrived at the
convent she could scarcely have been more oppressed with
a sense of sin, if she had murdered her grandmother and
eloped with the cavalier.

On her arrival in the convent court, the peaceful and
dreamy stillness contrasted strangely with the gorgeous
brightness of the day outside. The splendid sunshine, the
sparkling seas, the songs of the boatmen, the brisk passage
of gliding sails, the bright hues of the flowers that garlanded the rocks, all seemed as if the earth had been arrayed
for some gala-day; but the moment she had passed the
portal, the silent, mossy court, with its pale marble nymph,
its lull of falling water, its turf snow-dropt with daisies and
fragrant with blue and white violets, and the surrounding
cloistered walks, with their pictured figures of pious history, all came with a sad and soothing influence on her
nerves.

The nuns, who had heard the news of the projected pilgrimage, and regarded it as the commencement of that saintly
career which they had always predicted for her, crowded
around her, kissing her hands and her robe, and entreating
her prayers at different shrines of especial sanctity that she
might visit.

The Mother Theresa took her to her cell, and there hung
round her neck, by a golden chain, the relic which she

designed for her, and of whose genuineness she appeared
to possess no manner of doubt.

"But how pale you are, my sweet child!" she said.
"What has happened to alter you so much? Your cheeks
look so thin, and there are deep, dark circles round your
eyes."

"Ah, my mother, it is because of my sins."

"Your sins, dear little one! What sins can you be
guilty of?"

"Ah, my dear mother, I have been false to my Lord,
and let the love of an earthly creature into my heart."

"What can you mean?" said the mother.

"Alas, dear mother, the cavalier who sent that ring!"
said Agnes, covering her face with her hands.

Now the Mother Theresa had never left the walls of
that convent since she was ten years old, — had seen no
men except her father and uncle, who once or twice made
her a short call, and an old hunchback who took care of
their garden, safe in his armor of deformity. Her ideas
on the subject of masculine attractions were, therefore, as
vague as might be the conceptions of the eyeless fishes in
the Mammoth Cave of Kentucky with regard to the fruits
and flowers above ground. All that portion of her womanly
nature which might have throbbed lay in a dead calm.
Still there was a faint flutter of curiosity, as she pressed
Agnes to tell her story, which she did with many pauses
and sobs and blushes.

"And is he so very handsome, my little heart?" she
said, after listening. "What makes you love him so much
in so little time?"

"Yes, — he is beautiful as an angel."

"I never saw a young man, really," said the Mother
Theresa. "Uncle Angelo was lame, and had gray hair;
and papa was very fat, and had a red face. Perhaps he
looks like our picture of Saint Sebastian; — I have often

thought that I might be in danger of loving a young man that looked like him."

"Oh, he is more beautiful than that picture or any picture!" said Agnes, fervently; "and, mother, though he is excommunicated, I can't help feeling that he is as good as he is beautiful. My uncle had strong hopes that he should restore him to the True Church; and to pray for his soul I am going on this pilgrimage. Father Francesco says, if I will tear away and overcome this love, I shall gain so much merit that my prayers will have power to save his soul. Promise me, dear mother, that you and all the sisters will help me with your prayers; — help me to work out this great salvation, and then I shall be so glad to come back here and spend all my life in prayer!"

CHAPTER XXIV

AND so on a bright spring morning our pilgrims started. Whoever has traversed the road from Sorrento to Naples, that wonderful path along the high rocky shores of the Mediterranean, must remember it only as a wild dream of enchantment. On one side lies the sea, shimmering in bands of blue, purple, and green to the swaying of gentle winds, exhibiting those magical shiftings and changes of color peculiar to these waves. Near the land its waters are of pale, transparent emerald, while farther out they deepen into blue and thence into a violet-purple, which again, towards the horizon-line, fades into misty pearl-color. The shores rise above the sea in wild, bold precipices, grottoed into fantastic caverns by the action of the waves, and presenting every moment some new variety of outline. As the path of the traveler winds round promontories whose mountain-heights are capped by white villages and silvery with olive-groves, he catches the enchanting sea-view, now at this point, and now at another, with Naples glimmering through the mists in the distance, and the purple sides of Vesuvius ever changing with streaks and veins of cloud-shadows, while silver vapors crown the summit. Above the road the steep hills seem piled up to the sky, — every spot terraced, and cultivated with some form of vegetable wealth, and the wild, untamable rocks garlanded over with golden broom, crimson gillyflowers, and a thousand other bright adornments. The road lies through villages whose gardens and orange-orchards fill the

air with sweet scents, and whose rose-hedges sometimes
pour a perfect cascade of bloom and fragrance over the
walls.

Our travelers started in the dewy freshness of one of
those gorgeous days which seem to cast an illuminating
charm over everything. Even old Elsie's stern features
relaxed somewhat under the balmy influences of sun and
sky, and Agnes's young, pale face was lit up with a brighter
color than for many a day before. Their pilgrimage through
this beautiful country had few incidents. They walked in
the earlier and latter parts of the day, reposing a few hours
at noon near some fountain or shrine by the wayside, —
often experiencing the kindly veneration of the simple
peasantry, who cheerfully offered them refreshments, and
begged their prayers at the holy places whither they were
going.

In a few days they reached Naples, where they made a
little stop with the hospitable family to whom Jocunda had
recommended them. From Naples their path lay through
the Pontine Marshes; and though the malaria makes this
region a word of fear, yet it is no less one of strange, soft,
enchanting beauty. A wide, sea-like expanse, clothed with
an abundance of soft, rich grass, painted with golden bands
and streaks of bright yellow flowers, stretches away to a
purple curtain of mountains, whose romantic outline rises
constantly in a thousand new forms of beauty. The up-
land at the foot of these mountains is beautifully diversified
with tufts of trees, and the contrast of the purple softness
of the distant hills with the dazzling gold and emerald of
the wide meadow-tracts they enclose is a striking feature
in the landscape. Droves of silver-haired oxen, with their
great, dreamy, dark eyes and polished black horns, were
tranquilly feeding knee-deep in the lush, juicy grass, and
herds of buffaloes, uncouth, but harmless, might be seen
pasturing or reposing in the distance. On either side of

the way were waving tracts of yellow fleur-de-lis, and beds
of arum, with its arrowy leaves and white blossoms. It
was a wild luxuriance of growth, a dreamy stillness of solitude, so lovely that one could scarce remember that it was
deadly.

Elsie was so impressed with the fear of the malaria, that
she trafficked with an honest peasant, who had been hired
to take back to Rome the horses which had been used to
convey part of the suite of a nobleman traveling to Naples,
to give them a quicker passage across than they could have
made on foot. It is true that this was quite contrary to
the wishes of Agnes, who felt that the journey ought to be
performed in the most toilsome and self-renouncing way,
and that they should trust solely to prayer and spiritual
protection to ward off the pestilential exhalations.

In vain she quoted the Psalm, "Thou shalt not be afraid
for the terror by night, nor for the arrow that flieth by
day, nor for the pestilence that walketh in darkness, nor
for the destruction that wasteth at noon-day," and adduced
cases of saints who had walked unhurt through all sorts of
dangers.

"There's no use talking, child," said Elsie. "I'm
older than you, and have seen more of real men and women; and whatever they did in old times, I know that
nowadays the saints don't help those that don't take care
of themselves; and the long and the short of it is, we must
ride across those marshes, and get out of them as quick as
possible, or we shall get into Paradise quicker than we
want to."

In common with many other professing Christians, Elsie
felt that going to Paradise was the very dismalest of alter-
natives, — a thing to be staved off as long as possible.

After many days of journeying, the travelers, somewhat
weary and foot-sore, found themselves in a sombre and
lonely dell of the mountains, about an hour before the

going down of the sun.   The slanting yellow beams turned
to silvery brightness the ashy foliage of the gnarled old
olives, which gaunt and weird clung with their great,
knotty, straggling roots to the rocky mountain-sides.   Before them, the path, stony, steep, and winding, was rising
upward and still upward, and no shelter for the night appeared, except in a distant mountain-town, which, perched
airily as an eagle's nest on its hazy height, reflected from
the dome of its church and its half-ruined old feudal tower
the golden light of sunset.   A drowsy-toned bell was ringing out the Ave Maria over the wide purple solitude of
mountains, whose varying outlines were rising around.

"You are tired, my little heart," said old Elsie to Agnes,
who had drooped during a longer walk than usual.

"No, grandmamma," said Agnes, sinking on her knees
to repeat her evening prayer, which she did, covering her
face with her hands.

Old Elsie kneeled too; but, as she was praying, — being
a thrifty old body in the use of her time, — she cast an
eye up the steep mountain-path and calculated the distance of the little airy village.   Just at that moment she
saw two or three horsemen, who appeared to be stealthily observing them from behind the shadow of some large
rocks.

When their devotions were finished, she hurried on her
grandchild saying, —

"Come, dearie! it must be we shall find a shelter
soon."

The horsemen now rode up behind them.

"Good-evening, mother!" said one of them, speaking
from under the shadow of a deeply slouched hat.

Elsie made no reply, but hurried forward.

"Good-evening, pretty maid!" he said again, riding
still nearer.

"Go your ways in the name of God," said Elsie.   "We

are pilgrims, going for our souls to Rome; and whoever hinders us will have the saints to deal with."

"Who talks of hindering you, mother?" responded the other. "On the contrary, we come for the express purpose of helping you along."

"We want none of your help," said Elsie, gruffly.

"See, now, how foolish you are!" said the horseman. "Don't you see that that town is a good seven miles off, and not a bit of bed or supper to be had till you get there, and the sun will be down soon? So mount up behind me, and here is a horse for the little one."

In fact, the horsemen at this moment opening disclosed to view a palfrey with a lady's saddle, richly caparisoned, as if for a person of condition. With a sudden movement, two of the men dismounted, confronted the travelers, and the one who had acted as spokesman, approaching Agnes, said, in a tone somewhat imperative, —

"Come, young lady, it is our master's will that your poor little feet should have some rest."

And before Agnes could remonstrate, he raised her into the saddle as easily as if she had been a puff of thistle-down, and then turning to Elsie, he said, —

"For you, good mother, if you wish to keep up, you must e'en be content with a seat behind me."

"Who are you? and how dare you?" said Elsie, indignantly.

"Good mother," said the man, "you see God's will is that you should submit, because we are four to you two, and there are fifty more within call. So get up without more words, and I swear by the Holy Virgin no harm shall be done you."

Elsie looked and saw Agnes already some distance before her, the bridle of her palfrey being held by one of the horsemen, who rode by her side and seemed to look after her carefully; and so, without more ado, she accepted the services of the man, and, placing her foot on the toe of his riding-boot, mounted to the crupper behind him.

"That is right," said he. "Now hold on to me lustily, and be not afraid."

So saying, the whole troop began winding as rapidly as possible up the steep, rocky path to the mountain-town.

Notwithstanding the surprise and alarm of this most unexpected adventure, Agnes, who had been at the very point of exhaustion from fatigue, could not but feel the sensation of relief and repose which the seat in an easy saddle gave her. The mountain air, as they rose, breathed fresh and cold on her brow, and a prospect of such wondrous beauty unrolled beneath her feet that her alarm soon became lost in admiration. The mountains that rose everywhere around them seemed to float in a transparent sea of luminous vapor, with olive-orchards and well-tilled fields lying in far, dreamy distances below, while out towards the horizon silver gleams of the Mediteranean gradually widened to the view. Soothed by the hour, refreshed by the air, and filled with admiration for the beauty of all she saw, she surrendered herself to her situation with a feeling of solemn religious calm, as to some unfolding of the Divine Will, which might unroll like the landscape beneath her. They pursued their way in silence, rising higher and higher out of the shadows of the deep valleys below, the man who conducted them observing a strict reserve, but seeming to have a care for their welfare.

The twilight yet burned red in the sky, and painted with solemn lights the mossy walls of the little old town, as they plunged under a sombre antique gateway, and entered on a street as damp and dark as a cellar, which went up almost perpendicularly between tall, black stone walls that seemed to have neither windows nor doors. Agnes could only remember clambering upward, turning short corners, clattering down steep stone steps, under low archways, along narrow, ill-smelling passages, where the light that seemed so clear without the town was almost extinguished in utter night.

At last they entered the damp court of a huge, irregular pile of stone buildings. Here the men suddenly drew up, and Agnes's conductor, dismounting, came and took her silently from her saddle, saying briefly, "Come this way."

Elsie sprang from her seat in a moment, and placed herself at the side of her child.

"No, good mother," said the man with whom she had ridden, seizing her powerfully by the shoulders, and turning her round.

"What do you mean?" said Elsie, fiercely. "Are you going to keep me from my own child?"

"Patience!" replied the man. "You can't help yourself, so recommend yourself to God, and no harm shall come to you."

Agnes looked back at her grandmother.

"Fear not, dear grandmamma," she said, "the blessed angels will watch over us."

As she spoke, she followed her conductor through long, damp, mouldering passages, and up flights of stone steps, and again through other long passages, smelling of mould and damp, till at last he opened the door of an apartment from which streamed a light so dazzling to the eyes of Agnes that at first she could form no distinct conception as to where she was.

As soon as her eyesight cleared, she found herself in an apartment which to her simplicity seemed furnished with an unheard-of luxury. The walls were richly frescoed and gilded, and from a chandelier of Venetian glass the light fell upon a foot-cloth of brilliant tapestry which covered the marble floor. Gilded chairs and couches, covered with the softest Genoese velvet, invited to repose; while tables inlaid with choice mosaics stood here and there, sustaining rare vases, musical instruments, and many of the light, fanciful ornaments with which, in those days, the halls of women of condition were graced. At one end of the apartment was an alcove, where the rich velvet curtains were looped away with heavy cords and tassels of gold, displaying a smaller room, where was a bed with hangings of crimson satin embroidered with gold.

Agnes stood petrified with amazement, and put her hand to her head, as if to assure herself by the sense of touch that she was not dreaming, and then, with an impulse of curious wonder, began examining the apartment. The rich furniture and the many adornments, though only such as were common in the daily life of the great at that period, had for her simple eyes all the marvelousness of the most incredible illusion. She touched the velvet couches almost with fear, and passed from object to object in a sort of maze. When she arrived at the alcove, she thought she heard a slight rustling within, and then a smothered laugh. Her heart beat quick as she stopped to listen. There was a tittering sound, and a movement as if some one were shaking the curtain, and at last Giulietta stood in the doorway.

For a moment Agnes stood looking at her in utter bewilderment. Yes, surely it was Giulietta, dressed out in all the bravery of splendid apparel, her black hair shining and lustrous, great solid ear-rings of gold shaking in her ears, and a row of gold coins displayed around her neck.

She broke into a loud laugh at the sight of Agnes's astonished face.

"So, here you are!" she said. "Well, now, didn't I tell you so? You see he was in love with you, just as I said; and if you wouldn't come to him of your own accord, he must fly off with you."

"Oh, Giulietta!" said Agnes, springing towards her and

catching her hands, "what does all this mean? and where have they carried poor grandmamma?"

"Oh, never worry about her! Do you know you are in high favor here, and any one who belongs to you gets good quarters? Your grandmother just now is at supper, I doubt not, with my mother; and a jolly time they will have of it, gossiping together."

"Your mother here, too?"

"Yes, simple, to be sure! I found it so much easier living here than in the old town, that I sent for her, that she might have peace in her old age. But how do you like your room? Were you not astonished to see it so brave? Know, then, pretty one, that it is all on account of the good courage of our band. For, you see, the people there in Rome (we won't say who) had given away all our captain's lands and palaces and villas to this one and that, as pleased them; and one pretty little villa in the mountains not far from here went to a stout old cardinal. What does a band of our men do, one night, but pounce on old red-hat and tie him up, while they helped themselves to what they liked through the house? True, they couldn't bring house and all; but they brought stores of rich furnishing, and left him thanking the saints that he was yet alive. So we arranged your rooms right nobly, thinking to please our captain when he comes. If you are not pleased, you will be ungrateful, that's all."

"Giulietta," said Agnes, who had scarcely seemed to listen to this prattle, so anxious was she to speak of what lay nearest her heart, "I want to see grandmamma. Can't you bring her to me?"

"No, my little princess, I can't. Do you know you are my mistress, now? Well, you are; but there's one that's master of us both, and he says none must speak with you till he has seen you."

"And is he here?"

"No, he has been some time gone northward, and has not returned, — though we expect him to-night. So compose yourself, and ask for anything in the world, but to see your grandmother, and I will show that I am your humble servant to command."

So saying, Giulietta courtesied archly and laughed, showing her white, shiny teeth, which looked as bright as pearls.

Agnes sat down on one of the velvet couches, and leaned her head on her hand.

"Come, now, let me bring you some supper," said Giulietta. "What say you to a nice roast fowl and a bottle of wine ? "

"How can you speak of such things in the holy time of Lent ? " said Agnes.

"Oh, never you fear about that! Our holy Father Stefano sets such matters right for any of us in a twinkling, and especially would he do it for you."

"Oh, but Giulietta, I don't want anything. I could n't eat, if I were to try."

"Ta, ta, ta!" said Giulietta, going out. "Wait till you smell it. I shall be back in a little while."

And she left the room, locking the door after her.

In a few moments she returned, bearing a rich silver tray, on which was a covered dish that steamed a refreshing odor, together with a roll of white bread, and a small glass *flacon* containing a little choice wine.

By much entreaty and coaxing, Agnes was induced to partake of the bread, enough to revive her somewhat after the toils of the day; and then, a little reassured by the familiar presence of Giulietta, she began to undress, her former companion officiously assisting her.

"There, now, you are tired, my lady princess," she said. "I 'll unlace your bodice. One of these days your gowns will be all of silk, and stiff with gold and pearls."

"Oh, Giulietta," said Agnes, "don't! — let me, — I don't need help."

"Ta, ta, ta! — you must learn to be waited on," said Giulietta, persisting. "But, Holy Virgin! what is the matter here? Oh, Agnes, what *are* you doing to yourself?"

"It's a penance, Giulietta," said Agnes, her face flushing.

"Well, I should think it was! Father Francesco ought to be ashamed of himself; he is a real butcher!"

"He does it to save my soul, Giulietta. The cross of our Lord without will heal a deadly wound within."

In her heart, Giulietta had somewhat of secret reverence for such austerities, which the whole instruction of her time and country taught her to regard as especially saintly. People who live in the senses more than in the world of reflection feel the force of such outward appeals. Giulietta made the sign of the cross, and looked grave for several minutes.

"Poor little dove!" she said at last, "if your sins must needs be expiated so, what will become of me? It must be that you will lay up stores of merit with God; for surely your sins do not need *all* this. Agnes, you will be a saint some day, like your namesake at the Convent, I truly do believe."

"Oh, no, no, Giulietta! don't talk so! God knows I wrestle with forbidden thoughts all the while. I am no saint, but the chief of sinners."

"That's what the saints all say," said Giulietta. "But, my dear princess, when *he* comes, he will forbid this; he is lordly, and will not suffer his little wife" —

"Giulietta, don't speak so, — I cannot hear it, — I must not be his wife, — I am vowed to be the spouse of the Lord."

"And yet you love our handsome prince," said Giulietta;

."and there is the great sin you are breaking your little
heart about.   Well, now, it's all of that dry, sour old
Father Francesco.   I never could abide him, — he made
such dismal pother about sin; old Father Girolamo was
worth a dozen of him.   If you would just see our good
Father Stefano, now, he would set your mind at ease about
your vows in a twinkling; and you must needs get them
loosed, for our captain is born to command, and when
princes stoop to us peasant-girls, it is n't for us to say nay.
It's being good as Saint Michael himself for him to think
of you only in the holy way of marriage.   I'll warrant me,
there's many a lord cardinal at Rome that is n't so good;
and as to princes, he is one of a thousand, a most holy and
religious knight, or he would do as others do when they
have the power."

Agnes, confused and agitated, turned away, and, as if
seeking refuge, laid her down in the bed, looking timidly
up at the unwonted splendor, — and then, hiding her face
in the pillow, began repeating a prayer.

Giulietta sat by her a moment, till she felt, from the
relaxing of the little hand, that the reaction of fatigue and
intense excitement was beginning to take place.   Nature
would assert her rights, and the heavy curtain of sleep fell
on the weary little head.   Quietly extinguishing the lights,
Giulietta left the room, locking the door.

CHAPTER XXV

THE CRISIS

AGNES was so entirely exhausted with bodily fatigue
and mental agitation that she slept soundly till awakened
by the beams of the morning sun. Her first glance up at
the gold-embroidered curtains of her bed occasioned a bewildered surprise; — she raised herself and looked around,
slowly recovering her consciousness and the memory of the
strange event which had placed her where she was. She
rose hastily and went to the window to look out. This
window was in a kind of circular tower projecting from
the side of the building, such as one often sees in old Norman architecture; — it overhung not only a wall of dizzy
height, but a precipice with a sheer descent of some thousand feet; and far below, spread out like a map in the
distance, lay a prospect of enchanting richness. The eye
might wander over orchards of silvery olives, plantations
with their rows of mulberry-trees supporting the vines,
now in the first tender spring green, scarlet fields of clover,
and patches where the young corn was just showing its
waving blades above the brown soil. Here and there rose
tufts of stone-pines with their dark umbrella-tops towering
above all other foliage, while far off in the blue distance a
silvery belt of glittering spangles showed where the sea
closed in the horizon-line. So high was the perch, so distant
and dreamy the prospect, that Agnes felt a sensation of gid-
diness, as if she were suspended over it in the air, — and
turned away from the window, to look again at what seemed
to her the surprising and unheard-of splendors of the

apartment.   There lay her simple peasant garb on the rich
velvet couch, — a strange sight in the midst of so much
luxury.   Having dressed herself, she sat down, and, covering her face with her hands, tried to reflect calmly on the
position in which she was placed.

With the education she had received, she could look on
this strange interruption of her pilgrimage only as a special
assault upon her faith, instigated by those evil spirits that
are ever setting themselves in conflict with the just.   Such
trials had befallen saints of whom she had read.   They
had been assailed by visions of worldly ease and luxury
suddenly presented before them, for which they were
tempted to deny their faith and sell their souls.   Was it
not, perhaps, as a punishment for having admitted the love
of an excommunicated heretic into her heart, that this sore
trial had been permitted to come upon her?   And if she
should fail?   She shuddered, when she recalled the severe
and terrible manner in which Father Francesco had warned
her against yielding to the solicitations of an earthly love.
To her it seemed as if that holy man must have been
inspired with a prophetic foresight of her present position, and warned her against it.   Those awful words came
burning into her mind as when they seemed to issue like
the voice of a spirit from the depths of the confessional:
*"If ever you should yield to his love, and turn back
from this heavenly marriage to follow him, you will accomplish his damnation and your own."*

Agnes trembled in an agony of real belief, and with a
vivid terror of the world to come such as belonged to the
almost physical certainty with which the religious teaching
of her time presented it to the popular mind.   Was she,
indeed, the cause of such awful danger to his soul?   Might
a false step now, a faltering human weakness, indeed
plunge that soul, so dear, into a fiery abyss without bottom
or shore?   Should she forever hear his shrieks of torture

and despair, his curses on the hour he had first known her?
Her very blood curdled, her nerves froze, as she thought of
it, and she threw herself on her knees and prayed with an
anguish that brought the sweat in beaded drops to her forehead, — strange dew for so frail a lily! — and her prayer
rose above all intercession of saints, above the seat even of
the Virgin Mother herself, to the heart of her Redeemer,
to Him who some divine instinct told her was alone mighty
to save. We of the present day may look on her distress
as unreal, as the result of a misguided sense of religious
obligation; but the great Hearer of Prayer regards each
heart in its own scope of vision, and helps not less the
mistaken than the enlightened distress. And for that
matter, who is enlightened? who carries to God's throne a
trouble or a temptation in which there is not somewhere
a misconception or a mistake?

And so it came to pass. Agnes rose from prayer with
an experience which has been common to the members of
the True Invisible Church, whether Catholic, Greek, or
Protestant. "In the day when I cried Thou answeredst
me, and strengthenedst me with strength in my soul."
She had that vivid sense of the sustaining presence and
sympathy of an Almighty Saviour which is the substance
of which all religious forms and appliances are the shadows;
her soul was stayed on God, and was at peace, as truly as
if she had been the veriest Puritan maiden that ever worshiped in a New England meeting-house. She felt a calm
superiority to all things earthly, — a profound reliance on
that invisible aid which comes from God alone.

She was standing at her window, deep in thought, when
Giulietta entered, fresh and blooming, bearing the break-
fast-tray.

"Come, my little princess, here I am," she said, "with
your breakfast! How do you find yourself, this morning?"

Agnes came towards her.

"Bless us, how grave we are!" said Guilietta.   "What has come over us?"

"Giulietta, have you seen poor grandmamma this morning?"

"Poor grandmamma!" said Giulietta, mimicking the sad tone in which Agnes spoke, "to be sure I have.   I left her making a hearty breakfast.   So fall to, and do the same, for you don't know who may come to see you this morning."

"Giulietta, is he here?"

"He!" said Giulietta, laughing.   "Do hear the little bird!   It begins to chirp already!   No, he is not here yet; but Pietro says he will come soon, and Pietro knows all his movements."

"Pietro is your husband?" said Agnes, inquiringly.

"Yes, to be sure, — and a pretty good one, too, as men go," said Giulietta.   "They are sorry bargains, the best of them.   But you'll get a prize, if you play your cards well. Do you know that the King of Naples and the King of France have both sent messages to our captain?   Our men hold all the passes between Rome and Naples, and so every one sees the sense of gaining our captain's favor.   But eat your breakfast, little one, while I go and see to Pietro and the men."

So saying, she bustled out of the room, locking the door behind her.

Agnes took a little bread and water, resolved to fast and pray, as the only defense against the danger in which she stood.

After breakfasting, she retired into the inner room, and opening the window, sat down and looked out on the prospect, and then, in a low voice, began singing a hymn of Savonarola's, which had been taught her by her uncle.   It was entitled "Christ's Call to the Soul."   The words were conceived in that tender spirit of mystical devotion which characterizes all this class of productions.

"Fair soul, created in the primal hour,
          Once pure and grand,
    And for whose sake I left my throne and power
          At God's right hand,
      By this sad heart pierced through because I loved thee,
      Let love and mercy to contrition move thee !

"Cast off the sins thy holy beauty veiling,
          Spirit divine !
    Vain against thee the hosts of hell assailing :
          My strength is thine !
      Drink from my side the cup of life immortal,
      And love will lead thee back to heaven's portal !

"I, for thy sake, was pierced with many sorrows,
          And bore the cross,
    Yet heeded not the galling of the arrows,
          The shame and loss.
      So faint not thou, whate'er the burden be :
      But bear it bravely, even to Calvary ! "

While Agnes was singing, the door of the outer room was slowly opened, and Agostino Sarelli entered. He had just returned from Florence, having ridden day and night to meet her whom he expected to find within the walls of his fastness.

He entered so softly that Agnes did not hear his approach, and he stood listening to her singing. He had come back with his mind burning with indignation against the Pope and the whole hierarchy then ruling in Rome; but conversation with Father Antonio and the scenes he had witnessed at San Marco had converted the blind sense of personal wrong into a fixed principle of moral indignation and opposition. He no longer found himself checked by the pleading of his early religious recollections; for now he had a leader who realized in his own person all his conceptions of those primitive apostles and holy bishops who first fed the flock of the Lord in Italy. He had heard from his lips the fearless declaration, "If Rome is against me, know that it is not contrary to me, but to Christ, and its controversy is with God: doubt not that God will conquer;" and he embraced the cause with all the enthusiasm of patriotism and knighthood.   In his view, the most holy place of his religion had been taken by a robber, who reigned in the name of Christ only to disgrace it; and he felt called to pledge his sword, his life, his knightly honor to do battle against him.   He had urged his uncle in Milan to make interest for the cause of Savonarola with the King of France; and his uncle, with that crafty diplomacy which in those days formed the staple of what was called statesmanship, had seemed to listen favorably to his views, intending, however, no more by his apparent assent than to withdraw his nephew from the dangers in which he stood in Italy, and bring him under his own influence and guardianship in the court of France.   But the wily diplomate had sent Agostino Sarelli from his presence with the highest possible expectations of his influence both with the King of France and the Emperor of Germany in the present religious crisis in Italy.

And now the time was come, Agostino thought, to break the spell under which Agnes was held, — to show her the true character of the men whom she was beholding through a mist of veneration arising entirely from the dewy freshness of ignorant innocence.   All the way home from Florence he had urged his horse onward, burning to meet her, to tell her all that he knew and felt, to claim her as his own, and to take her into the sphere of light and liberty in which he himself moved.   He did not doubt his power, when she should once be where he could speak with her freely, without fear of interruption.   Hers was a soul too good and pure, he said, to be kept in chains of slavish ignorance any longer.   When she ceased singing, he spoke from the outer apartment, "Agnes!"

The name was uttered in the softest tone, but it sent

the blood to her heart, as if it were the summons of doom. Everything seemed to swim before her, and grow dark for a moment; but by a strong effort she lifted her heart in prayer, and, rising, came towards him.

Agostino had figured her to himself in all that soft and sacred innocence and freshness of bloom in which he had left her, a fair angel child, looking through sad, innocent eyes on a life whose sins and sorrows, and deeper loves and hates, she scarcely comprehended, — one that he might fold in his arms with protecting tenderness, while he gently reasoned with her fears and prejudices; but the figure that stood there in the curtained arch, with its solemn, calm, transparent paleness of face, its large, intense dark eyes, now vivid with some mysterious and concentrated resolve, struck a strange chill over him. Was it Agnes or a disembodied spirit that stood before him? For a few moments there fell such a pause between them as the intensity of some unexpressed feeling often brings with it, and which seems like a spell.

"Agnes! Agnes! is it you?" at last said the knight, in a low, hesitating tone. "Oh, my love, what has changed you so? Speak! — do speak! Are you angry with me? Are you angry that I brought you here?"

"My Lord, I am not angry," said Agnes, speaking in a cold, sad tone; "but you have committed a great sin in turning aside those vowed to a holy pilgrimage, and you tempt me to sin by this conversation, which ought not to be between us."

"Why not?" said Agostino. "You would not see me at Sorrento. I sought to warn you of the dangers of this pilgrimage, — to tell you that Rome is not what you think it is, — that it is not the seat of Christ, but a foul cage of unclean birds, a den of wickedness, — that he they call Pope is a vile impostor" —

"My Lord," said Agnes, speaking with a touch of some-

thing even commanding in her tone, "you have me at advantage, it is true, but you ought not to use it in trying to
ruin my soul by blaspheming holy things." And then she
added, in a tone of indescribable sadness, "Alas, that so
noble and beautiful a soul should be in rebellion against
·the only True Church! Have you forgotten that good
mother you spoke of? What must she feel to know that
her son is an infidel!"

"I am not an infidel, Agnes; I am a true knight of our
Lord and Saviour Jesus Christ, and a believer in the One
True, Holy Church."

"How can that be?" said Agnes. "Ah, seek not to
deceive me! My Lord, such a poor little girl as I am is
not worth the pains."

"By the Holy Mother, Agnes, by the Holy Cross, I do
not seek to deceive you! I speak on my honor as a knight
and gentleman. I love you truly and honorably, and seek
you among all women as my spotless wife, and would I lie
to *you?*"

"My Lord, you have spoken words which it is a sin for
me to hear, a peril to your soul to say; and if you had
not, you must not seek me as a wife. Holy vows are upon
me. I must be the wife of no man here; it is a sin even
to think of it."

"Impossible, Agnes!" said Agostino, with a start.
"You have not taken the veil already? If you had" —

"No, my Lord, I have not. I have only promised and
vowed in my heart to do so when the Lord shall open the
way."

"But such vows, dear Agnes, are often dispensed; they
may be loosed by the priest. Now hear me, — only hear
me. I believe as your uncle believes, — your good, pious
uncle, whom you love so much. I have taken the sacrament from his hand; he has blessed me as a son. I believe as Jerome Savonarola believes. He it is, that holy

prophet, who has proclaimed this Pope and his crew to be vile usurpers, reigning in the name of Christ."

"My Lord! my Lord! I must not hear more! I must not, — I cannot, — I will not!" said Agnes, becoming violently agitated, as she found herself listening with interest to the pleadings of her lover.

"Oh, Agnes, what has turned your heart against me? I thought you promised to love me a little?"

"Oh, hush! hush! don't plead with me!" she said, with a wild, affrighted look.

He sought to come towards her, and she sprang forward and threw herself at his feet.

"Oh, my Lord, for mercy's sake let me go! Let us go on our way! We will pray for you always, — yes, always!" And she looked up at him in an agony of earnestness.

"Am I so hateful to you, then, Agnes?"

"Hateful? Oh, no, no! God knows you are — I — I — yes, I love you too well, and you have too much power over me; but, oh, do not use it! If I hear you talk I shall yield, — I surely shall, and we shall be lost, both of us! Oh, my God! I shall be the means of your damnation!"

"Agnes!"

"It is true! it is true! Oh, do not talk to me, but promise me, promise me, or I shall die! Have pity on me! have pity on yourself!"

In the agony of her feelings her voice became almost a shriek, and her wild, affrighted face had a deadly pallor; she looked like one in a death-agony. Agostino was alarmed, and hastened to soothe her, by promising whatever she required.

"Agnes, dear Agnes, I submit; only be calm. I promise anything, — anything in the wide world you can ask."

"Will you let me go?"

"Yes."

"And will you let my poor grandmamma go with me?"

"Yes."

"And you will not talk with me any more?"

"Not if you do not wish it. And now," he said, "that I have submitted to all these hard conditions, will you suffer me to raise you?"

He took her hands and lifted her up; they were cold, and she was trembling and shivering. He held them a moment; she tried to withdraw them, and he let them go.

"Farewell, Agnes!" he said. "I am going."

She raised both her hands and pressed the sharp cross to her bosom, but made no answer.

"I yield to your will," he continued. "Immediately when I leave you your grandmother will come to you, and the attendants who brought you here will conduct you to the high-road. For me, since it is your will, I part here. Farewell, Agnes!"

He held out his hand, but she stood as before, pale and silent, with her hands clasped on her breast.

"Do your vows forbid even a farewell to a poor, humble friend?" said the knight, in a low tone.

"I cannot," said Agnes, speaking at broken intervals, in a suffocating voice, — "for *your* sake I cannot! I bear this pain for you, — for *you!* Oh, repent, and meet me in heaven!"

She gave him her hand; he kneeled and kissed it, pressed it to his forehead, then rose and left the room.

For a moment after the departure of the cavalier, Agnes felt a bitter pang, — the pain which one feels on first realizing that a dear friend is lost forever; and then, rousing herself with a start and a sigh, she hurried into the inner room and threw herself on her knees, giving thanks that the dreadful trial was past, and that she had not been left to fail.

In a few moments she heard the voice of her grandmother in the outer apartment, and the old wrinkled creature clasped her grandchild in her arms, and wept with a passionate abandonment of fondness, calling her by every tender and endearing name which mothers give to their infants.

"After all," said Elsie, "these are not such bad people, and I have been right well entertained among them. They are of ourselves, — they do not prey on the poor, but only on our enemies, the princes and nobles, who look on us as sheep to be shorn and slaughtered for their wearing and eating. These men are none such, but pitiful to poor peasants and old widows, whom they feed and clothe out of the spoils of the rich. As to their captain, — would you believe it? — he is the same handsome gentleman who once gave you a ring, — you may have forgotten him, as you never think of such things, but I knew him in a moment, — and such a religious man, that no sooner did he find that we were pilgrims on a holy errand, than he gave orders to have us set free with all honor, and a band of the best of them to escort us through the mountains; and the people of the town are all moved to do us reverence, and coming with garlands and flowers to wish us well and ask our prayers. So let us set forth immediately."

Agnes followed her grandmother through the long passages and down the dark, mouldy stairway to the court-yard, where two horses were standing caparisoned for them. A troop of men in high peaked hats, cloaked and plumed, were preparing also to mount, while a throng of women and children stood pressing around. When Agnes appeared, enthusiastic cries were heard: " *Viva Jesù!* " " *Viva Maria!* " " *Viva! viva Jesù! nostro Re!* " and showers of myrtle-branches and garlands fell around. "Pray for us!" "Pray for us, holy pilgrims!" was uttered eagerly by one and another. Mothers held up their children; and beggars and cripples, aged and sick, — never absent in an Italian town, — joined with loud cries in the general

enthusiasm. Agnes stood amid it all, pale and serene,
with that elevated expression of heavenly calm on her features which is often the clear shining of the soul after the
wrench and torture of some great interior conflict. She
felt that the last earthly chain was broken, and that now
she belonged to Heaven alone. She scarcely saw or heard
what was around her, wrapt in the calm of inward prayer.

"Look at her! she is beautiful as the Madonna!" said
one and another. "She is divine as Santa Catarina!" said
others. "She might have been the wife of our chief, who
is a nobleman of the oldest blood, but she chose to be the
bride of the Lord," said others: for Giulietta, with a woman's love of romancing, had not failed to make the most
among her companions of the love-adventures of Agnes.

Agnes meanwhile was seated on her palfrey, and the
whole train passed out of the court-yard into the dim, narrow street, — men, women, and children following. On
reaching the public square, they halted a moment by the
side of the antique fountain to water their horses. The
groups that surrounded it at this time were such as a
painter would have delighted to copy. The women and
girls of this obscure mountain-town had all that peculiar
beauty of form and attitude which appears in the studies of
the antique; and as they poised on their heads their copper
water-jars of the old Etruscan pattern, they seemed as if
they might be statues of golden bronze, had not the warm
·tints of their complexion, the brilliancy of their large eyes,
and the bright picturesque colors of their attire given the
richness of painting to their classic outlines. Then, too,
the men, with their finely-moulded limbs, their figures so
straight and strong and elastic, their graceful attitudes,
and their well-fitting, showy costumes, formed a no less
imposing feature in the scene. Among them all sat Agnes
waiting on her palfrey, seeming scarcely conscious of the
enthusiasm which surrounded her. Some admiring friend

had placed in her hand a large bough of blossoming haw-
thorn, which she held unconsciously, as, with a sort of
childlike simplicity, she turned from right to left, to make
reply to the request for prayers, or to return thanks for the
offered benediction of some one in the crowd.

When all the preparations were at last finished, the procession of mounted horsemen, with a confused gathering of
the population, passed down the streets to the gates of the
city, and as they passed they sang the words of the Crusa-
ders' Hymn, which had fluttered back into the traditionary
memory of Europe from the knights going to redeem the
Holy Sepulchre.

> " Fairest Lord Jesus,
> Ruler of all Nature,
> O Thou of God and man the Son !
> Thee will I honor,
> Thee will I cherish,
> Thou, my soul's glory, joy, and crown !
>
> " Fair are the meadows,
> Fairer still the woodlands,
> Robed in the pleasing garb of spring :
> Jesus shines fairer,
> Jesus is purer
> Who makes the woful heart to sing !
>
> " Fair is the sunshine,
> Fairer still the moonlight,
> And all the twinkling starry host :
> Jesus shines fairer,
> Jesus is purer,
> Than all the angels heaven can boast ! "

They were singing the second verse, as, emerging from
the dark old gateway of the town, all the distant landscape
of silvery olive-orchards, crimson clover-fields, blossoming
almond-trees, fig-trees, and grapevines, just in the tender
green of spring, burst upon their view. Agnes felt a kind
of inspiration. From the high mountain elevation she
could discern the far-off brightness of the sea, — all between
one vision of beauty, — and the religious enthusiasm which

possessed all around her had in her eye all the value of the
most solid and reasonable faith. With us, who may look
on it from a colder and more distant point of view, doubts
may be suggested whether this *naïve* impressibility to religious influences, this simple, whole-hearted abandonment
to their expression, had any real practical value. The fact
that any or all of the actors might before night rob or stab
or lie quite as freely as if it had not occurred may well
give reason for such a question. Be this as it may, the
phenomenon is not confined to Italy or the religion of the
Middle Ages, but exhibits itself in many a prayer-meeting
and camp-meeting of modern days. For our own part, we
hold it better to have even transient upliftings of the nobler and more devout element of man's nature than never
to have any at all, and that he who goes on in worldly and
sordid courses, without ever a spark of religious enthusiasm
or a throb of aspiration, is less of a man than he who sometimes soars heavenward, though his wings be weak and he
fall again.

In all this scene Agostino Sarelli took no part. He had
simply given orders for the safe-conduct of Agnes, and
then retired to his own room. From a window, however,
he watched the procession as it passed through the gates of
the city, and his resolution was immediately taken to pro-
ceed at once by a secret path to the place where the pilgrims should emerge upon the high-road.

He had been induced to allow the departure of Agnes
from seeing the utter hopelessness by any argument or per-
suasion of removing a barrier that was so vitally interwoven
with the most sensitive religious nerves of her being. He
saw in her terrified looks, in the deadly paleness of her
face, how real and unaffected was the anguish which his
words gave her; her saw that the very consciousness of her
own love to him produced a sense of weakness which made
her shrink in utter terror from his arguments.

"There is no remedy," he said, "but to let her go to Rome and see with her own eyes how utterly false and vain is the vision which she draws from the purity of her own believing soul. What Christian would not wish that these fair dreams had any earthly reality? But this gentle dove must not be left unprotected to fly into that foul, unclean cage of vultures and harpies. Deadly as the peril may be to me to breathe the air of Rome, I will be around her invisibly to watch over her."

CHAPTER XXVI

A VISION rises upon us from the land of shadows. We see a wide plain, miles and miles in extent, rolling in soft billows of green, and girded on all sides by blue mountains, whose silver crests gleaming in the setting sunlight tell that the winter yet lingers on their tops, though spring has decked all the plain. So silent, so lonely, so fair is this waving expanse with its guardian mountains, it might be some wild solitude, an American prairie or Asiatic steppe, but that in the midst thereof, on some billows of rolling land, we discern a city, sombre, quaint, and old, — a city of dreams and mysteries, — a city of the living and the dead. And this is Rome, — weird, wonderful, ancient, mighty Rome, — mighty once by physical force and grandeur, mightier now in physical decadence and weakness by the spell of a potent moral enchantment.

As the sun is moving westward, the whole air around becomes flooded with a luminousness which seems to transfuse itself with pervading presence through every part of the city, and make all its ruinous and mossy age bright and living. The air shivers with the silver vibrations of hundreds of bells, and the evening glory goes up and down, soft-footed and angelic, transfiguring all things. The broken columns of the Forum seem to swim in golden mist, and luminous floods fill the Coliseum as it stands with its thousand arches looking out into the city like so many sightless eye-holes in the skull of the past. The tender light pours up streets dank and ill-paved, — into

noisome and cavernous dens called houses, where the
peasantry of to-day vegetate in contented subservience.
It illuminates many a dingy court-yard, where the moss is
green on the walls, and gurgling fountains fall into quaint
old sculptured basins. It lights up the gorgeous palaces
of Rome's modern princes, built with stones wrenched from
ancient ruins. It streams through a wilderness of churches,
each with its tolling prayer-bell, and steals through painted
windows into the dazzling confusion of pictured and gilded
glories that glitter and gleam from roof and wall within.
And it goes, too, across the Tiber, up the filthy and noisome Ghetto, where, hemmed in by ghostly superstition,
the sons of Israel are growing up without vital day, like
wan white plants in cellars; and the black mournful obelisks of the cypresses in the villas around, it touches with
a solemn glory. The castle of St. Angelo looks like a great
translucent, luminous orb, and the statues of saints and
apostles on the top of St. John Lateran glow as if made of
living fire, and seem to stretch out glorified hands of welcome to the pilgrims that are approaching the Holy City
across the soft, palpitating sea of green that lies stretched
like a misty veil around it.

Then, as now, Rome was an enchantress of mighty and
wonderful power, with her damp, and mud, and mould,
her ill-fed, ill-housed populace, her ruins of old glory rising dim and ghostly amid her palaces of to-day.   With all
her awful secrets of rapine, cruelty, ambition, injustice, —
with her foul orgies of unnatural crime, — with the very
corruption of the old buried Roman Empire steaming up as
from a charnel-house, and permeating all modern life with
its effluvium of deadly uncleanness, — still Rome had that
strange, bewildering charm of melancholy grandeur and
glory which made all hearts cleave to her, and eyes and
feet turn longingly towards her from the ends of the earth.
Great souls and pious yearned for her as for a mother, and

could not be quieted till they had kissed the dust of her streets. There they fondly thought was rest to be found, — that rest which through all weary life ever recedes like the mirage of the desert; there sins were to be shriven which no common priest might forgive, and heavy burdens unbound from the conscience by an infallible wisdom; there was to be revealed to the praying soul the substance of things hoped for, the evidence of things not seen. Even the mighty spirit of Luther yearned for the breast of this great unknown mother, and came humbly thither to seek the repose which he found afterwards in Jesus.

At this golden twilight-hour along the Appian Way come the pilgrims of our story with prayers and tears of thankfulness. Agnes looks forward and sees the saintly forms on St. John Lateran standing in a cloud of golden light and stretching out protecting hands to bless her.

"See, see, grandmother!" she exclaimed, "yonder is our Father's house, and all the saints beckon us home! Glory be to God, who hath brought us hither!"

Within the church the evening-service is going on, and the soft glory streaming in reveals that dizzying confusion of riches and brightness with which the sensuous and color-loving Italian delights to encircle the shrine of the Heavenly Majesty. Pictured angels in cloudy wreaths smile down from the gold-fretted roofs and over the round, graceful arches; and the floor seems like a translucent sea of precious marbles and gems fused into solid brightness, and reflecting in long gleams and streaks dim intimations of the sculptured and gilded glories above. Altar and shrine are now veiled in that rich violet hue which the Church has chosen for its mourning color; and violet vestments, taking the place of the gorgeous robes of the ecclesiastics, tell the approach of that holy week of sadness when all Christendom falls in penitence at the feet of that Almighty Love once sorrowful and slain for her.

The long-drawn aisles are now full to overflowing with that weird chanting which one hears nowhere but in Rome at this solemn season. Those voices, neither of men nor women, have a wild, morbid energy which seems to search every fibre of the nervous system, and, instead of soothing or calming, to awaken strange yearning agonies of pain, ghostly unquiet longings, and endless feverish, unrestful cravings. The sounds now swell and flood the church as with a rushing torrent of wailing and clamorous supplication, — now recede and moan themselves away to silence in far-distant aisles, like the last faint sigh of discouragement and despair. Anon they burst out from the room, they drop from arches and pictures, they rise like steam from the glassy pavement, and, meeting, mingle in wavering clamors of lamentation and shrieks of anguish. One might fancy lost souls from out the infinite and dreary abysses of utter separation from God might thus wearily and aimlessly moan and wail, breaking into agonized tumults of desire, and trembling back into exhaustions of despair. Such music brings only throbbings and yearnings, but no peace; and yonder, on the glassy floor, at the foot of a crucifix, a poor mortal lies sobbing and quivering under its pitiless power, as if it had wrenched every tenderest nerve of memory, and torn open every half-healed wound of the soul.

When the chanting ceases, he rises slow and tottering, and we see in the wan face turning towards the dim light the well-remembered features of Father Francesco. Driven to despair by the wild, ungovernable force of his unfortunate love, weary of striving, overborne with a hopeless and continually accumulating load of guilt, he had come to Rome to lay down at the feet of heavenly wisdom the burden which he can no longer bear alone; and rising now, he totters to a confessional where sits a holy cardinal to whom has been deputed the office to hear and judge those sins which no subordinate power in the Church is competent to absolve.

Father Francesco kneels down with a despairing, confiding movement, such as one makes, when, after a long struggle of anguish, one has found a refuge; and the churchman within inclining his ear to the grating, the confession begins.

Could we only be clairvoyant, it would be worth our while to note the difference between the two faces, separated only by the thin grating of the confessional, but belonging to souls whom an abyss wide as eternity must forever divide from any common ground of understanding.

On the one side, with ear close to the grate, is a round, smoothly developed Italian head, with that rather tumid outline of features which one often sees in a Roman in middle life, when easy living and habits of sensual indulgence begin to reveal their signs in the countenance, and to broaden and confuse the clear-cut, statuesque lines of early youth. Evidently, that is the head of an easy-going, pleasure-loving man, who has waxed warm with good living, and performs the duties of his office with an unctuous grace as something becoming and decorous to be gone through with. Evidently he is puzzled and half-contemptuous at the revelations which come through the grating in hoarse whispers from those thin, trembling lips. The other man, who speaks with the sweat of anguish beaded on his brow, with a mortal pallor on his thin, worn cheeks, is putting questions to the celestial guide within which seem to that guide the ravings of a crazed lunatic; and yet there is a deadly, despairing earnestness in the appeal that makes an indistinct knocking at the door of his heart, for the man is born of woman, and can feel that somehow or other these are the words of a mighty agony.

He addresses him some words of commonplace ghostly comfort, and gives a plenary absolution. The Capuchin monk rises up and stands meekly wiping the sweat from his brow, the churchman leaves his box, and they meet face to face, when each starts, seeing in the other the apparition of a once well-known countenance.

"What! Lorenzo Sforza!" said the churchman. "Who would have thought it. Don't you remember me?"

"Not Lorenzo Sforza," said the other, a hectic brilliancy flushing his pale cheek; "that name is buried in the tomb of his fathers; he you speak to knows it no more. The unworthy Brother Francesco, deserving nothing of God or man, is before you."

"Oh, come, come!" said the other, grasping his hand in spite of his resistance; "that is all proper enough in its place; but between friends, you know, what's the use? It's lucky we have you here now; we want one of your family to send on a mission to Florence, and talk a little reason into the citizens and the Signoria. Come right away with me to the Pope."

"Brother, in God's name let me go! I have no mission to the great of this world; and I cannot remember or be called by the name of other days, or salute kinsman or acquaintance after the flesh, without a breach of vows."

"Poh, poh! you are nervous, dyspeptic; you don't understand things. Don't you see you are where vows can be bound and loosed? Come along, and let us wake you out of this nightmare. Such a pother about a pretty peasant-girl! One of your rank and taste, too! I warrant me the little sinner practiced on you at the confessional. I know their ways, the whole of them; but you mourn over it in a way that is perfectly incomprehensible. If you had tripped a little, — paid a compliment, or taken a liberty or two, — it would have been only natural; but this desperation, when you have resisted like Saint Anthony himself, shows your nerves are out of order and you need change."

"For God's sake, brother, tempt me not!" said Father Francesco, wrenching himself away, with such a haggard and insane vehemence as quite to discompose the churchman; and drawing his cowl over his face, he glided swiftly down a side-aisle and out the door.

The churchman was too easy-going to risk the fatigue of a scuffle with a man whom he considered as a monomaniac; but he stepped smoothly and stealthily after him and watched him go out.

"Look you," he said to a servant in violet livery who was waiting by the door, "follow yonder Capuchin and bring me word where he abides. He may be cracked," he said to himself; "but, after all, one of his blood may be worth mending, and do us good service either in Florence or Milan. We must have him transferred to some convent here, where we can lay hands on him readily, if we want him."

Meanwhile Father Francesco wends his way through many a dark and dingy street to an ancient Capuchin convent, where he finds brotherly admission. Weary and despairing is he beyond all earthly despair, for the very altar of his God seems to have failed him. He asked for bread, and has got a stone, — he asked a fish, and has got a scorpion. Again and again the worldly, almost scoffing, tone of the superior to whom he has been confessing sounds like the hiss of a serpent in his ear.

But he is sent for in haste to visit the bedside of the Prior, who has long been sick and failing, and who gladly embraces this opportunity to make his last confession to a man of such reputed sanctity in his order as Father Francesco. For the acute Father Johannes, casting about for various means to empty the Superior's chair at Sorrento, for his own benefit, and despairing of any occasion of slanderous accusation, had taken the other tack of writing to Rome extravagant laudations of such feats of penance and saintship in his Superior as in the view of all the brothers required that such a light should no more be hidden in an obscure province, but be set on a Roman candlestick, where it might give light to the faithful in all parts of the world. Thus two currents of worldly intrigue were uniting to push an unworldly man to a higher dignity than he either sought or desired.

When a man has a sensitive or sore spot in his heart, from the pain of which he would gladly flee to the ends of the earth, it is marvelous what coincidences of events will be found to press upon it wherever he may go. Singularly enough, one of the first items in the confession of the Capuchin Superior related to Agnes, and his story was in substance as follows. In his youth he had been induced by the persuasions of the young son of a great and powerful family to unite him in the holy sacrament of marriage with a *protégée* of his mother's; but the marriage being detected, it was disavowed by the young nobleman, and the girl and her mother chased out ignominiously, so that she died in great misery. For his complicity in this sin the conscience of the monk had often troubled him, and he had kept track of the child she left, thinking perhaps some day to make reparation by declaring the true marriage of her mother. That the residence of this young girl had been at Sorrento, where she had been living quite retired, under the charge of her old grandmother, — and here the dying man made inquiry if Father Francesco was acquainted with any young person answering to the description which he gave.

Father Francesco had no difficulty in recognizing the person, — and assured the dying penitent, that, in all human probability, she was at this moment in Rome. The monk then certified upon the holy cross to the true marriage of her mother, and besought Father Francesco to make the same known to one of the kindred whom he named. He further informed him, that this family, having fallen under the displeasure of the Pope and his son, Cæsar Borgia, had been banished from the city, and their property confiscated, so that there was none of them to be found thereabouts except an aged widowed sister of the young man, who, having married into a family in favor with the Pope, was allowed to retain her possessions, and now resided in a villa near Rome, where she lived retired, devoting her whole life to works of piety. The old man therefore conjured Father Francesco to lose no time in making this religious lady understand the existence of so near a kinswoman, and take her under her protection. Thus strangely did Father Francesco find himself obliged to take up that enchanted thread which had led him into labyrinths so fatal to his peace.

CHAPTER XXVII

THE SAINT'S REST

AGNES entered the city of Rome in a trance of enthusiastic emotion, almost such as one might imagine in a soul entering the heavenly Jerusalem above. To her exalted ideas she was approaching not only the ground hallowed by the blood of apostles and martyrs, not merely the tombs of the faithful, but the visible "general assembly and church of the first-born which are written in heaven." Here reigned the appointed representative of Jesus, — and she imagined a benignant image of a prince clothed with honor and splendor, who was yet the righter of all wrongs, the redresser of all injuries, the friend and succorer of the poor and needy; and she was firm in a secret purpose to go to this great and benignant father, and on her knees entreat him to forgive the sins of her lover, and remove the excommunication that threatened at every moment his eternal salvation. For she trembled to think of it, — a sudden accident, a thrust of a dagger, a fall from his horse, might put him forever beyond the pale of repentance, — he might die unforgiven, and sink to eternal pain.

If any should wonder that a Christian soul could preserve within itself an image so ignorantly fair, in such an age, when the worldliness and corruption in the Papal chair were obtruded by a thousand incidental manifestations, and were alluded to in all the calculations of simple common people, who looked at facts with a mere view to the guidance of their daily conduct, it is necessary to remember the nature of Agnes's religious training, and the absolute

renunciation of all individual reasoning which from infancy
had been laid down before her as the first and indispensable prerequisite of spiritual progress.   To believe, — to believe utterly and blindly, — not only without evidence, but
against evidence, — to reject the testimony even of her
senses, when set against the simple affirmation of her superiors, — had been the beginning, middle, and end of her
religious instruction.   When a doubt assailed her mind on
any point, she had been taught to retire within herself and
repeat a prayer; and in this way her mental eye had formed
the habit of closing to anything that might shake her faith
as quickly as the physical eye closes at a threatened blow.
Then, as she was of a poetic and ideal nature, entirely differing from the mass of those with whom she associated,
she had formed that habit of abstraction and mental reverie
which prevented her hearing or perceiving the true sense
of a great deal that went on around her.   The conversa-
tions that commonly were carried on in her presence had
for her so little interest that she scarcely heard them.   The
world in which she moved was a glorified world, — wherein
to be sure, the forms of every-day life appeared, but appeared as different from what they were in reality as the
old mouldering daylight view of Rome is from the warm
translucent glory of its evening transfiguration.

    So in her quiet, silent heart she nursed this beautiful
hope of finding in Rome the earthly image of her Saviour's
home above, of finding in the head of the Church the real
image of her Redeemer, — the friend to whom the poorest
and lowliest may pour out their souls with as much freedom
as the highest and noblest.   The spiritual directors who
had formed the mind of Agnes in her early days had been
persons in the same manner taught to move in an ideal
world of faith.   The Mother Theresa had never seen the
realities of life, and supposed the Church on earth to be all
that the fondest visions of human longing could paint it.

The hard, energetic, prose experience of old Jocunda, and the downright way with which she sometimes spoke of things as a trooper's wife must have seen them, were repressed and hushed down, as the imperfect faith of a half-reclaimed worldling, — they could not be allowed to awaken her from the sweetness of so blissful a dream.   In like manner, when Lorenzo Sforza became Father Francesco, he strove with earnest prayer to bury his gift of individual reason in the same grave with his family name and worldly experience.   As to all that transpired in the real world, he wrapped himself in a mantle of imperturbable silence; the intrigues of popes and cardinals, once well known to him, sank away as a forbidden dream; and by some metaphysi cal process of imaginative devotion, he enthroned God in the place of the dominant powers, and taught himself to receive all that came from them in uninquiring submission, as proceeding from unerring wisdom.   Though he had begun his spiritual life under the impulse of Savonarola, yet so perfect had been his isolation from all tidings of what transpired in the external world that the conflict which was going on between that distinguished man and the Papal hierarchy never reached his ear.   He sought and aimed as much as possible to make his soul like the soul of one dead, which adores and worships in ideal space, and forgets forever the scenes and relations of earth; and he had so long contemplated Rome under the celestial aspects of his faith, that, though the shock of his first confession there had been painful, still it was insufficient to shake his faith.   It had been God's will, he thought, that where he looked for aid he should meet only confusion, and he bowed to the inscrutable will, and blindly adored the mysterious revelation.   If such could be the submission and the faith of a strong and experienced man, who can wonder at the enthusiastic illusions of an innocent, trustful child?

Agnes and her grandmother entered the city of Rome

just as the twilight had faded into night; and though
Agnes, full of faith and enthusiasm, was longing to begin
immediately the ecstatic vision of shrines and holy places,
old Elsie commanded her not to think of anything further
that night.   They proceeded, therefore, with several other
pilgrims who had entered the city, to a church specially set
apart for their reception, connected with which were large
dormitories and a religious order whose business was to
receive and wait upon them, and to see that all their wants
were supplied.   This religious foundation is one of the
oldest in Rome; and it is esteemed a work of especial
merit and sanctity among the citizens to associate themselves temporarily in these labors in Holy Week.   Even
princes and princesses come, humble and lowly, mingling
with those of common degree, and all, calling each other
brother and sister, vie in kind attentions to these guests
of the Church.

When Agnes and Elsie arrived, several of these volunteer assistants were in waiting.   Agnes was remarked
among all the rest of the company for her peculiar beauty
and the rapt enthusiastic expression of her face.

Almost immediately on their entrance into the reception
hall connected with the church, they seemed to attract the
attention of a tall lady dressed in deep mourning, and
accompanied by a female servant, with whom she was
conversing on those terms of intimacy which showed
confidential relations between the two.

"See!" she said, "my Mona, what a heavenly face is
there! — that sweet child has certainly the light of grace
shining through her.   My heart warms to her."

"Indeed," said the old servant, looking across, "and
well it may, — dear lamb come so far!   But, Holy Virgin,
how my head swims!   How strange! — that child reminds
me of some one.   My Lady, perhaps, may think of some
one whom she looks like."

"Mona, you say true. I have the same strange impression that I have seen a face like hers, but who or where I cannot say."

"What would my Lady say, if I said it was our dear Prince? — God rest his soul!"

"Mona, it *is* so, — yes," added the lady, looking more intently, "how singular! — the very traits of our house in a peasant-girl! She is of Sorrento, I judge, by her costume, — what a pretty one it is! That old woman is her mother, perhaps. I must choose her for my care, — and, Mona, you shall wait on her mother."

So saying, the Princess Paulina crossed the hall, and, bending affably over Agnes, took her hand and kissed her, saying, —

"Welcome, my dear little sister, to the house of our Father!"

Agnes looked up with strange, wondering eyes into the face that was bent to hers. It was sallow and sunken, with deep lines of ill-health and sorrow, but the features were noble, and must once have been beautiful; the whole action, voice, and manner were dignified and impressive. Instinctively she felt that the lady was of superior birth and breeding to any with whom she had been in the habit of associating.

"Come with me," said the lady; "and this — your mother" — she added.

"She is my grandmother," said Agnes.

"Well, then, your grandmother, sweet child, shall be attended to by my good sister Mona here."

The Princess Paulina drew the hand of Agnes through her arm, and, laying her hand affectionately on it, looked down and smiled tenderly on her.

"Are you very tired, my dear?"

"Oh, no! no!" said Agnes, — "I am so happy, so blessed to be here!"

"You have traveled a long way?"

"Yes, from Sorrento; but I am used to walking, — I did not feel it to be long, — my heart kept me up, — I wanted to come home so much."

"Home?" said the Princess.

"Yes, to my soul's home, — the house of our dear Father the Pope."

The Princess started, and looked incredulously down for a moment; then noticing the confiding, whole-hearted air of the child, she sighed and was silent.

"Come with me above," she said, "and let me attend a little to your comfort."

"How good you are, dear lady!" said Agnes.

"I am not good, my child, — I am only your unworthy sister in Christ;" and as the lady spoke, she opened the door into a room where were a number of other female pilgrims seated around the wall, each attended by a person whose peculiar care she seemed to be.

At the feet of each was a vessel of water, and when the seats were all full, a cardinal in robes of office entered, and began reading prayers. Each lady present, kneeling at the feet of her chosen pilgrim, divested them carefully of their worn and travel-soiled shoes and stockings, and proceeded to wash them. It was not a mere rose-water ceremony, but a good hearty washing of feet that for the most part had great need of the ablution. While this service was going on, the cardinal read from the Gospel how a Greater than they all had washed the feet of His disciples, and said, "If I, your Lord and Master, have washed your feet, ye also ought to wash one another's feet." Then all repeated in concert the Lord's Prayer, while each humbly kissed the feet she had washed, and proceeded to replace the worn and travel-soiled shoes and stockings with new and strong ones, the gift of Christian love. Each lady then led her charge into a room where tables were spread with a plain and wholesome repast of all such articles of food as the season of Lent allowed. Each placed her *protégée* at table, and carefully attended to all her wants at the supper, and afterwards dormitories were opened for their repose.

The Princess Paulina performed all these offices for Agnes with a tender earnestness which won upon her heart. The young girl thought herself indeed in that blessed society of which she had dreamed, where the high-born and the rich become through Christ's love the servants of the poor and lowly; and through all the services she sat in a sort of dream of rapture. How lovely this reception into the Holy City! how sweet thus to be taken to the arms of the great Christian family, bound together in the charity which is the bond of perfectness!

"Please tell me, dear lady," said Agnes, after supper, "who is that holy man that prayed with us?"

"Oh, he — he is the Cardinal Capello," said the Princess.

"I should like to have spoken with him," said Agnes.

"Why, my child?"

"I wanted to ask him when and how I could get speech with our dear Father the Pope, for there is somewhat on my mind that I would lay before him."

"My poor little sister," said the Princess, much perplexed, "you do not understand things. What you speak of is impossible. The Pope is a great king."

"I know he is," said Agnes, — "and so is our Lord Jesus; but every soul may come to him."

"I cannot explain to you now," said the Princess, — "there is not time to-night. But I shall see you again. I will send for you to come to my house, and there talk with you about many things which you need to know. Meanwhile, promise me, dear child, not to try to do anything of the kind you spoke of until I have talked with you."

"Well, I will not," said Agnes, with a glance of docile affection, kissing the hand of the Princess.

The action was so pretty, — the great, soft, dark eyes looked so fawn-like and confiding in their innocent tenderness, that the lady seemed much moved.

"Our dear Mother bless thee, child!" she said, laying her hand on her head, and stooping to kiss her forehead.

She left her at the door of the dormitory.

The Princess and her attendant went out of the church-door, where her litter stood in waiting. The two took their seats in silence, and silently pursued their way through the streets of the old dimly-lighted city and out of one of its principal gates to the wide Campagna beyond. The villa of the Princess was situated on an eminence at some distance from the city, and the night-ride to it was solemn and solitary. They passed along the old Appian Way over pavements that had rumbled under the chariot-wheels of the emperors and nobles of a bygone age, while along their way, glooming up against the clear of the sky, were vast shadowy piles, — the tombs of the dead of other days. All mouldering and lonely, shaggy and fringed with bushes and streaming wild vines through which the night-wind sighed and rustled, they might seem to be pervaded by the restless spirits of the dead; and as the lady passed them, she shivered, and, crossing herself, repeated an inward prayer against wandering demons that walk in desolate places.

Timid and solitary, the high-born lady shrank and cowered within herself with a distressing feeling of loneliness. A childless widow in delicate health, whose paternal family had been for the most part cruelly robbed, exiled, or destroyed by the reigning Pope and his family, she felt her own situation a most unprotected and precarious one, since the least jealousy or misunderstanding might bring upon her, too, the ill-will of the Borgias, which had proved so fatal to the rest of her race. No comfort in life remained to her but her religion, to whose practice she clung as to her all; but even in this her life was embittered by facts to which, with the best disposition in the world, she could not shut her eyes. Her own family had been too near the seat of power not to see all the base intrigues by which that sacred and solemn position of Head of the Christian Church had been traded for as a marketable commodity. The pride, the indecency, the cruelty of those who now reigned in the name of Christ came over her mind in contrast with the picture painted by the artless, trusting faith of the peasant-girl with whom she had just parted. Her mind had been too thoroughly drilled in the non-reflective practice of her faith to dare to put forth any act of reasoning upon facts so visible and so tremendous, — she rather trembled at herself for seeing what she saw and for knowing what she knew, and feared somehow that this very knowledge might endanger her salvation; and so she rode homeward cowering and praying like a frightened child.

"Does my Lady feel ill?" said the old servant, anxiously.

"No, Mona, no, — not in body."

"And what is on my Lady's mind now?"

"Oh, Mona, it is only what is always there. To-morrow is Palm Sunday, and how can I go to see the murderers and robbers of our house in holy places? Oh, Mona, what can Christians do, when such men handle holy things? It was a comfort to wash the feet of those poor simple pilgrims, who tread in the steps of the saints of old; but how I felt when that poor child spoke of wanting to see the Pope!"

"Yes," said Mona, "it's like sending the lamb to get spiritual counsel of the wolf."

"See what sweet belief the poor infant has! Should not the head of the Christian Church be such as she thinks?

Ah, in the old days, when the Church here in Rome was poor and persecuted, there were Popes who were loving fathers and not haughty princes."

"My dear Lady," said the servant, "pray, consider, the very stones have ears. We don't know what day we may be turned out, neck and heels, to make room for some of their creatures."

"Well, Mona," said the lady, with some spirit, "I'm sure I have n't said any more than you have."

"Holy Mother! and so you have n't, but somehow things look more dangerous when other people say them. A pretty child that was, as you say; but that old thing, her grandmother, is a sharp piece. She is a Roman, and lived here in her early days. She says the little one was born hereabouts; but she shuts up her mouth like a vise, when one would get more out of her."

"Mona, I shall not go out to-morrow; but you go to the services, and find the girl and her grandmother, and bring them out to me. I want to counsel the child."

"You may be sure," said Mona, "that her grandmother knows the ins and outs of Rome as well as any of us, for all she has learned to screw up her lips so tight."

"At any rate, bring her to me, because she interests me."

"Well, well, it shall be so," said Mona.

CHAPTER XXVIII

THE morning after her arrival in Rome, Agnes was awakened from sleep by a solemn dropping of bell-tones which seemed to fill the whole air, intermingled dimly at intervals with long-drawn plaintive sounds of chanting. She had slept profoundly, overwearied with her pilgrimage, and soothed by that deep lulling sense of quiet which comes over one, when, after long and weary toils, some auspicious goal is at length reached. She had come to Rome, and been received with open arms into the household of the saints, and seen even those of highest degree imitating the simplicity of the Lord in serving the poor. Surely, this was indeed the house of God and the gate of heaven; and so the bell-tones and chants, mingling with her dreams, seemed naturally enough angel-harpings and distant echoes of the perpetual adoration of the blessed. She rose and dressed herself with a tremulous joy. She felt full hope that somehow — in what way she could not say — this auspicious beginning would end in a full fruition of all her wishes, an answer to all her prayers.

"Well, child," said old Elsie, "you must have slept well; you look fresh as a lark."

"The air of this holy place revives me," said Agnes, with enthusiasm.

"I wish I could say as much," said Elsie. "My bones ache yet with the tramp, and I suppose nothing will do but we must go out now to all the holy places, up and down and hither and yon, to everything that goes on. I saw enough of it all years ago when I lived here."

"Dear grandmother, if you are tired, why should you not rest? I can go forth alone in this holy city. No harm can possibly befall me here. I can join any of the pilgrims who are going to the holy places where I long to worship."

"A likely story!" said Elsie. "I know more about old Rome than you do, and I tell you, child, that you do not stir out a step without me; so if you must go, I must go too, — and like enough it's for my soul's health. I suppose it is," she added, after a reflective pause.

"How beautiful it was that we were welcomed so last night!" said Agnes; "that dear lady was so kind to me!"

"Ay, ay, and well she might be!" said Elsie, nodding her head. "But there's no truth in the kindness of the nobles to us, child. They don't do it because they love us, but because they expect to buy heaven by washing our feet and giving us what little they can clip and snip off from their abundance."

"Oh, grandmother," said Agnes, "how can you say so? Certainly, if any one ever spoke and looked lovingly, it was that dear lady."

"Yes, and she rolls away in her carriage, well content, and leaves you with a pair of new shoes and stockings, — you, as worthy of a carriage and a palace as she."

"No, grandmamma; she said she should send for me to talk more with her."

"*She* said she should send for you?" said Elsie. "Well, well, that is strange, to be sure! — that is wonderful!" she added, reflectively. "But come, child, we must hasten through our breakfast and prayers, and go to see the Pope, and all the great birds with fine feathers that fly after him."

"Yes, indeed!" said Agnes, joyfully. "Oh, grandmamma, what a blessed sight it will be!"

"Yes, child, and a fine sight enough he makes with his

great canopy and his plumes and his servants and his trumpeters; — there is n't a king in Christendom that goes so proudly as he."

"No other king is worthy of it," said Agnes. "The Lord reigns in him."

"Much you know about it!" said Elsie, between her teeth, as they started out.

The streets of Rome through which they walked were damp and cellar-like, filthy and ill-paved; but Agnes neither saw nor felt anything of inconvenience in this: had they been floored, like those of the New Jerusalem, with translucent gold, her faith could not have been more fervent.

Rome is at all times a forest of quaint costumes, a pantomime of shifting scenic effects of religious ceremonies. Nothing there, however singular, strikes the eye as out-of-the-way or unexpected, since no one knows precisely to what religious order it may belong, or what individual vow or purpose it may represent. Neither Agnes nor Elsie, therefore, was surprised, when they passed through the doorway to the street, at the apparition of a man covered from head to foot in a long robe of white serge, with a high-peaked cap of the same material drawn completely down over his head and face. Two round holes cut in this ghostly head-gear revealed simply two black glittering eyes, which shone with that singular elfish effect which belongs to the human eye when removed from its appropriate and natural accessories. As they passed out, the figure rattled a box on which was painted an image of despairing souls raising imploring hands from very red tongues of flame, by which it was understood at once that he sought aid for souls in Purgatory. Agnes and her grandmother each dropped therein a small coin and went on their way; but the figure followed them at a little distance behind, keeping carefully within sight of them.

By means of energetic pushing and striving, Elsie contrived to secure for herself and her grandchild stations in
the piazza in front of the church, in the very front rank,
where the procession was to pass. A motley assemblage
it was, this crowd, comprising every variety of costume of
rank and station and ecclesiastical profession, — cowls and
hoods of Franciscan and Dominican, — picturesque head
dresses of peasant-women of different districts, — plumes
and ruffs of more aspiring gentility, — mixed with every
quaint phase of foreign costume belonging to the strangers
from different parts of the earth ; — for, like the old
Jewish Passover, this celebration of Holy Week had its
assemblage of Parthians, Medes, Elamites, dwellers in
Mesopotamia, Cretes, and Arabians, all blending in one
common memorial.

Amid the strange variety of persons among whom they
were crowded, Elsie remarked the stranger in ·the white
sack, who had followed them, and who had stationed himself behind them, — but it did not occur to her that his
presence there was other than merely accidental.

And now came sweeping up the grand procession, brilliant with scarlet and gold, waving with plumes, sparkling
with gems, — it seemed as if earth had been ransacked and
human invention taxed to express the ultimatum of all that
could dazzle and bewilder, — and, with a rustle like that
of ripe grain before a swaying wind, all the multitude went
down on their knees as the cortege passed. Agnes knelt,
too, with clasped hands, adoring the sacred vision enshrined
in her soul ; and as she knelt with upraised eyes, her cheeks
flushed with enthusiasm, her beauty attracted the attention
of more than one in the procession.

"There is the model which our master has been looking
for," said a young and handsome man in a rich dress of
black velvet, who, by his costume, appeared to hold the
rank of first chamberlain in the Papal suite.

The young man to whom he spoke gave a bold glance at Agnes and answered, —

"Pretty little rogue, how well she does the saint!"

"One can see that with judicious arrangement she might make a nymph as well as a saint," said the first speaker.

"A Daphne, for example," said the other, laughing.

"And she would n't turn into a laurel, either," said the first. "Well, we must keep our eye on her." And as they were passing into the church-door, he beckoned to a servant in waiting and whispered something, indicating Agnes with a backward movement of his hand.

The servant, after this, kept cautiously within observing distance of her, as she with the crowd pressed into the church to assist at the devotions.

Long and dazzling were those ceremonies, when, raised on high like an enthroned God, Pope Alexander VI. received the homage of bended knee from the ambassadors of every Christian nation, from heads of all ecclesiastical orders, and from generals and chiefs and princes and nobles, who, robed and plumed and gemmed in all the brightest and proudest that earth could give, bowed the knee humbly and kissed his foot in return for the palm-branch which he presented. Meanwhile, voices of invisible singers chanted the simple event which all this splendor was commemorating, — how of old Jesus came into Jerusalem meek and lowly, riding on an ass, — how His disciples cast their garments in the way, and the multitude took branches of palm-trees to come forth and meet Him, — how He was seized, tried, condemned to a cruel death, — and the crowd, with dazzled and wondering eyes following the gorgeous ceremonial, reflected little how great was the satire of the contrast, how different the coming of that meek and lowly One to suffer and to die from this triumphant display of worldly pomp and splendor in His professed representative.

But to the pure all things are pure, and Agnes thought

only of the enthronement of all virtues, of all celestial charities and unworldly purities in that splendid ceremonial, and longed within herself to approach so near as to touch the hem of those wondrous and sacred garments. It was to her enthusiastic imagination like the unclosing of celestial doors, where the kings and priests of an eternal and heavenly temple move to and fro in music, with the many-colored glories of rainbows and sunset clouds. Her whole nature was wrought upon by the sights and sounds of that gorgeous worship, — she seemed to burn and brighten like an altar-coal, her figure appeared to dilate, her eyes grew deeper and shone with a starry light, and the color of her cheeks flushed up with a vivid glow; nor was she aware how often eyes were turned upon her, nor how murmurs of admiration followed all her absorbed, unconscious movements. "*Ecco! Eccola!*" was often repeated from mouth to mouth around her, but she heard it not.

When at last the ceremony was finished, the crowd rushed again out of the church to see the departure of various dignitaries. There was a perfect whirl of dazzling equipages, and glittering lackeys, and prancing horses, crusted with gold, flaming in scarlet and purple, retinues of cardinals and princes and nobles and ambassadors all in one splendid confused jostle of noise and brightness.

Suddenly a servant in a gorgeous scarlet livery touched Agnes on the shoulder, and said, in a tone of authority, —

"Young maiden, your presence is commanded."

"Who commands it?" said Elsie, laying her hand on her grandchild's shoulder fiercely.

"Are you mad?" whispered two or three women of the lower orders to Elsie at once; "don't you know who that is? Hush, for your life!"

"I shall go with you, Agnes," said Elsie, resolutely.

"No, you will not," said the attendant, insolently. "This maiden is commanded, and none else."

"He belongs to the Pope's nephew," whispered a voice
in Elsie's ear. "You had better have your tongue torn
out than say another word." Whereupon, Elsie found
herself actually borne backward by three or four stout
women.

Agnes looked round and smiled on her, — a smile full
of innocent trust, — and then, turning, followed the servant into the finest of the equipages, where she was lost
to view.

Elsie was almost wild with fear and impotent rage; but
a low, impressive voice now spoke in her ear. It came
from the white figure which had followed them in the
morning.

"Listen," it said, "and be quiet; don't turn your head,
but hear what I tell you. Your child is followed by those
who will save her. Go your ways whence you came.
Wait till the hour after the Ave Maria, then come to the
Porta San Sebastiano, and all will be well."

When Elsie turned to look she saw no one, but caught
a distant glimpse of a white figure vanishing in the crowd.
She returned to her asylum, wondering and disconsolate,
and the first person whom she saw was old Mona.

"Well, good-morrow, sister!" she said. "Know that
I am here on a strange errand. The Princess has taken
such a liking to you that nothing will do but we must
fetch you and your little one out to her villa. I looked
everywhere for you in church this morning. Where have
you hid yourselves?"

"We were there," said Elsie, confused, and hesitating
whether to speak of what had happened.

"Well, where is the little one? Get her ready; we
have horses in waiting. It is a good bit out of the city."

"Alack!" said Elsie, "I know not where she is."

"Holy Virgin!" said Mona, "how is this?"

Elsie, moved by the necessity which makes it a relief to

open the heart to some one, sat down on the steps of the
church and poured forth the whole story into the listening
ear of Mona.

"Well, well, well!" said the old servant, "in our days,
one does not wonder at anything, one never knows one day
what may come the next, — but this is bad enough!"

"Do you think," said Elsie, "there is any hope in that
strange promise?"

"One can but try it," said Mona.

"If you could but be there then," said Elsie, "and take
us to your mistress."

"Well, I will wait, for my mistress has taken an especial
fancy to your little one, more particularly since this morning, when a holy Capuchin came to our house and held a
long conference with her, and after he was gone I found
my lady almost in a faint, and she would have it that we
should start directly to bring her out here, and I had much
ado to let her see that the child would do quite as well
after services were over. I tired myself looking about for
you in the crowd."

The two women then digressed upon various gossiping
particulars, as they sat on the old mossy, grass-grown steps,
looking up over house-tops yellow with lichen, into the
blue spring air, where flocks of white pigeons were soaring
and careering in the soft, warm sunshine. Brightness and
warmth and flowers seemed to be the only idea natural to
that charming weather, and Elsie, sad-hearted and forebod-
ing as she was, felt the benign influence. Rome, which
had been so fatal a place to her peace, yet had for her, as
it has for every one, potent spells of a lulling and soothing
power. Where is the grief or anxiety that can resist the
enchantment of one of Rome's bright, soft, spring days?

CHAPTER XXIX

THE NIGHT-RIDE

THE villa of the Princess Paulina was one of those soft, idyllic paradises which lie like so many fairy-lands around the dreamy solitudes of Rome. They are so fair, so wild, so still, these villas! Nature in them seems to run in such gentle sympathy with Art, that one feels as if they had not been so much the product of human skill as some indigenous growth of Arcadian ages. There are quaint terraces shadowed by clipped ilex-trees, whose branches make twilight even in the sultriest noon; there are long-drawn paths, through wildernesses where cyclamens blossom in crimson clouds among crushed fragments of sculptured marble green with the moss of ages, and glossy-leaved myrtles put forth their pale blue stars in constellations under the leafy shadows. Everywhere is the voice of water, ever lulling, ever babbling, and taught by Art to run in many a quaint caprice, — here to rush down marble steps slippery with sedgy green, there to spout up in silvery spray, and anon to spread into a cool, waveless lake, whose mirror reflects trees and flowers far down in some visionary underworld. Then there are wide lawns, where the grass in spring is a perfect rainbow of anemones, white, rose, crimson, purple, mottled, streaked, and dappled with ever varying shade of sunset clouds. There are soft, moist banks where purple and white violets grow large and fair, and trees all interlaced with ivy, which runs and twines everywhere, intermingling its dark, graceful leaves and vivid young shoots with the bloom and leafage of all shadowy places.

In our day, these lovely places have their dark shadow ever haunting their loveliness: the malaria, like an unseen demon, lies hid in their sweetness. And in the time we are speaking of, a curse not less deadly poisoned the beauties of the Princess's villa, — the malaria of fear.

The graveled terrace in front of the villa commanded, through the clipped arches of the ilex-trees, the Campagna with its soft, undulating bands of many-colored green, and the distant city of Rome, whose bells were always filling the air between with a tremulous vibration. Here, during the long sunny afternoon while Elsie and Monica were crooning together on the steps of the church, the Princess Paulina walked restlessly up and down, looking forth on the way towards the city for the travelers whom she expected.

Father Francesco had been there that morning and communicated to her the dying message of the aged Capuchin, from which it appeared that the child who had so much interested her was her near kinswoman. Perhaps, had her house remained at the height of its power and splendor, she might have rejected with scorn the idea of a kinswoman whose existence had been owing to a *mésalliance;* but a member of an exiled and disinherited family, deriving her only comfort from unworldly sources, she regarded this event as an opportunity afforded her to make expiation for one of the sins of her house. The beauty and winning graces of her young kinswoman were not without their influence in attracting a lonely heart deprived of the support of natural ties. The Princess longed for something to love, and the discovery of a legitimate object of family affection was an event in the weary monotony of her life; and therefore it was that the hours of the afternoon seemed long while she looked forth towards Rome, listening to the ceaseless chiming of its bells, and wondering why no one appeared along the road.

The sun went down, and all the wide plain seemed like the sea at twilight, lying in rosy and lilac and purple shadowy bands, out of which rose the old city, solemn and lonely as some enchanted island of dream-land, with a flush of radiance behind it and a tolling of weird music filling all the air around. Now they are chanting the Ave Maria in hundreds of churches, and the Princess worships in distant accord, and tries to still the anxieties of her heart with many a prayer. Twilight fades and fades, the Campagna becomes a black sea, and the distant city looms up like a dark rock against the glimmering sky, and the Princess goes within and walks restlessly through the wide halls, stopping first at one open window and then at another to listen. Beneath her feet she treads a cool mosaic pavement where laughing Cupids are dancing. Above, from the ceiling, Aurora and the Hours look down in many-colored clouds of brightness. The sound of the fountains without is so clear in the intense stillness that the peculiar voice of each one can be told. That is the swaying noise of the great jet that rises from marble shells and falls into a wide basin, where silvery swans swim round and round in enchanted circles; and the other slenderer sound is the smaller jet that rains down its spray into the violet-borders deep in the shrubbery; and that other, the shallow babble of the waters that go down the marble steps to the lake. How dreamlike and plaintive they all sound in the night stillness! The nightingale sings from the dark shadows of the wilderness; and the musky odors of the cyclamen come floating ever and anon through the casement, in that strange, cloudy way in which flower scents seem to come and go in the air in the night season.

At last the Princess fancies she hears the distant tramp of horses' feet, and her heart beats so that she can scarcely listen: now she hears it, — and now a rising wind, sweeping across the Campagna, seems to bear it moaning away.

She goes to a door and looks out into the darkness. Yes, she hears it now, quick and regular, — the beat of many horses' feet coming in hot haste along the road. Surely the few servants whom she has sent cannot make all this noise! and she trembles with vague affright. Perhaps it is a tyrannical message, bringing imprisonment and death. She calls a maid, and bids her bring lights into the reception-hall. A few moments more, and there is a confused stamping of horses' feet approaching the house, and she hears the voices of her servants. She runs into the piazza, and sees dismounting a knight who carries Agnes in his arms pale and fainting. Old Elsie and Monica, too, dismount, with the Princess's men-servants; but, wonderful to tell, there seems besides them to be a train of some hundred armed horsemen.

The timid Princess was so fluttered and bewildered that she lost all presence of mind, and stood in uncomprehending wonder, while Monica pushed authoritatively into the house, and beckoned the knight to bring Agnes and lay her on a sofa, when she and old Elsie busied themselves vigorously with restoratives.

The Lady Paulina, as soon as she could collect her scattered senses, recognized in Agostino the banished lord of the Sarelli family, a race who had shared with her own the hatred and cruelty of the Borgia tribe; and he in turn had recognized a daughter of the Colonnas. He drew her aside into a small boudoir adjoining the apartment.

"Noble lady," he said, "we are companions in misfortune, and so, I trust, you will pardon what seems a tumultuous intrusion on your privacy. I and my men came to Rome in disguise, that we might watch over and protect this poor innocent, who now finds asylum with you."

"My Lord," said the Princess, "I see in this event the wonderful working of the good God. I have but just learned that this young person is my near kinswoman; it was only this morning that the fact was certified to me on the dying confession of a holy Capuchin, who privately united my brother to her mother. The marriage was an indiscretion of his youth; but afterwards he fell into more grievous sin in denying the holy sacrament, and leaving his wife to die in misery and dishonor, and perhaps for this fault such great judgments fell upon him. I wish to make atonement in such sort as is yet possible by acting as a mother to this child."

"The times are so troublous and uncertain," said Agostino, "that she must have stronger protection than that of any woman. She is of a most holy and religious nature, but as ignorant of sin as an angel who never has seen anything out of heaven; and so the Borgias enticed her into their impure den, from which, God helping, I have saved her. I tried all I could to prevent her coming to Rome, and to convince her of the vileness that ruled here; but the poor little one could not believe me, and thought me a heretic only for saying what she now knows from her own senses."

The Lady Paulina shuddered with fear.

"Is it possible that you have come into collision with the dreadful Borgias? What will become of us?"

"I brought a hundred men into Rome in different disguises," said Agostino, "and we gained over a servant in their household, through whom I entered and carried her off. Their men pursued us, and we had a fight in the streets, but for the moment we mustered more than they. Some of them chased us a good distance. But it will not do for us to remain here. As soon as she is revived enough, we must retreat towards one of our fastnesses in the mountains, whence, when rested, we shall go northward to Florence, where I have powerful friends, and she has also an uncle, a holy man, by whose counsels she is much guided."

"You must take me with you," said the Princess, in a tremor of anxiety. "Not for the world would I stay, if it be known you have taken refuge here. For a long time their spies have been watching about me; they only wait for some occasion to seize upon my villa, as they have on the possessions of all my father's house. Let me flee with you. I have a brother-in-law in Florence who hath often urged me to escape to him till times mend, — for, surely, God will not allow the wicked to bear rule forever."

"Willingly, noble lady, will we give you our escort, — the more so that this poor child will then have a friend with her beseeming her father's rank. Believe me, lady, she will do no discredit to her lineage. She was trained in a convent, and her soul is a flower of marvelous beauty. I must declare to you here that I have wooed her honorably to be my wife, and she would willingly be so, had not some scruples of a religious vocation taken hold on her, to dispel which I look for the aid of the holy father, her uncle."

"It would be a most fit and proper thing," said the Princess, "thus to ally our houses, in hope of some good time to come which shall restore their former standing and possessions. Of course some holy man must judge of the obstacle interposed by her vocation; but I doubt not the Church will be an indulgent mother in a case where the issue seems so desirable."

"If I be married to her," said Agostino, "I can take her out of all these strifes and confusions which now agitate our Italy to the court of France, where I have an uncle high in favor with the King, and who will use all his influence to compose these troubles in Italy, and bring about a better day."

While this conversation was going on, bountiful refreshments had been provided for the whole party, and the attendants of the Princess received orders to pack all her jewels and valuable effects for a sudden journey.

As soon as preparations could be made, the whole party left the villa of the Princess for a retreat in the Alban Mountains, where Agostino and his band had one of their rendezvous. Only the immediate female attendants of the Princess, and one or two men-servants, left with her. The silver plate, and all objects of particular value, were buried in the garden. This being done, the keys of the house were intrusted to a gray-headed servant, who with his wife had grown old in the family.

It was midnight before everything was ready for starting. The moon cast silver gleams through the ilex-avenues, and caused the jet of the great fountain to look like a wavering pillar of cloudy brightness, when the Princess led forth Agnes upon the wide veranda. Two gentle, yet spirited little animals from the Princess's stables were there awaiting them, and they were lifted into their saddles by Agostino.

"Fear nothing, Madam," he said, observing how the hands of the Princess trembled; "a few hours will put us in perfect safety, and I shall be at your side constantly."

Then lifting Agnes to her seat, he placed the reins in her hand.

"Are you rested?" he asked.

It was the first time since her rescue that he had spoken to Agnes. The words were brief, but no expressions of endearment could convey more than the manner in which they were spoken.

"Yes, my Lord," said Agnes firmly, "I am rested."

"You think you can bear the ride?"

"I can bear anything, so I escape," she said.

The company were now all mounted, and were marshaled in regular order. A body of armed men rode in front; then came Agnes and the Princess, with Agostino

between them, while two or three troopers rode on either
side; Elsie, Monica, and the servants of the Princess followed close behind, and the rear was brought up in like
manner by armed men.

The path wound first through the grounds of the villa,
with its plats of light and shade, its solemn groves of stone-
pines rising like palm-trees high in air above the tops of
all other trees, its terraces and statues and fountains, — all
seeming so lovely in the midnight stillness.

"Perhaps I am leaving all this forever," said the Princess.

"Let us hope for the best," said Agostino. "It cannot
be that God will suffer the seat of the Apostles to be subjected to such ignominy and disgrace much longer.   I am
amazed that no Christian kings have interfered before for
the honor of Christendom.   I have it from the best authority that the King of Naples burst into tears when he heard
of the election of this wretch to be Pope.   He said that
it was a scandal which threatened the very existence of
Christianity.   He has sent me secret messages divers times
expressive of sympathy, but he is not of himself strong
enough.   Our hope must lie either in the King of France
or the Emperor of Germany: perhaps both will engage.
There is now a most holy monk in Florence who has been
stirring all hearts in a wonderful way.   It is said that the
very gifts of miracles and prophecy are revived in him, as
among the holy Apostles, and he has been bestirring himself to have a General Council of the Church to look into
these matters.   When I left Florence, a short time ago,
the faction opposed to him broke into the convent and took
him away.   I myself was there."

"What!" said Agnes, "did they break into the convent
of the San Marco?   My uncle is there."

"Yes, and he and I fought side by side with the mob
who were rushing in."

"Uncle Antonio fight!" said Agnes, in astonishment.

"Even women will fight, when what they love most is attacked," said the knight.

He turned to her, as he spoke, and saw in the moonlight a flash from her eye, and an heroic expression on her face, such as he had never remarked before; but she said nothing. The veil had been rudely torn from her eyes; she had seen with horror the defilement and impurity of what she had ignorantly adored in holy places, and the revelation seemed to have wrought a change in her whole nature.

"Even you could fight, Agnes," said the knight, "to save your religion from disgrace."

"No," said she; "but," she added, with gathering firmness, "I could die. I should be glad to die with and for the holy men who would save the honor of the true faith. I should like to go to Florence to my uncle. If he dies for his religion, I should like to die with him."

"Ah, live to teach it to me!" said the knight, bending towards her, as if to adjust her bridle-rein, and speaking in a voice scarcely audible. In a moment he was turned again towards the Princess, listening to her.

"So it seems," she said, "that we shall be running into the thick of the conflict in Florence."

"Yes, but my uncle hath promised that the King of France shall interfere. I have hope something may even now have been done. I hope to effect something myself."

Agostino spoke with the cheerful courage of youth. Agnes glanced timidly up at him. How great the change in her ideas! No longer looking on him as a wanderer from the fold, an enemy of the Church, he seemed now in the attitude of a champion of the faith, a defender of holy men and things against a base usurpation. What injustice had she done him, and how patiently had he borne that injustice! Had he not sought to warn her against the danger of venturing into that corrupt city? Those words

which so much shocked her, against which she had shut
her ears, were all true; she had found them so; she could
doubt no longer.   And yet he had followed her, and saved
her at the risk of his life.   Could she help loving one who
had loved her so much, one so noble and heroic?   Would
it be a sin to love him?   She pondered the dark warnings
of Father Francesco, and then thought of the cheerful, fervent piety of her old uncle.   How warm, how tender, how
life-giving had been his presence always! how full of faith
and prayer, how fruitful of heavenly words and thoughts
had been all his ministrations! — and yet it was for him
and with him and his master that Agostino Sarelli was
fighting, and against him the usurping head of the Christian Church.   Then there was another subject for pondering during this night-ride.   The secret of her birth had
been told her by the Princess, who claimed her as kinswoman.   It had seemed to her at first like the revelations
of a dream; but as she rode and reflected, gradually the
idea shaped itself in her mind.   She was, in birth and
blood, the equal of her lover, and henceforth her life would
no more be in that lowly plane where it had always moved.
She thought of the little orange-garden at Sorrento, of the
gorge with its old bridge, the Convent, the sisters, with a
sort of tender, wondering pain.   Perhaps she should see
them no more.   In this new situation she longed once
more to see and talk with her old uncle, and to have him
tell her what were her duties.

Their path soon began to be a wild clamber among the
mountains, now lost in the shadow of groves of gray, rustling olives, whose knotted, serpent roots coiled round the
rocks, and whose leaves silvered in the moonlight whenever
the wind swayed them.   Whatever might be the roughness
and difficulties of the way, Agnes found her knight ever at
her bridle-rein, guiding and upholding, steadying her in
her saddle when the horse plunged down short and sudden

descents, and wrapping her in his mantle to protect her from the chill mountain-air. When the day was just reddening in the sky, the whole troop made a sudden halt before a square stone tower which seemed to be a portion of a ruined building, and here some of the men dismounting knocked at an arched door. It was soon swung open by a woman with a lamp in her hand, the light of which revealed very black hair and eyes, and heavy gold earrings.

"Have my directions been attended to?" said Agostino, in a tone of command. "Are there places made ready for these ladies to sleep?"

"There are, my Lord," said the woman, obsequiously, "the best we could get ready on so short a notice."

Agostino came up to the Princess. "Noble Madam," he said, "you will value safety before all things; doubtless the best that can be done here is but poor, but it will give you a few hours for repose where you may be sure of being in perfect safety."

So saying, he assisted her and Agnes to dismount, and Elsie and Monica also alighting, they followed the woman into a dark stone passage and up some rude stone steps. She opened at last the door of a brick-floored room, where beds appeared to have been hastily prepared. There was no furniture of any sort except the beds. The walls were dusty and hung with cobwebs. A smaller apartment opening into this had beds for Elsie and Monica.

The travelers, however, were too much exhausted with their night-ride to be critical; the services of disrobing and preparing for rest were quickly concluded, and in less than an hour all were asleep, while Agostino was busy concerting the means for an immediate journey to Florence.

CHAPTER XXX

"LET US ALSO GO, THAT WE MAY DIE WITH HIM"

FATHER ANTONIO sat alone in his cell in the San Marco in an attitude of deep dejection. The open window looked into the garden of the convent, from which steamed up the fragrance of violet, jasmine, and rose, and the sunshine lay fair on all that was without. On a table beside him were many loose and scattered sketches; and an unfinished page of the Breviary he was executing, rich in quaint tracery of gold and arabesques, seemed to have recently occupied his attention, for his palette was wet and many loose brushes lay strewed around. Upon the table stood a Venetian glass with a narrow neck and a bulb clear and thin as a soap-bubble, containing vines and blossoms of the passion-flower, which he had evidently been using as models in his work.

The page he was illuminating was the prophetic Psalm which describes the ignominy and sufferings of the Redeemer. It was surrounded by a wreathed border of thorn-branches interwoven with the blossoms and tendrils of the passion-flower, and the initial letters of the first two words were formed by a curious combination of the hammer, the nails, the spear, the crown of thorns, the cross, and other instruments of the Passion; and clear, in red letter, gleamed out those wonderful, mysterious words, consecrated by the remembrance of a more than mortal anguish, "My God, my God, why hast thou forsaken me?"

The artist monk had perhaps fled to his palette to assuage the throbbings of his heart, as a mourning mother flies to the cradle of her child; but even there his grief

appeared to have overtaken him, for the work lay as if
pushed from him in an access of anguish such as comes
from the sudden recurrence of some overwhelming recollection. He was leaning forward with his face buried in his
hands, sobbing convulsively.

The door opened, and a man advancing stealthily behind
laid a hand kindly on his shoulder, saying softly, "So, so,
brother!"

Father Antonio looked up, and, dashing his hand hastily
across his eyes, grasped that of the new-comer convulsively,
and saying only, "Oh, Baccio! Baccio!" hid his face
again.

The eyes of the other filled with tears, as he answered
gently, —

"Nay, but, my brother, you are killing yourself. They
tell me that you have eaten nothing for three days, and
slept not for weeks; you will die of this grief."

"Would that I might! Why could not I die with him as
well as Fra Domenico? Oh, my master! my dear master!"

"It is indeed a most heavy day to us all," said Baccio
della Porta, the amiable and pure-minded artist better
known to our times by his conventual name of Fra Bartolommeo. "Never have we had among us such a man, and
if there be any light of grace in my soul, his preaching first
awakened it, brother. I only wait to see him enter Paradise, and then I take farewell of the world for ever. I am
going to Prato to take the Dominican habit and follow him
as near as I may."

"It is well, Baccio, it is well," said Father Antonio;
"but you must not put out the light of your genius in
those shadows, — you must still paint for the glory of
God."

"I have no heart for painting now," said Baccio, deject-
edly. "He was my inspiration, he taught me the holier
way, and he is gone."

At this moment the conference of the two was interrupted by a knocking at the door, and Agostino Sarelli entered, pale and disordered.

"How is this?" he said, hastily. "What devils' car-
nival is this which hath broken loose in Florence? Every
good thing is gone into dens and holes, and every vile thing
that can hiss and spit and sting is crawling abroad. What
do the princes of Europe mean to let such things be?"

"Only the old story," said Father Antonio, — "*Prin-
cipes convenerunt in unum adversus Dominum, adversus
Christum ejus.*"

So much were all three absorbed in the subject of their
thoughts, that no kind of greeting or mark of recognition
passed among them, such as is common when people meet
after temporary separation. Each spoke out from the fullness of his soul, as from an overflowing bitter fountain.

"Was there no one to speak for him, — no one to stand
up for the pride of Italy, — the man of his age?" said
Agostino.

"There was one voice raised for him in the council,"
said Father Antonio. "There was Agnolo Niccolini: a
grave man is this Agnolo, and of great experience in public
affairs, and he spoke out his mind boldly. He told them
flatly, that, if they looked through the present time or the
past ages they would not meet a man of such a high and
noble order as this, and that to lay at our door the blood
of a man the like of whom might not be born for centuries
was too impious and execrable a thing to be thought of.
I'll warrant me, he made a rustling among them when he
said that, and the Pope's commissary — old Romalino —
then whispered and frowned; but Agnolo is a stiff old fellow when he once begins a thing, — he never minded it,
and went through with his say. It seems to me he said
that it was not for us to quench a light like this, capable
of giving lustre to the faith even when it had grown dim

in other parts of the world, — and not to the faith alone, but to all the arts and sciences connected with it. If it were needed to put restraint on him, he said, why not put him into some fortress, and give him commodious apartments, with abundance of books, and pen, ink, and paper, where he would write books to the honor of God and the exaltation of the holy faith? He told them that this might be a good to the world, whereas consigning him to death without use of any kind would bring on our republic perpetual dishonor."

"Well said for him!" said Baccio, with warmth; "but I'll warrant me, he might as well have preached to the north wind in March, his enemies are in such a fury."

"Yes, yes," said Antonio, "it is just as it was of old: the chief priests and Scribes and Pharisees were instant with loud voices, requiring he should be put to death; and the easy Pilates, for fear of the tumult, washed their hands of it."

" And now," said Agostino, "they are putting up a great gibbet in the shape of a cross in the public square, where they will hang the three holiest and best men of Florence! "

"I came through there this morning," said Baccio, "and there were young men and boys shouting, and howling, and singing indecent songs, and putting up indecent pictures, such as those he used to preach against. It is just as you say. All things vile have crept out of their lair, and triumph that the man who made them afraid is put down; and every house is full of the most horrible lies about him, — things that they said he confessed."

"Confessed! " said Father Antonio, — "was it not enough that they tore and tortured him seven times, but they must garble and twist the very words that he said in his agony? The process they have published is foully falsified, — stuffed full of improbable lies; for I myself have read the first draught of all he *did* say, just as Signor

Ceccone took it down as they were torturing him. I had it from Jacopo Manelli, canon of our Duomo here, and he got it from Ceccone's wife herself. They not only can torture and slay him, but they torture and slay his memory with lies."

"Would I were in God's place for one day!" said Agostino, speaking through his clenched teeth. "May I be forgiven for saying so!"

"*We* are hot and hasty," said Father Antonio, "ever ready to call down fire from heaven; but after all, 'the Lord reigneth, let the earth rejoice.' 'Unto the upright there ariseth light in the darkness.' Our dear father is sustained in spirit and full of love. Even when they let him go from the torture, he fell on his knees, praying for his tormentors."

"Good God! this passes me!" said Agostino, striking his hands together. "Oh, wherefore hath a strong man arms and hands, and a sword, if he must stand still and see such things done? If I had only my hundred mountaineers here, I would make one charge for him to-morrow. If I could only *do* something," he added, striding impetuously up and down the cell and clenching his fists. "What! hath nobody petitioned to stay this thing?"

"Nobody for him," said Father Antonio. "There was talk in the city yesterday that Fra Domenico was to be pardoned; in fact, Romalino was quite inclined to do it, but Battista Alberti talked violently against it, and so Romalino said, 'Well, a monk more or less is n't much matter,' and then he put his name down for death with the rest. The order was signed by both commissaries of the Pope, and one was Fra Turiano, the general of our order, a mild man, full of charity, but unable to stand against the Pope."

"Mild men are nuisances in such places," said Agostino, hastily; "our times want something of another sort."

"There be many who have fallen away from him even in our house here," said Father Antonio, "as it was with our blessed Lord, whose disciples forsook Him and fled. It seems to be the only thought with some how they shall make their peace with the Pope."

"And so the thing will be hurried through to-morrow," said Agostino, "and when it's done and over, I'll warrant me there will be found kings and emperors to say they meant to have saved him. It's a vile, evil world, this of ours; an honorable man longs to see the end of it. But," he added, coming up and speaking to Father Antonio, "I have a private message for you."

"I am gone this moment," said Baccio, rising with ready courtesy; "but keep up heart, brother."

So saying, the good-hearted artist left the cell, and Agostino said, —

"I bring tidings to you of your kindred. Your niece and sister are here in Florence, and would see you. You will find them at the house of one Gherardo Rosselli, a rich citizen of noble blood."

"Why are they there?" said the monk, lost in amazement.

"You must know, then, that a most singular discovery hath been made by your niece at Rome. The sister of her father, being a lady of the princely blood of Colonna, hath been assured of her birth by the confession of the priest that married him; and being driven from Rome by fear of the Borgias, they came hither under my escort, and wait to see you. So, if you will come with me now, I will guide you to them."

"Even so," said Father Antonio.

CHAPTER XXXI

MARTYRDOM

In a shadowy chamber of a room overlooking the grand square of Florence might be seen, on the next morning, some of the principal personages of our story. Father Antonio, Baccio della Porta, Agostino Sarelli, the Princess Paulina, Agnes, with her grandmother, and a mixed crowd of citizens and ecclesiastics, who all spoke in hushed and tremulous voices, as men do in the chamber of mourners at a funeral. The great, mysterious bell of the Campanile was swinging with dismal, heart-shaking toll, like a mighty voice from the spirit-world; and it was answered by the tolling of all the bells in the city, making such wavering clangors and vibrating circles in the air over Florence that it might seem as if it were full of warring spirits wrestling for mastery.

Toll! toll! toll! O great bell of the fair Campanile! for this day the noblest of the wonderful men of Florence is to be offered up. Toll! for an era is going out, — the era of her artists, her statesmen, her poets, and her scholars. Toll! for an era is coming in, — the era of her disgrace and subjugation and misfortune!

The stepping of the vast crowd in the square was like the patter of a great storm, and the hum of voices rose up like the murmur of the ocean; but in the chamber all was so still that one could have heard the dropping of a pin.

Under the balcony of this room were seated in pomp and state the Papal commissioners, radiant in gold and

scarlet respectability; and Pilate and Herod, on terms of
the most excellent friendship, were ready to act over again
the part they had acted fourteen hundred years before.
Now has arrived the moment when the three followers of
the Man of Calvary are to be degraded from the fellowship
of His visible Church.

Father Antonio, Agostino, and Baccio stood forth in
the balcony, and, drawing in their breath, looked down, as
the three men of the hour, pale and haggard with imprisonment and torture, were brought up amid the hoots and
obscene jests of the populace. Savonarola first was led
before the tribunal, and there, with circumstantial minute-
ness, endued with all his priestly vestments, which again,
with separate ceremonies of reprobation and ignominy, were
taken from him. He stood through it all serene as stood
his Master when stripped of His garments on Calvary.
There is a momentary hush of voices and drawing in of
breaths in the great crowd. The Papal legate takes him
by the hand and pronounces the words, "Jerome Savonarola, I separate thee from the Church Militant and the
Church Triumphant."

He is going to speak.

"What says he?" said Agostino, leaning over the balcony.

Solemnly and clear that impressive voice which so often
had thrilled the crowds in that very square made answer, —

"From the Church Militant you *may* divide me; but
from the Church Triumphant, *no*, — *that* is above your
power!" — and a light flashed out in his face as if a smile
from Christ had shone down upon him.

"Amen!" said Father Antonio; "he hath witnessed a
good confession," — and turning, he went in, and, burying
his face in his hands, remained in prayer.

When like ceremonies had been passed through with
the others, the three martyrs were delivered to the secular

executioner, and, amid the scoffs and jeers of the brutal crowd, turned their faces to the gibbet.

"Brothers, let us sing the Te Deum," said Savonarola.

"Do not so infuriate the mob," said the executioner, "for harm might be done."

"At least let us repeat it together," said he, "lest we forget it."

And so they went forward, speaking to each other of the glorious company of the apostles, the goodly fellowship of the prophets, the noble army of martyrs, and giving thanks aloud in that great triumphal hymn of the Church of all Ages.

When the lurid fires were lighted which blazed red and fearful through that crowded square, all in that silent chamber fell on their knees, and Father Antonio repeated prayers for departing souls.

To the last, that benignant right hand which had so often pointed the way of life to that faithless city was stretched out over the crowd in the attitude of blessing; and so loving, not hating, praying with exaltation, and rendering blessing for cursing, the souls of the martyrs ascended to the great cloud of witnesses above.

CHAPTER XXXII

CONCLUSION

A FEW days after the death of Savonarola, Father Antonio was found one morning engaged in deep converse
with Agnes.

The Princess Paulina, acting for her family, desired to
give her hand to the Prince Agostino Sarelli, and the interview related to the religious scruples which still con-
flicted with the natural desires of the child.

"Tell me, my little one," said Father Antonio, "frankly
and truly, dost thou not love this man with all thy heart?"

"Yes, my father, I do," said Agnes; "but ought I not
to resign this love for the love of my Saviour?"

"I see not why," said the monk. "Marriage is a sacrament as well as holy orders, and it is a most holy and venerable one, representing the divine mystery by which the
souls of the blessed are united to the Lord. I do not hold
with Saint Bernard, who, in his zeal for a conventual life,
seemed to see no other way of serving God but for all men
and women to become monks and nuns. The holy order
is indeed blessed to those souls whose call to it is clear and
evident, like mine; but if there be a strong and virtuous
love for a worthy object, it is a vocation unto marriage,
which should not be denied."

"So, Agnes," said the knight, who had stolen into the
room unperceived, and who now boldly possessed himself
of one of her hands "Father Antonio hath decided this
matter," he added, turning to the Princess and Elsie, who
entered, "and everything having been made ready for my

journey into France, the wedding ceremony shall take place on the morrow, and, for that we are in deep affliction, it shall be as private as may be."

And so on the next morning the wedding ceremony took place, and the bride and groom went on their way to France, where preparations befitting their rank awaited them.

Old Elsie was heard to observe to Monica, that there was some sense in making pilgrimages, since this to Rome, which she had undertaken so unwillingly, had turned out so satisfactory.

In the reign of Julius II., the banished families who had been plundered by the Borgias were restored to their rights and honors at Rome; and there was a princess of the house of Sarelli then at Rome, whose sanctity of life and manners was held to go back to the traditions of primitive Christianity, so that she was renowned not less for goodness than for rank and beauty.

In those days, too, Raphael, the friend of Fra Bartolommeo, placed in one of the grandest halls of the Vatican, among the Apostles and Saints, the image of the traduced and despised martyr whose ashes had been cast to the winds and waters in Florence. His memory lingered long in Italy, so that it was even claimed that miracles were wrought in his name and by his intercession. Certain it is, that the living words he spoke were seeds of immortal flowers which blossomed in secret dells and obscure shadows of his beautiful Italy.